COBALT ROGUE
VOL. 01: THE DEAD BLUE

ALEXANDER ENGEL-HODGKINSON

COBALT ROGUE, VOL. 1: THE DEAD BLUE

COBALT ROGUE, VOL. ONE: THE DEAD BLUE

ISBN 978-0-9952174-9-2

Art by Alexander Engel-Hodgkinson

Published by
Dark Brothers Incorporated

COBALT ROGUE, VOL. 1: THE DEAD BLUE

COBALT ROGUE, VOL. 1: THE DEAD BLUE

The first volume in the Final Apocalypse Saga

PARENTAL ADVISORY

'Cobalt Rogue, Vol. 1: The Dead Blue' contains strong violent content, disturbing horror content, frequent profanity, strong crude and sexual content, and other themes intended for mature readers ages 17 and up.

Author's Comment

I'd written this once before... when I was between the ages of ten and thirteen. And that story was utter crap. It ridiculously tried to one-up itself the whole way through. And the plot scattered in all directions beyond my control. It was fun writing it at the time, but it was an embarrassing re-read years later. After Volume 13, I thought "Screw this; I don't know where the hell the plot's going! I plan for it to go one way but my hands throw it in the EXACT OPPOSITE DIRECTION!"

It was a disaster!

Oh, and the name was different. Before, it was called 'Dark-Boy,' as was the protagonist. And it was more of a generic superhero YA series.

So this is a re-write. Or reboot. Or whatever you want to call it. It's everything I'd ever wanted to do with the character, but never had the guts to for fear of my parents closing the laptop lid and washing my mouth out with soap for my characters' 'grammar problems.' It would seem even worse when they speak to me like an escaped mental patient just for the amount of violence/gore, or ask questions like "How do you know that?" whenever they encounter some sort of sexual reference or whatever. Now I don't have to worry, because I realized I can say: "My characters speak for themselves! Wash their mouths out with soap!"

I probably know what you're thinking: "'Dark-Boy'? What the hell kind of name is that?" I know, it sounds lame. Well, that's the name of the original character. Give me some credit; I was

seven, and Damian was just a teenager who wore tights and fought crime. He was like my version of Teen Titans' Robin, except with blue hair and a crappier attitude and darker colours in his costume. I can assure you this story bears little to no resemblance to that whatsoever. Why, even the name is different now!

The blue hair is an exception. And the crappy attitude. And, like, a couple of original character names.

Honestly, I kept the name for the first two volumes of this series for nostalgia's sake. I didn't realize it'd serve me so poorly later on, for several reasons—few of which I'll never get into. Mainly, it just didn't suit the story I was telling anymore. It was no longer a super-childish superhero story with black-and-white morality and lighter themes. This was a dark, violent, mature, and sometimes horrific coming-of-age sci-fi fantasy. There was no longer a need for superheroes. Not in this world.

Anyway, this story's completely different from that 13-volume crap-fest I'd written before. Hopefully I'll do it right this time.

All in all, I hope you enjoy this series!

COBALT ROGUE, VOL. 1: THE DEAD BLUE

Intro:

The beginning of the 20th Century is when it all began. For an unknown reason, a rift opened between two polar opposite dimensions, causing a portion of one version of Earth to crash into the other.

The dimension that survived the catastrophe, called Solaria, was inhabited by humanity alone until a race called Dehons arrived with the remains of their planet. For a while, the two races had managed to maintain a shaky peace between one another, although tensions never ceased.

Over time, war ripped the two races apart, and the fear of the opposite race caused the Dehons to flee, leaving behind the results of Dehon/human pairings: the Dehues; the kin race of the Dehons formed when Dehons and humans mated.

But the fear that compelled humanity soon took control, and one man neither human nor Dehue led a brutal year-long campaign of genocide against the Dehues. He thought he was protecting humanity from absolute destruction. He considered it not an act of destruction, but an act of salvation.

That 'salvation' became known as the 'Dehue Extermination Project.'

The man fought for what he thought was right and soon had humanity under his control. The Dehues were left with an ultimatum: fight or die. The war for survival consisted of three long, agonizing battles, two in the city-state of Cloverfield and one at the Dehue sanctuary in the Gomai Sea. The first was at the Cloverfield Harbour, the world's largest known harbour, and it was called The Battle of the Waves. The second in the Gomai Sea was called the Invasion of Sanctuary.

The third and final battle, named The Battle of Yesterday, was the Dehues' last desperate attack against humanity's main forces, but they were eliminated in the battle that lasted for two months. Some Dehues remained in hiding, but they're believed to be dead by most, and no longer pose a threat. They're no longer hunted.

Except for one: the worst of them all. There weren't many that

knew what his real name was, but many called him the Dead Blue—the Killer of Twenty Million People. Although none knew where he disappeared to after the end of the war, his legacy was never forgotten.

COBALT ROGUE, VOL. 1: THE DEAD BLUE

COBALT ROGUE, VOL. 1: THE DEAD BLUE

Episode 000

Prologue

The sun shone brightly over the dry yard. Kites with radiant patterns and colours fluttered majestically through the clear sky. The breeze was perfect for kite flying, shifting them about in wonderful rainbow collages. The cheerful laughter of their young owners spread across the town. Many of the townspeople would sit on the grassy hills and watch the kites soar through the sky like panicked flocks of birds. Two individuals in particular stood out—a man and his son—for their appearances and reputation alone. They were both born with unusual cobalt blue hair, but it was the boy who stood out the most. The town was populated by two Dehue clans, with their basic appearances being mainly human in nature, although they would also have black spaded tails protruding from their lower backs. The boy, however, was the only Dehue to not have a tail because his father had wed a human woman instead of a Dehue woman, which broke the regulations of the clan.

The boy looked up at his father, holding a blue and white diamond-shaped kite in his small hands, eager to join the other children and his siblings. "Dad," he said, "I made you a good one."

His father looked down at him, unconvinced. "A good one, you say?"

"I-it's good enough to fly now. Can I join the others?"

"Let me see it." The man took his son's creation, briefly inspected it...

...and then he dropped it to the ground and crushed it under his foot.

The boy gulped down a lump of disappointment, watching sadly as his father lifted his foot off the smashed mess of papier-mâché and twigs. As the boy knelt down to pick up the remains, he heard his father say the one thing he hated to hear. Every year he'd hear it, like it was mocking his efforts to please his father with his modified kite, only to see it destroyed once more.

"You can do better."

And now, an important message from our sponsors...

The Systems Corporation logo - a red biohazard symbol with a snarling skull in the center - explodes onto the TV screen.

ANNOUNCER:

Every day, brave men and women leave their homes, their offices, and their comfort zones to defend mankind from total annihilation by the Dehue threat. They make our race proud by fighting for what's right! They show the Dehue invaders that mankind won't EVER give up the planet, our home, to such unforgiving scum! YOU can join today, and show these freakish scumbags that mankind means business!

CUT TO:
EXT. SYSTEMS CORP. POW CAMP - DAY

Three individuals stand in a straight line in front of a Dehue POW chained to an upright slab of concrete. They're clearly in the desert. The Dehue prisoner is labelled DEHUE FREAK by subtitles.

SOLDIER #1:

[As he FIRES on the POW]

Dehue scum! This is for our homes!

SOLDIER #2:

[Joins in, SHOOTS the screaming POW alongside his comrade]

This is for our families!

YOUNG KID IN SOLDIER UNIFORM

[SHOOTS FIRE from a flamethrower onto the POW]

And this is for all of mankind, you scum!

DEHUE POW

[writhes in agony on the slab]

Aaaaaaaah! They sure showed ME!

ANNOUNCER:

If you're not for us, then you're against us. Join today! Be proud, humanity!

FADE TO BLACK

[A message from Systems Corporation]

Cloverfield City, Friday, January 1st, 2021: Exactly one year after the beginning of the Dehue Extermination Project.

The snow lightly descended into the blackened urban horizon that went on farther than the eye could see. Thick columns of smoke still rose from the concrete wasteland. The deep, forty kilometre-wide crater in the center of the city belched plumes of black smoke and radiated with the light of glowing blue ember. The grey sky hung over the city in solemn silence; watching as humanity began its process of healing from the battle that finally ended the day before.

The Battle of Yesterday, dated November 3rd, 2020 at 10:37

AM to January 1st, 2021 at 12:01 AM. That was what the final battle of the Dehue Extermination Project was dubbed by all who fought it, all who escaped it, all who witnessed it and all who survived it. Its title originated as a joke when a now-dead war hero stopped the battle to declare his disapproval to the enemy for their timing, since the Dehues were expected to attack by November 2nd. Because they were a day late, the soldiers managed to amuse themselves with this short-but-lasting dose of black comedy.

Now it was over.

The Dehue Extermination Project was over.

2020. It was the worst year in recorded human history.

The city was an endless mountain range of smoking rubble and totalled machines of war; artillery guns, tanks, even battleships lay in waste, protruding from the dunes of rubble and debris. The larger machines, bulky robots that once belonged to the Dehue race, laid in scattered pieces above and beneath the vast No Man's Land. Giant shell casings littered the pocked wasteland; they once poured out of the giant Gatling guns that were equipped to the Dehues' large robots called Battle Automatons, or 'terrain marchers.' These machines were five storeys tall, standing on hoof-like jet boosters and fat bodies for the pilots to safely reside in.

The Dehues were the kin race of the Dehons, who came from an alternate earth in a parallel dimension. Not much is known about their world, since the Dehons were secretive where their pasts were concerned. Even the cause of the mysterious black hole that swallowed their world and blasted its remains into the Solaria Dimension—where this world resides—remains unknown. Like opposing magnets, the giant chunks of their planet hovered over the surface of the human earth, serving as sky islands that orbited the planet in the safety of its atmosphere; hence why mankind wasn't wiped off the face of the earth over a hundred years earlier.

On this day, even the sky islands seemed devoid of life now.

What was left of the weary human battalions were transporting the endless dead and wounded out of the wasteland and cleaning up the ruins like an army of bustling ants.

"Agggghhhh! Damn it, you morons!"

"Steady! Don't hurt him." General Zero Fraden supervised two soldiers getting ready to pull a soldier out from under a large chunk of concrete as soon as ten others would lift it. Zero was a substitute general of the CGSDF (Cloverfield Ground Self-Defence Force) from the main headquarters of Cloverfield Heart. Cloverfield Heart was the elite government/military organization run by Prime Minister John Whitaker, representative of the World Alliance and leader of Cloverfield itself—a grungy city-state that was already going to hell before the war even began.

The ten soldiers grunted as they lifted the concrete slab off the soldier's legs, giving the other two soldiers enough time to quickly pull their wounded comrade out to safety before they dropped the concrete into the charred ground.

"Oh, Christ," the wounded soldier moaned pitifully as his two companions supported his arms. "Look at my legs! I'll never walk again!"

"Oh, come off it," the man holding his left arm said. "Don't be so over-dramatic."

"*Look* at this shit! My kneecaps are crushed!"

"Just a flesh wound."

Zero sighed and observed the wasteland full of soldiers and workers. He had natural white hair and blue eyes. His green uniform was muddy, ragged and coated in patches of soot and dried blood. He was relatively short; around four and a half feet. Despite his discouraging size he'd proven to all of his soldiers that he was a formidable general, even if he was a substitute. He took off his cap and wiped sweat off his brow with his sleeve. "Those Dehues really gave us a good beating. How aren't we the ones facing extinction?"

"Sir! First Lieutenant Queen, reporting for my debriefing," announced a tall, broad-shouldered woman standing at least a foot over him with green eyes and black hair. Her uniform was just as tattered as his. She stood to attention when he turned to her.

"At ease," he replied wearily. He was too tired to even stand after the battle, and with that passing thought, he sat down on a twisted robot thumb with gnarled wires hanging out from the broken joint. He beckoned her to do the same, but she refused with a dutiful head shake. "Any sign of Captain Elm's party yet?"

"No sir."

"What about Jonathon Silverstein's body?"

She shook her head and answered formally, "No, sir. The only soldiers known to be associated with Systems Corporation all seem to be dead. No sign of Jonathon Silverstein or any of his assassins except for…"

He looked at her calmly. "'Except for…' who?"

"We've found Aria Knight, one of Jonathon Silverstein's rogue assassins."

"Rogue?"

"She turned rogue, yes."

"Is she dead?"

"Barely alive, but *that* shouldn't be a problem for her."

The image of the fiery-haired fourteen year old girl being thrown from a burning plane flashed through his mind. He closed his tired eyes to envision it more clearly. "Rejuvenation, huh?"

"Yessir," she said. "She's resting in a different sector." Beat. "We also found a girl a little younger than her nearby, and *she's* alive and awake. But she doesn't look too good in terms of physical appearance."

"I didn't peg you for the judgemental type, First Lieutenant."

"I apologize, General. I suppose I wasn't clear enough. I didn't mean it in a judgemental way, just… she's physically healthy, but she doesn't *look* like it. Her mental state, on the other hand..."

"Who can blame her? She was probably caught in the middle of the chaos." He stood up. "I'm not feeling too healthy either, at the moment. Not with this smell."

"Sir?"

"Take me to her."

Queen nodded in acknowledgement and turned. "Very well, sir. Follow me."

He stared down at her in half-concealed horror. She was just ten years old. Her body was thin, with more bone than muscle from what Zero could see. She sat in the far corner of the tent with a blanket wrapped around her. The table and chair in the center of the tent remained neglected, as did the sandwich and unopened milk carton provided for her. Her eyes were like pits, hidden under the shadow of her dulled, spiky red hair as she stared lifelessly at the charred dirt.

A male middle-aged doctor and a young adult female nurse sat on a crudely constructed stone bench on the opposite side of the tent. The doctor turned to Zero, his face softened with concern and pity.

"What happened to her?" asked Zero, watching the girl tremble.

"She won't speak to me," he answered. "She'll only talk to Nurse Lana. Whenever I go a few paces near her, she becomes very aggressive and quite frightened. Doesn't help that she's a pyrokinetic. She burned the last tent down."

Nurse Lana stood up and walked past Zero. "I must speak with you outside. See if the First Lieutenant can calm her down. She'll only talk to women, from the looks of it."

Zero nodded to Queen and turned to leave the tent with Lana walking beside him. "So what happened to her?"

"Her father died in the Battle of the Waves. As for her mother... she mentioned the mafia, but remained vague on the details. And then there's her sister..."

"Mafia?" Zero raised an eyebrow. "I'm surprised she told you *that* much."

"She and her sister, along with a few remaining friends, looked for shelter among other survivors of the attack, but they were ambushed by Systems Corporation soldiers and captured. Their friends were killed before their eyes and the girls were…" Lana hesitated, trying to find the right words. "…Assaulted repeatedly. The other girls actually ended up pregnant, but they were killed by Multiplier and his group. She was crying when she told me everything else leading up to today. I can't... I can't imagine, I mean... she's just a *kid*."

"How do you know for sure?"

Lana stopped and looked at him with sadness. He stopped three steps ahead of her and looked back. "What do you mean?"

"These days, you can't trust anybody. Not even kids. That's just the way things are now."

"…You didn't see her eyes, general. No one could go through so much undefeated, especially at her age. Her spirit's been crushed."

Zero nodded understandingly and straightened. "I'm sorry."

Lana looked over her shoulder at Queen, who was kneeling in front of the girl, smiling kindly and speaking comforting words that Lana couldn't hear. The girl was looking up into Queen's eyes but the sadness and pain were still there.

"What's her name?"

"Jenny. Jenny Knight."

Zero went silent for a moment. Then he said, "If her sister's still alive—"

Kablam!

Suddenly dirt and shrapnel erupted under a Humvee, slinging the exploding vehicle into an artillery crater full of rainwater. Muddy water showered the area as machine gun fire rang through the air.

"What the hell?!" Zero ran for the trench, toward the gunfire. Soldiers alarmed by the sudden racket rushed to the scene alongside him with their assault rifles ready.

"Where is she?!" a familiar voice shouted. It was young, and it was shrill and desperate.

Zero stepped onto the edge of the trench to see another girl stepping back with her arm wrapped around a struggling soldier's neck, jabbing a pistol against his temple. Soldiers all around her aimed their assault rifles at her, barking orders.

"Drop your weapon!"

"Surrender! The war is over!"

"Step away from the hostage and put down your weapon!"

"Don't give me that crap! Where the fuck is my sister?!" she screamed.

Her body was bloody and broken and her clothes were burnt and torn. She was soaked head-to-toe in blood, both eyes wide open and frantic. She had fiery red hair tied back by a green and yellow polka-dotted bandanna with the exception of a couple spiky bangs hanging over her eyes. Her eyes were jet black and bloodshot.

Her hostage clawed at her arm, trying to stay on his feet while bent back due to her shorter height. "Your arms are like steel, girl."

"Shut up!" she shouted.

"Make me, bitch! Just wait till I get outta this grip you got me in."

"Oh yeah?!" she replied, jerking back on his neck.

"Yeah, I ain't afraid to strangle a little bitch!"

"An' I ain't afraid to kneecap a tall jackass!" And then she shot him in his left kneecap.

The hostage screamed in agony and writhed in her hold, trying to reach his wounded leg, "AH! Oh, my leg! Oh Jesus, *God*, my leg! One day I'll have my revenge! I'll skewer you like a fish! A sweet, moist *salmon*! Agh!"

"Aria," Zero spoke her name, instantly turning her crazed eyes toward him.

"YOU! Zero! Where's my sister? Give her back, or I swear to God, I'll scatter this bastard's brains all over the crater!"

"Your sister's safe. Drop the gun."

"Give her back! She's all I have left! I know you have her, Zero!"

"Aria, calm down—"

"SHUT UP!"

"Drop your weapon, girl!" a soldier shouted.

"Don't shoot!" barked Zero. "Stand down, men!"

The soldiers looked at Zero with uncertainty. "General…?"

"Drop your weapons," he ordered calmly. "And back out of the trench with your hands up over your heads."

They hesitated. One of them exclaimed, "What, are you actually fucking serious?"

"That's an order."

They exchanged worried looks before tossing their weapons to the ground and backing out of the trench with their hands up. Aria pressed her back to the wall, watching as they raised their hands over their heads, being sure to keep them in her sight. Zero calmly watched her tremble. He tossed aside his H&K Mk 23 pistol and threw his hands up.

"Where's my sister?" she asked.

"Let the soldier go first."

"Give me my sister first."

"No," he said stubbornly.

Aria fingered the trigger, jabbing it against the soldier's head roughly. "Care to rethink that answer? I'm not in the mood for games, and I sure as hell don't trust any government organization at the moment."

"Sir!" another soldier shouted as he reached the edge of the trench, pointing his gun at Aria. "I got her, sir! Permission to shoot!"

"For Christ's sake," Zero yelled, "put the gun down! *Now*!"

The soldier hesitated. "But she's—"

"PUT. IT. *DOWN*." Zero thrust his index finger toward the ground. "*NOW*!"

The soldier's eyes shifted to Aria, then to Zero, then back to Aria, then to Zero once again. "But—"

A disarmed soldier smacked his shoulder. "Damn it son, put it down!"

"We're all good here," said Zero, as calmly as he could manage. "I think we're all a little on the edge here. Hey, a war just ended, who the hell wouldn't be?" He chortled nervously. "This girl's got every reason to be panicking. Aria, you've got every reason to be panicking."

Aria made a half-shrug.

Zero continued: "But I'm being reasonable here. Clean slate, you guys. Clean slate. She didn't do a damn thing to incur our distrust."

The soldier trembled. "B-but sir…!"

Zero growled through gnashed teeth, "Damn it soldier, if you don't put that gun down *right freaking now*, I'll lynch your ass myself! Do you understand me?!" He jabbed his finger toward the ground with every word: "PUT. IT. *DOWN*."

The soldier let out a frustrated yell before throwing his gun aside.

Zero sighed and nodded with approval. "Good. Much better. We're good?" He looked at Aria. "Are we good?"

Aria half-shrugged again. "I-I…"

"We're good," said Zero. "No cause for alarm. Your sister's safe with us. She's in a tent. No unreliable men are around. No psychos, no lunatics, no bad guys."

"Yeah," Aria said, scoffing, "like I'm going to trust your word on that."

"You don't trust me? That's too damn bad. But if trust is the issue here, then take me as your hostage and I'll take you to your sister. And then we can talk like civilized people and maybe even have some of my mom's delicious tea and chocolate chip cookies. Does that sound like a good deal or what?"

That answer caught Aria off guard, but the surprised look in her crazy eyes didn't last long. She recovered quickly and slowly pushed the soldier across the trench toward the sloping wall with her gun still fixed on his head. When they reached the top of the wall beside Zero, she kicked the soldier back down and moved behind Zero, hoisting her arm around his neck and pressing her gun against his head in one swift, blurry motion. She looked around for any signs of movement she wouldn't like from the soldiers, but they remained rooted to their spots with their hands in the air. "Take me to my sister. And no funny business."

"Okay. Much better." Zero nodded and slowly walked for the tent with her stumbling in tow, struggling to keep a good pace while she restrained him. She cursed his shortness, since she was half a foot taller, and let go of him, proceeding to follow him with her gun trained on the back of his head. The soldiers and workers shifted out of their path, watching with silent anxiety as they crossed the sector.

They reached the tent, and Jenny saw Aria first and gasped with relief. "Aria! You're...!"

Zero stepped to the side, allowing Aria to run to her sister and wrap her arms around her. "Jenny! Oh, thank God you're alive!"

Jenny buried her face into Aria's bosom and burst into tears. "Aria..."

Aria smiled, stroking her younger sister's hair with motherly tenderness. "Shh… it's all right now. You're okay. You're okay."

First Lieutenant Queen watched their reunion with a distant expression. She turned to Zero. "What should we do with them, sir?"

Zero decided upon his decision quickly, crossing his arms—an expression that told anyone who knew him that what he was about to say would his final decision. He said, "They'll be my responsibility from here on out."

Aria glanced over her shoulder at Zero, as if she knew she could trust him. Zero looked back at her and turned to Queen again. He uncrossed his arms and headed out of the tent.

"Forgive me, General, but if I may be so bold," said Queen as she followed him out of the tent, "why would you do that? Can't we do anything else?"

Zero stopped and looked up at the sky. "What else *can* we do with them? Their future is for them to decide."

"But… what about their actions? How—"

"You just let *me* worry about that, *First Lieutenant*," he said curtly.

"...Of course. I apologize, sir."

An armoured Humvee pulled up nearby, and a man in a black suit stepped out of the vehicle, instantly surrounded by bodyguards.

The man looked at him urgently, and Zero nodded to him. "Excuse me, First Lieutenant."

"Of course." She returned inside the tent.

Zero approached the man with his hands clasped behind his back. He saluted. "Prime Minister Whitaker, sir. What a coincidence, I was just about to—"

"Is the Dead Blue taken care of?"

Instantly the mood changed between them. Zero looked around to make sure no one was watching. All he saw were soldiers moving bodies onto the trucks and paramedics tending to the wounded, and then there were also Whitaker's bodyguards, but they weren't anything to be concerned about. He turned back to Whitaker. "We don't have him, sir."

"What happened?"

"He vanished shortly after the Fate Star exploded."

"There are many unanswered questions, General, and none of them are safe to answer out in the open like this."

"Sir?"

"The Dead Blue's capture is of the utmost importance. I want him found alive. He's far too dangerous to be out there on his own in his current state. You've seen what he's capable of, General. You know that compared to Jonathon Silverstein or Aria Knight, the Dead Blue is much more important?"

Zero nodded. "Yes sir."

"See to it that he's found," said Whitaker. "If he goes on another killing spree before you capture him, *you* will be held accountable for his actions and I will expect your resignation the day after. Do you understand?"

The wind blew the stench of burning flesh and death across the city as they stared at one another.

"Do I make myself clear?" Whitaker repeated impatiently.

After another brief pause, Zero nodded, "Yes sir."

"Good," said Whitaker as he returned into the back seat of the Humvee. "And as for Aria Knight, General…"

"About that, sir, that's what I was about to ask about. I need a favour…"

One Week Later

"Here we are." Zero eased his sedan to the side of the dirt road in a sleepy suburban neighbourhood on a moderately raised hillside. A blanket of snow spread across the front lawn. Zero looked at the house across that lawn; it was simple, with a path darting through the lawn from the sidewalk to the patio at the front door. A mailbox hung over the curb, covered in snow and dripping with sparkling icicles. The driveway was coated with a sheet of ice beside the picket fence that separated the property from the neighbour's.

"My brother used to live here," said Zero. "Now *you* will."

The Knight Sisters looked at him with surprise from the back seats. Aria asked, "Wha…? Why're you helping us?"

Zero pulled off his sunglasses and leaned back, pondering Aria's question for a few silent moments. "I don't really know. It's not exactly pity. Maybe it's just because I feel that it's my duty."

Aria stared at him. "Your... duty?"

"That's right," he said.

Aria blinked, trying to figure out what he meant.

Then Zero gave her a goofy grin. "And also my sweet little sister who lives down the road. You could all be good friends!"

Aria jabbed a pistol against his forehead with a scowl on her face. "I'm not in a friend-making mood."

Zero froze. "I-I was just kidding—where did that come from…?"

Zero unlocked the door and led the girls inside the kitchen. The dining room was on the other side of the large rectangular room, with a sliding door leading into another room and stairs that curved left into the hallway on the second floor. Zero showed them around, opening the sliding door for them to see the large living room with a foldout couch sitting under a glass tile roof that curved down the wall.

"Whoa…" Aria couldn't help but say that.

He said, "And upstairs…" Zero led them up the stairs and opened the first door on the left. "This is the bathroom."

The bathroom was completely white; pearly floor and wall tiles, and a grey ceiling. The mirror was screwed into the wall above the counter that sat across from the bathtub/shower, with the toilet wedged in a niche between the shower and the far wall.

Zero closed the door and opened the closet door on the right, already full of towels and washcloths before moving on to the second door beside the closet, revealing the study. The study already had a desk and chair with bookshelves of manga volumes of all types and genres standing against both walls. Zero laughed with slight embarrassment. "He was one of those otaku types…"

He moved on to the door across the hall on the left, revealing the first bedroom about seven feet wide and six feet across. He moved on to the door at the end of the hallway and opened it, revealing a washing machine and a dryer.

"And finally, the last bedroom." He opened the last door on the right side of the hallway to reveal a bedroom slightly wider than the first one. "And that's everything. Most of this stuff is my brother's, so please treat it with respect. And please don't break the plasma screen TVs in the bedrooms and living room… those were gifts from me to him. And they were expensive."

Jenny was rendered speechless.

Aria was nearly as stunned. "Th-thanks… we won't."

Zero sighed and handed them each a card. "Well, since you're in my care now, here's my number for emergencies only. I'll send you each a hundred bucks a week for food and whatever else you might want or need. I'll get you enrolled in the academy up the road once things settle down. You need an education if you want a future, after all. They'll help you control your abilities so that you're not a danger to yourselves or those around you. And I'd like to see you two make some friends. My sister included."

They scowled at the last remark, but it was obvious to them that he was really proud of his younger sister.

Aria asked bluntly, "Do you have a sister complex?"

Jenny chimed in, eyes narrowing, "Are you a pervert?"

Zero stared at them in disbelief for a beat. "No... and *no*."

The girls didn't look away or change their expressions.

"Anyway," Zero said quickly, "the sheets have been washed, the windows cleaned, the dishes done and put away. I expect you two to keep this place in top shape, got it?"

They nodded in response.

Zero smiled. "Good. Taking care of you two should be easy, then."

Silence filled the air as Zero kept his confident grin. The girls never stopped staring at him.

Suddenly Zero's shoulders fell in discouragement. He was

already feeling emotionally drained. "Who am I kidding…? This is gonna be hard!"

Aria smiled. "Don't feel *too* worried. I only killed about four thousand people and my reputation for collateral damage isn't *too* bad. I'm not that hard to get along with."

Zero raised his head, showing the girls his exhausted frown and droopy eyes.

"What? Better than five thousand."

"Just don't be such hassles… I'm only nineteen…"

Aria blinked, staring at him in disbelief. "A nineteen-year-old general? How?"

Zero shook his head. "No idea. It just happened."

"Well, I'm off! If you need anything, just give me a shout." Zero opened the front door and stepped out into the cold January snow.

"Um, Zero…"

Zero looked at Aria over his shoulder. "Huh?"

Aria smiled at him as kindly as she could. "Thanks for everything. But I have to ask again: why are you helping us? There's always a reason, isn't there?"

"...You want a reason?" Zero paused. "I knew your dad. He was a good man and I made a promise to him to take care of you two if something happened. I keep the promises I make, Aria. And... hopefully by doing this, I'll keep you out of that world. You still have so much life ahead of you." He placed his hands on her shoulders and looked her straight in the eyes. "*Please*... I can't do this without you. Promise me you'll make the effort to stay out of that world. Promise me you'll try to live a life that's... relatively *normal*."

"...What about Silverstein?"

He sighed. "We haven't found Silverstein yet. If he shows up here, don't try to take him on yourself. I want you to run. I want you to run and call me as soon as you can."

She scoffed. "Running? Where's the fun in that?"

"I'm serious, Aria," he said. "Just say 'okay'."

Aria cocked her head to the left and shrugged her left shoulder playfully. "Okay."

"Promise me *that* much."

"I promise. Now close the door. We're not heating the outside."

Zero chuckled and released her shoulders, "Alright. I'm off. Take care of your sister. I'll be back later to check up on you two."

"Alright, then," she replied with a smile. She waved. "Bye."

Zero smiled and closed the door before walking to his car. *"Relatively normal," huh... it's probably too much to ask.*

Zero approached his car and stopped on the curb. He stared at the roof of his sedan, which gleamed despite the bleak colour in the sky. A very thin sheet of snowflakes coated it. *I hate the idea of spying on people. I hate the thought of it. But I have to put them under surveillance. It's how I'll know... they'll never do anything that will land us in a heap of trouble.*

He turned and looked at the house again. He spotted Jenny's face staring behind the frosted window above the front door. She was staring right at him with a blank, fatigued expression on her face.

I guess she picked her room, he thought.

Zero smiled kindly and waved. She didn't wave back.

A loud flapping sound reverberated over his head, causing him to stop and look up. In the dull, ashen skies he spotted an Apache helicopter flying above the suburbia toward the top of the hill where the fortified Cloverfield High Academy proudly sat. He watched it ascend the mountainous hill for a few seconds with scrunched eyebrows. The first thing he looked for was the infamous Systems Corporation logo on the side. Nothing. He got back into his car, buckled up, and thought, *What's going on there?*

Cloverfield High Academy—Rooftop

The helicopter landed on the roof of the academy's left wing where five men waited. Four of them were members of the Elite Infantry of Systems Corporation; soldiers clad in thick body armour and gas masks with round, blood-red lens; armed with M-16 assault rifles, they stood like dutiful statues, flanking the fifth man. Kirk, a middle-aged man in a black suit with short blonde hair and blue eyes, seemed out of his elemental between the soldiers. Flurries of snow buffeted the small group as the helicopter landed on the rooftop—their attempts at keeping statue-still weren't very successful due to the helicopter's strong rotor wash.

They stood to attention as the hatch slid open and revealed a fearsome man. He wore all black—a cloak and a wide-brimmed hat and ragged bulky pants; a modified Smith & Wesson Volcanic strapped to each leg. Beneath his cloak were a soot-stained flak jacket, a thick belt where four more holstered Volcanic pistols were strapped, and two ammo belts that took the shape of an X across his chest. His eyes glowed red and his skin was stained dark crimson like a skin-tight mask. He looked like a demon from their worst nightmares; even the way his cloak shifted with his ghostly movements, gave him the appearance of a ghastly vapour or a dark shadow.

"Commander Silverstein, sir!"

Jonathon Silverstein looked up at them, his cold eyes sending chills down their spines. "At ease," he ordered in a gravelly voice. "Kirk, get your men to carry this kid downstairs."

Kirk nodded to the men that flanked him, and they immediately ran to the chopper, hesitating briefly due to Silverstein's appearance before climbing into the helicopter and pulling out a coffin-like tube of metal and glass—a cryogenic incubator. There was a small body inside—the body of a boy. The pill-shaped capsule was fairly light; it was practically anti-gravitational, which surprised the soldiers as they carried it out of the helicopter. Kirk watched the soldiers carry the capsule through the door and down the stairs before turning to Silverstein. "Sir—permission to speak freely?"

"Granted."

"Why are you storing him here?"

"Here, *they* wouldn't even think about looking for him. Provided no one saw us get here in the first place, they'll never find him." Silverstein crossed his arms and took in the view of the silent neighbourhood as a thin mist of snowflakes gently cascaded the grey sky. "You can relax, Kirk. He's sleeping soundly in cryostasis. There's no waking him up unless I *want* him woken up."

"That's not the point. Why under a school for children? He's a killer…"

"Indeed, he's a killer. But your students also have Dehue genes in their blood. It wouldn't matter if he killed them or not. To make my answer to your previous question clearer, no one would think to look at a school for children to find the Killer of Twenty

Million People. That capsule is designed to keep him asleep for decades. No one will find him. No one will wake him. Stop worrying."

"But it would be bad on my part. I'd be the one responsible. And what if he wakes up?"

"He *won't* wake up," He said quickly. "No one will look for him anyway. As far as the world is concerned, he died when the Fate Star hit. Although he deserves a nice 'thank you' for saving the world from the destruction the star could've caused." Silverstein snickered, lighting the cigarette he put in his mouth while he spoke. "That sounds so stupid. A *Dehue* being the saviour of mankind. The very thing I campaigned to destroy saved us all in its dying breath. The whole damn thing leaves a bitter taste in my mouth."

"My only question is *why* he would save us."

Silverstein shrugged. "Hell if I know. Just keep him asleep and don't wake him up, otherwise there will be hell to pay. From me *and* from him. Got it?"

Kirk nodded. "Understood, sir."

Silverstein climbed back into the helicopter. He turned and glared at Kirk and said, "If he wakes up, it'll be *your* head—though it would all depend on who gets it first; me or him." He slammed the hatch shut, and all Kirk could do in response was watch the helicopter take off into the grey sky.

Fraden Residence

Zero knocked on the door to a white two-storey house and waited patiently for a forty-year-old woman to open the door. She stared at him in disbelief, tears welling up in her eyes. She gasped happily and hugged him tight. "Zero! Thank God you're all right."

"Mom, are you okay? Is everyone safe?"

She nodded and let go. Then she let him in the house and quickly closed the door behind him. Zero took off his muddied boots and stepped into the living room. "The battle didn't reach this far, miraculously. But we could hear it from the basement. I thought it would reach us…"

"The war is over now. We won."

Zero's mother sat down on the couch, trying to digest the news. "It just doesn't feel right to me. If feels like they were only trying to survive."

"They were," he answered solemnly.

"What about your friends? Weren't some of them Dehues?"

Zero froze, as if he'd seen a ghost.

"I-I'm sorry," she said, putting her hand over her mouth. "I didn't… I didn't mean…"

Then he snapped out of it, sat down on the couch beside her, and held her hand. "I'm a coward."

"Don't say that, Zero. You did what you had to."

"I had to kill my own friends to prove that I was loyal to my country and my race. But if I didn't kill them, my family wouldn't be safe. You and Marner. The punishments were too severe, damn it." He buried his face in his hands and shuddered. "They all trusted me to do the right thing. I failed them."

"You did what you had to. It's not your fault." She was fighting back tears, trying to comfort him with her own words. "No one deserves any of this."

Zero broke into a sob. "But I still failed them! I killed them. They trusted me, and I killed them. I shot them in the back, every one of them!"

She patted him on the back. "All you can do now is move on. Stop blaming yourself for that."

"Stop saying that," he snapped. "I could've done something else. I could've protected them. I… I could've hid them somewhere. I could've smuggled them out, or disguised them, or, or… *something*—"

"Zero?" A small girl in a night gown hesitantly walked into the living room. She had long silver hair and blank eyes. Blank, but not stupid—they made her look blind, when in fact she wasn't. Marner looked at Zero. Her doubtful expression turned into tears of joy and relief. "Zero!" She dashed around the couch and leaped into his arms. "I was so worried!"

He stared down at her with disbelief, as if a total stranger hugged him instead. The recognition quickly came. He relaxed, and smiled. "It's all right, little sister. The war's over now." He lifted her off his lap and set her down in front of him. "I adopted two girls that you can be friends with."

His mother looked at him in surprise. "You did?"

Zero nodded, smiling proudly. "They're gonna grow up to be such sweet girls."

COBALT ROGUE, VOL. 1: THE DEAD BLUE

Episode 001

Astral Demon

Cloverfield High Academy; Thursday, October 1st, 2026

It was the fifth largest recorded private academy ever built on earth; its brick perimeter walls stood thirty feet high and stretched out to a kilometre in each direction. The academy itself was a fortress with a glass dome jutting up from the center of its angular rooftops. Reaching up from the dome was a tall metal spire that pierced the clouds; a gold angel with its arms and wings spread out had perched itself vigilantly on the tip. Each floor wrapped around the dome's base in quarter-kilometre chunks; the angular, terra cotta rooftops consisted of solar shingles to generate the academy's own electricity. Under the dome, the vortex-themed, yellow-brick courtyard provided a quiet place for students to think and study. An oversized sword-in-the-stone fountain spewed water into a pond that circled its base in the vortex's center. Oak trees stood high in the patches of grass scattered around the courtyard. The courtyard was always peaceful.

The halls, less so.

"YOU SICK, PERVERTED SON OF A BITCH!"

WHAM!

Jenny's fist slammed her fellow student's head right through the door of his locker with enough ferocity to kill him. And if he didn't have rejuvenation powers included with his ability to manipulate ice and snow, she would have succeeded. Even with his skull cracking and his jaw flying off, he would live. It would just shift and snap right back into place like a Lego set.

Most of the students in the hall casually walked around the scene while others calmly and quietly observed, as if what she was doing to her schoolmate was normal.

And it was. For the past three years, Jonny Kyle would get his face pounded into the floor, a locker, a wall, a set of stairs, a drinking fountain, a bookshelf, the ceiling, a toilet, a microwave, a blender, and many other things because of his endless sexual harassment of the female students. Jenny was among the few who outright beat him for it. He was like Wile E. Coyote. He was too stupid to give up, and too immortal for his target of harassment to succeed in ending the tedious cycle. The only difference that existed between the two was that Jenny was trying to kill her stalker.

"Jesus Christ, get a fucking life! Don't you have anything better to do than grab my tits day in and day out? Do I look like a goddamn whore to you? Well, DO I?!" She kicked him in the stomach, momentarily snapping his spine in half with a resounding *CRACK*.

Despite this, Jonny still managed to snap his jaw back into place. The tissue quickly grew back, and his face looked like new again in a matter of seconds. Then Jenny arched back and slammed her foot into his face, pushing him back into the locker.

"Aww, come on, I was just having a little fun," he protested into the sole of her shoe.

"What is so appealing about me that you have to grope me and harass me every day? Huh? When are you gonna learn? *Huh*?"

A muffled, echoing, "I don't know" was all she could hear from inside the locker. "They're just big for your age. I like—"

She kicked him through the wall, sent him tumbling into the next classroom in an avalanche of bricks.

The ninth-grade health and nutrition teacher, Mrs. Amy, sighed and closed her text book. She had long green hair and light green eyes; she was dressed in a green and white blouse and matching miniskirt. "Oh dear, not again. Lars, when they're finished, can you repair the wall?"

A boy with black hair sitting in the third row of the classroom nodded.

Jenny grabbed Jonny by the collar and shook him angrily. "The only thing that's pissing me off more than your usual bullshit is that stupid fucking grin on your face! Get that look off your face *right* now! *NOW*! You hear me?!"

Jonny continued grinning and replied stupidly, "My sweet Jenny is holding me close… in her arms."

"*UGH*!" Jenny slammed him into the marble floor, knocking him unconscious, with a dumb smile frozen on his blank comatose face. His twisted body twitched in a pool of blood that spread from his fractured skull.

"Ms. Knight, may I make a suggestion?" asked Mrs. Amy. "Not to be rude, but perhaps the reason for him to constantly harass you is the inappropriate outfit you're wearing. It's quite aggravating and—pardon my French—a little, um, slutty."

Jenny's 'inappropriate outfit' was a black leather tube top with a built-in bra under her brown jacket. She also wore black jeans with white pockets, and black spandex gloves. Of course, Mrs. Amy was pointing at the tube top.

"You shut up!" Jenny yelled defensively, jabbing a hostile finger at her. "I should be able to wear whatever the hell I want without worrying about some perverted dipshit groping me like I'm his sex doll!" She started kicking his twisted body again, angrily stomping him deeper and deeper into the floor. "Asshat! Fuckman! You want tits so bad, go milk a cow and see what happens!"

Mrs. Amy shrugged, maintaining her kind, patient smile. "I'm just saying, dear."

Jenny growled angrily and stormed out of the room through the opening she made. The second period bell rang, so she proceeded down the hall to attend her science class.

"Hi, Jenny!" Marner's high pitched voice caught up with her as she stomped down the hall. Marner's appearance hadn't changed much in five years, except that she had grown a few inches taller. Now she was about five feet, one inch tall. "I heard what happened."

"That idiot ought to give up already," she snarled.

"Have you told Aria about it?"

"All Aria did was laugh and tell me to take it as a compliment. She was no help at all." Jenny continued grumbling to herself as she turned the corner and marched up the two sets of stairs leading to the second floor. "Some sister *she* is. She won't even defend her little sister from grabby perverts!"

Marner Fraden wore the school uniform; a white shirt with a blue bandanna around her shirt collar and a blue pleaded skirt. She was a ghost whisperer and often had visions and visits from ghosts that need her help and support. Even though her tolerance for ghosts popping out of nowhere was high, she was timid and frightened easily by other things. Despite being Jenny's polar opposite, nothing could stop them from becoming the best of friends.

Jenny reached her locker and entered the combination. Opened it. Took out her science text book.

"Hey, Jenny?"

"What?"

"I had another strange dream last night."

"Same guy?"

Marner nodded.

Jenny looked at her and closed her locker door. "What'd he want this time?"

"He just told me that he needs my help and… he said the strangest thing."

"What?" Jenny pressed.

Marner looked at her with concern. "He said he'd tell me in science class."

Jenny blinked. "Oh, I see. I'll let you copy my notes after class, then. Let's go." Jenny turned and headed for the stairs.

"Hey, wait!" Marner ran after her. "Do you think he's been watching for long?"

"What d'you mean?"

"Well, he knows my schedule..."

"Oh. Probably."

Elsewhere...

An endless plain of tall green grass and rainbow-coloured flowers, bending from side to side in calm waves with the breeze. The sky, an empty black void, though somehow the Spirit Core was as bright as a cloudless day. Children enveloped in white light auras laughed and played in the vast fields, chasing each other through the flowers and tall grass.

The Spirit Core.

It was all that was left of the Dehon dimension; the only thing that still existed. Now it served as a home for the dead until they were judged to go to either Heaven or Hell. Even the evil and misunderstood spirits were calm here. Paradise, in every sense of the word.

A young man's voice with a barely noticeable Russian accent pierced the air: "You sure I can trust her?"

"Oh, yes, definitely!"

"How can I know for sure?"

"You can't."

The boy scowled at him. "*What?*" He wasn't enveloped in white light like the others.

The white wispy ghost grinned stupidly. "Weeeellll she's helped out lots of ghosts, including a lot of Dehues after the Dehue Extermination Project, but nothing like you."

"Well what's wrong with *me*?"

"You *did* kill a lot of people, you know."

"Wasn't my fault."

"Still…"

"Shut up, Dave."

Dave was a ghost, obviously. A very unusual one. He had a bashed-in top hat with googly eyes bouncing back and forth on the antennas poking out of it. Strapped in a strait jacket. His teeth were like huge piano keys, shining with a cartoonish gleam every time he grinned. He had no legs, only a wispy end, and his skin was that of a classic ghost's—white and transparent. "No, *you* shut up. Just because I can't see through you doesn't mean you can be a bully, Damian." He stuck out his floppy, dog-like tongue. "*Nyeh*!"

Damian had messy cobalt hair that hung over his cold blue eyes and pale face in spiky, uneven bangs. He wore a red T-shirt and blue jeans. His height was nothing special; he was about five feet, eight inches, and his build was athletic, but somehow still allowed him to have the look of a child just entering his teenage years. His emotionless expression lacked something... *human*, which quietly concerned Dave.

"Whatever. As long as your niece is reliable, I don't give a damn."

"Oh yes, of course!" He laughed heartily.

Damian sighed. *It's gonna be a long afternoon.*

Cloverfield High Academy—The Living World

Jenny watched with an amused smirk at the back of the science class as Marner slumped down on her desk in the front row. *Asleep already, huh? That was fast.*

Just like all the classrooms in the academy, this classroom ramped upward as it approached the back, making it easier for the teacher to monitor all students during lectures. Marner was a good student, so teachers rarely monitored her activity.

Jenny leaned on her elbow, maintaining her smirk. *Sweet dreams.*

The Spirit Core

Marner opened her eyes when something brushed against her face. She found herself lying in a soft bed of long rustling grass. She felt at peace here, as if all her stress and fear were washed away from her body. She got up and looked around.

"You wanna know an interesting fact?" a familiar voice said behind her.

Startled, Marner gasped and leaped away from Damian, who was sitting in the grass with his legs crossed and his cold blue eyes fixed on her. He glanced up at the sky and continued, "You might already know this—or maybe not—but this place is like... what's left of our dimension. Bet you didn't know that the Spirit Core was made up of our world, did ya?"

"You…" she sputtered. "You're the boy from my dreams."

"I'll take that as a compliment." he said with a slight smirk. His reply made her blush.

"I-I know what this place is. I've been here before," she said, referring to his brief explanation. "So... what's your story?"

He looked at her. "My story?"

Marner nodded and sat down on her knees with her feet tucked under her, careful not to let the breeze blow her skirt up. "Yes, your story. Why did you contact me?"

"Because you can help me." He scratched the back of his head. "Y'see, I'm not dead."

Marner blinked. "Then what are you? Astral?"

"Oh, *no*," he said sarcastically. "Frozen. Stuck. A random camper who got his ass caught in a bear trap," he said with a scowl. His eyes alone looked as if they were saying 'Are you really *that* retarded?'

"Please be serious."

"No, seriously."

"Where are you?"

"Below you."

Marner jumped back defensively. "I picked a bad day to wear a skirt. Oh dear!"

A scowl stretched across his face. "…No. I mean I'm under

the ground in a cryogenic capsule thing. I can't wake up; the air in that thing is drugged with something that keeps me asleep. So because I'm pretty much dead physically, I'm able to do astral projection. I can go wherever I want, whenever I want, and see whoever I want. Cool, yes?"

"S-sure..." she agreed uneasily. *He's cute but weird... and really mean.*

"*NO*," he said sharply, making her jump. "It's *not* cool. Not at all! It's annoying, and restraining, and it just downright pisses me off. And I have the worst itch ever." His expression softened. "So I was wondering if you could get me out. Your principal kinda buried me underneath the academy. Somewhere in a dingy basement."

Marner was starting to distrust him. That sounded like a lie, and his behaviour wasn't very convincing either. "Why would Principal Kirk do that?"

"Principal Kirk would do that because he was once a Systems Corporation supporter and Jonathon Silverstein's loyal bitch." Damian leaned back and gave her an annoyed frown. He crossed his arms. "You don't believe me, do you?"

Marner sighed. "Well, it sounds very... unbelievable."

Damian heaved an exasperated sigh; his shoulders fell in discouragement. He was starting to wonder if Dave was as reliable as he claimed. "Yeah, well, the idea of alternate dimensions sounded stupid a hundred years ago too, but *now* look at the world."

He has a point, she admitted to herself. "How can you prove all of this?"

"Well, I've been watching the academy grounds for two years, despite the fact that I've been down there for about *five* years. But hey, I just figured out I could float around in astral projection about two years ago, and since I've had nothing else to do, that's all I've been doing. Just floating around, minding my own business, maybe goofing off even though no one could see me. It was fun at first, but then... it started feeling a little too familiar. Not being noticed by anyone, I mean... and I found something interesting..."

"Does it have to do with the private dorms for the teachers?" she asked quickly.

Damian paused. "No... but I went near one once and the sounds I heard were not pleasant. For me, anyway. Hell, I was curious once and actually went in there. All I have to say is that anyone who plants a video camera in there will make millions in the porn industry." He paused again. "Then again, I guess some students wouldn't mind doing that shit. Like Jonny."

Okaaay, that's more than I needed to know. Marner shook her head, hoping to shake the disturbing mental images out of her brain. "Okay, so what did you find interesting?"

The stray hair that stuck upward from the rest of his hair twitched, as if it had a life of its own. With a serious expression, he said, "Gym class."

"...Gym class?"

"What happens at the beginnings and ends of every gym class?"

Marner blinked. Then she turned red. "You... you mean...!"

Damian's ahoge stood upright, although his expression remained unchanged. "Change rooms. And showers. And a couple staff members fucking in the teacher's lounge. That shit was awesome."

Marner nearly swooned from the shock and embarrassment.

"Also, after school, the school's almost completely empty. BUT!" He yelled the last word, making Marner jump, which seemed to make him feel clever judging by the mischievous smirk on his face. "You know Tim, the academy heartthrob?"

Marner noted the hint of malice that Damian tried to hide when he said Tim's name. "Tim Sahara Ryan?"

"From now on, as long as you're speaking to me about him, he won't be known as 'Timothy Sahara Ryan, the Cloverfield High Academy Heartthrob' anymore. Instead, he will be known as 'That Pussy Who Wasn't Even Remotely Involved in my Capture and Still Acts Like a Big Shot'." Damian turned, muttering several bitter, vulgar phrases under his own breath—all of which involved Tim, including: "That little cunt, I shoulda ripped his balls off and shoved 'em up his ass when..."

"Yes?"

Damian snapped his head back to her. "He comes down every night to check up on me. He and I were big enemies during the war and we fought a lot. And I beat his worthless ass every time. Just follow him down into the basement of the academy, and when you see me, yell my name. *Shout* it like you were an extra on the set of *Braveheart*."

"*Braveheart*?"

"*Braveheart*," he repeated with a nod.

Marner blinked. "How do I know I can trust you? You must be locked down there for a reason."

"Well, yeah," he scoffed. "I got caught."

Marner scowled at him. *Smart aleck.* "Why did they go after you in the first place?"

"Because I'm special in a lot of ways," he answered quickly.

"How?"

Klunk!

He smacked the top of her head with a text book. She shot him with an agitated glare. "Wake up."

"Huh?"

"Wake up, Ms. Fraden!" he yelled.

Marner sleepily raised her head, her ears ringing with the class's laughter. "Huh? What?" She looked up to see Mr. Harris, the huge, plump science teacher that dwarfed her with his menacing size. He gripped the text book until it squeaked like rubber in his thick fingers. "Eep," she said.

"Are my lectures really *that* boring, Ms. Fraden?" His voice was loud and thunderous, making her shake.

"N-no."

"Then PAY ATTENTION!"

Marner sat trembling in the chair, nodding until her head was a blur. "Y-y-y-yes sir!"

"So what'd you see? Anything good?" Jenny asked between mouthfuls of a meat pizza. They sat in the huge cafeteria packed with chattering students, eating at a table by themselves. The walls, floors and ceilings were coated in white tiles depicting various acts of kindness and friendship around the air vents and lights through crude painted pictures.

Marner looked at her, concerned. "He has a knack for telling me strange things..."

"Strange things, like…?"

"He said he was trapped under the academy. He said that Tim goes down there every day after school to check up on him."

Jenny blinked. "Tim? Tim Sahara Ryan? *That* jackass? I

knew he was odd." She leaned on her elbow with a reminiscent scowl. "I knew he was hiding something."

Marner nodded.

"Who knew he had *those* types of fetishes? Like I wasn't good enough for him. I'll admit though... those extra-curricular activities *do* sound fun."

Marner's jaw dropped. "That's not it at all!"

Jenny laughed. "I was joking! Jeez! You never have a sense of humour when you're trying to fix something."

"I'm not into that sort of thing," Marner stated seriously.

Jenny snickered. "Well, you're a ghost whisperer, so you probably have some secret, effed-up fetishes hidden in that innocent-looking head of yours. Heeheeheehee! Guilty secrets!" She grinned as if she knew Marner's dirty little secret and was about to blackmail her with it. "Messed-up secrets! Un-innocent secrets!"

Marner turned red and shook her head. "Stop that!"

Jenny laughed and finished with a sigh. "So what should we do? Do you trust this ghost?"

"He said he was still alive, just trapped in a cryogenic capsule. I'm not quite sure if I trust him. Usually I can tell if a spirit is innocent or not, but for him… I couldn't tell."

"Was it a bit of both?"

"Not really…"

"What do you mean, not really?"

"He didn't really have a feeling… he just…" Marner shook her head. "I don't know. But it felt like I could trust him, despite the fact that he's one of the most arrogant people I've ever spoken to. And rude."

"So should we do the impulsive thing and stalk Tim after school to spring this guy?"

Marner nodded. "Sounds like we have a plan."

Jenny's mischievous grin returned. "Who knows, it might even be fun."

"Stop that!"

Final Period—Math Class

Jenny sat in the second row up next to one of her best friends, Elsie Karan. Elsie had short snow-white hair with black trims at the tips of the spiky bangs hanging over her forehead. She usually wore different coloured T-shirts with the same cartoon skull slapped over two overlapping rollerblades, similar to a skull and crossbones design; and faded blue jeans.

Marner sat on the other end of the second row, by the windows that overlooked the quiet neighbourhood of the school district. She stared anxiously out at the suburban district.

Jenny looked at Elsie, who leaned against the desk. She gazed at their twelfth-grade math teacher, Mr. James Anderson—spellbound. An oblivious Anderson went on to explain the fraction problems he'd drawn on the Smart Board: "C'mon, you guys, you should've learned this in ninth grade…"

"You know," Jenny whispered, "there are much better guys out there."

"He's the one," Elsie breathed.

Oh, for God's sake.

"He's a *teacher*, Elsie!" Jenny whispered with a shriller pitch. "Like, come on."

"He's a *good* teacher," she said.

Jenny's eyebrow twitched in disgust. Then with a bored sigh she turned her head to the front of the room and scrutinized the teacher.

Mr. James Anderson was fairly tall, about six and a half feet, with broad shoulders, short brown hair, athletic build, aqua blue eyes, and a handsome smile. Sure, the man was attractive, but Jenny didn't consider him to be dating material, especially for one of his students. Elsie may have been eighteen years old, but it would still cause uproar if what Jenny knew ever got out.

"I dunno what you see in him, but whatever. Just make sure you don't get caught by anyone with a big mouth."

Elsie's head suddenly twisted in her direction. "What?"

Jenny gave her a mischievous smirk. "Don't worry, though. I won't tell anyone. Your secret's safe with me. Heheheheheheh…"

"J-Jenny…! It's not like that!"

"Suuuuure."

"I-it's not!"

"*Suuuuuuuuuuuurree*!"

Elsie's face turned red. "I… I…"

Jenny leaned closer. Her expression hard and serious. "I guess you forgot the time when he was supposedly tutoring the both of us at his place, and you two went upstairs and *totally* ditched me for an hour."

Elsie went silent, staring at Jenny with raised eyebrows.

Jenny placed her hands on her cheeks, swayed back and forth, and mockingly whispered, "Oh, Monsignor! Oh, *Monsignor*!"

"S-stop that!"

"Never!"

Mr. Anderson's voice of authority shook the room as he spoke up, "Miss Knight, Miss Karan, is something the matter?"

Elsie turned to him and flashed an embarrassed grin his way. "Oh, no, no, nothing's wrong, sir!"

"Then pay attention, please," he said with a fond smile that was obviously directed toward Elsie. Then he turned back to the board and continued his lecture.

Jenny scowled at him, then looked at Elsie's blushing face and shuddered in absolute disgust.

BBBBBRRRRRIIINNNGGGG!

Mr. Anderson glanced at the clock above the intercom for a moment before announcing, "That's the bell." Chatter filled the room as the students gathered their things and packed up their books. Just before the first student could get themselves out the door, with the rest quickly following, Mr. Anderson continued, "There will be no homework tonight. Everyone, enjoy yourselves and stay safe out there!"

Jenny leaned against the wall outside the classroom with her hands stuffed into her jacket pockets as the remaining students filtered into the hall. Marner emerged from the crowd and approached Jenny with the same concerned expression she had on during class. Jenny hardly noticed her, preoccupied with observing Elsie's interaction with Mr. Anderson. Elsie leaned on his desk as Mr. Anderson packed his books and laptop into his bag, occasionally stopping to smile at her. Then he said something that made Elsie draw back suddenly with her hand over her mouth. Flustered.

Jenny exhaled with disgust and rolled her eyes. Then she looked at Marner. "You sure you wanna wait until everyone leaves?"

Marner nodded. "What other choice is there?"

"We could just walk away."

"Why?"

Jenny shrugged. "I dunno, I just… have a bad feeling."

"…Is it about Tim?"

Jenny gave her a bitter scowl. Marner faltered slightly and continued, "I-I mean, well… maybe it's just awkward for you…"

"That's not what I meant," Jenny said agitatedly. "I couldn't care less about that. It's this other guy… what's his name?"

"Damian. He said his name was Damian."

"Damian, huh?" Jenny blew a spike of hair away from her mouth. "I just dunno about this… a prisoner in a cryogenic capsule under our school is fascinating an' all, but let's just think for a minute here. *Why* is he in there? What'd he do? He must've done something. And *who*, exactly, put him there? And why *here*? Whoever hid him here didn't think he'd be found here, and if he's here in the first place, that means someone in the school's involved—or *all* of them are involved—which would just make things worse for us if we let him out. They've got staff and students guarding the place like a bunch o' guards or something. Doesn't that bother you at all?"

"…You don't have to come with me if it bothers you."

"You don't have to go. I'm not letting you go down there by yourself. Fuck that. I just think it's fishy. And I can't shake the feeling that we'll be in over our heads if we help this guy."

Marner took a moment. True, it was a suspicious situation, and there was obviously something else going on, but…

"I can't," she finally said.

"What?"

Marner gave Jenny a serious, dutiful look. "I can't just abandon a spirit in need of help. I refuse to leave him down there."

Jenny stared at her with raised eyebrows. She didn't say anything until Elsie left the classroom, with Mr. Anderson locking the door with his bag in hand. "Alright, then. I guess it's settled. I'm going too."

Later that Afternoon…

Tim Sahara Ryan was the 'cool and silent' type. Some liked his spiky blood-red hair while others found the hardened look of resolve in his ruby-coloured eyes appealing. Some even liked the X-shaped scar running across his cheek and cutting from below his left eye to his jaw. He always wore red, which just added to the 'mystery'. He was also the type that made all the guys jealous and the entire population of female students chase after him…

…Or stalk him. Not that *anyone's* curiosity would give them the boldness to follow him to see what he *really* did when no one was in the school.

And that made him careless.

"There he is," Jenny whispered, leaning around the corner as Tim silently marched down the hallway, bathed in the fiery glow of the sunset.

"Ready?"

Marner nodded. "Once he turns the corner, let's go."

They waited until he disappeared around the corner and quickly-but-quietly jogged down the hall. When they reached the corner, they stopped with their backs against the lockers that lined the wall and peeked around the corner. Tim stood in front of a row of lockers and typed the four-digit combination into the middle locker. It beeped and he yanked it open. He looked around cautiously. The girls retreated behind the corner. Jenny waited a moment, then looked around again. Tim had vanished, and the locker door was closing.

Jenny gasped, dashed down the hall, *dived*, arm out-stretched. The door closed painlessly on her fingers. She sighed with relief and waited until Marner reached her and fully opened it before getting back up to her feet. "Safe."

Marner smiled proudly. "Nice save, Jenny."

Jenny bowed sarcastically. "Thank you, thank you. Ladies first."

Marner shook her head and peered inside to see a narrow staircase running down into pitch blackness. She shivered and carefully went down the stairs with Jenny close behind. "I can't see."

"Neither can I."

"Well, you can manipulate fire. Can't you light the room?"

"And risk getting caught by Mr. Sunshine down here? Noooo thank you."

"What are you two doing here?" Tim asked.

Hesitant silence.

"Um… Marner… please tell me you just hit puberty…"

"N-no… that's wasn't me."

"Nah, that was definitely you. My, your voice got deep."

"I asked you a question," said Tim, rather impatiently. "Jenny, is that you? Marner, too, following like a lost puppy."

"Maybe if we pretend we're not here, he'll forget about us. Shh!"

"I asked you a damn quest—"

"SHH!"

More silence, longer this time.

"I'm still here."

"QUICK ESCAPE!"

Whack!

Crash!

"Ow!"

"RUN! RUUUUUUN!"

Tim stayed silent.

Bam!

Crash!

SMASH!

"Hey, a doorknob!"

"Don't go in there!" Tim shouted desperately.

"Bite me, bitch!" Jenny fired back.

Bam!

Jenny kicked the door down and dived inside a room with a dim blue glow, yanking Marner in with her. She slammed the door shut and threw a metal shelf down in front of it. Tim banged against the door yelling for them to "open the damn door!" but Jenny pushed against the shelf.

"No way in hell, buddy!"

"Jenny…" Marner said, fear and awe in her voice.

"What?" Jenny looked over her shoulder to see the very object that illuminated the small room with its dim blue glow. "Whoa."

Damian lay inside the glass tube, his hair moving on its own as if submerged in water. He breathed steadily, strapped inside the capsule with metal restraints wrapped tightly around him. Marner thought he looked peaceful inside there.

"He's actually kinda hot," said Jenny.

Marner frowned.

"Yipe!" Jenny leaped back as Tim sliced an X through the crude barricade and kicked everything across the room. Some bits of metal hit the girls while other debris pelted Damian's capsule without leaving a dent.

Marner shielded herself from the fragments of metal with her arms, as did Jenny. *His instructions!* She screamed, "DAMIAAAAANN!"

To her horror, nothing happened.

Jenny went stiff, staring at Tim, breathing steadily.

Tim froze and watched Damian intently, waiting for something—*anything*—to happen. His body tensed as his eyes searched for any movement.

Nothing.

Tim relaxed. An arrogant smirk appeared on his face as he approached the girls. A red telekinetic energy blade materialized in his hand. "Well, well, well. Looks like you didn't wake up that blue-haired freak after all. Do you know what would've happened if you did? Honestly, you two." He paused. Arched an eyebrow. Then his eyes narrowed. "How did you even *know* about...?"

BOOM!

The capsule and the restraints exploded in a blast of blue light, and before anyone knew what happened, As if in slow motion, Damian hung suspended in midair above Tim, eyes wide with fury. "MORNING, SLEEPYHEAD!"

With a powerful kick, Damian sent Tim's flying back out the door and crashing into the main basement lobby. Damian landed on the floor without a sound and followed him out the door. His hands went up. Two black blades with bluish auras appeared in his fists as he stepped over the remains of the shelf. "Welcome to my happy home." He raised the blades for Tim to see. "So glad you could come to the party. I was beginning to think no one was coming." He scoffed. "*That* would've been a fucking bummer." Damian sprang toward Tim, who scrambled to his feet.

Tim threw his hands up and screamed, "WAAAIIT!"

Damian stopped abruptly, just a few paces away from Tim. "…What?"

Tim pointed at the blade in his left hand and said, "That one's shorter than the other."

"What? Seriously?" Damian looked at his blades—

WHAK!

—only to receive Tim's surprise uppercut under his jaw. His head snapped back. Blades flew out of his hands and dissipated into nothing without their master. "*OW*!"

Tim lurched forward. Tackled Damian to the floor. The two of them started rolling around; kicking, punching, yelling. "Get back in the capsule!" Tim barked. "Do it!"

"Fuck you!"

"Do it!"

"Suck my dick!"

"Get back in the fucking capsule!"

"*You* get back in the capsule!"

Jenny and Marner watched with wide eyes as the two of them comically rolled back and forth on the floor, knocking over mops, buckets, and other cleaning supplies.

"Fucking *twat*!"

"Shit-faced *dweeb*!"

"Whoa… talk about a short fuse," said Jenny.

Marner gulped. "Y-you think we did the wrong thing?"

Jenny watched as Damian caught Tim in a headlock and repeatedly punched him in the stomach until Tim swung two fingers over his shoulder to poke Damian in the eyes, causing him to retract and yell with rage. She shrugged and smirked. "Who cares? It's funny."

"Pisshead!"

"Shit-fucker!"

"Dick muncher!"

"*Freak*!"

"I'm gonna shove that capsule up your fucking ass, *pizda*!"

"I couldn't agree more, you commie shit-stain!"

Marner cringed when Tim swung a mop into Damian's head, and then she cringed again when Damian picked up a nearby bucket and hurled it into Tim's face. "Whatever you say…"

Somewhere else…

"How many are there?"

"Thermal readings counting an approximate thirty."

"Quite the gathering we have here. So here's the plan: squad one, take out the enemy in warehouse eighteen. Squad two, warehouse nineteen. Squad three, take out the last warehouse. Squad four, their main HQ is nearby—I want all three floors of that building reduced to a single storey of rubble. Are your infantry units out of there yet?"

"My stealth soldiers have successfully planted the explosives inside their HQ without being noticed. You were right; the 'leader' inside the HQ was a dummy. The real one's probably in one of the warehouses."

"Thought as much. Good. Now on my mark, I want all of you to detonate the explosives, and squads one to three, I want you to move in and take the rest of them out. Mop the floor with their faces. Do you copy?"

"Yes, sir," each squad leader answered over the transmitters in their gas mask helmets, signalling his squad members to ready themselves.

"Ready?"

"Ready, sir."

"Alright… five… four… three… two… one… *initiate*!"

KABOOM!

The three-storey building near the three warehouses popped and crumbled to the ground in a fiery conflagration.

The charges set in the front and back doors of the warehouses disintegrated the doors and sprayed the occupants with shreds of metal, taking the gang members inside by surprise. Systems Corporation Elite Infantry poured in through both entrances, shooting everything in sight. The startled gang members blindly returned fire, but they were quickly mowed down by the trained soldiers' heavy fire. The situation was the same in each warehouse. In less than twenty seconds, the soldiers had nothing left to look at than mangled corpses and shredded furniture sprawled over pools of blood.

"Squad one is clear. No casualties to report."

"Squad two is clear. No casualties to report."

"Squad three is clear. No casualties to report."

"Squad four is clear. No casualties to report."

As expected of elites, Silverstein thought as he nodded with approval, sitting in the driver seat of his black Mercedes-Benz. He watched his soldiers nail a flag to the wall of one of the warehouses and load themselves into a handful of black vans. The flag had a red biohazard symbol with a skull in the center over a black background. He watched the vans file out of the compound and speed off down the road until they were out of sight. "Alright. Report back to base, men. Good work."

Cloverfield High Academy

Jenny sighed impatiently, sitting with her legs crossed and leaning on her hand, her elbow resting on her knee. She and Marner quietly watched Damian and Tim continuing brawl. Marner didn't like watching the fight from the very beginning, but Jenny had been enjoying it, finding it to be the funniest thing she'd seen all week.

That was half an hour ago.

"This is getting old," she croaked.

Marner gasped and placed her hand over her mouth when Tim pinned Damian to the ground and heard a sickening snap; she thought Tim broke his neck. She was somewhat relieved when Damian kicked him away and dived after him, yelling, "BANZAI, BITCH!"

"Why won't you give up already?!" Tim parried Damian's bull thrust and side-kicked him in the jaw, slamming his face into the wall.

Damian grabbed his ankle and counter-attacked with a kick to the vulnerable crotch.

With a squeak, Tim was down and rolling on the ground, moaning in pain, grasping his throbbing crotch. "That's fighting dirty!"

FINISH HIM!

Damian lifted him by the throat and grunted as he hurled Tim at the nearby wall. Tim bounced off the wall and landed on his back, rendered unconscious.

FACEPLANTALITY!

Damian sighed wearily and said, "I beat you! You're still a weak little bitch, Tim!"

Jenny rolled her eyes. "Finally."

Marner rushed to Damian's side when she saw blood trickling from the side of his mouth, dripping off his chin. More blood dribbled down the right side of his head and oozed over his closed left eye. His bruised knuckles cracked when he bent them. To top it all off, he made a sputtering noise before spitting blood onto the wall. “Are you okay?” she asked.

Damian wiped the blood off his chin and said, “Peachy.” He stopped, gave them both a blank, wide-eyed stare.

And then it hit him like a runaway truck into an oblivious three-year-old.

He fell flat on his face.

Jenny stepped beside Marner and observed the somewhat comical scene before her amused gaze stopped at Damian. “You alive down there?”

“Feels like I haven’t eaten in years,” he answered with a dead, emotionless tone in his voice. “What do you think…?”

Marner sighed and helped him up, slinging his arm over her shoulder and assisting him up the stairs. “Let’s get you something to eat.”

“And what about this one?” Jenny asked, pointing her thumb over her shoulder in Tim’s direction. “He’s out cold. Can we leave him? Let’s throw him in the capsule.”

Yes, Damian thought, *throw him in the capsule.*

Marner sighed as she steadily progressed up the stairs. “Please bring him, too.”

Goddamn it!

“And where do you plan on bringing them?”

“Your place.”

“Wait, what? What the hell?! You know how I feel about stuff like that! And Tim’s an asshole! Why would I want my ex in my house again?”

“I’ll be there too. Besides, Damian isn’t bad. Are you?” she asked him, flashing a kind smile his way.

“Foooooood,” he absently groaned. “Feed me. I want some food… Some nice steak... and waffles... and a nice stack of pie slices. Pumpkin would be nice...”

Jenny snarled with frustration, lifted Tim, and slung him over her shoulder with one arm. “Damn boys. Hey, Marner! Marner!”

“What?” Marner asked patiently. She knew it was coming: Jenny’s complaining fit.

“How would you like to have your ex over to *your* house, huh? Especially under these mysterious circumstances!”

“It’s only until he comes to.”

“Oh, yeah, right, I’ve heard that one before. Isn’t that right, you stupid man-whore?! Why do I have to carry *you*?! I'd rather carry the cute one! At least *he* isn't a psycho dickhead!"

Marner ignored her fit as she treaded up the steps. She was thankful that Damian at least helped her with the steps, only leaning on her shoulder for support.

"Foooood," Damian moaned again.

"Shut up," Jenny snapped behind them.

"Pumpkin pie."

"Fuck you, you get apple!"

Damian moaned in dismay.

The girls arrived at Jenny's house half an hour later.

"Okay, Damian's in the foldout bed in the living room and Tim's in the bathtub," Jenny announced as she descended the stairs.

Marner looked at her with slight disappointment, though she certainly wasn't surprised by Jenny's choice. "The bathtub? *Really*?"

Jenny glared at her. "Hey, it's bad enough they're staying here in *my* house. But there's no way in hell that creep is going to sleep in *my* room. In *my* bed. If he was there right now, he'd probably 'magically' regain consciousness and snoop through my underwear like the perverted dick-face that he is."

Oh boy, here we go, Marner thought to herself.

"Or worse: he could be planting tiny little spy cameras in the bedroom."

"Bathrooms are more common, you know…"

"Or *worse*!"

What's worse than that?!

"He could be taking pictures of every page in my journal or… or…" she looked at Marner with wide terror-filled eyes. "My *secret collection*!"

Oh. That. Marner laughed and waved it off. "That's too ridiculous, Jenny. What kind of boy would look at yaoi manga?"

"The really fucked-up kind, that's what," she answered. "The Tim-Sahara-Ryan kind."

Marner shook her head and went to the fridge next to the stairs. She opened it and peered inside, looking through the shelves until she discovered a package of bacon and a carton of eggs. She gathered them up in her arms and placed the food onto the stove embedded between the fridge and the counter.

"Um, what're you doing?" Jenny asked, pulling a chair out from under the wooden table beside the living room door. She slumped into it with a sigh and propped her feet up on the table, leaning on the back two legs of the chair. "You're cooking my food for my unwanted guests again, aren't you?"

"Yes. Damian needs food. I'm surprised he's lasted this long without passing out."

"Just give him a banana and he'll be your best friend."

Marner paused. "I should include some bananas in his meal," she squeaked excitedly. "Add some nutrition to his first meal since he was put in that horrible thing! I hope he enjoys my cooking."

Jenny shrugged. "He probably will. He doesn't look like the type to pick mushrooms off his pizza, you know?"

"I know."

Jenny sniffed the air. Her face darkened with disgust. "Something smells."

The living room door slid open, startling them both. Damian stalked in like a moaning zombie, his mouth watering and his eyes staring blankly ahead. "I smell bacon and eggs…"

Marner blinked. "I… didn't even turn the stove on…"

"Bacon and eggs."

He tried to sit in the chair near the wall but ended up tripping over it, smacking his face off the table, and falling to the floor.

Jenny shook her head and looked down on him as if he were the most pathetic thing she'd ever seen.

"Ow."

"Are you okay down there?" Marner rushed beside him and pulled him up onto the chair, satisfied with him sitting straight before he wobbled and did a face plant on the table. Marner gasped and lifted his head up in her arms. "Are you okay?" she repeated worriedly.

"I'm fine. Where's Tim?"

"Upstairs."

"I see…" he said slyly. Every hint of fatigue suddenly gone. He stood up. "'Scuse me."

"Where do you think you're going?" Jenny asked him.

"Gotta take a piss."

"Don't start anything," she said suspiciously. "And don't plant any cameras, either."

Damian whirled around and raised an eyebrow at her. "Cameras?"

Jenny shot him a sinister glare.

Damian blinked and said, "What?"

"I'll castrate you with my foot if you even *think* of doing that."

"How in the hell are you going to castrate me with your *foot*?"

"Don't push me."

"No, I wanna know how you're gonna castrate me with your foot. I'm genuinely curious."

Jenny scowled. She hated him already. Pissing her off with his smartass attitude and that condescending smirk. "Go take your piss."

"Not until you explain it! I have *no* idea how you'd castrate someone with your foot!"

Marner adopted a warning tone, "Damian..."

Beat.

Damian asked, "With or without shoes?"

Jenny cracked her knuckles, seething. "*URGH*!"

Marner snapped at him, "Go do your business and stop aggravating her!"

"And stay the fuck out of my room," Jenny added on her behalf.

"Got it." He headed for the stairs.

"Are you listening to me?"

"No."

He remembered every night as if it was happening all over again. He remembered the blinding walls of fire rising from the black mountains of corpses and rubble, stretching as far as the horizon. He remembered the horrible stench that invaded his nostrils. He remembered the blood-soaked earth, how it felt like mud under his feet. He remembered the chilling chorus of screams that filled the charcoal night illuminated by the lesion of radiant red light.

The Dehue screams. The freak screams.

They haunted him every night. That lingering, high-pitched ringing sound that never seemed to have any end to it. It went on and on as he slept.

He remembered how the men were lined up and shot, or gunned down in the heat of battle. He remembered how the women would be divided into categories to meet different horrible fates; the ones deemed attractive were raped repeatedly—sometimes by more than one soldier—and shot to death, while the ones deemed ugly would be thrown into the fires that greedily devoured their towns and villages. He remembered how the children would be thrown into massive craters, piled on top of each other until those unfortunate enough to be stuck on the bottom suffocated to death. And he remembered how those children would be shot if any of them tried to climb out, and he remembered watching in horror as the soldiers drowned them with gasoline and torched them.

Oh, God. The children.

Even as Tim watched the hundred or so children writhe in the flaming pit, he knew that he still hadn't witnessed the extent of the terror of the Dehue Extermination Project.

What is this I'm feeling? What is this burning heat? What is this pull on my face? Why does it feel like I'm soaking beneath the fires of hell while some round object tries to suction my face off? The thoughts poured through Tim's mind and constantly repeated over and over again as he began to regain consciousness; although that consciousness was fading away as quickly as it came.

Terror struck Tim as the sudden realization hit him. Submerged in boiling hot water. Something round and slimy pressed down on his face, keeping him under. He flailed his arms and kicked his legs desperately; splashing around in the small, narrow space he was trapped in. Sliding around on the slick surface.

Damian sat on a stool beside the bathtub with a fashion magazine in his right hand and a toilet plunger in his left. He blatantly ignored Tim's desperate struggles while he casual skimmed the magazine pages. "So shirts that emphasize breast sizes and tight jeans that emphasize ass sizes are the latest fashion trends these days… huh... interesting. Hey, Dave, lookit this."

Dave peered closely at the magazine over his shoulder as Damian held it up for him. "Ooh...!"

"Nice, right?"

Still looking at the magazine, Dave said, "I didn't know fashion trends interested you."

"They don't, really. But hey, I've been asleep for five years. May as well find out what's been going on in the world today. Starting with what's trendy nowadays."

Bubbles fizzled from beneath the toilet plunger as Tim grabbed the handle with both hands and pulled, but Damian kept pressing it down on his face.

Damian turned the page with his thumb. "Hey, there are bras built into shirts now?"

Dave leaned closer, squinting as he studied the page spread with newfound fascination.

Jenny knocked on the door. "Damian, why's the water running?"

"Later!" Dave disappeared with a pop.

Oh, shit.

"Giving Tim a bath," he replied with his eyes fixed on the magazine.

"What?!" she called back in disbelief. "A bath?!"

"That's right. He forgot his scuba gear so he's relying on suction."

"Suction?!" The door flew open, and the sight of Damian drowning Tim with the toilet plunger made her gasp in disbelief. A wave of steam hit her, and after blinking from the sudden humidity, and that awful smell she complained about earlier, she looked at Damian through the haze. "What're you doing with that?!"

"With what?" he asked, looking up.

"That magazine! It's *mine*! *Not* yours! Why're you touching my things without my permission?"

Tim's head managed to surface. Without turning away from Jenny, Damian shoved Tim's head back under before he could catch a breath. "I was asleep for five years. One would think I'd wanna catch up on all the latest trends so I'm not *completely* in the dark."

"Oh, I see," she said with a weary sigh. Her exhausted scowl shifted to Tim's flailing arms and legs. "What about the jackass?"

"It's not a jackass, it's just some gunk stuck in your bathtub. So I'm plunging it."

Jenny crossed her arms. "And you didn't think that plunging said 'gunk' would turn my bathroom into a crime scene?"

"Who cares? As long as you get the gunk out and dispose of it efficiently, you'll be fine."

"Yeah, right."

Silence fell between them. The only noise was the sound of water rushing into the tub and Tim's limbs splashing about.

"Do you mind going back downstairs?" she asked.

"Why?"

"Because I don't want any dead bodies in my bathroom."

Damian looked at her.

She looked back at him.

Then he said, "We don't have to keep it in here."

"GET OUT!" she shouted as she grabbed him and hurled him out of the bathroom as if he were weightless—much to his surprise.

Damian hit the wall across the hallway and fell on his back. He rubbed his aching face and craned his neck back to see upside down Jenny turning the facet off and letting the water out of the tub. Tim's head resurfaced and Damian could hear him gasp for air.

"Thank God!" Tim gasped.

"Be quiet," Jenny retorted.

"Oh, come on," Damian called with frustration. "If you keep the garbage from getting thrown out, people will think you're a pack rat!"

"Go downstairs!" Jenny shouted. "I am *this* close to tossing your asses out on the street!"

Damian sat at the table with his head resting on his hands when Jenny came back. Without warning, she grabbed the back of his head and bashed his face into the table. "*Suka*!" he shouted as he sat back up and massaged the back of his throbbing head, giving her a piercing glare. "What the actual fuck was *that* for?"

"For being an inhospitable guest," she replied bluntly. She sat down at the opposite end of the table, placed her elbows on the blue and white checkered tablecloth, and glowered at him.

"Asshole? Me?" Damian hissed defensively. "Do me a favour and keep your mouth shut."

Marner scowled at him. *Oh, goodness, he's really something, isn't he?*

Jenny's eyes narrowed menacingly. "Watch your mouth."

"*You* watch *your* mouth," he snapped back.

Jenny gnashed her teeth angrily. "You're asking for an ass-kicking—"

Marner gasped when Damian suddenly bounded out of the chair with an energy blade in his hand, and quick as a blue flash he threw the blade at the stairs.

SPANG!

Tim cocked his head to the side just before the blade hit the wall a mere an inch from his face like a dart. He stood on the middle step like an emotionless doll, his pupils glowing blood red.

Damian glared at him with blue eyes that shimmered like dark water, frozen in his stance.

The tension thickened.

Each one watched the other for the slightest movement, waiting for the precise moment to strike.

Marner stayed rooted to her spot in front of the stove.

Jenny grabbed Damian's head, yanked him back, and slammed his face into the table again. "You goddamn jerk! Now *I* have to fix that!"

The boys said nothing.

Jenny sighed and left Damian as he got back to his feet. She went around the table and sat back in her chair, crossing her arms. She then shot resentful glares at the boys and said, "If you're gonna fight, take it outside! You're not gonna mess up my house just because of a little feud. If you damage even *one* floor tile I'm gonna kick your faces into the ceiling. Got it?"

"Whatever," Tim snapped back.

Damian rubbed his reddening forehead, glaring at Tim again. "As long as I can kick the shit out of 'im, I'm fine with that."

Jenny nodded. "Good. Fighting is good as long as it's outside. And frankly," she started, glancing over at Damian, "the fact that you obviously don't like my ex makes me like you a little more. Could almost make me forgive you for that mouth of yours."

"I have a pretty mouth, thank you," Damian said sarcastically.

"They'd *love* you in prison," Jenny said with equal sarcasm.

Marner exchanged worried glances from Damian to Tim, her hand almost over her mouth. "You shouldn't be fighting. Why don't you sort it out? Like friends?"

Jenny looked at the two of them as disbelief swept across their faces. *That's so like her.*

"Say what?!" they replied in unison. "You don't mean that, do you?"

"Yes!" Marner smiled as she skipped in between them excitedly. "Why don't you shake hands and apologize for whatever you're angry at each other for? You never know, you could become best friends."

"'Friends'," Damian spat, "with *him*?"

"Yes, of course," Marner said. "Friendship is good, you guys."

"Not with *him*, it isn't," Tim said.

"Sure it is," Marner said. "And do you know what's just as good as friendship? *Pacifism*."

The two boys' faces twisted in disgust. Jenny slapped her forehead.

"How about violence?" Damian said, eyeing Tim.

"No," Marner said. "Violence isn't the answer."

"Violence is *always* the answer."

"That's nonsense."

"Pacifism's nonsense," Damian said. "Violence, when acted out on certain people, is *good*."

"That's baloney," Marner said, folding her arms across her chest. "Violence is a horrible, hateful thing. It only makes things worse. I know you two would feel better about yourselves if you resolved this peacefully. I'm sure the only reason this feud between you has gone on for so long because you're always trying to solve it with violence. Trying to solve your problems with violence is like trying to dry a block of ice with a damp cloth. Now, does *that* sound productive to you?"

"No," Tim said slowly.

Damian said, "Who in their right mind would try to dry *ice*?"

Marner frowned. "Alright, I'll demonstrate. Try to open your minds. I want you to shake hands and call it a night."

Silence filled the room.

"Wouldn't it be great if we could get rid of this menacing atmosphere?" Marner continued cheerfully. "I-it's probably just something silly anyway. It doesn't matter who started it. Why don't you be the mature ones and just bury the hatchet?"

Tim gave in and, grinding his teeth, hesitantly stepped down the stairs.

Marner nodded in encouragement and looked at Damian. "Come on, Damian. Don't make Tim look so alone."

"Why not? That's his specialty."

"*Go*," she ordered sternly.

Damian growled and reluctantly stepped forward. Both of them glared at each other as they slowly approached one another, one step at a time; one in sync with the other's movements.

They stopped, eyes locked, as if a Western-style duel was about to go down between them.

Jenny raised an eyebrow as she watched with slight amusement.

Marner stood beside them in front of the living room door, silently encouraging them both with a pleased smile.

Damian looked at her.

She nodded for him to continue.

Tim looked at her.

She nodded again.

They looked at each other again, and finally, Damian extended his trembling hand forward—but he did so cautiously.

Tim looked at his hand, unsure. He looked back up into Damian's eyes as he smiled innocently and said, "I'm sorry for what I did back then."

Tim hesitated.

Marner looked at him. "Go on…"

Tim scratched the back of his head anxiously. "...I'm sorry, too."

"Friends?"

Tim smiled and took his hand. "Friends."

Marner cheered silently.

Jenny frowned, waiting for something bad to happen.

Ka-SMASH!

And there it was.

Their grips tightened as both of them thrust their fists into the others' faces with enough force to crack the floor beneath them. The items around them shattered.

"Like *fuck* I'll forgive you, you cobalt faggot!" Tim growled.

"I'll bury the hatchet in your *balls*, whore!" Damian snarled.

Jenny roared, "NOT IN MY HOUSE!"

KRAM!

Jenny launched their faces into the ceiling with a single high kick to their jaws.

Marner watched them struggle to get down as their bodies dangled and swayed from the ceiling, their heads on the second floor. She flinched as she heard their muffled cursing and swearing, still kicking and slapping each other as they began with the insults again. She sighed and drew a strand of her silver ear back behind her ear. "Why can't they get just along?"

"Because they're boys—" Jenny punched Damian in the crotch, which incited a muffled, pained moan from the second floor "—and they're stupid!" She did the same with Tim, creating more cries of anguish from the ceiling. They grasped their throbbing crotches and crossing their legs, rocking back and forth steadily, and whining.

"Again with solving violence with violence." Marner looked at her with disappointment. She watched as Jenny yanked them both down from the ceiling by their ankles, dragged them through the kitchen, opened the door, and threw them out before they could figure out what the hell just happened. "You don't need to do that…"

"If you want them here, you better make damn sure they don't break anything with some impossible force like what they just did," she said as she slammed the door shut, crossed the kitchen again, approaching the table. "I mean, *look* at this!" Jenny held up a sheet of paper with cracks running through it. "They *cracked the paper*! How much fucking tension was in the room just now?! Do you know how *impossible* that is?"

"I know, I know."

"It's fucking *impossible*, *that's* how impossible that is! How could anyone possibly crack *paper*?! Even Aria hasn't figured out how to do that one!"

Marner went for the door. "Well, I can't leave Damian out there to starve." She grabbed the straw broom that leaned on the wall beside the door and opened the door. "Damian?"

Tim was on top of Damian with his hands around his neck. Damian had his thumb pressed into Tim's right eye. Both of them stopped and stared at her like two cats caught in the act.

Swack!

Marner swatted Tim's head with the broom. "Go on! Shoo! Go home!"

Tim hissed like a man possessed and scurried across the front lawn, crossed the driveway, and up the road out of sight behind the fence.

Damian pointed and laughed mockingly. "Yeah, you *better* run!"

Swack!

Damian scowled when Marner hit him over the head with the broom. "*You* be quiet."

"Yes ma'am."

Marner sighed and stood the broom up beside her. She pulled the door shut behind her and looked down at him with slight sympathy. "You know, you should try to watch your temper around Jenny. You should also watch what you say. When it comes to boys, she has a very short fuse. But then again, after what just happened, I'm sure you already figured out that she's not exactly fond of the opposite sex."

"*Sex*?!" Jenny's startled shout cut through the door. "Not on *my* front lawn!"

Marner turned red with embarrassment and quickly yelled back, "That's not what I said!"

Damian crossed his arms dutifully. "Alright. I'll do it."

Marner leaped back, holding the broom defensively. "That's not what I was getting at!"

"Not *that*!" Damian yelled. "I was talking about watching my temper. I'll do it. If it means that I won't get my masterpiece face kicked into the second floor again."

"Ooohh." Marner loosened up, standing the broomstick back up beside her. "Well, that's good to hear."

"Uh-huh."

All sorts of things went through Marner's mind. Like how he ended up in that capsule in the first place or why Tim kept checking on him or why the both of them can't be in the same room together without one trying to break the other's neck. She also wondered why he was in the Spirit Core if he wasn't dead. She'd been to the Spirit Core many times before, but astral projections were extremely rare. "Damian."

"Yeah?" He crossed his legs, sitting on the front step without looking up at her.

"What happened to you?"

She knew that question struck a nerve. He was almost

shaking, looking down at the ground. Silence filled the air between them as Marner waited.

Guess it was inevitable for her to ask. Still, she caught me off guard with the question. It's like when kids ask their parents about 'the talk'. Strikes 'em dumb and nobody knows what the fuck to say right away. I mean, what am I supposed to say? Can't tell her to piss off. That'll just make things worse. So...

"...You ask what happened?" His voice startled her.

Marner nodded. "Uh-huh?"

He looked up at her with one of the most serious expressions she'd ever seen on the face of a sixteen-year-old boy. "It all started before the war..."

Episode 002

Settling In

WHAM!

Younger Damian kicked younger Tim into a pile of trash cans and laughed. Then, he snatched a video game from Tim's hands and said, "Don't worry. I'll return it before the due date so you won't have to pay the late fee."

"…And I never did," Damian finished. "He's never forgiven me since."

A pause.

Marner scowled. She knew he was hiding something a lot bigger than that. But for now, just to be on the safe side, she was going to keep quiet about it. He didn't seem too dangerous at first, but after the incident in the kitchen, she wasn't so sure about him. He looked gentle enough, and he did avoid hurting her and Jenny when he tried to skewer Tim, but she couldn't help but worry about him.

"Are you hungry?" she asked, trying to hide her worry and suspicion.

Damian looked up at her with a look pathetic enough to put a puppy begging for table scraps to shame. "Yeeeeeeeesssss."

Marner smiled at him kindly. "Come inside. I'll fix you something to eat." She turned around and opened the door. "Agh!"

Jenny stood in the doorway with a scowl, and she quickly grabbed Damian by the shirt collar and dragged him into the kitchen. "C'mere. I need you."

Marner was quick to protest as she shut the door behind her. "A-aren't you jumping in too fast, Jenny?"

"Quiet, Marner," she hissed as she let go of Damian, turned, and looked into his confused eyes.

Damian blinked and said sarcastically, "What's with the well-deserved attention all of a sudden? I know I 'm amazing an' all but come on."

Marner took a step forward. "Uh... Jenny...?"

Jenny sniffed the air and frowned. Then, she took two more steps back and sniffed the air. The same disgusted frown appeared on her face. She walked backward until she was standing beside the table and sniffed the air again. "Hm…" She took three more steps backward, her back touching the sliding door to the living room. Then, she opened the door, walked in, and closed it. All Marner and Damian could hear were Jenny's footsteps fading to silence behind the door.

Jenny opened the door, approached Damian, and leaned over him. Glaring at him, she pointed an accusatory index finger in his face. "You *stink*!"

Damian blinked again. "…Huh?"

"You stink so bad I could smell you from across the house! I *knew* something smelled awful! I *knew*!"

"So? Don't blame me; I couldn't shower when I was sleeping for… how many years?" he asked, glancing over his shoulder at Marner.

"When were you put in there?" Marner asked.

"The day… after the end of the war, I think."

"The Dehue Extermination Project?"

"No, the 1974 Viceeper Civil War," Damian said sarcastically, clearly agitated.

Marner said patiently, "Five years."

"Five years," Damian repeated, turning back to Jenny. "I knew it."

Jenny pointed to the stairs. "Shower. Now."

Damian leaped into defense mode, terror-stricken.

"I will wash your clothes. They stink too."

"NEVER!" he protested.

"Fine." Jenny crossed her arms, turning away from him and giving him a sideways smirk. "No shower, no food."

Damian's shoulders fell, horror frozen on his face. "The fuck?!" he sputtered. "Y-you wouldn't!"

"No, I wouldn't let you touch a single carrot until you shower," she said smugly. "Not a crumb of bread, or an ounce of fat, or a teensy, tiny little sliver of shit from the toilet."

"And what about my clothes?! What am I going to wear?"

"You're gonna stay in there until the laundry's done. You're lucky I didn't wash my load yet. Otherwise I would just be wasting water."

"Staying in the shower for two hours is a waste of fuckin' water!" he snapped back, throwing his hand over his mouth when he remembered to keep his temper in check.

Jenny smiled. "And if you last long enough for me to put them in the dryer, I'll give you a delicious reward."

Damian's eyes widened. *A delicious reward, eh?* His eyes dropped down to her chest.

Jenny scowled. "Get your head outta the gutter. What kind of a whore do you take me for?"

His eyes shot back up to her face. "I'm still not showering," he said defiantly. He crossed his arms and puffed out his chest. "Just try an' fuckin' make me."

The impatience on Jenny's face intensified. "Okay, I'll make you a deal." She uncrossed her arms, placing her hands on her hips, and smirked triumphantly, as if she'd already won the challenge she was about to declare. "If you can smell the inside of your shoe and stay on your feet, you can eat before you take a shower."

You act as if I'm staying here, he thought.

"Well, what other place do you have to go to?"

She can read minds?!

"No, I could tell by the stupid look on your face.

She's figured me out already?!

"Yup."

Lies!

"Well basically, anyway. I'm damn good at reading people."

Damian looked down at his shoes and cringed. He never noticed how much they were squeezing his feet like circulation-blocking cocoons. "Fine. I'll do it." *Then I can eat! This'll be as easy as sharpening a pencil.* He pulled off his shoe, held it at arm's length, and began to inhale through his nose.

Squish!

"NO CHEATING!" Jenny shoved the shoe into his face. The terrible green stench clogged his nostrils, forcing him to breathe in through his mouth, causing him to accidentally suck in the deathly stench that would surely make Chuck Norris himself cry for mercy.

Jenny laughed evilly as Damian collapsed. Marner gasped and rushed beside him. "He's not breathing!"

Jenny stopped laughing. "Oh." Then she laughed even harder. "Now we can put the food back in the fridge! HOORAY!"

Damian stood in the shower, pouting under the hot water. "Damn it all to hell."

Knock, knock!

"I'm coming in to get your clothes," Marner called nervously.

"Okay, whatever. They're in a pile next to the sink."

"O-okay." She quickly opened the door, her face completely red. She looked around quickly in search of his clothes and nervously struggled to decide which task she wanted to fulfill first. "Uh…um…"

"What?" he asked behind the curtain. "Care to join me?"

"A-Absolutely not! Um... Ummm... now what was it? Oh yeah! J-Jenny told me to give you this." She approached the shower curtain and hesitated. Looking in the other direction, she poked a cookie inside the shower and waited anxiously for him to take it.

"Oh." He took it and she quickly withdrew her hand. He ate it quickly, before the shower water made it soggy. *Guess this is my 'delicious' reward.*

Marner quickly gathered his clothes up in her arms and left the bathroom, stepped into the hallway and clumsily dropped his clothing. "Shoot." She gathered up his clothes and quickly rushed down the hall where Jenny waited by the washing machine. "Here."

"Did you empty out his pockets?"

"I didn't want to intrude…"

Jenny rolled her eyes and went through all the pockets, pulling out a dog-eared cut-out photo from a newspaper. "Wouldn't wanna intrude, but then you'd just be washing his clothes and destroying whatever he's got in his pockets. Hm? What's this?"

Marner stepped beside her and looked at the object she'd discovered with her. It was a photo of a crowd of people with cat ears sticking out of their heads standing in front of a cathedral. "Mews?"

Mews.

A race that resembled ordinary humans, with the exception of their cat-like features; mainly cat ears and tails.

"Hey, who's that?"

"Who?" asked Marner, looking to where Jenny was pointing.

She saw a short, pink-haired girl with light pink eyes smiling in the front row of the crowd. "Oh… she's beautiful."

Jenny shrugged. "Eh. She's alright." She handed the photo to Marner and stuffed Damian's clothes into the washing machine.

Marner looked at the photo again and walked back down the hall. *I wonder who she is.*

"Beats me."

"Ack!"

"Oh yeah, another thing," she said as she snatched the picture and stuffed it in her pocket. She headed down the hall, brushing past Marner.

"What?" asked Marner, following her.

"You forgot to close to bathroom door." Jenny sighed. "I swear you were born blonde, Marner."

They reached the door, and Jenny looked into the bathroom and froze. Damian was stepping out of the shower, freezing mid-step to look at her. Naked. Jenny looked down, then back up, maintaining a blank expression on her face.

"Can I help you?" he asked.

"N-nice... trinket you got there."

Then Damian did something unexpected. He smiled and gave her the thumbs up. "Magnificent, aren't I?"

"Why are you getting out of the shower?"

"Hm?" Damian asked, not making any attempt to cover himself. "What do you mean?"

"The… the laundry just started."

"I gotta take a piss. But hey, you're both welcome to join in."

A pause.

Jenny stared at him. He maintained his smirk.

She grabbed the door knob, pulled it shut, and stared at the door, standing completely still. Marner was amazed by Jenny's coolness. "Wow, Jenny... you handled that really well."

CRACK! CRACK! CRACK! CRACK!

Jenny started bashing her head against the door, startling Marner. "Jenny, stop that!"

Ding-dong!

Residence of James Anderson

Mr. Anderson opened the door and discovered Elsie on his

doorstep with a smile on her face. She grasped the handle of her backpack in front of her.

She beamed when she asked, "Ready to tutor me, Mr. Anderson?"

Mr. Anderson quickly ushered her inside. He took one last look out the door, surveying the empty street, before closing the door shut and locking it. He turned around and looked at Elsie, who had busied herself with scraping dirt off her boots on the rug. He was about to say something. Elsie scampered off into the living room. He sighed and followed her into the living room, in time to see her hop on the couch against the wall opposite the TV. A stone fireplace adorned with family photos and soccer trophies stood on the other side of the room, just a few feet away from the kitchen entrance.

Elsie bounced up and down lightly with her hands on her knees. She wore mostly black; a pleaded skirt and a white long-length tank top with a cartoon skull emblem on its chest under an unzipped denim jacket. She also wore laced boots that reached up to her knees and two leather studded wristbands.

Mr. Anderson cleared his throat nervously as he approached the coffee table. He scratched the back of his head and said, "Listen, Elsie…"

"Hm?" She looked at him with that enticing stare, sprawling herself onto the couch like a lazy cat. She raised her leg slightly in a way that would flash a small portion of her panties in Mr. Anderson's direction. She knew wearing white in the right places would make the parts of her she wanted him to notice stand out more.

Mr. Anderson tried to pry his eyes away, even taking a brief glance at her panties, then tearing his eyes away from her skirt entirely before his sight settled on her breasts, which seemed to roll out of her jacket under her tank top. Somehow the tightness of the shirt greatly emphasized their large size. To Mr. Anderson, they were the perfect proportions… everything about her was perfectly proportionate.

"Ugh," he said, scratching the back of his head again. "Elsie, we can't keep doing this."

"Doing what, Monsignor?" she asked innocently, stretching her arms up over the arm of the couch she had her head rested on.

Mr. Anderson couldn't pry his eyes away from her breasts as

they moved up to her collar while she stretched. "I… I… we're not Catholic, is that even accurate? Uh… just… I mean… *this*. We can't keep doing *this*."

"What?" she asked. She sat back upright. "We're just tutoring."

"My wife's gonna be home with the kids shortly, so—"

"It's Thursday. Soccer practice. They won't be home for another three hours."

"Uh… yeah… but—"

"So just relax. You get to tutor me… for *three… whole… hours*." She traced a few overlapping loops into the unoccupied couch cushion beside her with her index finger. "C'mon, Monsignor. Tutor me."

Mr. Anderson started to sweat. His heart raced. He had to resist the urge.

"Monsignoooorrr," she sang playfully as she slid down on the couch and placed her feet on the edge of the coffee table, just far enough apart to reveal what was under her skirt.

Mr. Anderson gulped.

She blushed and gave him a lustful smile. "Come play with me, Monsignor," she purred, arms extended outward.

Mr. Anderson hesitated.

She pursed her lips lustily, although her expression became slightly sterner. "Come here, or else."

"O-or else what?"

She winked slyly, spreading her legs out a little farther. "Or else I'll tell everyone that a teacher at the renowned Cloverfield High Academy is having an affair with one of his students."

Mr. Anderson's eyes widened.

"And I'll tell them how it all started."

Play along. It's all you can do. "Oh, you're mean, Miss Karan."

"I can't help it." She giggled. Then she opened her legs even wider. "Come to me."

Guess I have no choice.

Mr. Anderson stepped between her legs and stooped down on one knee. She leaned forward and touched his cheeks with her warm, slender hands. Her legs closed around him. She inched closer until her lips touched his. They were locked together for a moment before she moved away.

Then, with a seductive smile, she said, “Let’s go upstairs.”

OOOHHH MMMYYYYY GGAAAAAAWWWWWDD! PHONE CALL! PHONE CALL! PPPHHHOOOOOOOONNE CAAAAAAAAAAALLLL! BAHAHAHAHAHAHAAA! CAN YOU BELIEVE IT!? SOMEONE ACTUALLY CARED ENOUGH TO CALL YOU!

Before Mr. Anderson could lift Elsie off the couch, the roar of Bill O’Brien killed the mood.

Elsie sighed and answered her phone. “*What*, Jenny? I’m busy.”

“Hey to you too, bitch. What’s up with you?”

“I said, I’m a little busy right now, Jenny…”

“Ooohhh, did I catch you in bed with your loving ‘Monsignor’?”

“N-no! Of course not!”

“Riiiiiight.”

“I’m not!”

“Riiiiiiiiiight!”

Elsie groaned in embarrassment. “What do you waaaaaant?” she moaned.

“I need some advice.”

“On?”

“…Well… you see… there’s a guy I really don’t like. And I don’t just mean ‘don’t like,’ I mean I don’t trust him, either.”

“What do you mean?”

“He’s too suspicious.”

“Who is this guy?” A wry smile crossed Elsie’s face.

“Some douchebag named Damian.”

“Does he go to our school? Is he cute?”

“Not exactly…”

“Huh?”

“I mean, he’s cute, sure, but he doesn’t exactly go to our school…”

“What do you mean?”

“It’s complicated, Elsie. I’m just calling you for advice because he needs a place to stay and for some stupid reason he’s staying at my place, using my shower, and—”

“Whoa, whoa, whoa, *whoa*, stop right there!”

A pause.

Then Jenny said, “Huh?”

“You scold me for *my* relationship choices but then you have the nerve to ask *me* for advice about letting a guy you don’t like stay with you!”

“It’s not like that, damn it!”

“Suuuuuure,” Elsie replied, mocking Jenny.

“It’s not!” Jenny protested.

“Suuuuuuuurrrreee!” Elsie scowled. “And then you call *me* a slut, you hypocrite! In fact, I might even go so far as to say that *you’re* a hypocritical slut, you... you... hypocritical slut! Haha! That’s right, bitch!”

“You *are* a slut, goddamn it! And don’t deny it! Also, *I’m* not the one sleeping with a married man with two kids and a wife! Now are you gonna give me some advice or not?!”

“Advice on *what*? Keeping him? Why should you keep him around if you don’t like him? It’s even worse if he’s actually trouble. And since when did you trust guys, anyway?! Why is he using your shower? Where did you even *find* him if he doesn’t go to our school? Just what the hell’s going on? I wanna know *everything*.”

“Ugh… never mind. Sorry I asked.”

“No, no, what is going on? Don’t leave me hangin’, now! Your Elsie is curious.”

A sigh could be heard from the other end. Then Jenny said, “Okay, well, Marner and I were walking home from school and we found him passed out on the curb. Marner wanted to help him out and stuff—you know how Marner is—so we took him to my place an’ we found out that he doesn’t have a place to stay so for some stupid reason I offered to let him stay with me! What possessed me to do that?!”

Elsie blinked a few times. Then she said, “Um. Do I look like a shrink to you?”

“No, but that’s not why I was calling. Aside from Marner and Zero and Aria, you’re the only person who knows me well enough to form a valid opinion, and hey, I don’t hang around Zero that often anymore and Aria’s got her own place. I figured I’d talk to you.”

Elsie chuckled. “I’ll tell you what it is. You want the ‘D’.”

“*Excuse* me?!”

"Hmm," Elsie said thoughtfully as she withdrew her legs away from Mr. Anderson. Mr. Anderson immediately went into the kitchen to fix up a pot of coffee to calm his nerves. "Maybe you finally found a guy you like?"

"I already told you, I *don't* like him."

"Well maybe you're telling yourself that. You see, Jenny… your problem is that you're so uptight about the endless possibilities of guys breaking your heart and stabbing you in the back. I mean, *really* uptight. You get wound up over the slightest thing a guy could say."

"So what?"

"Soooo… have fun, for once. If that guy in your shower is hot then do to him exactly what he would probably do to you."

"I'm afraid to ask…"

"Fuck 'im and ditch 'im."

"Oh, nice, Elsie."

"I'm serious. Why do you think I'm always relaxed? I have my fun and that's all it is. Just mindless, harmless fun. You don't have enough fun in your life. That's your problem. And it's like your brain is telling you to have fun, because secretly, you *crave* it. All of us chicks do, you know, even if you don't wanna admit it."

"Okay, well, thanks for classing it up for me."

"Another suggestion is that you could stop taking me seriously and find that special someone. I think I've found mine."

"Mr. Anderson is *not* the one, Elsie, I'm telling you."

"Whatever you say, Jenny. Whatever you say."

"He's got a family, Elsie. How low can you go?"

"Hey, I don't criticize *you* for *your* behaviour."

"I'm still entitled to my opinion."

"You know what I like about you? The fact that you know how to keep your mouth closed."

"Too bad I can't say the same about your legs," Jenny replied with a chuckle.

Elsie couldn't stop herself from grinning. "Hey, fuck you, bitch."

"Meh."

"But seriously, though. It's not like you know the guy personally. You just never know. He could turn out to be something else… maybe even a total beast in bed."

"Or a total flop."

"Ha! True. *That* would be embarrassing."

"Well, look, I just got out of a relationship—"

Elsie scoffed, cutting her off. "Oh, please. You broke up with Tim last year. He's a thing o' the past."

"It doesn't make the pain go away any faster."

"Sure, you trusted him and he stabbed you in the back with some other bitch. That's what most boys do. But forget about him already. Move on, girl. Maybe go on a date with this Damian guy."

"…Heh. It's funny…"

"What?"

"Damian and Tim hate each other. They're total enemies."

"Is that right?"

"As a matter of fact, they both got in a fight when we were on our way home. I mean, we ran into him and stuff, and Damian just beat the living shit right out of him."

"Perfect!" Elsie laughed. "He's a keeper! Go for it! Now, I gotta go. Don't wanna keep my Monsignor waiting."

"Alright, alright. Have fun, I guess. Ugh…"

Click!

Still maintaining her amused grin, Elsie tucked her cell phone away, propped her elbows up on the couch, and called out, "Oh, Monsignoooorr!"

Jenny's Place

Jenny snapped her cell shut and scowled. Why does everyone sound so insensibly stupid?

Six Years Ago

"What have I done…?" He kept repeating the words to himself as he stared at the blood coating his trembling hands; running down his fingers and dripping off his knuckles. "What have I done?"

"You killed him, boy."

He gasped and looked up to see nothing but the darkness that enveloped him. "W-who—"

"I am."

"…But I don't see you."

"Look up."

He did as he was told and saw a grinning child's face staring back down at him. Its right eye, gone. Only a black gaping hole remained, oozing blood that ran down his face and dripped off his chin.

He screamed in terror and scurried away from it, but the dark figure clad in robes darker than a starless night followed him like a shadow. "Stay away from me!"

"Now why would you want that? Why are you afraid of me?"

"You're evil!"

The figure suddenly grabbed him by the back of his shirt and yanked him back with a snicker. "You're the one who just killed someone. And I know... you can't help but admit you enjoyed tearing him apart; separating the... squishy stuff from bone."

He pressed his knees against his chest, closed his eyes tightly, and clamped his hands over his ears. "No, no, no, no, NO!"

"ADMIT IT! Those adorable, innocent blue eyes of yours aren't your real eyes, are they? No, no, no... they're just for show, aren't they?"

"No... mom... dad... help me..."

"Awww, crying for mommy and daddy? They won't save you. No one will."

"Stay away from me... stay away..."

The figure growled impatiently and slapped him, sending him flying through the darkness. He splashed in some thick liquid, and when he opened his eyes, he found himself sitting in a shallow pool of blood. A doll's severed head bobbed along the surface around him. Or maybe it was a little girl with a doll-like face. He gasped and screamed in terror.

Let me out.

He looked around. Even the figure had vanished. "H-hello?"

Let me out.

"Where are you?" He looked down into his reflection. It stared back up at him.

But it wasn't him.

It had the same basic features as him, but its hair was wilder and its eyes were red with narrowed pupils. Its skin was jet black. "Let me out," his reflection said. "Come on, Damian. Let me out. Get me out of here. You can do it, can't you?"

He couldn't move. Frozen with fear. All he could do was

watch in terror as the reflection reached for him. "No... no!"

A hand shot out of the blood. Grabbed his ankle. Yanked him under, as if it was never shallow. He had to hold his breath. He wouldn't last long. He opened his eyes, the dark crimson world around him slowly rising to meet him. But it wasn't his imagination going wild.

They were bodies. Thousands of them. People he knew, people who died. All of them whispered his name and begged him to join them as they all rose up to meet him. Reaching for him.

"Join us. Join us, Damian."

"We want you with us, Damian."

Terrified, Damian flapped his arms and kicked his legs, trying to reach the surface. He desperately clawed for the surface. They were coming up after him. Mom, dad, his brothers and sister, his arranged fiancé—everyone. He wasn't going to make it. Running out of air; his lungs hollow and empty. Heart racing. Terrified.

Then **she** *dived into the blood, bubbles fizzling around her as she descended the crimson liquid above him. An angel, engulfed in heavenly light. She reached for him, calling his name. It echoed.*

But it couldn't be...

The one reaching for him wasn't anyone he knew six years ago. Somehow she was the one reaching for him.

Jenny.

Knock, knock!

Damian's eyes snapped open, still standing in the shower. "Yeah?"

Jenny called back, "Your clothes are done. I'm bringing them in."

"Okay."

"Don't jump out an' surprise me now."

"You'd like that, wouldn't you?"

"In your dreams," Jenny said as she opened the door and set the clothes down beside the counter, carefully slipping the photo back in the same pocket she found it in. "Dinner's ready too, so hurry up before it gets cold."

"Okay."

She walked out without another word and shut the door.

Damian sighed and shut off the water. He wondered how he

wasn't more wrinkled than a prune. At least he was clean enough to avoid any more complaints from Jenny.

Jenny.

Why the hell was she there?

Damian stared at the food on the table like it was a gift from God. A bowl of garden salad drizzled with ranch dressing, a platter of leftover barbeque ribs, a bowl of home-cut fries, and a bottle of ketchup.

Marner sat at the far end of the table and Jenny sat on the right side of her. The chair for the left side (closest to the living room door) of the table had been pulled out for Damian.

Jenny scowled at him. "Well, don't just stand there gawking at it like an idiot. Dig in. There's plenty there."

Damian sat in the chair and started eating, trying to brush off the awkward feel of the situation. "Thanks. Looks awesome." He felt nervous about eating it until they also started eating, which loosened the tension a little.

"So how is it?" asked Marner before stuffing her mouth with a forkful of lettuce and sliced tomato.

Damian had already finished the ribs. "Huh? What?" he asked with his mouth full.

Jenny raised an eyebrow. "Did you even *taste* it?"

Damian nodded. "Yeah, and it's good. *Really* good."

"Well, eat till you're full, because you're not going to be eating a midnight snack tonight," she said before ripping a chunk of meat from the bone with her teeth.

Damian stopped. "Wait, what?"

Jenny glared at him. "What? I'm sure you don't have any other place to go, so until you settle down, you're staying here. Unless you're one of the few kids in this part of town to actually have parents."

Damian shook his head. "No. Everyone I knew died. Except the faggot she chased off earlier." He cocked his head toward Marner.

Marner couldn't help but feel sorry for him, but she couldn't believe he could say that so bluntly and easily.

Jenny leaned back in her chair. "Then it's settled. You're staying here."

That confused Marner even more. The one person she knew who had an uncanny hatred towards all males was offering a boy to stay in her house. "But, Jenny, are you sure?"

She gave her a deathly glare, shutting her up. "He's. Staying."

Damian blinked. "Okay…"

Jenny turned her deathly glare towards him. "Is there a problem?"

"Eep."

"That's what I thought."

Marner smiled. Whatever he did, he obviously wasn't that dangerous if Jenny's glare shut him up.

Of course, no one ever dared to resist it with success. Resistance was futile.

"You'll be staying in that room." She pointed her fork to the door behind Damian. "The door has a lock, so you can do whatever manly things you would usually do when you're alone."

Damian blinked before leaning forward, glaring at her with suspicion. "And what's *that* supposed to mean?"

Uh-oh.

Jenny shot forward, hitting her forehead off his like a bull, grinning evilly. "You tell me."

Damian slunk back in his chair, gaping at her. Words nearly failed him. "I-I don't know."

Jenny smiled triumphantly and sat back into her chair. "Okay then. There's a TV in there and a Fun Station 4 to use. The games and DVDs are on a shelf in there. Watch or play anything you want, just keep the volume down when I'm trying to sleep. Or else."

"Or else what?" he asked. He wasn't being sarcastic, he was actually curious.

Jenny pointed her fork at the two holes in the ceiling.

Damian nodded understandingly. "The volume will be kept low."

Jenny smiled innocently. It was a smile that would fool anyone who didn't know her. "Good boy. Here's a cookie." She handed him a chocolate chip cookie.

He scowled at it and looked at her with a 'do you seriously think I'd stoop so low' look. Then, unexpectedly, he took it and ate it in two bites before continuing on with his dinner.

Marner smiled at his simplicity. He probably didn't care what happened, as long as it didn't involve him getting his face launched into the ceiling like the next Apollo. "You really love those cookies, don't you?"

Damian nodded and finished his plate, immediately loading it up with more food and eating it with a little more dignity than the first plate. "Not as much as waffles, though. Nothing beats waffles."

"Great," a voice in Damian's mind said. *"Now I think I have an idea. I think I know what we've gotten ourselves into now. Marner's fine. She seems innocent enough. It's Jenny we have to watch out for. First she's complaining about you showing up, but now, suddenly, she insists you stay over for the night? Better watch your back, Damian. Watch your back. She's a fuck-load of trouble. I can feel it."*

Damian narrowed his suspicious eyes, glaring at her unnoticed. *What are you planning?*

Meanwhile…

"Ah. Tonight is a splendid night." The expensive silk suits and dresses the pale vampires wore were just as colourful and brilliant as the domed ceiling remodelled to look similar to the Chapel of the Church of Santo Domingo they sat under. They sipped sparkling blood from their wine glasses and lounged in golden chairs at their leisure. Each member of the vampiric Lorenzo Family sat in their own solid gold throne with their names engraved into the top. Immigrants from the country of Maxino, now a supernatural crime family in South Cloverfield.

Roberto poured more blood into his glass from a golden pitcher and took a controlled gulp. "This one had low blood sugar."

"Roberto." His pale wife, Abila approached him. Her snow white hair matched the paleness of her skin, curled in thick locks. Her eyes were deep red but her face was gentle. "Have you seen Diego?"

"That fool? He left in search of his own blood an hour before sundown," he answered before taking a sip from his glass. "He hasn't returned since."

"I'm getting worried."

"Don't be. Why would you worry?"

"He usually makes it a point to be back before three."

"So he ran a little late, so what? It is nothing for you to fret over."

Creeaakk!

Everyone turned toward the door to see Silverstein materialize from the shadows, approaching Roberto. A sense of unease filled their cold, dead hearts as he sat down, selecting a wine bottle and pouring himself some fresh blood. Everyone watched nervously as he elegantly inhaled the faint scent rising from his cup. Then he gulped it down. He sighed with satisfaction when he finished and tossed the glass at the wall. It shattered against a wall, causing everyone to flinch.

"Well, don't stop the party on my account," he said with a frightening smile.

"Silverstein," Roberto said, trying to conceal his unease, "what business brings you to us?"

Silverstein took a bottle of blood by the neck and rotated it, swishing its contents around. "I heard about your recent contract with President Truman. As long as his soldiers protect you from any uprisings that could occur during the day, you would provide him with vampire soldiers. When I heard the news, I couldn't quite believe it myself. So I thought I'd stop by to say hello... and perhaps ask you to clarify it in person."

Roberto tensed up. "Our business was concluded when you assisted us in dealing with Southern Cloverfield's law enforcement two years ago."

"It was."

"So why are you here?"

Silverstein took a gulp from the bottle and wiped his mouth. "Yuck. Diabetic."

Roberto pursed his lips, waiting impatiently for an answer.

"President Truman and I have had a little disagreement when he didn't uphold his end of our bargain. Have you heard about the recent events on the news? Quick and efficient… events. Surely you're aware?"

"I had a feeling that was all your doing."

Silverstein laughed abruptly, making them all jump. "What gave me away?"

"The Systems Corporation marker you left behind at each

crime scene."

"Of course," said Silverstein, taking another gulp.

"Cockiness, or...?"

"A message. To scum like you." Silverstein maintained his smile, but he was obviously furious. "Do you know why I'm here, Roberta?"

"It's *Roberto*, and yes, I do know why," he hissed. "And I do not have any interest in fighting you, Jonathon Silverstein."

"Why the hell not?"

"A boar knows that it stands no chance when it charges towards a battle, but it is stubborn and continues to charge headlong toward its death. I am no boar, and therefore I will not fight you."

"No, you're not a reckless boar. You're a coward. So you're just gonna turn tail and run, huh? Well, at least you're smart enough to know that you can't win against my organization. I'll give you that much credit."

"Forgive me for saying so, but you're starting to sound unbelievably cocky."

"Sure," said Silverstein. "It's the victories. They're probably getting to my head. But I won't let them influence me completely. Don't *you* worry about that."

"Believe me when I say I am no coward. I still think of you as an ally and continue to be indebted to you for what you did for us two years ago. To fight you would be like breaking my contract with President Truman. He wants you for himself. I admit I have thrown my family into a dark pit that we may not be able to climb out of. But I would appreciate it if you just left us in peace. Now if you'll please excuse me—" Roberto stood up out of his chair "—I have urgent matters to attend to." He turned and walked with his wife towards the door with fearful haste.

"Like finding your son?"

Roberto stopped, and after a brief moment, he turned on his heel and looked at Silverstein with a grin. "Boys will be boys. I'm sure you know how teenagers are from your experiences with your own son before he... I apologize." Roberto sighed. "But I digress… I believe my daughter Maria is going down a brighter path for her future."

Silverstein scratched the back of his head under his hat. "Yeah… teenagers are crazy these days. You never know when they might lose their heads and do something completely stupid."

Roberto watched him take another gulp of blood. "What do you mean?"

Silverstein placed the bottle back on the table, reached under his cloak, and pulled out a severed head by the hair. He tossed it across the room to Roberto and watched the shock spread across his face as it bounced to his feet. "I found your son. Nice kid, but not very smart..."

Abila shrieked at the sight of her son's severed head, and Roberto's face twisted with rage. "Damn you, Jonathon Silverstein!"

"Also, regarding that remark about your daughter," Silverstein said casually, "she's the only family member unaccounted for here, so it seems your comment is more accurate than you thought!" He chuckled, and cold hands gripped their hearts and sent chills down their spines as his snicker escalated into a maniacal laugh. His laughter echoed through the chamber and shook the ceiling like a swarm of shrieking bats.

BOOM!

The windows suddenly burst inward, and blinding rays of light shone into the room. All the vampires shrieked as they burst into flames, scrambling around in blind terror and agony, flailing their arms as they burned alive and sought out the shadows in vain.

Systems Corporation Elite Infantry charged into the room from every direction, shooting down the members of the Lorenzo Family as they burned. A deafening *POW*. Roberto cowered in Silverstein's shadow as Abila's left arm and half her ribcage exploded into nothing. Courtesy of the explosive rounds fired from Silverstein's Volcanic pistol.

Roberto roared and lunged at Silverstein with blind rage. "Damn you!"

Smack!

He stopped when Silverstein pressed the smoking barrel of his Volcanic against his forehead. Silverstein gave him a fearsome yellow-fanged grin. "I'm sorry about this. But I'm afraid I couldn't let you live. You see, if you're an ally of Truman, then you immediately became my enemy. Letting you live would just complicate things later on."

Roberto shook with fear and fury. "Why aren't you dying

from the light!?"

"Ah! *Finally* someone asks me that question!" Silverstein laughed. "Well, do you know why my skin is red?"

Roberto gazed into his eyes, trembling with terror.

Silverstein's evil, gleeful grin widened and said dramatically, "It's permanently stained with the blood of all my victims. Thus, I am protected from the wrath of God that burns away *all* evil."

The terror-stricken vampire blinked. "…Hunh?"

"I'm immune to that shit," Silverstein said nonchalantly.

"Oh." Roberto blinked. Then his eyes widened as Silverstein pulled the trigger. "Wait that makes no sense—"

BLAM!

Jenny's Place

Damian awoke with a start, staring up the barrel of a revolver. Light from the street leaked in through the checkered window tile ceiling that curved over the headboard of the bed. Damian blinked, staring at the gun. Then his eyes followed the arm that held it until they discovered Jenny's face, which was partially concealed within the shadows. Her blue eyes burned ominously in the darkness. Her other hand was under the covers, holding something cold and hard against his naked crotch. Damian's clothes were folded up neatly on the floor by the bedside table, where the digital clock and the lamp were. The feel of whatever else she held instantly warned him not to move.

Damian stared at Jenny with silent surprise. And then he said, "If only you knew just how fucking creepy you look right now. It's almost arousing. *Almost*."

"What do you feel under the covers, Damian?" she asked.

Damian paused. "Do I get a hint?"

"No."

"Can I look?"

"*No*," she repeated curtly.

Damian frowned. After another brief pause to think, he said, "It feels like you're holding a pair of gardening sheers to my dick."

"Close. *Scissors*. I'm holding a pair of *scissors* to your dick."

"...And why are you threatening my dick with a pair of scissors?"

"I want answers. That's why."

"Oh, so this is an interrogation?" He jolted slightly when he felt the scissors slither across his skin. "T-this is some kinky shit."

"First question," Jenny said, getting straight to the point, "why the hell were you put in that capsule?"

"I got caught. Isn't it obvious?"

Jenny narrowed her eyes. It actually sent chills down Damian's spine. The feeling of the scissors tightening added to his nervousness. "I'm not in the mood for games."

"Hey, I wonder what Marner would say about this. Marner wouldn't stand for this kind of abuse! I have rights! She'll save me!" He started screaming at the top of his lungs, "MARNER! I'M UNDER ATTACK! RED ALERT! IT'S A TRAP! SOYLENT GREEN IS PEOPLE!"

A sinister grin crossed Jenny's face as he hopelessly quieted down from lack of response. "Marner went home an hour ago. It's just you... and me... and a cold, silent night in October. And these scissors. It was pretty stupid to go to bed naked. ...And really, really gross. I don't think I'll ever sit on this couch again."

"Gotta admit, it's cozier this way."

"Shut the fuck up. Why'd you go to bed *naked*?"

"Well actually, I usually wear telekinetic clothing because it's got fewer problems. But it disappears when I sleep, so..."

"Whatever. Answer my other question."

"What was the question again?"

"Why were you down in our school basement?"

Damian blinked, staring at the gun. "...I don't remember."

Jenny scowled impatiently. "Have it your way."

He could feel the scissor blades sliding over his thighs. More than enough to make his skin crawl. "NO! NO! NO! I'm serious!" Damian shouted quickly. "I was in this fight, then I got shot by somebody, and then I passed out. Next thing I knew, I was walking around in the Spirit Core! I seriously thought I was dead until Dave showed up!"

"Dave?"

"M-Marner's uncle!"

"Oh, right. Marner's uncle. And that's how you knew about Marner?"

Damian nodded.

"Next question: why's Tim after you, and why was he

guarding the place? And don't you *dare* tell me it was because of an overdue video game rental."

"L-look, I don't remember much aside from little bits here and there. I don't even know why I was under the school. Or why Tim was guarding me. For all I know, he's the cocksucker who shot me in the first place!"

"Where'd he shoot you?"

"I-in the back, because he's a fucking pussy!"

"Show me."

"What?"

"I wanna see the bullet wound. Show me."

"What's *that* gonna prove? I have rejuvenation; it's already healed up by now."

"I still want to see your back."

Damian scrunched his eyebrows and exclaimed, "Why?!"

"TURN OVER," she growled.

Damian quickly did as he was told, rolling on his stomach. "You better not shove those scissors up my ass."

"Don't be retarded—" she stopped and stared at his back with surprise and newfound curiosity. She'd discovered a set of black angel wings tattooed on his shoulder blades, extending to his lower back and his elbows. "Jesus..."

"What?"

"What do these tattoos mean? You part of a gang or something?"

"No," he said. "I don't remember where I got them from. They're just random tattoos."

"They're a little too elaborate to be 'random tattoos'."

He looked over his shoulder at her. Then he quickly returned to a sitting position. "I don't *remember*. Just fuck off already," he snarled angrily. "Or else I'll shove those goddamn scissors down your fucking throat."

Hit a nerve there, did we? She thought as she stood up straight, maintaining her glare. "I'll be watching you. Don't start anything and nothing will happen."

"Fine."

"But I'm warning you: if you *do* start something, there will be no place you can run where I won't catch up to you. There will be no place for you to hide where I can't find you. There won't even be a spot for you to climb up to without me already waiting for you at the top. And when I catch you, bad things will happen. *Very. Bad. Things*." She leaned in close with the gun a few inches from his chin and the scissors a short distance from his throat. "There will be no escape. If I find that you were even thinking about fucking with me or the people I care about... I WILL GUT THE FUCKING SHIT OUT OF YOU AND MAKE YOU CHOKE TO DEATH ON YOUR DICK! YOU'RE MY BITCH, NOW! *UNDERSTAND*?!"

Damian quickly nodded, wide-eyed with newfound fear.

"Well, now that we understand each other and have got *that* out of the way..." she said. She smiled innocently and said, "Have a good night, okay? Sweet dreams." And, with that, she left the living room and slowly slid the door closer to the jamb, staring at him with crazy wide eyes through the narrowing gap. "Enjoy... your... stay."

Thunk!

Left once again in the dimly lit room courtesy of the streetlights, Damian shrank into the covers with the blanket up to his chin, staring fearfully at the door like a child expecting a monster to come out of the closet.

COBALT ROGUE, VOL. 1: THE DEAD BLUE

Episode 003

Trouble

"I... I didn't do it."

"...Do what?"

"I didn't..."

"What didn't you do?"

"I... I tried to stop it..."

"You mean you tried to stop... it... from getting out?"

"I-I didn't mean to let him out! I just..."

"'Just' what?"

"...I just..."

"Listen. You're still quite young. To go through so much at a young age would traumatize any young child. It's understandable to be upset about these things. Things such as... your lack of control over him. Have you ever been afraid that you are losing the fight? Do you feel as though he's winning?"

"...Sometimes."

"He invades your thoughts... and somebody else from another realm... speaks to you?"

"I just told you this. I just told you this!"

"I'm just making sure we're on the right page. Enlighten me."

Flash!

The boy jerked in his chair and shut his eyes as a blinding light stabbed into his eyes. The boy, teary-eyed and trembling in fear, opened his eyes a crack, trying to peer through the light to find the face of the man sitting across from him.

"What did the voice from another realm say to you?"

"I... I can't tell you."

"Why is that?"

"...He knows where I am... who I am... almost everything about me. Almost all of my secrets and thoughts." The boy started to whisper: "If I tell, he'll kill me."

"How could he kill you if he's trapped in another realm?"

"...No one likes a tattletale."

*

Friday, October 2nd, 2026

RING, RING!

Two figures nestled under the bed sheets stirred slightly at the phone's obnoxious ringing on the bedside table. A long, slender leg hanging over the side of the bed retreated under the covers. A mature woman's sleepy moan interrupted the brief, silent pauses between rings.

RING, RING!

A tall, thin figure almost completely maintained her elegant posture, even in her half-sleep. Held down firmly by the muscular arm of the second figure—a man with black hair and an athletic build, keeping her naked body close to his. He squirmed as the phone's disturbance droned on.

RING, RING!

The woman shifted, slipped out from under his arm, which flopped on the space she'd occupied most of the night. "Sorry babe, just a sec."

RING—

The woman picked up. "The bitches are always right—who's this?" she croaked sleepily.

"Hey, Sis, listen—"

"Jenny, do you know what freakin' time it is?"

"It's… 6:33."

"…Right. Uh, um… let me just get straight to the point and ask you why in God's name you're breaking our little agreement and calling me this early in the morning?"

"Well, I need you to do me a favour…"

"Are you pregnant?"

"What? *No*! I haven't slept with anybody in months!"

"That's the answer I like to hear. But now I'm more suspicious. Are you injured?"

"No…"

"Is there a boy with you?"

"Sort of."

"What do you mean, 'sort of'?"

"I-I'm not sleeping with him. He's in the guest room."

"Why? That your idea of a doghouse for him when you saw the test?"

"I'M *NOT* PREGNANT!"

"So then why the hell are you calling? And who's the boy? Do I know him? Is he cute?" Aria's black eyes narrowed to curious, mischievous slits. "Or is he *sexy*?"

"Funny story… y'see, we kind of found that Damian guy in a cryogenic capsule under the school and now he's staying at our place…"

Aria placed her feet on the floor and leaned forward, perched on the edge of the bed. Her grip tightened on the phone, but her expression didn't change. "Damian… *who*?"

"…Warkowski?"

Aria stared at the *Smackin' Aces* movie poster tacked to the wall on the other side of the room. She blinked, said nothing for a brief moment as she processed what she'd just heard. "I, uh, um. ...What?"

"...Damian Warkowski?"

"Uuuuuhhhh," Aria moaned tiredly. "I heard Roman Orlovsky. Max, did you hear Roman Orlovsky?"

The man lying on his side behind her groaned, "I sure as fuck hope so."

"Yup," Aria said. "So you like the European musicians now, huh? Europeans are *sexy*."

"What?" Jenny replied. "NO! Damn it! Damian Warkowski! DAMIAN! *WARKOWSKI*! DA-MI-AN WAR-*FUCKING*-KOW-SKI! Understand?!"

"...You *better* not've slept with him. That fucker's trouble."

"Aria. I *did not* sleep with him. Try thinking with your brain instead of your nonexistent dick for a second here."

"I'm listenin', I'm listenin'. I'm just asking a bunch of questions first!"

Max turned over and cracked his eyes open sleepily. "Everythin' alright, babe?"

Aria turned to him and waved it off. "Yeah, yeah. Sorry 'bout that, Max. Get back to sleep, sweetheart." She turned around again and ordered curtly: "Explain."

"I see," she said after taking a moment to process the story Jenny had just told her. "That escalated quickly."

"Yeah, probably," Jenny said. "Explains where he disappeared to, I guess."

"Yep. Listen. After our last little meeting with him I don't trust him. In fact, I don't want him anywhere near you, or Marner. Go to school tomorrow. I'll be down there as soon as I can."

"I was just getting ready in case you said that."

"Good girl. Now get going."

She hung up, and with a weary sigh she crawled back under the covers to snuggle with her lover. "Sorry 'bout that, hon'."

"That your sister again?"

"Yeah… you still going on that mission in Cemetery City?"

"I have to," he said, kissing her. "Whatever puts food on the table, right, babe?"

"Yeah," she said with a smile. "I suppose blowing people up is a good way to make some money."

He chuckled and kissed her again. "Only the bad guys."

Jenny's Place—A Few Hours Later

Damian woke up with the sunshine stabbing into his eyes. "Fuck," he groaned, sitting up. Golden rays of sunlight shone brightly through the glass tiles in the roof. Felt like a firecracker had exploded in his brain. "Ugh, Jesus Christ."

Dave hovered above the foot of his bed, smiling as usual. "I'm bettin' it's because you've been down in that basement for so long."

"Dave, do me a favour and shut the hell up," Damian grumbled, rubbing his head, running his hands through his sweat-dampened hair. He looked at the digital clock beside him.

10:30 AM. Jenny and Marner would probably be at school now. Damian rolled over and clamped his eyes shut. The sunlight persisted on keeping him wide awake and irritated.

He gave up on the idea of sleeping in, and with a tired sigh he sat back up. Sweating, naked, and feeling like trash. The perspiration owed to the heat, or the weird dream he'd had. Maybe both.

GrrrrrrOOOOOWWWWLLLL…

His stomach grumbled. He felt like he hadn't eaten in years.

But first things first.

He spread his arms out, and thought of clothes. Black shadows started to swirl out from under the bed and spin around him like jellyfish swimming under the sea. They latched onto him, diving under the covers, wrapping around his limbs and torso, and forming a T-shirt, pants, and sneakers—all black with white-trim edges.

Dave stared at Damian's new clothes with raised eyebrows and said, "Nifty."

"Oh, I'm so glad you think so," Damian replied sarcastically. "Christ, it's autumn but it feels like I just woke up in the middle of summer." He exited the living room and entered the kitchen with Dave floating close behind. There, he found a written note and a cell phone waiting for him on the table. "Huh?" He picked it up and read it:

Damian,

There's plenty of food in the fridge for you to eat. Don't touch the meat in the freezer or else there will be an extra hole in the ceiling. Marner and I will be back from school at around 3:30. My sister Aria is coming over to check up on you soon. Make sure you get along with her because being on her bad side is a worse idea than getting on my bad side.

Also, don't go upstairs unless you need to use the bathroom (obviously), or if you want to read the manga in the study, if you're into that. My cell phone number is on the fridge in case of emergencies, but Aria should be able to help you out with everything. You can call the number on the new cell phone I got you. Aria put a plan on it for me. You're covered.

Clean up everything when you're finished with it, including the dishes.

Be good and I'll give you another cookie

P.S-Don't bother trying to look for them. They're very well hidden.

-Jenny

Damian set down the note and searched the fridge door for the phone number on it. He found it written on a sticky note, memorized it, and then opened the fridge and peered inside. "Now let's see… I kinda feel like… oh!" He took out a cup of yogurt and a bottle of maple syrup and set them down on the table. He kicked the door shut and searched the freezer. "Waffles!" He snatched the box and took two waffles out. Tossed them on the countertop. They rotated like giant quarters before vibrating to a standstill.

He opened the bottom drawer below the oven. Rummaged through pots and pans until he found a skillet. He placed the skillet on the bottom-left element on the stove and turned the nozzle to high.

Dave snorted. Damian frowned and turned to him. "What's so funny?"

"You've never made waffles by yourself, have you?"

Damian glared at him. "Hey, don't make fun of my cooking skills. I once survived in the tropical forest by myself with two days' worth of rations and half the wildlife trying to kill me for a month. By the end of that month, only a third of that wildlife was left over."

"Yeah, but that's meat. Did you ever make *waffles* on your own?"

"...My mom always made them for me, but I'll figure it out. How hard can it be?" Damian studied the waffles on the countertop. "No idea why they've got these indents in them, though." He looked at Dave, confused. "I remember when my mom would make the batter from scratch, and then she'd have a hard time getting these into shape, but look! They've even got these grid indentations in them now. Must be a new thing or something." He lifted the waffles off the counter and scowled. "Even more evidence that humans waste their time and resources on pointless things. Why change something that was fine the way it was? Whose fucking idea was it to punch grids into waffles?"

An amused grin crossed Dave's face. "Do you think you're confusing pancakes with waffles?"

Damian looked at him, arching an eyebrow. "Pancakes? The fuck are those?"

"I rest my case."

Damian rolled his eyes, ignoring him. Beat. "Hey... I have powers. I should use them."

Dave snickered. "Well, good luck with that. I've got stuff to do, people to haunt. That sort of fun stuff. I'll see you later." He vanished in a theatrical puff of smoke.

"Who the hell needed you anyway?" Damian looked at the waffles and concentrated on moving them. *Move... move!*

They didn't budge.

He pointed at one of them. "Move, you whole wheat son of a

bitch!"

The waffle jumped off the counter and smacked him in the face like a professional boxer's right hook.

"*Yob*!" he shouted as he stumbled sideways, hand over his right eye, hitting the back of the chair tucked under the table. "Cunt!" Leaning on the table, Damian glared at the waffle with his good eye between his fingers. The waffle landed on the counter. *Okay... let's try thinking positive... positive... positive.* "Move onto the pan," he ordered impatiently.

The waffle didn't budge.

"Move onto the pan... please?"

The waffle still didn't move. It silently mocked his inability to move it.

Dehues had several special abilities. One in particular: advanced telekinesis—to move objects and form whatever object they desired using their own energy and imagination, manifested as black energy.

Right now, Damian's mastery of such abilities was all but forgotten.

The waffle still didn't move.

Damn it! This thing is pissing me off. Damian angrily glared at it, and to his amazement, a dim black aura surrounded it. "Yes!"

The aura vanished.

Discouragement seeped through him. Then, rage. "FUCK YOU, you... you...!" He pointed at it. "Stuck-up, cheaply priced, unyielding piece of glucose *shit*!"

He tried again, feeling the same anger and frustration as before. Black energy enveloped the waffle again. He concentrated on how much it pissed him off, and it started to rise off the counter. He watched it float over the skillet and fall in it. "That's better. It's all coming back to me."

He smiled, pleased, and tried a second attempt with the second one. The second time proved to be much easier than the first. A newfound sense of pride brightened up his mood.

Then the skillet burst into flames.

"WHAT THE CRAP!?"

The front door opened. The first thing Aria saw was Damian pouring a glass of water all over the flaming stovetop. She smirked, amused. She wore jean overalls over a red T-shirt. Her fiery red hair had been tied back with her green-with-yellow-polka-dotted bandanna; sharp bangs dangled over her jet black eyes. She gnawed on the end of a toothpick, like she always did. "Well, well, well, this is something else."

Damian looked at her. He blinked. It took him a moment to recognize her. "Aria..."

"I thought it was you," she said. "So where ya been? You disappear for six years after a battle of epic proportions, and I see you again… trying to make waffles... on the stove." She glanced over at the smoking skillet. "To no avail, I see," she added, looking back at him. "I don't know why you'd try to make waffles like pancakes, but whatever." She shrugged. "Anyway, Jenny called me today and told me to check up on you." She kicked the door shut behind her. "Still as useless as ever when the situation's got nothin' to do with death and chaos."

Damian scowled at her. "Kitchen duty's for bitches."

Aria opened the overhead cupboard and selected a glass for herself. "Still got the misogyny down pat, I see. Not much has changed, has it? So tell me something…"

Damian kept his eyes on her as she walked around him, opened the fridge, and took out a carton of orange juice. "What d'you wanna know?"

She filled the glass with juice before flicking the cap back on with her thumb and sliding the carton between a jug of milk and a Tupperware container full of last night's dinner. She straightened and closed the fridge door, took a sip from her glass, and said, "Why're you *here*?"

"Long story."

"It's always a long story with you. You always say that. Then it ends up being something that could be summed up in one or two sentences."

"Okay, well, first off, help me with these waffles."

Aria yanked out the toaster, dropped two waffles in, and pushed the lever down. Then she looked at him, sipping from her glass and smacking her lips. "Go."

Damian looked at the toaster, then at her, then at the toaster again, then at her—

"*Go*," she said.

"It's *that* easy?"

"Yeah, you dumbass." Aria frowned. "Now *go*."

"Well, last thing I remember, I was killing a bunch of soldiers back when the war just ended. Some asshole shot me in the back, and I was out like a light. Then, I'm walking around the Spirit Core for a few years and doing all this astral projection stuff with a *really* irritating ghost named Dave. He's the one who recommended I call Marner, by the way. So, I called Marner, and I told her where I was. The whole astral projection thing shed some light on just where the hell I was, and just *who* in the hell shot me."

"Where were you?"

"Under the school."

Aria stared at him, unconvinced. She pointed at the fridge. "*That* school? The academy?"

"Yep. Turns out Tim was there to stand guard like a watchdog. Unfortunately for him, Jenny and Marner got down there anyway and let me out. I kicked Tim's ass, they brought us here, fed me, I kicked his ass again, and then I slept here."

"*Where* did you sleep?" Aria asked quickly.

Damian pointed over her shoulder. "Living room."

"Where did *she* sleep?"

"I don't fucking know. I didn't think to ask, especially when she was threatening to cut my dick off with a pair of scissors *and* paint the couch bed thing I was sleeping in with my fucking brains! Your sister's crazier than *you* are!"

"Oh, good," she said, looking relieved.

Damian scowled, knowing that Aria wasn't the least bit concerned about Jenny's threatening behaviour last night. "Why d'you ask?"

"Oh, well, you know how teenagers are. Especially girls. Always sleeping around."

Damian stared at her blankly. "You mean I could've gotten laid last night?"

"*NO*." Aria sighed. "On a different subject: I thought you were dead after that last battle. Thought Silverstein killed you."

"Fat chance," he replied. "You're the one who got caught in an explosion." Damian hopped up and sat on the counter beside the toaster and stared at the waffles sitting inside it. He crossed his arms. "Well. All I know is that Silverstein kept me alive for a reason."

"That pentagram thing?"

"Mhm." Damian nodded. "He just needs to get it from Truman. Still. After six years, one would think he would've gotten it by now—"

BAM!

The waffles popped out of the toaster.

"SON OF A FUCKING WHORE!" Damian leaped off the counter, drew a black energy Model 500 revolver and pointed it at the toaster. His trigger finger, just a tiny breadth away from blowing the toaster to smithereens.

Aria chortled, made a snorting sound, then burst out laughing. She spilled some of her orange juice. "AHAHAHAHAHAHAAAA! What's this? The fucking Dead Blue is afraid of toasters?"

Damian scowled. The gun vanished in a wisp of black smoke. He kicked the bottom cupboards in frustration. "It's not funny."

"It's hilarious!"

"Fuck you."

"Lighten up. I'm just messing with you. Don't worry—" she placed her hand on his shoulder and leaned in close, making a serious expression "—I won't let the toaster hurt you."

Damian's frown widened when she started chuckling again.

"HEY, HEY, HEEEYYYY!" Dave screamed, popping out of nowhere.

Damian let out another startled shout and fired his energy Model 500 at Dave. The energy bullets zipped right through Dave with no effect on him; instead they blasted holes in the wall. Damian gasped in horror. *Jenny's gonna be pissed!*

"Jesus," Aria said, calm as a cucumber, "chill."

Dave snickered.

"Goddamn it!" Damian growled and gave him the finger. "Fuck *you*, asshole! It's *my* ass Jenny's gonna ream when she gets home!"

"Listen, listen, *listen*!" Dave exclaimed as he fluttered through the kitchen. "Seriously, there's something bad going on! There are soldiers everywhere! I think the girls are in trouble up there!"

"Yeah?" Damian asked irritably. "How d'you figure?"

Aria scrunched her eyebrows. "Who...?"

"It's *your* fault!" Dave shouted, bursting into tears. "We're all gonna die!"

"What the hell are you going on about?!" Damian shouted. "And *you* can't die! You're already dead!"

Aria stared at him with wide eyes. "Me? Uhh… I'm just drinking juice."

"Not you," Damian hissed at her. "Marner's friggin' uncle."

"Oh. Dave, right?"

"Yeah." He turned to Dave. "Now what the hell are you talking about?"

"Systems soldiers," Dave sputtered. "T-they're c-coming! You gotta get to the school! You gotta save my niece!"

Damian took a waffle and bit into it, eyes half open, conveying the scowl he would be giving if not for the waffle in his mouth. "No," he said.

"*Coooooome ooooooooooooooooonnnn,*" Dave groaned. "Pretty please?!"

"No."

"Pretty, pretty, *pretty* please!?"

"No."

Aria looked at him. "What does he want?"

"Nothing," Damian said as he quickly gathered up his waffles and headed to the front door. "Well, thanks for the hospitality an' all, but I must be going. Be sure to thank Marner for me."

"NO!" Dave shrieked. "You can't go! You owe them this much!"

"I don't owe them shit," Damian said with a mouthful of waffle in his mouth as he opened the door.

Dave trembled like gelatine on a washing machine. Then he exclaimed, "If Jenny and Marner die because of you, Aria will know!"

Damian froze in mid-step, now standing on the patio.

Dave crossed his arms. He knew he'd won. Smiling triumphantly, he growled, "And guess who'll be the first one she comes after once she figures it all out?"

Damian's head slowly rotated toward Dave and an oblivious Aria, waffle still hanging out of his mouth. "Aw, *mofferfocker*," he grumbled.

"Anyone gonna fill me in on what's goin' on?" Aria asked impatiently.

Damian sighed, took the waffle out of his mouth. "He wants

me to go up to the school to protect Jenny and Marner, because apparently Systems soldiers are looking for us."

"*What*!?" she exclaimed, bolting upright. "Then we gotta go!"

"No, you."

Aria snapped. "C'mon, big boy!" With a sharp grunt, she marched past him out the doorway, grabbing him by the hair on her way out. He screamed, struggled, and complained as she dragged him with her.

Cloverfield High Academy

Jenny sat in her history classroom, third row from the top between Ray Monocle, one of Jonny's friends, and Elsie. Unlike Jonny, Ray left Jenny alone, and only spoke to her when she spoke to him, which wasn't very often. Jenny didn't mind Ray at all, but she didn't trust him, either. Elsie sat on Jenny's right, fiddling around with her portable video game and occasionally stealing a glance in Jenny's direction.

Finally: "Hey," Elsie said, leaning toward Jenny. "Tim was looking for you this morning. He was even asking Ronny if he'd seen you."

"Was he now?" she asked. She wasn't at all surprised, considering the events that went on the night before. "How surprising."

"Are you two a thing again or something?"

"Hell no," she replied quickly.

"Or is this about that fight you told me about?"

"What fight?"

"The fight between him and this Damian guy?"

"Right, right. Yeah, it's probably about that."

"He seemed pretty pissed. Guess Damian isn't so bad after all, if he put Tim's reputation on the line. ...Hey, you're not holdin' out on me, are you?"

"What the hell are you talking about?" Jenny asked with a frown.

Elsie smirked. Jenny knew exactly what she was thinking. "Damian must've really impressed you last night."

"...What?" Jenny blinked, eyebrows raised. "You better not be thinking what I think you're thinking."

"Oh, come on." Elsie said with a huff and leaned her elbow on the desk. "Did you fuck 'im or not?"

"*No*. I'm not you, you freaking nympho," Jenny hissed with disgust. "*You're* the slut of the pack, not me."

"Oh, so you mean he's available?"

"If you want 'im, you can have 'im, but I wouldn't recommend it."

"Why not? He's the only guy who actually beat Tim up. Tim's undefeated streak is over and I didn't even get to see it! What a jip. But hey, Damian's cute, right?"

"Sure," Jenny said, leaning forward on the desk.

"Lots of muscles? Is he strong? Handsome face?" she asked playfully.

The image of Damian stepping out of the shower flashed through her mind. Jenny's heart skipped a beat. She surprised herself with that thought. She let out a long groan and said, "Sure, he's alright. ...Boyish, I guess. Kinda short, though. I'm almost as tall as he is."

"Oooohh," Elsie said with a grin. "He sounds like a total stiff. And you *didn't* let him plug you? Shame. Sounds like you also could've had a wild time in the sack last night."

"What, like you and our math teacher before his wife and kids came home? Ugh. Why don't you stop with the interrogation and go fuck yourself already," Jenny snapped. "You're not gonna hear any more from me."

"Someone's jealous."

"Jealous? Of you or Mr. Anderson?"

"Bit of both, maybe?"

"Gimme a break."

"Oh, relax. I'm just messing with you. God, you get agitated so easily; you're jumpier than a scrawny white child molester in a high-security prison full of big black guys."

"Somehow I don't find that funny coming from someone like you."

"It wasn't meant to be funny." Elsie leaned closer to her, adopting a more serious tone. "Did he try something last night?"

"No, aside from doing some damage to my house and trying to kill Tim three times in fifteen minutes."

"Wait, I thought you said you an' Marner found them on the road?"

"Uhh... Tim showed up at the house later."

Elsie's eyes narrowed with suspicion. "What're you hiding?"

Jenny looked at her. "What?"

"I can tell when you're hiding something from me."

"Am not."

"Oh, come on. I'm your second-best friend. I've been your second-best friend for two years. I know when you're hiding something. And I know you're covering something up. Tell me what it is, man!"

"I'm not hiding anything," Jenny protested. "Seriously, I'm fine. I was just a little weirded out by him. And I'm trying to figure out what he and Tim have against each other."

"Okay then." Elsie said, her voice laced with concern. "Still, you don't look so good."

"I'm fine. I'm also a little pissed."

"At who?"

"Who do you think? His buddy." She jutted her thumb toward Ray.

Ray looked at her. "Have you ever even considered going out with him at least once? You never know, you might actually like him."

"Not in a million years. Out of the few years I've been here, and out of the few guys I've dated, I learned that I can't seem to stop hating them. And I hate perverts especially."

"Ah well," he said with a shrug. "He's just gonna keep trying, you know."

"And I'm just gonna have to keep pummeling him. Can't you tell him to lay off or something?"

Elsie chuckled. "If you told him that, I'm sure he'd get the wrong idea."

Jenny's eyebrow twitched with irritation. "Lemme rephrase that: tell him to piss off."

"If it were that easy, he would've given up long ago. He thinks you're special. I think he's in—" Ray crept closer to her with a creepy grin on his face, as if he'd been stalking her himself "—*loooooooooooove*."

Whack!

Jenny half-gently chopped him in the forehead with a scowl. "God, don't be so creepy."

Ray sat back and smiled. "But seriously though, maybe he really is in *looooooove.* Could explain why he's constantly harassing you."

"Ugh! Don't say that; it gives me the creeps!"

"Hey, Jenny!" a male student from the top row called. "Your boyfriend was lookin' for you!"

Jenny whirled around and gave him the finger. "Get bent, Ron! He's not my boyfriend!"

Ronny, a football jock with short blonde hair and green eyes. Another 'heartthrob,' mainly because he was good at being the quarterback on the academy's extreme football team, the Clover Knights. He wasn't very smart, though, and it showed.

Jenny noticed right away that a boy just a few seats down the row from Ronny had been staring daggers at him, sweating and shaking. James Nitwig, a constant victim of Ronny's bullying. Jenny felt sorry for him. James seemed on edge today, more so than usual. Jenny noticed him grab something under his fall jacket. He started to rise from his seat.

Ronny snickered, looking down at her as if she were inferior to him in every way. He regained Jenny's attention. "Aw, what, was he too big for you?"

"*WHAT*?!" Jenny exclaimed furiously. Her outburst seemed to have startled James. He twisted his head in her direction quickly, eyes wide. Lost his nerve. He sat back down and stared into his lap for a moment before stuffing something back into his jacket.

"I'm sure you're a slut just like your sister. She was always bringin' guys from the chess club home. She must have a thing for smart guys, and you must have a thing for big, macho guys. If that's the case, why don't you come to my house tonight? I'll rock your world, baby." His friends, also football jocks that sat beside him, laughed raucously and exchanged high-fives.

"Hell," one of his jock buddies added, "we could *all* rock your world!"

"And blow your mind, too!"

This is what Ronny had in mind:

Ker-thump! Ker-thump! Ker-thump!

Jenny sat outside of the room with a horror-struck expression frozen on her face while Aria shouted within the room, "OH, YES,

CHESS MASTERS ARE SO GOOOOOOD!"

This is what really happened:

The same scenario every time, with every member of the club. Aria would be sitting at the table with the chess club member sitting on the other side, staring at the board between them in horror. She had taken control of most of the board without even breaking a sweat.

Then she moved a pawn one space forward and said casually, "Checkmate. You lose."

And thus, the club member bowed his head sullenly in defeat.

Checkmatality!

Jenny, literally set ablaze with anger, cracked her knuckles and grinded her teeth. "I *dare* you to say that again! I *fucking dare* you!"

Ray lurched away from her to avoid the sudden burst of flame. "Whoa!"

"Hey, hey," Elsie said nervously. "Calm down, Jenny. Ignore him. Go with the flow in a different river!"

"C'mon! Say it again! I'll plant your face on the fucking moon, asshole!"

"Only in your wildest dreams, babe." Ronny winked at her, fuelling her anger.

Elsie placed her hand on Jenny's shoulder, unscathed by the flames. "Just ignore him, Jenny. Jenny! Cool it!"

Jenny was ready to pound Ronny's face into the ground. She heaved a heavy, exasperated sigh, growled with frustration, and sat back down with a loud thump. The flames went out, dissipating like cigarette smoke. "Stupid asshole," she muttered.

"So," Elsie started casually, immediately intent on getting her mind off Ronny and Tim, "are you lookin' at someone in particular to bring to the fair?"

Jenny shot her with a surprised sideways glance. "What?"

"The fair," Elsie repeated. "Are you going to the Tiberius Day Fair next Tuesday?"

"…What?" Jenny asked again.

"You don't remember?"

"I have trouble remembering those kinds of holidays."

Elsie rested on her elbow. "The Memorial Day celebration? You know, the war hero? Doesn't 'Tiberius Marckinson' ring a bell to you?"

"Oh. Maybe."

"The fair starts next Tuesday. You really ought to remember these things, Jenny. They're kind of important. I even got a date; you should get one, if you don't already. Maybe Damian could be your date."

"Yeah, yeah," she said passively. "No, I don't have anyone in mind. Why?"

"Double-dates are always fun."

"Ugh," Jenny replied, rolling her eyes. "You're actually taking Mr. Anderson on a date?"

"Of course not… I'm taking Ray."

Ray straightened with alarm when he heard this. "What?"

"All right everyone; sit down, calm down, shut up—" Ms. Elm's no-nonsense voice silenced the classroom as she entered. She went straight to her desk, just like every other day, and placed her text book down on it. "—and don't *any* of you start any crap today." She had black angular glasses and straight black hair pinned back in a ponytail. She always dressed in a grey button-up blazer and a long skirt that went down to her knees. She clacked around in her black high heel shoes, but she would never wear the fancy ones to work. Her unfriendly, business-like exterior kept the students in line most of the time.

"Today, we will be learning from a personal experience of mine in the Dehue Extermination Project. I hope you read the pages I assigned to you in your books yesterday about the 'Killer of Twenty Million People.' Over the course of the war, he managed to kill an estimated twenty million, seven thousand eighty-three. That's just an *approximate* number. It could be a lot more than that, but who the hell knows for sure.

"Of course, calling him the 'Killer of Twenty-Million-Seven-Thousand-Eighty-Three People' would just be lame and too much of a mouthful for the average person, so they just named him the 'Legendary Killer of Twenty Million People,' Another infamous nickname for him is the 'Dead Blue,' or the less popular name adopted by most media stations at the time: 'Dark-Boy.' No one knows his true name, or where he disappeared to. The only solid facts about him are that he was a Dehue and he wasn't even an adult. He was a *child.* If you don't find this uniquely disturbing even a *little*, you should get yourself checked out by a psychiatrist."

A few chuckles and laughs resonated from the students, mostly from the jocks. One of them said, "Yeah, we're psychos! Psychos! Psychos! Psy—"

"Be quiet," she barked.

They immediately fell silent.

"Anyway, I've witnessed one of the events mentioned in the text book, believe it or not. It was January 1st, 2021. I was trudging through the ruins thickened with snow, mud, blood and bile of Western Cloverfield with what remained of my platoon. Only four of us were left. We were assigned to defend the western shores of Tina Beach from the oncoming wave of Dehue soldiers. Their intentions, I assume, were to take control of the entire shoreline for a tactical advantage. Millions of us defended that shore. I've seen horrors there that you wouldn't want to imagine. Their giant Gatling guns tore through our ranks, shredding the soldiers I once trained with like grated cheese. It wasn't pretty in the slightest. I lost most of my friends that day.

"And you know what," she said with a weary sigh, "I thought I'd seen everything by that point… until I saw him the day after the war was declared over. The 'Killer of Twenty Million People.' When he moved, it was like lightning; you'd see a blue flash, and in the next instant, all those around him would be dead—hence the other nickname, 'Dead Blue.' That's how I knew it was him when I saw him battling a platoon of infantrymen.

"Well, I guess 'fighting' isn't the correct way to put it. It was more like... *slaughter*. My comrades and I hid while we watched this bloodbath. A small army against one. Just imagine it for a moment: twelve men circle him. A blue streak surrounds him. Their bodies came apart instantly, like paper. It was unlike anything I'd ever seen before."

Ms. Elm closed her eyes, as if picturing the horrors she was talking about. She opened them again. "And then he disappeared, and no one's seen him since."

Jenny frowned. She believed her, since she saw something similar back then, but she still wondered how much of that was truth, and how much was sensationalized. And without emotion. It bothered her just how robotic Ms. Elm sounded. She should've been a writer instead of a teacher. Jenny wanted to laugh at the idea. Her books would probably bore her to death.

"After that, I reported it to General Zero Fraden, the youngest person ever recorded to be ranked at general, substitute or not, and the Dead Blue was considered dead by some and missing in action by others."

"And what do you think?" asked a student.

Ms. Elm shrugged. "I honestly couldn't tell you. He vanished at the end of the war as quickly as he appeared at the beginning. Like an apparition."

"Sounds like bullshit!" Ronny shouted.

His jock friends laughed.

Elm scowled and pointed at him. "And *you* sound like an unintelligent prick that's about to get a piece of chalk in the eye if you don't keep your mouth shut. That goes for the rest of you idiots back there, as well."

Ronny and his friends went quiet again, slinking behind their desks like frightened dogs that'd just been threatened with shotguns.

"I heard he got shot," Jenny found herself saying. Everyone in the room turned to her. Surprised and embarrassed, Jenny slowly shrank into her chair.

Ms. Elm raised an eyebrow. "Where'd you hear that, Jenny?"

"Um... the, uh... a documentary I watched."

"Which was...?"

"I don't remember the name for it. I saw it a while ago, flipping through channels."

Jenny thought she'd caught a brief suspicious look from Ms. Elm. Then Ms. Elm adjusted her glasses and said, "...Perhaps. I heard that as well. That someone had gunned him down with special Dehue-proof rounds."

As Ms. Elm continued her lecture, Jenny's mind drifted elsewhere. She couldn't help but wonder about Damian now. He was a child back then, and when he moved to kill Tim last night she *did* see a blue flash. And if that wasn't enough, Damian was captured— presumably by Systems Corporation—and imprisoned inside the cryogenic capsule. It made complete sense that Damian was the Dead Blue.

And she freed him. She fucking *freed* him. "FUCK!"

All eyes converged on her—some shocked, others surprised and amused. Elm herself arched an eyebrow and said, "Are we going to have a problem with outbursts today, Miss Knight?"

Jenny sank into her chair, squeaking a high-pitched, "No..."

Principal Kirkpatrick August sat in his office with his back to the window, typing reports on the computer at his desk. A mountain of paperwork blocked his view of the door. He only stopped occasionally to take a sip from his coffee mug before returning back to work. His eyes were already starting to throb and glaze over from the glare of the holographic computer screen. "Ugh." With a weary sigh, he reached for his coffee mug again, only to find that it had inexplicably vanished. "What the—"

SMASH!

Someone smashed the mug of hot coffee over his head, and before he could scream from the boiling liquid burning his skin, they grabbed his head roughly. "Not the face!" Too late; his assailant slammed his face into the keyboard.

Silverstein turned him around in his chair and grabbed him by the collar. With a vicious snarl, he hurled him through the stacks of paper on his desk. "You… *FOOL*! Where's the boy?!"

Kirk struggled to get up, only for Silverstein to grab a fistful of his hair and hurl him across the office into the framed diploma hanging on the wall. Before Kirk could hit the floor, a black tendril from Silverstein's shadowy cape coiled around his neck like a snake, just under the Adam's apple, and lifted him off his feet, pressing his body against the wall. The glass shards from the picture dug into his back as he slid up the wall, kicking and choking.

"I should kill you. Do you have any idea what your negligence has unleashed?"

Kirk struggled to breathe. He somehow managed to wheeze, "Can't… breathe…"

Silverstein's cape tendrils flipped him through the air and slammed Kirk on the desk with a loud *THUD*. It released him once he'd landed.

Knock, knock!

"Principal Kirk, is everything alright in there?" his worried secretary, Ms. Jane, called out from the other side of the door.

More spiked tendrils from the shredded ends of Silverstein's cape circled his head. "Everything is fine!" he called, keeping his eyes fixed on Silverstein. When they were sure she was gone, Kirk groaned in pain and clambered back into his chair, massaging his throat. Once he was seated, he asked, "Now what the hell are you talking about?!"

Silverstein snarled back, "Damian is gone! Tim reported that two girls found him and released him!"

Kirk's eyes widened. "What…? But how? Why?! *What*?!"

"How the hell should I know?" Silverstein approached the window and looked to the courtyard below. "My soldiers are scouring the neighbourhood for any sign of him. If he's in the academy—"

"He wouldn't be. Tim attended today and hasn't seen any sign of him. He's most likely hiding." Kirk groaned, still rubbing his neck.

"My men searched the Knight Residence. No sign of him, aside from a burnt waffle in a skillet. He was there, but he isn't now." Silverstein put a cigarette in his mouth and lit it. Then he looked back out the window, scowling. "Why he would try to make waffles on the stove is beyond me." He turned, jutted his forefinger at Kirk. "I told you what would happen if you let him escape. I trusted you to at least keep him in one place. Damn it, Kirk, you had *one* job. Your life is hanging by a thread—"

"L-look, Tim told me something went wrong last night, but when I asked what happened he told me that you would fill me in with the details."

Silverstein looked over his shoulder at him. "So you were expecting me?"

"I didn't expect you to break my coffee mug over my head and crush my keyboard with my face, if that's what you mean. Plastic surgery isn't cheap, you know."

"So why'd you remodel your face? Afraid it would scare the children away?"

Kirk cringed at Silverstein's insult. "My... *other* face isn't exactly under-the-radar material."

"A hundred grand is a lot of money. Be glad I'm not a rat. I also may still have a use for you."

"Why's that?"

"Our list of allies is growing thin."

"Probably because you keep killing them all."

"Only the ones who screwed up."

"There's something called 'forgiveness.' Look it up. The dictionary should on the floor... along with everything else you mopped off the desk with my body." Kirk let out a weary sigh. "Who knows, it might even help you improve your social and business skills."

"President Truman obviously isn't happy that I've been taking out all of his contacts in Cloverfield. He may launch an attack against us. That scenario is a little far-fetched now, but trust me. It'll happen. I just need to aggravate him a little more..."

"And then what?"

"The whole city will be turned against us once that happens, unless I do something about it first..."

"The city's *already* against us. Do you know how many death penalties you deserve for what you did? Genocide, homicide, assassinations, terrorism, arson; the list goes on for quite a long ways. And anyway, so what if Troyas wages a war against us? Let the military handle it."

"It's not that simple, Kirk." Silverstein moved away from the window and looked through each row of books on the shelf leaning against the far wall. "Truman won't hesitate to level this entire country with his special Elemental Five. He needs Damian as a weapon, and until today, he would never have been able to find him."

"Then call one of your assassins to eliminate him."

"I can't do that."

"Why not?"

"He and I made a deal in the Dehue Extermination Project. In exchange for the artifact of my choosing, he would assist me in the war. At that time, I had the weapons capable of destroying Troyas. But since I lost everything, he hasn't upheld his end of the bargain."

"Is one pentagram really worth all this trouble?"

"It is."

"Why? What do you intend to do with it once you get it?"

Silverstein stopped looking through the books. "I plan on summoning Diablo."

Kirk turned in Silverstein's direction and stared at him with wide eyes. "You're not serious…"

Silverstein looked at Kirk. "Once I get my hands on that pentagram, I need Damian's blood to release Diablo back into the world. I believe, with his power, that I can restore the world back to its former glory, before the arrival of the Dehons."

"But why Damian?"

"Damian is the reincarnation of the warrior that sealed him within the Hell Pentagram. And so I need his blood to release him. …They say that the original incarnation was sucked into the dimensional rift that sent a portion of the Dehon planet to earth… they say he's still floating around in space, orbiting the planet." Silverstein chuckled.

"And you didn't do the blood thing earlier because…?"

"Without the pentagram, Damian is useless. But once I get the pentagram, Damian is useful. I need that pentagram, and once Truman gives it up, or I steal it from him, Damian's blood will be all I need. But now that he's free, it's going to be extremely difficult to extract fresh blood from him."

"Oh."

"First things first: I need to find those girls. If something happens in the academy, keep the halls clear of staff and students. Don't want a riot to break out."

"Kids are curious creatures. How do you expect me to keep them all from the site?"

"Just initiate your lockdown. Isn't that one of the protocols schools practice?"

"Well, yes, I guess I could do that."

Silverstein sighed. Then he hissed, "Damn... it's all because you got careless! You let the worst of the monsters in this world go free! You might as well've obliterated mankind yourself! I… DAMN!" Silverstein grunted in frustration and turned back to the window. "He's probably out there right now, causing mayhem and destruction on the very people I mean to save! God help us all if Truman's found out about him."

"Isn't that why you've been blowing things up and starting shootouts at every corner of the city-state?" Kirk asked with a scowl.

"Yes, Truman's spies. But even I don't know just how many of them remain out there. Still lurking in the streets, watching my every move, reporting everything I do to that coward. I can't even begin to estimate. Lately, it seems like the list of allies is getting shorter."

"Again, it's because you keep *killing* them!" Kirk snapped.

"If I killed them, I killed them for a reason," Silverstein retorted sharply. "*Everything* I do is for a reason. Did you forget? Did you really think I'd risk the lives of every human being on this planet for no good reason? Answer me truthfully."

"I just think *how* you go about it is... excessively unnecessary."

Silverstein glanced over his shoulder at him with a raised eyebrow.

Kirk shrugged. "I get it. Sacrifices must be made. But holy shit, Jon." He chortled. "That last major campaign of yours decimated three quarters of life on this planet. Scionia, out in the east... it's just an uninhabitable forest with... with... infected... *things* roaming around due to the radiation."

Silverstein's gaze returned to the courtyard. "Everything is just... cause and effect. A former friend of mine lived by a unique philosophy. He believed the world wouldn't exist without chaos. One little event would unexpectedly branch out into billions of different situations. Everything has a cost. He believed that chaos created the world and everything in it, and he believed it would eventually lead to the world's end. He lived and died by that philosophy. He even put it to the test at one point, and it's what killed him in the end."

"Are you referring to Lan Vixen and the High School Bizarre incident? Lan Vixen *was* crazy, as I recall."

"Yes, he was. But his philosophy made sense," Silverstein said. "Chaos makes the world go 'round. Think of Damian as the cause. When the effect kicks in, it's not going to be pleasant for any of us."

The Halls

"Freakin' Elm, giving us homework..." Jenny grumbled, walking through the halls alongside Marner.

"You're not having a very good day, are you?" Marner asked.

"*No*," she snapped, making her flinch. She sighed, calming down a little. "Sorry. I didn't mean to take it out on you—"

The intercom squealed, then Kirk's voice echoed through the

halls: "Jenny Knight and Marner Fraden, report to the office immediately. Jenny Knight and Marner Fraden, please report to the office immediately."

Jenny thought for a moment. "You really think the principal's in on it?"

Marner shrugged, looking at her nervously. "I-I don't know. That's what Damian said."

"So far Damian's told the truth and stated the obvious. Tim's a dick, and he's in on something big. I'd like some answers. But if we're going in there, we're gonna need some extra insurance."

"What kind of insurance?"

Jenny smiled. "Remember James Nitwig? The kid who's always gettin' picked on by Ronny and his gang?"

"Yes? What about him?"

Under the Bleachers of the Soccer Field, South Yard

Wham!

Jenny pushed the short, timid boy against the support beams under the bleachers. He wore the school uniform—a grey shirt and jeans, though the red and white jacket worn over it was his—and his messy brown hair almost concealed his sad green eyes completely. He made a whimpering noise as he slid down the beam to the dirt, as if he were helpless to defend himself, reaching into his open jacket. Trembling with fear as if he were facing his murderers.

"Alright, James," Jenny began, "cough it up."

"W-what?" James sputtered. "Cough what up? I-I don't know… I don't know what you're talking about."

Jenny crossed her arms impatiently. "I know you, James. We started attending this academy at the same time. Ronny and his faggots've been picking on you for almost as long. I see you're finally starting to snap, though. I noticed you in class earlier. Don't think for a second I didn't know what you were up to."

"What are you talking about?" he asked with a shaking voice.

"The gun, James," said Jenny. "Your dad's gun… give it to me."

"W-what?!"

"You brought it to school to teach those assholes a lesson, right? Hate to break it to ya, but they're too thick-skulled to get it.

You'd be wasting your time and energy, not to mention your dad's bullets."

James looked up at her, startled and wide-eyed. "How do you know about…?"

"I'm not stupid," she said. "You've been hiding it in your locker for weeks. I've seen it before in elementary school. The only person who would be super-defensive of their locker would be someone with a gun. And the way you acted in history today kinda cements my suspicions. 'Cept, I need it more than you do—"

"Get away!" he shouted, drawing a CZ-75B pistol on Jenny.

Marner yelped and leaped away. "Jenny!"

Jenny didn't flinch. She glared at him. "C'mon, James. Don't be like that."

James trembled. The gun rattled in his shaking hand. Tears welled up in his eyes. "I-I don't wanna shoot you! Just stay the hell out of my way!"

"You're not gonna shoot me," she said calmly. "You like me too much for that."

She reached for the gun.

He lurched back, grasping the gun with both hands now. "Stop! Don't! I'll—"

"You'll *what*?" she snapped. "You think shooting me's gonna make you feel better? Try it, if it'll make you feel better! Do it, you bitch! Do it!"

Marner quickly protested, "J-Jenny…!"

"Shut up, Marner!"

James quivered. He burst into tears and moaned with defeat, dropping his head and pointing the gun to the ground. "I don't want to…"

She knelt down and took the gun out of his hands. "I'm saving your future here, bud. Those pricks aren't worth going to prison for."

"…I guess this means I won't be seein' you around for a while, huh?" He sniffled, trying to wipe the tears away with his sleeve.

"Probably, but not for the reasons you're thinking."

"Huh?" He looked up at her.

She smiled at him. Then she winked. "I'm not telling a damn soul."

He stared at her, as if he were mesmerized by her smile.

"Believe me; I need this a lot more than you do." She stood up straight and stuffed the gun in her pants behind her back, tucked safely under her jacket. She looked down at him as he pressed his knees against his chest and cried. "Go home, okay?"

Marner breathed a sigh of relief.

They were back in the halls. Jenny seemed to be looking for something—or someone. Marner grew more worried with every passing minute. She didn't like how things were turning out.

"Hey, um," she said, hesitated.

"What is it, Marner?" Jenny asked as she continued treading down the empty hallway.

"W-why did we need the gun?"

"I told you, didn't I? It's insurance."

"Insurance for *what*? All the principal did was call us down to his office—"

Jenny whirled around and grabbed Marner's shoulders. "Marner! Listen. Don't be daft. Kirk's in on it. I'm sure of it. The gun is for *our* protection." She straightened and looked around. "But first, we need to get everyone out."

"Huh?"

"Sound an alarm. Something that'll get everyone outta here. Then no one will be in the way if shit hits the fan."

They stopped. The frosted glass wall stretched down the corridor on their right. The windows overlooking the soccer field on their left. Jenny looked up at the sprinklers. Then she turned to the frosted glass wall where the faint chatter of the tech class students reached her ears.

Then she heard footsteps. Looking back down, she saw Jonny turn the corner and head toward them. She smirked and called out, "Hey, Jonny!"

Jonny paused, surprised to see her. "Oh, hey there."

"C'mere for a minute. I need you to do me a favour."

Jonny smiled, figuring today would be his lucky day. "Oh, yeah? What kinda favour?"

"I want you to cause some mischief for me."

Having reached them, Jonny stopped and asked, "Mischief? What kinda mischief are we talking about?"

Jenny smirked. "I'll give you a challenge. If you can make

everyone run out of this school in panic or something, I'll give you a delicious reward."

Delicious reward, he thought. His eyes went straight for her cleavage and didn't move from there.

Jenny smirked, hiding her disgust. "You're on the right track."

Jonny scratched the back of her head. "But wait. Why, exactly?"

"'Why' isn't important," she said as she began to strut provocatively around him. "Think about it. It'll give us a bit of a rush. And we'll have the whole school to ourselves."

Marner took a step back, hands locked in silent distress. She didn't know what to think.

"It'll be fun," Jenny said. "Live for today, wait for tomorrow."

Jonny grinned. Apparently he was sold on the idea. "Got any ideas?"

Jenny pointed at the frosted glass wall of the library and said, "Oh, go over there and shout something that would cause an evacuation. Anything. Maybe controversial song lyrics or some shit."

"I don't listen to music that often," he said as he approached the glass. "Anything specific you want me to say?"

"Maybe something like 'Jenny's got a gun. Her dog day's just begun. Now everybody, run.' But make it sound scary. Also, it might be more convincing to pound on the wall or something. Got it?"

Jonny glanced over his shoulder at her with a raised eyebrow, obviously still a little suspicious of this sudden special treatment. "Can I have anything I want if I do this?"

"Yep," she said with a sly wink.

"*Anything*?"

"*Yes*, you little pervert. *Anything*. And believe me—I know what you're thinking, boy."

Jonny excitedly turned back around and raised his hands. "Alright. I'm gonna do it." He hesitated, then started banging furiously on the glass wall screaming, "HELP! HELP! JENNY'S GOT A GUN! HER DOG DAY'S JUST BEGUN!"

Jenny whipped out her newly acquired pistol and shot him through the back of his head, propelling him through the window, which shattered. Marner exploded into a screaming fit, covering her face and cowering from the spectacle.

Jenny approached Jonny's limp form sprawled out on a carpet of glass shards and fired three more bullets into his back. Then she looked up at the horrified faces of the tech class. She roared, "NOW EVERYBODY RUN!" and fired another shot into the ceiling. The entire tech class immediately scrambled for the nearest exit like a stampede of squealing elephants. Within thirty seconds, the library was empty, and the code red alarm wailed deafeningly through the corridors.

Jenny laughed, clearly pleased by her work.

Marner breathed heavily, shocked by what Jenny had done. "My God... oh my God..."

Jenny turned to her and tucked the gun away. "Hey, hey, it's okay, buddy."

"ARE YOU *INSANE*?!" Marner squealed. "You just shot our classmate in our school!"

"He's fine. Aren't you, Jonny?"

Jonny groaned on the floor, gave her the thumbs-up without moving the rest of his body, wheezing, "Just... great."

Jenny smirked. "What, you think I'd shoot someone I didn't know was an immortal?"

"If it was Jonny, you would!"

"And I *did* shoot Jonny, so what's the problem?"

Marner fell to her knees, hands over her head. "I-I don't believe this..."

Jenny turned back to Jonny and said, "You mind playing possum till you're sure everyone's out? Just in case someone runs down these halls and spots you. Want this to be as authentic as possible so that no bullshitters stay behind."

"...Sure. Whatever... you say..."

"Good! I owe you one! You're cool in my book now!" And with that, she snatched Marner's wrist and bolted down the hall. "Sorry I shot you!"

Jonny, face pressed into the glass, made a high-pitched "*Uuuuuuuuuuuuggggghhhhh*?"

Jenny and Marner stood at the door of the principal's office now. Marner was more than a little nervous. Jenny could tell. They were both shaking, although Jenny managed to hide it semi-successfully.

"This is it," Jenny breathed. "Time for the final showdown." Jenny gave her a comforting smile. "It'll be alright. Don't worry about it. Pretty soon it'll all be over and we'll probably just hang out at Aria's garage for a while."

Marner nonetheless took a cautionary step back as Jenny knocked on the door.

"Enter," Kirk's voice called out from the other side.

Jenny gulped, hesitated, and opened the door slowly. Kirk sat at his desk with his hands clasped together. She stepped inside. Marner followed her.

WHACK!

Suddenly a gloved fist flew in from the side and hit Jenny in the face, drawing blood immediately. Another hand shot out of the doorway and snatched Marner's wrist. Marner screamed. Jenny yanked out her pistol and pointed it at the first thing that stood out on her attacker.

A red eye lens on the gas mask.

"Hands off!" she roared before she popped a bullet through the mask, killing the infantry unit instantly.

"Jesus Christ!" Kirk yelped.

Marner managed to wriggle her arm free. Jenny whirled around. Another soldier behind her reached for the gun. She squeezed off another shot before a third man's arm wrapped itself around her neck and tightened on her throat. "MARNER!" Jenny shouted. "*RUN*!"

With an angry grunt, Tim slammed Jenny's head against Kirk's desk and turned to the second soldier, just as Marner disappeared from his sight. "Get her!"

The second soldier dashed out of the room, slamming the door shut behind him.

Tim took a deep breath, and punched Jenny in the face. "BITCH! And people wonder why I dumped you." He knelt down and picked the gun up off the floor. "What the hell is this?"

"A Super Soaker," Jenny responded defiantly.

In his anger, Tim crushed the gun in his grip until it shattered into several small pieces. Then he hit her across the face again. "Drop the goddamn attitude!"

Kirk raised his voice, "Can you two pipe down for a minute? I need to repeat my announcement." He waited until Tim cuffed Jenny's hands behind her back and slapped his hand over her mouth to keep her quiet before speaking into the receiver: "Code red, code red. Initiate lockdown and evacuation. Please proceed to the nearest exit in an orderly fashion."

He hung up.

Jenny bit down on Tim's fingers, drawing blood, much to his dismay. Tim quickly withdrew his hand before smacking her with his backhand.

Kirk sighed. "You are a very violent boy." His eyes shifted to Jenny. "And *you* are a very stubborn—and violent—girl. How the relationship between the two of you didn't work out is beyond me."

Jenny scoffed. "Feh! Probably because the only thing more limp than his two-inch dick is his stale personality."

With another angry growl, Tim smacked her.

Jenny chuckled. "Tim... you stupid faggot. Didja forget already? Slapping the shit outta me is only gonna turn me on."

"Oh yeah," Tim said with disgust. "I forgot. You're a masochistic little bitch."

"And you're an abusive one-inch fuckhead."

Tim pulled her head up by her hair and planted his fist in her face. "Still satisfying enough!"

Jenny laughed, even as blood started trickling from her nose and the side of her mouth. "Bitch, please. You think I'll tell you anything? I won't let you get off so easily, because I know you won't be satisfied until I've run outta smartass comebacks to give you. But seeing as how that's never gonna happen, I guess we'll be doing this all day."

"Oh yeah?" Tim replied angrily. "We haven't *been* at it all day, *yet*."

"If you couldn't even establish yourself as the domme in the sack, how in the fuck do you expect to do it now?"

Before Tim could respond, Kirk went straight to business. "Listen, Jenny... I won't call the cavalry if you just answer a few questions. Silverstein and his men have the place surrounded. There's no escape. Really, waking Damian up was an accident. We all know you and Marner didn't have a clue what you were getting yourselves into. We can fix this in a matter of mere hours. Then you and your friend can walk away as if nothing ever happened.

What do you say?"

Jenny's head lowered. She panted. She took a few breaths to stabilize herself and stop the shaking at least a little. Then she looked up at Kirk with a serious, innocent expression and said, "Who's Damian?"

WHACK!

Tim hit her again.

"Told ya so."

"About what?" Tim hissed.

"The smartass thing. I've got a whole bunch of 'em left."

"Don't bother using them," Tim said.

"And you hit like one of those bitches in the fashion club."

WHACK!

Kirk sighed again and continued, "Where do you think Damian is now?"

Jenny didn't say anything.

WHACK!

Tim hit her again. "Answer him!"

Jenny coughed, and spat blood into her lap. Then she said, "For Christ's sake, isn't your arm tired yet?"

He hit her again. "SHUT UP!"

"Just sayin'," she said.

Kirk scowled. "I'll ask again: *where is Damian*?"

Without hesitation, she shrugged and answered, "Last I checked, he was booking a flight to the moon."

WHACK!

"Nope, it was Europia."

WHACK!

"My bad, Sky Japan."

WHACK!

"…It was definitely Sky Japan."

WHACK!

"OKAY!" she screamed. "I-I'll tell you everything… just… stop hitting me! It's too much for a poor, weak, helpless girl like me to take!"

Silence.

Kirk stared at her expectantly.

Tim crossed his arms and glared at her.

Jenny sniffled as blood dripped down her face. Then she said with a defiant smile, "He's in your mom's room in the whorehouse down the road. Fifty-dollar discount, incoming!"

With an impatient grunt, Tim hit her again.

Cloverfield High Academy Main Entrance

Systems infantry units now guarded the main entrance. A silver-haired man named Seth supervised the group. He stood in the lobby, turning around just as another soldier walked through the doors and approached him.

"Ah," he said, "finished with your search?"

The soldier nodded.

"No luck?"

The soldier shook his head.

Marner darted down the hall, almost completely blinded by tears. She knew the soldier was hot on her heels. Her shoes squeaked with every hasty step pounding against the marble floor. She careened around the corner, nearly slipping off her feet in the process, and bolted toward the stairs.

The soldier skidded when he made the turn, bouncing off the wall of lockers on the other side before stumbling and continuing his chase. "Come back here, you!"

She reached the stairs and bounded down recklessly, skipping three or four steps at a time, reaching the intermediate landing in a second and stumbling down the second flight of stairs. The soldier jumped after her, skipping every step on the way down to the intermediate landing.

CRASH!

But he landed wrong, tripped, and fell headlong through the window, where his startled scream slightly faded and ended abruptly. "FUUUU—"

Crunch!

Marner didn't stop. She reached the bottom and dashed down the hallway toward the nearest emergency exit indented in the middle of a row of lockers. She ran to it and pushed it open.

Stopped.

Stared at the two soldiers standing idly by, smoking cigarettes with their gas mask helmets off. She gulped.

The soldiers looked at her. One of them said, "Hey, it's

lockdown. Didn't you hear the announcement? You lost or somethin'?"

That's when she realized something: they didn't know who she was. She hesitated, then said, "I-I want to go home."

"Home? No one leaves the premises till the principal gives the announcement," said the soldier. His partner continued smoking, leaning against the fence, looking through to the dusty baseball diamond on the other side. "Evacuation only applies to the buildin' itself and not the school grounds. Sorry, sweetheart," he said. "Here, lemme escort you inside—"

She jumped inside and pulled the door shut. She watched the door shake as the soldier banged against it on the other side, shouting for her to open it.

Marner started to panic. She ran toward one of the classroom doors and tried the knob. Locked. With a panicked whimper she started hitting the door with her fists shouting, "Let me in, please! Someone, please! These people are trying to kill me! I know someone's in there! I'm begging you—"

SMASH!

She turned to see her pursuer jump through the window with a pistol in his hand. Wooden splinters and shards of glass poured into the hallway as he charged toward her. "Now you've done it, you little cunt!" He squeezed off a shot as he ran.

Marner ducked instinctively and screamed as the glass trophy case down the hall shattered. She whirled around and ran in the opposite direction. Two more deafening cracks followed her.

"Get back here, bitch!"

She reached the corner and scrambled around it—

—only to stop when she saw Seth, the two guards, and the extra soldier that had just arrived; all standing at the front door.

Thirty paces away from them. She didn't know what to do. She could hear her pursuer's swearing and death threats getting closer. Her eyes were fixed on the surprised soldiers and Seth especially.

Seth, dressed in a white leotard with two sheathed rapiers strapped to his sides, asked with sick amusement, "Going somewhere, miss?" He looked at the soldiers, grabbing their attention immediately. He cocked his head at Marner. The soldiers exchanged acknowledging nods, then pointed their assault rifles at her.

Marner gasped, stunned. She clamped her eyes shut. Threw her hands over her head and dropped to the ground. She screamed again. "NO!"

Her pursuer turned the corner.

BANG!

The first shot rang out. Marner jolted.

"Urk…!" Blood oozed from the shattered right eye lens of Marner's pursuer, and with a final wheeze, the soldier slipped on the floor, flipped backwards, and fell in a crumpled heap.

The two guards whirled around. Seth himself, shocked, looked at the third soldier with the smoking gun. "Are you blind?!" Seth shouted. "What the fuck was that?"

The third soldier ignored him and shot the other two soldiers in the eyes.

Seth realized it too late. "Oh, shit!" He drew his rapiers and zipped toward the third soldier, running at lightning speed. "Die—"

Then he froze, coming face to face with the muzzle of a China Lake Launcher. The end of the barrel exploded, shooting a grenade into Seth's chest. The force of the launch sent Seth spiralling down the hall, screaming, until he reached the far corner of the building and exploded, blasting a massive hole through the west corner of the front hall.

Marner opened her eyes, trembling, staring at the third soldier.

The third soldier yanked the tube out of the gas mask and popped the helmet off, revealing a familiar mix of green, yellow, and red.

"I'm always saving you," Aria said with a smirk as she tossed the helmet aside.

Marner heaved a sigh of relief. "A-and I'm always thankful for it."

"Good," she replied in a no-nonsense manner. "Now where's Jenny?"

Tim's assault on Jenny's hadn't let up; his fists knocked her head back and forth with enough force to tear a normal human's head off. "For fuck's sake, Jenny! Stop being retarded and just tell us! You have no idea what you're defending, and believe me when I say that you do *not* want this situation to end with Damian getting away! Do you understand me?!"

Jenny was losing consciousness. The room spun and spun; her ears rang, and her face and clothes were dampened with her own blood. Her mind and vision went blank for a second before Tim lightly slapped her cheek, snapping her out of a possible blackout.

"Okay," she mumbled tiredly. "I-I…"

Tim leaned in close. "Yeah?"

"Come closer. I'm too tired to raise my voice anymore…"

Tim moved in until his face was mere inches from hers.

She spat blood in his eye. Tim shrieked in agony, "MY EYES!" and reeled backwards into the bookshelf on the other side of the room. "Fuck!" He fell to the ground, still screaming, "I'm blind, you—"

WHAM!

The bookshelf fell on him, and Tim's screams were reduced to angry groans.

Jenny snickered. "You asked for it. But I guess you didn't see that coming."

Tim's head poked out from under the shelf. He was still wiping blood from his teary eyes. "I didn't ask to be temporarily blinded, damn it!"

Jenny shrugged. "You said, 'spit it out.'" She added innocently, "I'm just doing what I was told."

Kirk sighed and took a sip from his coffee. "I need a vacation…"

The far corner of the office darkened, as if the sun's light had strayed away from that particular spot. Jenny noticed it right away, and watched with increasing horror as a black and crimson shadow as dark as blood on a pitch black night materialized from the corner. A grinning face, red and twisted like a demon, under a wide-brimmed hat; a thousand shredded claws of the darkest fabric writhing from his black coat; a voice as gravelly and broken as a group of dying souls moaning in unison.

Jonathon Silverstein, in the flesh.

"Are we having difficulties?" Silverstein stepped on the fallen shelf, much to Tim's annoyance.

Jenny's eyes went wide. She started to tremble. *I'm gonna die,* she thought, *I'm gonna die. I'm gonna die...*

Kirk gestured toward her. "She's just as stubborn as her sister."

Silverstein looked at her with dark, crimson eyes that seemed to look straight into her soul, searching for the fearless defiance that seemed to have abandoned her the second he entered the room. "Is that right?" he said.

"Think you can get her to talk?"

"If she's anything like her sister, then no. And if I know her sister, we're in for a good fight shortly." He stepped off the shelf. Tim pushed the shelf off and got up to his feet, brushing himself off and wiping blood from his eyes.

"Aria's here?" Kirk asked quickly, alarmed. "Would she *really* start a shootout in a school of all places?! Even her?"

"She's already started it. An explosion in the front section was just reported. She doesn't care. And in the chance that Damian *is* with her, and he most likely is with her, I suggest you call off the lockdown and initiate an immediate evacuation off the property."

"R-right!" Kirk picked up the receiver immediately. "Attention staff and students, this is your principal speaking. Please evacuate the academy premises in an orderly fashion, ASAP! This is not a drill; this is an emergency situation! Leave the school immediately!"

He hung up and cocked his head toward Jenny. "What about her?"

Silverstein leaned over the desk, looming over her like a hungry predator. Jenny could smell the rancid mixture of cigarette smoke and blood in his breath. "Seeing as how you ignorantly released a monster who is famous for slaughtering millions of people within a year and has a notorious reputation of causing mayhem and destruction wherever he goes—hell, it took me a year to track him down and capture him—I hope you understand how seriously pissed off this little situation has made me. You understand, do you not?"

Jenny nodded, shaking violently in her chair, staring at him in a petrified trance.

"I see stubbornness is not the only trait you have in common with your sister. Oddball girls like you two are rare nowadays. But—" he brandished his Volcanic, making her heart nearly pound through her chest "—that admirable trait alone won't save you. No—" he gently pressed the pistol's muzzle against her forehead, making her break into a sweat that soaked her in under a minutes' time "—you'll have to convince me not to kill you. I'm not the type to enjoy this kind of thing—threatening children, I mean—but this is merely a necessity and nothing more. Now speak! Why did you and Marner Fraden let him out?! Were you or were you not aware of the consequences of doing such a thing?"

Jenny gulped down a lump of panic. She trembled. She opened her mouth slightly; her jaw quivered, and she made a slight whimpering noise. She hesitated, then she managed to smile, and said, "I dunno… w-why did you come up with the stupid idea of stashing him in a school basement?"

"Because it would be the last place anybody would look, or so I thought."

"What if there was a power-outage for an… e-extended period of time?"

"We've got several batteries to keep it going independently for years without the support of the city's power supply."

"But you didn't take *everything* into consideration."

Silverstein paused, scowling. "What are you talking about?"

"It's all *your* fault Damian's loose, really," Jenny caught herself saying, much to her disbelief. *Now you've done it, Jenny.*

"Oh?" he asked, raising an eyebrow.

"T-the only reason Marner and I found out about him was because he was able to do astral projection. But that's not all… and believe me when I say that this is probably the dumbest aspect of your plan to keep him hidden down there…"

"Go on."

"…Why not make the secret entrance a broom closet or something?"

Silverstein blinked.

"I-I mean, a locker? Really? What if some punks picked on this one kid and shoved him in lockers as a sick sorta hobby, and they locked him in *that* one? Sure, it's padlocked, but in a school full of degenerates with superpowers, a freakin' *padlock* isn't gonna do shit-for-dick to keep out a nosy ninth-grade freshman. Also, it's the *only* locker to have a padlock in the entire academy… that wouldn't strike you as even a *little* odd? It's like trying to stash a donut in a police station by gift-wrapping it."

The side of Silverstein's mouth curled upward.

"Also," Jenny continued, "you let a sixteen-year-old dipshit guard the place—"

"Hey!" Tim shouted.

"Suck my dick, you fuckwit!" Jenny yelled at him, before turning back to Silverstein. "Was *he* really the only qualified guard? The only thing that could possibly make sense about this 'secret basement section' would be the fact that a student is the one guarding it. That part makes sense, because he blends right in. But again—a locker? I'm not gonna ask you to forgive me for being bold, but… out of all those retarded, bullshit campaigns and plans and strategies and decisions you've made, and all the things I'm aware of, that locker thing is, by far, the most ridiculously stupid thing you've *ever* done! *Ever*! And I'm including the entire Dehue Extermination Project in your list of stupid accomplishments when I say this!"

Both of Silverstein's eyebrows went up.

"A broom closet is less likely to be discovered than a locker. But then again, the ultimate method of hiding a secret room is… is…"

"'Is'…?" He said, urging her on, grinning from ear to ear.

"…A healthy beverage soda machine."

He blinked again.

"See, nobody likes all that tomato juice, mineral water, apricot-pineapple bullshit. That stuff tastes like garbage. Even anorexic girls who think they need to go on a diet stay away from that shit. Today, many girls would want to go healthy… and nothing scares a dieter more than calories and artificial flavouring. Take my word for it—if you want to make a successful secret door that will never, *ever* be discovered, make it healthy and nutritious, and inorganic, because people like organic despite the fact that it's expensive as hell. Oh, and add a dash of artificial flavours. That might help, too..."

Silverstein stared at her. Then he chuckled. Then he broke out into a full-scale laughing fit. Jenny almost sighed with relief when he holstered his pistol. "Clever girl," he said with a grin. "You've got your sister's smartass personality traits, as well."

Jenny watched him anxiously as he turned his back to her. "Let her go."

"What?!" Tim exclaimed. "Let her go?"

"Let her go," he repeated sharply. "She won't be of any value to us… and besides, keeping her as a hostage would only cause more problems. Remember the last hostage situation we had with Aria on the opposing side?"

Tim scoffed, strolling toward the window when he heard a few students shouting in the courtyard below. "What a load of shit." He crossed his arms and watched the staff and students pour into the street through the front gate. "Where the hell is that freak asshole, anyway? You know what? I bet he's halfway across the world right now, terrorizing third world countries and insulting minorities."

KRASH!

Something burst through the window and hit Tim in the face. The large black object barrelled through the office with Tim pinned to the front, and—Kirk had to dive out of his office chair and Jenny had to tip her chair to the side to avoid it—crashed through the office door into the hallway.

Tim's back hit the lockers, blood spurting from his face.

Damian straddled a black motorcycle—made of pure energy—which skidded to a stop directly in front of Tim. Damian glared at him, grinding his teeth furiously with an almost exaggerated look of rage on his face. "Do you like artificial flavouring, Tim?"

"You...!" Tim sputtered.

"Hey, you showed up," Jenny said. "I'm shocked."

"Did someone say the one word I hate *most*?!" Damian snarled. "You racist bitches should know better than to use that word when referring to me!" He kicked Tim in the face repeatedly as he continued, "And what the fuck did you mean by 'terrorizing third world countries and insulting minorities'?! I *love* Asians! Well... most of them. And Thai food is fucking awesome! And don't you forget those foreign action movies!" With one last surge of kicks, Damian added, "How *dare* you insult my list of favourite things! Don't you know who I am?! *I'm the fucking Dead Blue*!"

"Yes, indeed you are." Silverstein appeared in the doorway of the office with two pistols drawn. He squeezed off a few shots.

Damian bent backward on the motorcycle. Silverstein's explosive rounds blasted holes through the lockers. An energy Model 500 revolver (4" inch barrel model) materialized in Damian's hand, which he used to return fire at the doorway. Silverstein took the bullets, jolting, stumbling backwards with every bloody hole that ripped through his body. The holes quickly closed up, but Damian continued shredding him with his relentless volley of energy projectiles as if it were a minigun ; the guns' cylinder spun furiously as he fired. Jenny shouted with alarm and forcibly tilted the chair over to get out of the line of fire. Kirk screamed and dived out the window as the energy projectiles tore his desk to burning splinters.

Tim wrapped his arm around Damian's neck and yanked him off the motorcycle, slamming him into the locker. Swiftly kicked Damian's body through the wall, sent him sliding across a desk in the classroom on the other side.

Damian threw his feet up and flipped backwards over the side of the desk as another shot rang out from the hall. Tim, shooting into the desk through the gap in the wall with a red energy Beretta 92F, shouting furiously at his enemy.

Damian, crouched behind the desk Tim was assaulting, turned his head—

—and saw Elm standing by her desk, staring at him with a shocked expression on her face. The classroom was empty with the exception of those two.

*Well fuck **me**!*

"YOU!" Damian yelled. "This day just keeps getting better and better!" He shot at her. She instantly dived behind her desk as sections of the chalkboard exploded.

Elm opened the top left drawer of her desk, keeping her head low as the gunfire continued; books and papers and her laptop flew off the desk as energy projectiles pelted it. She reached into the drawer, pulled out an M9 pistol with a magazine, loaded the gun, cocked it, pulled the slide, and returned blind fire.

Damian tucked his legs against his chest as Elm's rounds took chunks out of the corner of the desk he hid behind. "Damn it!"

Tim jumped onto the desk and charged to the other side, firing away. His last round skinned Damian's knee before Elm shot Tim in the kneecap. Damian took the chance to dive behind the next desk on his left as Tim shouted in agony and tumbled right through the desk, which splintered under his weight.

Tim's rapid healing factor only bought Damian a few seconds. Damian kept his head low, speed-walking in a crouch as he fired his revolver over the surface of the desk in Elm's direction.

Elm bolted to the classroom door and stood in front of it,

foiling Damian's plan. She pointed her gun at the spot he hid behind, and barked, "Get out! *NOW*! Up with your hands where I can see them! No guns!"

Damian growled with frustration behind the desk, grunting, "Shit, shit, *SHIT*!"

"Do it now!"

Damian sighed and stood up with his hands raised. The revolver vanished in a plume of black smoke. He glared at her. "Don't shoot, you four-eyed skank."

BLAM!

A gunshot from a few feet beside Damian rang out. Blood splattered from Elm's shoulder, throwing her off. She reflexively shot a round into the desk. Damian drew two revolvers from thin air, pointed one at Tim, who had shot Elm, and one at Elm, who recovered quicker than expected. Tim pointed a pistol at Damian, and another pistol appeared in his free hand, which he pointed at Elm. Elm drew a backup pistol from a holster fastened to her upper thigh and pointed it at Tim; her M9 already maintaining its aim on Damian.

And the three of them froze.

Silverstein appeared in the gap in the wall, pointing one pistol at Damian and another at Elm. He was smoking a cigarette, as if the entire situation was part of a normal day.

K-chak!

Jenny stepped behind Silverstein and aimed the muzzle of one of his fallen soldiers' assault rifles at the back of his head.

Silverstein acknowledged with a frown and a low growl in his throat.

"Well." Damian exchanged annoyed glances with Elm, Tim, Silverstein, and Jenny. With a scowl, he said, "*That* escalated quickly."

COBALT ROGUE, VOL. 1: THE DEAD BLUE

Episode 004

Jeremy's Scrap Yard

The Spirit Core

The girl knelt down on one knee, humming a sweet tune as she sifted through the multi-coloured roses swaying in the grass field. Her long braided ponytail swayed with the wind, batting against her curved back that was concealed under a luminous white dress. The black sky's empty pattern spiralled mysteriously over the Spirit Core's endless rainbow fields that shimmered in a vast array of radiant colours. A soft breeze bent the flowers and the grass to the west in near-rhythmic patterns.

The girl's cat ears pricked up between uneven bangs of pink hair, and she raised her shimmer rose-coloured eyes at the sky. She sniffed the air and smiled.

"Welcome back to the world of the living, Damian."

Cloverfield High Academy

Systems Corporation Elite Infantry surrounded the academy grounds in ten-by-ten square formations, assault rifles poised. Apache attack helicopters buzzed over the academy grounds like angry hornets. Snipers were perched around the courtyard's glass dome. Mobile Gun System tank destroyers were lined up at each entrance with a handful of soldiers standing by; the 105 mm cannons jutted toward the academy. The fully evacuated staff and students, save for Elm, were gathered in the street behind road blocks, staring at the academy in awe and confusion.

"Why don't we cut a deal?" Silverstein asked. "Save us a bit of trouble and a lot of blood stays *in* us. Why don't you—" he jerked his revolver toward Damian "—come with me, and I'll be sure to let you on your way once I get what I need. Will that make you feel better?"

Damian scoffed. "I've got a better idea, Goldstein."

"It's *Silverstein,*" he corrected with a hint of annoyance.

Damian ignored him. "Crawl back under whatever rock you crawled out from, and let me go on my way *now* instead of later."

"I'm afraid I can't do that," Silverstein said.

"Hold up," Jenny interrupted as she peaked around Silverstein. "Why is our history teacher holding a gun? Elm!"

"What?" Elm asked, keeping her eyes trained on Damian.

"Why the hell are you holding a gun?!"

"That's confidential information. Sorry."

"What the hell! So you're like a secret agent or something?!"

Silverstein cautiously glanced over his shoulder at Jenny. "It seems as though she's a double agent."

"Double agent? What?"

"Isn't that right, Maria Elm?" Silverstein asked, turning back to Elm. "And here I thought you were a captain loyal to the cause. You're with Division 9, aren't you?"

"I'm not answering any questions," Elm said.

Damian spoke up again: "And another thing: they aren't my friends. I just needed someone to spring me from that thing. Worked perfectly, I say!"

"Oh, *that's* nice," Jenny shouted as she poked her head out from behind Silverstein again, still keeping her assault rifle trained on his head. "So you tricked us, huh? Used us like your own personal get-out-of-jail-free cards, is that it?"

"Well, you got me out, so I guess so?"

"Oho, *no*, you didn't just..." Jenny chuckled. Pissed. Her superficial smile couldn't quite conceal her anger. "Just so you know... if we get outta this alive, I'm gonna kill you."

"You do that," Damian replied, disinterested.

"Ooooh, you think I'm joking, do ya?" she said. Her temper was getting hotter by the second. "Who the hell would trick women into springing them out of a prison and taking them back to their house?!"

Damian blinked. "…Lots of people, actually."

Jenny growled. She shouted, "I'm gonna kill you!"

"You're really loud, holy shit," he said casually, raising his eyebrows.

"Say that again, you bastard! What was that word—*freak*!"

Damian's ahoge twitched. . "You know what? You're saying something, but all I'm hearing is bullshit! Get back in the kitchen before I shove your own bullshit back down your throat!"

Silverstein sighed, shoulders slouching. "Are you two quite done?"

Tim scowled. "Dude. She's getting mad—"

"You *really* wanna open this can of worms right up?" Jenny snarled.

Tim said, "You don't wanna open that can of worms right up."

Damian laughed, not taking either of them seriously. "Is the can labelled 'Bluffing Spam'?"

KBLAM!

Jenny fired a bullet into Silverstein's head—"Ow," he said nonchalantly as he fell—and pushed his crumpling body out of her way.

Before Tim could react, Jenny zipped across the desk and kicked him in the stomach. "*Ough*," he groaned before she grabbed his head and slammed his face into her knee. Tim fell back, clutching his bleeding nose and shouting in agony. Jenny advanced, aiming her M-16 at Damian.

"Freeze, motherfucker."

Damian gave her an amused smirk and pointed his revolver at her. "Oho, you wanna play, eh? Well, c'mon, then. Make a move." She didn't do anything. He scoffed arrogantly. "Yeah, that's what I—"

KBLAMBLAMBLAM!

A three-round burst from Jenny's assault rifle sent Damian sprawling against the wall. Blood spurted from the holes in his shredded left hand. He let out a pained yell and roared, "*Sookin syn*! Fuck! That was my favourite hand, you heartless bitch!"

Jenny glared at him, raising her right hand. A fireball materialized in her palm, hovering between her fingers. "I'm sorry," she said, hard as nails, cocking her arm back for a damn good throw. "I don't give a fuck."

Elm abandoned the classroom door and dived for cover behind her half-decimated desk. She knew when Jenny lost it, it was time to go.

Jenny pumped three rounds at a time. Damian threw his arms up, forming a black translucent shield, holding it up as he fled toward the door.

Jenny hurled the fireball at him. It hit the shield with a

deafening *BOOM.* More than enough impact to blast Damian through the classroom door in a spray of splinters. He scrambled to his feet, saw another fireball in her hand, said, "Fuck this!" and darted down the hallway.

BAMFBAMFBAMF!

Large portions of the wall exploded into the hallway in hot pursuit. Decimated the lockers on the other side. A pulsating flash-fire chased him to the end of the corridor. "CRAZY BITCH ALERT!" He leaped, dived—

BOOM!

The flash-fire swelled, destroying everything from lockers to walls in a fiery conflagration. The force hurled him across the connected hall. He skidded over the top of the stairs. He fell a step, grabbed the railing to prevent himself from falling down the entire staircase. He grunted as he pulled himself up, and yanked a splinter of metal out of his shoulder. "Agh! Stupid little bitch! Who do you think you're shooting at!?"

Jenny leaped through the wide opening where the wall once stood and landed in the blazing inferno that burned in the hallway. She fired her assault rifle at the stairs in three-round bursts until the gun clicked empty.

Damian laughed mockingly, sitting at the midway point on the staircase, out of her sight. "You're outta bullets! What're you gonna do…"

He looked up.

She loomed above him at the top of the stairs, holding a massive fireball as big as a piano above her head.

Damian's jaw dropped. "Shi—"

Jenny slammed the fireball into the staircase, blasting Damian right through to the first floor. The impact of his body sent cracks through the marble. She jumped through the burning hole in the stairs and landed right in his gut.

"*BLAUGHK*!"

She properly mounted him, and mercilessly assailed his face with two tight fists, shouting an obscenity at him with each hit that landed. Left. Right. Left. Right. Left. Right. "Bastard! Asshole! Douchebag! Turd! Dickwad! Freak—"

Damian blindly lashed out, grabbed her arms, and lurched

forward, head-butting her.

She went slack. He curled up, launched his feet into her stomach and slammed her into the wall. Then he got up, grabbed her by the wrists, flipped her over his head, and chucked her across the hallway into one of the lockers on the other side of the hall.

Jenny recovered quicker than he had anticipated. Before she could make another move, Damian shouted with his hands held up, "*WAIT*!"

"What do you want?" she snapped. "Make it quick!"

Damian chuckled. "This is ridiculous. I don't see why we can't help each other out."

"'Help each other out'…? What do you have that *I* could ever want?"

Damian shrugged. "A dick?"

Jenny burst out laughing. Then she said, "No."

He crossed his arms with a scowl. "What? Not pretty enough for you?"

"Heh. Your looks are all you've got goin' for you. Unfortunately, you've got a *liiiiiiittle* too much baggage for my taste."

"You're the one who threatened to cut my dick off with a pair of scissors over a few 'assumptions.' Fine. Let's cut the crap, then: I can help you find your mother."

Jenny went stiff. Her heart skipped a beat. Her eyebrows shot up. "H-how do you—?"

"Help me out until everything's resolved between me an' Systems an' anybody else. I mean, with me getting off scot-free, and I'll help you find her. Alive."

Jenny trembled with sudden rage. "BULL*SHIT*! How do you expect me to believe you!? *You*! Someone who's famous for lying and killing to save himself from any situation?"

"I lie about a lot of things. But I wouldn't lie about family. Hell, even I have morals and values, you know."

Jenny scoffed. "*That's* a shocker." Then she stopped. The certain glimmer in his cold blue eyes almost forced her to believe him right away. He looked serious, almost determined. She paused, thinking it over. A slight hesitation followed. "…Why me? Wouldn't Aria be more able to help you? Or her boyfriend?"

"The more, the merrier," Damian said. "It's kind of a big

deal."

"I know that. We're talking about going up against an entire organization *and* anyone else who might trouble you. This could take years. It could kill us!"

"Don't worry about stuff like that. I've got your back on that."

"You stay the hell away from my ass."

Damian sighed. "Whatever. Just think: do you want to see your mother again?"

"How do I know you're telling the truth? How do I know you're not bluffing to save your own sorry ass?"

"Would I lie to you?"

"I dunno. *Would* you?"

"Look, it's a simple yes-or-no question, Jenny."

"Prove it."

"Seriously?"

"Seriously."

"Right *now*?"

"*Yes*, now."

"We don't have time for—"

"*Now*."

"B—"

"*NOW*!" she barked.

"*OKAY*," Damian said, exasperated. "Jesus!"

Jenny scowled.

"It's amazing what you can do in the Spirit Core. You can look into the past and the future. You can contact certain types of people, you know, like Marner. Example: last time you saw your mom, she was protecting your house from a pair of loan sharks. And then she disappeared."

Jenny's eyes went wide with astonishment. "How did you...?"

"And do you *honestly* think I would lie to *the* sister of the Aria Knight; the Crimson Bitch that has spread fear and chaos throughout the entire world without losing so much as a finger? Sure, lots of people would challenge her, fight her, manipulate her… but not me. *Fuck* that. I don't feel like dying with a shotgun shoved up my ass." His eyebrows scrunched together. "That sound like a bluff to you?" He added sarcastically, "Or maybe I'm telling a big, fat, bald-eagled lie."

Jenny stared at him, dumbfounded. "I..."

"You help me get the hell outta here, and I'll help you find your mom. We can even do both at the same time. Multi-tasking. What d'ya say?" He held out his hand, maintaining his no-nonsense scowl. "Deal?"

Jenny looked at his hand, unsure. "I dunno..."

Elm had already gone when Silverstein got back up. The bullet that burrowed itself in his brain slipped out of the hole from which it entered, and the hole in his skull sealed itself up. He groaned and rubbed his head as it throbbed with its own heartbeat. "Damn," he said to himself, "What a headache…"

Chak!

He froze when he felt the barrel of a revolver against his head. He sighed with annoyance. "For Christ's sake."

Aria jabbed the .44 magnum against his head, just behind his ear, and said, "What're you doing here, Jonathon?"

"I can assure you, I'm not after you or your sister."

"Oh?"

"Your sister and her friend unwittingly woke Damian up. I'm simply trying to close Pandora's Box. Unfortunately, that ex-military captain teacher and your sister are making that task more difficult than it ought to be. If you stay out of this, no harm will befall you. But if you continue to persist, I'm afraid I *will* have to kill you."

Marner hid behind Aria, trembling with fear.

Aria bit down on a toothpick hanging out the side of her mouth. "That it, then?"

"Pretty much."

"I see." She withdrew the gun from his head. "You better still be a man of your word."

He took out a cigarette and fired it up. "Whenever I can."

"Sir!" a voice said urgently over the radio. "Commander Silverstein! Are you there?"

Silverstein fished the radio out from his inner breast pocket and answered, "Silverstein here. What is it?"

"We've surrounded the Dead Blue! He's taken a hostage with him, sir; we can't get close, and our snipers can't get a clear shot without hitting the hostage!"

Silverstein and Aria exchanged concerned glances. Then he

picked his hat up off the floor and placed it back on his head. "I'm on my way," he said.

The Courtyard

The dome echoed with Damian's maniacal laughter. "Haha! That's right, I've got murderous urges! I've got demands! I've got a hostage! And I've got a *really* short fuse! Back off! Did I mention I'm unstable? I'm nitroglycerin on a fucking rocky road."

The soldiers had Damian surrounded. Damian had his right arm wrapped around Jenny's neck, pressing her body against his with inhuman strength that she couldn't escape without putting in the effort. With his left hand he held a revolver to her temple with his finger on the trigger.

"Drop the gun, kid!" an infantryman shouted.

"There ain't no way out!"

"Let 'er go!"

Jenny screamed unenergetically, with obvious sarcasm in her voice, "Oh God. I'm so scared. Help me. I'm going to die."

Damian scowled and whispered in her ear, "You're not helping."

"Meh."

One of the soldiers shouted, "Drop it! Drop it now!"

"*I've* got the situation under *my* control," Damian shouted for all to hear. "*You* drop *your* guns, or I'll blow this bitch's brains all over this courtyard!"

Aria, Marner, and Silverstein rushed onto the courtyard. Damian immediately turned to them with a smug look on his face.

Aria immediately pumped a Remington shotgun. Damian took a step back, pulling Jenny with him. "Not another move, Aria," he said. "You don't want your sister's head to pop like a balloon, do you?"

Aria looked at Jenny, and noticed right away that something wasn't right. "Jenny, what the hell're you doing?"

"What do you mean?" she asked.

"Don't screw with me. You know what I mean. How in the hell did you get captured?"

Jenny shrugged. "Guess I'm the damsel in distress or somethin'."

"That's retarded! Flip 'im over or something!"

"He's a little too strong for that…"

"Elbow him in the gut! Kick him in the dick! C'mon, you useless whore! Do *something*! What'd I train you for?"

Damian blinked. "I'm like… *right* here."

Silverstein ordered, "Let her go, Damian. No good will come out of this."

Damian scoffed. "No good would come out of letting her go, either."

"Exactly," said Silverstein. "It's a lose-lose situation for you."

Damian jabbed the gun against Jenny's ear. "Do you not see the massive pistol pressed against my *hostage's* head?"

Aria chimed in, "That's a revolver, you nimrod."

"Whatever!"

Silverstein said, "Do you honestly think you're going to get out of this? Once you kill your hostage, this little farce is over."

"Oh, *come on*," Damian said, agitated. "I've got a hostage!"

"And I've got snipers," Silverstein replied. "Very skilful snipers that could blow your head clean off without so much as *scratch* your hostage. Besides, we all know you wouldn't dare kill Aria Knight's sister. Even *you* are afraid of her."

"…N-no I'm not! YOU ARE!"

"Yeah, but at least I'm man enough to admit it."

"Don't gimme that crap! I know when you're bluffing!"

"And I know when you're bluffing. Put down the gun. I doubt any of us want two shootouts in one day."

Damian paused. Jenny struggled slightly, but he only restricted her breathing further with his arm. Then a slight, sinister smile sliced across his face. "…You think I'm bluffing?" He threw his left hand up over his head; the revolver transformed into a black ball of energy— "DOES *THIS* LOOK LIKE A BLUFF!?" —and he shoved it into Jenny's stomach. Jenny gasped, nearly vomiting, as the ball sank into her stomach. Its luminescent glow died as soon as it sank in. Then, the revolver reappeared in Damian's hand, and he pressed the barrel against her temple again.

"*Guuuunnnhhh*," Jenny moaned, before breaking into a violent coughing fit. "What… what the hell… did you do?!"

"I just shoved a ball of compressed explosive energy into your body. If I die, or if anything happens that I don't like, that bomb's gonna explode like a nuclear bomb." The smile on his face widened. "This entire neighbourhood will be nothing but a giant crater, and I'll be the only survivor. Everyone here will be completely disintegrated without a trace. Forget the fact that we're on a hill. If it blows, there won't *be* a hill. Got it?"

Enraged, Aria shouted, "You son of a bitch! Take it out! Take it out *now*!"

Silverstein sighed and put another cigarette in his mouth. "Checkmate, huh…"

Damian watched impatiently as Silverstein lit his cigarette. "Well…?"

"What are your demands?" Silverstein asked.

Aria looked at Silverstein in disbelief. "You can't be—"

"I *am* serious," he said, cutting her off calmly. "He's got us. You and I both know all bets are off when he gets like this."

Aria turned back to Damian and Jenny and cursed under her breath, her grip on the shotgun tightening.

Marner kept her hands over her mouth the entire time, watching the scene in horror.

Jenny turned her head, and whispered, "H-hey… this wasn't part of the… damn deal…"

"Just shut up," he hissed. He raised his voice for everyone to hear: "I want an armoured vehicle to make a quick getaway. I'm taking this girl here, her sister, and that ghost girl there."

Marner jolted. Pointed at herself. "M-me?"

"Yes, you!"

"…Eep." She hid behind Aria, trembling.

Silverstein's eyes narrowed. *So he wants to take three hostages with him? And why those three, specifically?*

"Also I want a box of waffles," Damian added.

"Anything else?" Silverstein asked.

"Maple syrup. Aaaaaaaaand… a bag of nachos. And salsa. And jelly beans. Make that waffle demand… *four* waffle boxes. That's right. I want *four* boxes of waffles. And a few twenty-four packs of Broweiser beer. Actually, get us more than one bag of nachos, too. You better hope that armoured car's got a full tank, too. Nobody wants it to sputter on empty in the middle of any populated areas, do they? And I don't want anybody following us! If I see *one* gas mask or machine gun or cop or helicopter or airplane or sniper scope or flying rocket this bitch'll explode like Neo-Tokyo! You got that?!"

"Alright, then," said Silverstein. He looked at one of the soldiers, who had a pen and a notepad in his hands. "You get all that?"

"Yessir," said the soldier. "But… um… what kind of hostage demands are these? They ain't even hostage-related; they're just items for a shopping list!"

"Get the boy what he wants!" Silverstein barked.

"You heard the man! Go to the grocery store! *Now*!"

Fresh Basket Mart

Two soldiers burst through the sliding doors of the grocery store with their assault rifles raised high above their heads. One of them had the list, leading the way through the aisles. Another pushed shoppers out of the way for the third soldier, who wheeled the shopping cart behind them at a manic speed.

"Move! Move! Move!"

The soldier with the list turned into the snack section. "This way!"

They reached the shelves fully stocked with different bags of nacho chips; a wide assortment of flavours and labels lined the shelves.

The soldiers froze.

"…Which flavour did he want?!"

"Doesn't matter! Throw them *all* in!"

The soldiers emptied the shelf into the cart as they zipped down the aisle. The cart was overflowing with chip bags in no time.

The soldier with the list pointed at the other empty-handed soldier. "YOU! Get the salsa!"

"Got it!" The soldier ran out of the aisle.

"What's next on the list?" Cart Soldier asked hastily.

The other soldier looked at the list and exclaimed, "Four boxes of waffles!"

Cart Soldier abandoned the cart and dashed down the aisle, pushing an old lady into a shelf in his desperate flight.

"Hey, where ya goin'?! Don't abandon your post, goddamn it!"

"I'm getting another cart!"

"Oh! Good thinking!" List Soldier grabbed the chip cart and wheeled it out of the aisle.

Cloverfield High Academy

"You've got it all under control," the voice said. *"Things're going nice an' smooth, and nothing's gonna stop us now. Those snipers on the rooftops are looking more anxious than you are, but their fingers aren't on the triggers. They didn't want to risk pissing off their boss. You have all the right cards in your hands... you just have to play them at the right time. Those articles on war and crime that Dad made us read have taught us a lot. Remember, Damian... hostage situations are like cold wars... no one's gonna wait forever."*

Jenny looked at her watch impatiently. Damian's hold on her neck continued to gradually tighten. She could tell Damian's anxiety was starting to peak; she felt the same way. The only difference between them—*she* didn't have a fucking time bomb lodged in her stomach.

His hold tightened. A pleasurable pang coursed from her neck to below her waist. She turned red. She moaned—more like *squeaked.*

Damian jumped at the sound, and looked at her. "What's your problem?"

She looked back at him and blushed. "This is kinda turning me on…"

Damian scowled. "Oh, God. You're one of *those* types. Fantastic."

"Wanna make the restraints a little tighter?"

"*NO*. Now shut up. You're giving me a boner."

"Ew."

"Hey, don't chastise *me* for it when you're acting like this."

"You sure you don't wanna tighten...?"

"*No*, goddamn it."

Jenny looked away, disappointed. "Aw, man…"

"And I thought *I* was screwed up," Damian grumbled.

Aria hadn't moved from her spot. She stared Damian down with her fierce black eyes, still pointing the shotgun at him, waiting for him to make a move she wouldn't like.

Silverstein also hadn't moved, but he seemed a lot calmer than anyone else present in the courtyard. He casually dragged on his cigarette.

Marner sat on the steps leading up to the south entrance of the academy, nervously staring at Damian and Jenny. Then, surprising herself, she blurted out, "You're not going to hurt her, are you?"

Damian looked at her over Jenny's head. Marner wanted to disappear. She faltered under his intense stare. "That depends on how this is gonna turn out," he said. "Things're going smoothly for now."

"For now," said Silverstein. "I'm only worried about one thing."

Damian turned to him. "What's that?"

"…Where's Tim?"

"Right here," Tim said as he emerged from the north doorway, energy sword in hand. He approached Damian. Damian turned Jenny around to face him and tapped the barrel of his revolver against her temple. "Stay the hell back, or your girlfriend gets it!"

Jenny piped up, "I'm not his girlfriend!"

"Shut up!" Damian snapped.

Tim shrugged. "Go ahead and kill her. Wouldn't bother me one bit."

"No, but it'll bother your boss." Damian glanced over at Silverstein.

Tim scoffed. "Maybe, but unlike Silverstein, I won't care what happens to anyone, as long as I achieve my goal. Necessary sacrifices and stuff."

"That a fact?" Damian said. "Good for you."

Tim stepped forward.

"Not another step, dickhead."

Tim smirked arrogantly. "What're you gonna do? You can shoot her for all I care."

Silverstein curtly chimed in, "If she dies, *everyone* dies."

Tim stopped and looked at him. "What?"

"Damian planted a bomb in her. If we don't comply to his demands, we'll all be reduced to a crater that will be approximately twenty kilometres in diameter."

Tim whistled. "Wow. Quite a bomb you've got inside you, Jenny."

Jenny chuckled. "Givin' me more of a rush than you ever did, that's for damn sure."

Damian went slack-jawed. "Ooooohhhh *buuuurrrrrn*."

Tim gnashed his teeth. "You shut up!"

"Make me."

"I'll kill you both!"

"Sure you will," she said, rolling her eyes. "How're you gonna do that? You're ten feet away and only two inches long."

Damian burst out laughing.

"Ow," Jenny said, cringing, "that's *right* in my ear."

Tim's grip tightened on his sword until it cracked. "You bitch!"

Damian glanced over at Aria. "I'm starting to like her!"

Aria retorted, "Get bent."

"I always liked your sense of humour," he went on. "Glad your sister's got it. Holy crap. This is the best hostage situation ever!"

"Yeah?" Aria said. "Why don't you give 'er back?"

"And end the good times? No can do."

Jenny said to Tim: "And from I've seen… your performance in battle is more impressive than your skills in bed."

Damian paused. "I don't get it."

Jenny slightly turned her head to look at Damian. "Have you ever seen him *win* a battle?"

Damian blinked. Then he smiled. "Oooohhhhhh, I get it now!"

Silverstein said with a scowl, "Do you mind *not* aggravating him?"

Damian ignored him. "I feel sorry for you, Ms. Hostage."

"Hunh?"

"Those must've been some really uneventful nights."

Jenny frowned. "What'd you call me?"

"Ms. Hostage."

"What kind of retarded name is that?"

"One that fits."

"No, it doesn't!"

"Yes it does!"

"*No*, it *doesn't*!"

"*Yeah*, it kinda *does*!"

Jenny sighed. "Nope. It's lame. It doesn't fit me at all."

"Fits you more than his artificially flavoured dick."

Tim retorted, "Will you people *stop* with the dick jokes?!"

Damian raised his middle finger in Tim's direction. "Now, now. Can't deny the truth when the secret is out… with sufficient evidence, I might add."

"There *isn't* any evidence!"

"Dude, your reactions give us all the evidence we need." Damian nudged Jenny's head with his chin. "Hey. You got the time?"

Jenny looked at her wristwatch. "11:32 AM. And stop breathing down my neck."

Damian looked at Silverstein impatiently. "What the hell's taking so long?"

Silverstein replied, "They've only been gone for ten minutes."

"Ten minutes is too long."

"I once had a hostage situation that lasted a week," Silverstein hissed whilst tapping ash off the end of his shrinking cigarette. "You don't have the right to complain."

"Freedom of speech, you scraggly-haired retard!"

One of the soldiers perched on the roof of an armoured vehicle turned to another sitting beside him. "Is it just me, or is this more entertaining than *The Growing Family*?"

"Pfft," said the other soldier, "that show's been going downhill since season seventeen. And Debra's an annoying bitch."

"That she is."

Jenny: "My legs are getting tired."

Damian replied, "Well, deal with it. You think *your* legs are tired? *I'm* tired. You've been leaning most of your weight against me for the past fifteen minutes. How can *you* be tired!?"

"I didn't sleep much last night."

"That's your own damn fault."

"No, it's yours."

"How's it *my* fault you didn't sleep last night!?"

Aria's head pricked up. She glared at Jenny. "Oh, you didn't…!"

"What?" Jenny looked at her, curiously studying the shocked expression on Aria's face. Then when the realization hit her, she blushed and said, "NO! *NO*! Absolutely not! I wouldn't sleep with a psychopath! Why would I do that? I've only known him for a day or so!"

"I resent that remark," said Damian.

"Keep resenting it," Jenny replied to him. Then she turned back to Aria and shook her head. "Nothing happened!"

"If you get pregnant, I'm kicking your ass!"

"What part of 'nothing happened' don't you understand!?"

Damian smirked at Aria. "Hey, how're you and Max?"

"We're considering marriage," she said.

"Oh!" Damian beamed, though the sarcasm remained. "Congratulations on your engagement!"

"We're not engaged."

Damian blinked. "But you just said—"

"I said we're considering it."

"Oh. Still. Awfully hypocritical of you to judge your sister based solely on her sex life."

"What're you implying?"

"I'm willing to bet Max trampolines you every night!"

Aria tilted her head to the side passively. "When he's home."

"HA!" Damian shouted, pointing at her. "I *knew* it! I fucking *knew*!"

Jenny cringed. "Stop screaming in my ear."

Aria said, "There's a difference between me an' her, though. She's a teenager in school. I'm an adult and a high school graduate, and I have two well-paying jobs. I can handle a sex life and a baby or two. She can't. And if she *did* have a baby, I would probably kill her and the guy who impregnated her no matter how fast he can run."

Jenny squirmed in Damian's restraining hold with embarrassment. "Okay, I fail to see what my sex life has to do with this situation."

Silverstein said with an ever-widening frown, "I agree." He flicked his cigarette butt aside.

"Bitch, please. You enjoy humiliation. Enjoy it while it lasts."

She was about to protest. Then she nodded slightly and said, "I still don't see why we have to talk about my sex life…"

Damian paused. "How did it even come up again?" He looked at Tim. "Oh, yeah."

"Screw you!" Tim exclaimed angrily, sticking up his middle fingers in Damian and Jenny's direction. "Screw you both!"

Damian sighed. "Awful shame that your fingers are longer than your—"

"STOP! Just *stop*, for fuck's sake!"

Damian snickered mockingly at Tim's rage.

Jenny thought about Damian's statement for a moment. "Heeeyyy, that's actually a really good point."

"Hunh?" said Damian.

"His fingers gave me more pleasure than his twig ever did!"

Damian burst out laughing again.

"I told you to stop screaming in my ear," she said.

Marner seemed to be the only one truly bothered by the situation. "Why isn't anyone taking this seriously?"

Aria looked at her. "Hm? What's the matter?"

"Jenny's got a bomb inside her! You've got a… a shotgun pointed at both of them! We could all die, and we're all just sitting here joking about it!"

"Nobody's joking. Nobody's having fun here. We're just trying to ease the tension a little by making fun of Tim. That always works."

Tim scowled at Aria. Aria gave him the finger. Tim responded to it: "Fuck you, bitch."

"No thanks. You're not my type." She smirked when his enraged face flushed a new shade of red.

"I dunno," said Damian. "I'm kinda having fun."

"*You* shut up!" Aria snapped at him. Then she turned back to Marner and took a toothpick out of her breast pocket to gnaw on. "You don't need to worry. It'll be over before you know it."

"*That's* what I'm worried about," said Marner.

SKRREEEEEEE!

An armoured car swerved off the road and skidded through the open gate, grinding to a halt just inches away from the water fountain. The three soldiers—List Unit, Cart Unit, and Salsa Unit—climbed out of the vehicle.

List Unit announced, "We got it! We got everything on the list!"

Salsa Unit added on his behalf, "And we only had to kill the cashier lady to get it out without paying!"

"*WHAT*?!" Silverstein roared. "Why didn't you pay!?"

"It was three hundred dollars!"

"How much stuff did you get!?" he shouted in disbelief.

List Unit stroked the chin of his gas mask. "Weeeell… he wasn't very specific about different flavours, labels, etcetera… so we just grabbed them all." He turned to Damian. "Are fifty boxes of waffles okay?"

"For Christ's sake!" Silverstein shouted. Then he slapped his forehead and groaned. "And you killed the cashier… goddamn it."

Damian stared at List Unit with wide eyes. "I… guess…? Wait, how much maple syrup did you get?"

The infantrymen exchanged glances before List Unit said, "Um… around seventy bottles… I think."

Aria raised an eyebrow.

Silverstein sighed and rubbed his temples with agitation. "God, why?"

Damian turned to Aria and Marner and cocked his head toward the armoured car. "Get your asses in there."

The girls complied with slight hesitation. They knew they couldn't argue with him, given the current situation. When the girls got into the back seats, Damian turned to Silverstein and Tim and slowly started backing toward the car, dragging Jenny—who stumbled to keep herself from falling—with him. "Now remember, gentlemen," Damian said smugly, "there is always a next time."

"I'll be sure to remember that for the next time we meet," Silverstein replied calmly.

Damian almost shuddered at the harsh tone in his voice, but he maintained his under-control smirk. "I'll kill you later."

Tim scoffed. His blade shattered in his clenched fist. "After this shit, I'm going on vacation leave."

The armoured car sped off down the road, swerving from side to side, rear-ending cars, barrelling through telephone booths and bus stops, and sending an assortment of vehicles careening off the road. The armoured car didn't stop for anything, running red lights and narrowly avoiding serious collisions.

Damian gripped the wheel with both hands, spinning it back and forth, constantly glancing into the rear-view mirror until he side-swiped a truck, which ripped the side view mirror right off the door. It didn't take long for a highway patrol cruiser to start tailing the armoured car with its sirens wailing.

"North Cloverfield Police! Pull over to the side of the road!" an officer's voice boomed on a megaphone.

Damian ignored it, continuing to swerve into vehicles to knock them off the road or into the cruiser's path. The cruiser persevered, expertly manoeuvring through and everything Damian left for it.

"Pull over *now*!"

"Stubborn son of a bitch," Damian grunted. Then he swerved off the road. The armoured car vaulted through a trimmed hedge and sailed over a short concrete wall. Touched down in a full parking lot.

Jenny bounced in her seat, shouting when she hit her head off the ceiling, "Can't you drive?!"

"Never got a license," he said, flooring the gas as the car approached the glass doors of the Cloverfield Eater Centre Mall. Solicitors near the entrance scrambled out of the car's path.

Marner screamed as the doors got closer and buried her face in her hands.

CRASH!

The armoured car slammed through the glass doors, bolting straight for an information kiosk without slowing down. The robot operator (called an operatroid), which closely resembled a human, stood inside the kiosk. It held up a pamphlet and said, "Hello, sir! Would you be interested in—" before the car smashed through the information kiosk, flinging the operatroid onto the hood. Jenny let out a startled yell as the operatroid clung onto the windshield on her side of the car. "—a tour of the mall," it continued cheerfully, "to show you that we—"

"Get that fucking thing off the car!" Jenny screamed. "Oh God, it's giving me the creeps!"

Aria started laughing in the back seat.

Jenny continued screaming, "Don't look into its eyes!"

The police cruiser followed them into the mall.

Damian turned the armoured car to the left, just barely avoiding a fall down the escalator and instead zooming along the side of the atrium, revealing the other three underground levels of the mall. The police cruiser ran down the opposite side of the atrium, keeping up with Damian's pace. The driver kept his eyes forward, honking his horn to alert people that were already scrambling out of the way, while his partner pointed his shotgun out the passenger window at Damian. People of all ages jumped through storefront windows and bounded over benches to avoid getting run down by the armoured car.

The operatroid continued, "—qualify for two weeks' vacation. My name is Seltz—"

Damian's heart skipped a beat when he saw the shotgun. "Don't you—"

BLAM!

Shotgun pellets scraped across Damian's hand and threw the operatroid off the hood. Enraged, Damian drew his revolver from the blackness in his jacket and returned fire.

"Cocksuckers!"

BOOM!

The police cruiser's rear tires exploded, causing it to swerve uncontrollably and burst through the guardrail, plummeting to the bottom of the atrium. The crowd on the bottom level shrieked and scattered. The cruiser landed upside down on a row of soft drink vending machines, crushing them under its battered model.

The operatroid, now severely damaged, lay in a twisted sprawl in the armoured car's wake, twitching and whining, its voice becoming more distorted with every word, "Two weeks... two *weeks... two... weeks...*"

Damian breathed a heavy sigh and kept his foot down on the gas. He could feel Jenny's glare coming from the passenger seat and did his best to ignore her.

"You have some serious issues," she said.

"Yeah?" he replied. "Don't piss me off and that won't happen to you."

Police had every entrance of the mall blocked with their cruisers. However, the officers retreated when the doors of the south entrance exploded. The armoured car speared through the barricade and smacked aside two cruisers as it fishtailed into the parking lot. The police officers fired their weapons at the fleeing vehicle until it was out of range.

The armoured car sped down the freeway. Damian longer swerved from side to side. No police cruisers had been sighted since the mall incident either, which made everyone relax a little.

Damian muttered angrily to himself, occasionally smacking the steering wheel. "I told that son of a bitch 'no cops.' 'No cops'! What's the first thing I see? *Cops*! Like I have to blow up a few cars for 'im to get the fucking message! Apparently 'no fucking cops' isn't specific enough! I thought I was fucking specific! *NO*! I *was* fucking specific!" He turned to Jenny. "Wasn't I pretty fucking specific?"

Jenny shrugged her right shoulder calmly. "You were pretty fucking specific."

"Exactly! Like ears don't exist anymore!"

"The cops aren't gonna ignore you if you're tearing up highways and malls with an armoured car," Jenny explained bluntly.

"What are they getting paid for if not to ignore criminals?!"

"Um," said Jenny.

"What?"

"Mind getting this bomb out of my stomach now? The coast is clear."

He smiled at her. "Nah, you hold on to it for now."

She started trembling. "Hey. Hey. Hey. *Hey*! *That* wasn't part of the damn deal!"

"Well if I don't maintain the hostage part of this situation then I'm alone. And if I'm alone, I'm screwed. And if I'm screwed, I will die. And if I die, I will return and haunt the shit out of you! I will watch your every move, and *nothing* will make me turn away! *And* I will remind you of my presence!"

Jenny stared at him.

Damian sighed and wiped sweat from his forehead with his sleeve.

"W-where are you taking us?" Marner asked. Her voice trembled with fear.

Damian sighed again. "Listen. I'm not gonna hurt you guys. Might as well get comfortable because we'll be spending a lot of time together for the next little while. But you're all too valuable as hostages for me to kill you without a really good reason."

"Then what's with the bomb in my stomach?!" Jenny asked quickly.

"Just a little insurance. As for where we're going… we're going to a friend of mine's. Name's Jeremy. He specializes in machines; robot suits, planes, cars, tanks, blah, blah, blah. He'll give us a ride out of here. But first, we need to ditch this armoured car. It sticks out like a wart on a porn star's ass."

"Why are you so vulgar?" Jenny asked with disgust.

"Because I'm eccentric. Fuck you."

"Yeah. 'Eccentric.'"

Damian looked around, searching the freeway lanes for any flashing sirens, and scanning the sky every few seconds for a helicopter or a police hovercraft. His eyes stopped when he spotted a semi bearing a Black Cola logo on the side. "Bingo. Found our replacement."

"You're gonna steal *that*?" Jenny asked.

"Hell, yeah."

He floored the gas. The armoured car moved up, outrunning the semi. He was about to cut it off when the Black Cola tractor trailer took an off-ramp, leaving the armoured car to continue its run through an underpass. Damian swore as the semi disappeared from his sight. Jenny and Aria couldn't help themselves, and laughed at Damian's misfortune.

Damian ignored them, having locked onto another semi up ahead, and floored the gas until the armoured car was beside it. Then Damian turned the wheel and rammed the car into the side of the cab, which caused it to grind into the guardrail and abruptly skid to a stop.

Damian pulled up in front of the parked truck and got out. "Wait here."

The bearded truck driver climbed out of the cab and stomped toward Damian. "Hey, man! What the hell is your problem—wait a minute. What the fuck? You're just a kid!" He pointed at the armoured car. "Is that a tank?"

"It's not a tank, it's a car," Damian corrected. "Hey listen, I need to borrow your truck—"

"You stole that from somewhere, didn't you!?"

"I—"

"Little bastard steals a tank and hits my truck! Hell, it ain't even *my* truck, it's my employer's!"

"It's not a tank, it's a car. And secondly, I don't—"

"Damn, what the hell am I gonna do?! You better be ready, you little shit, I'm gonna sue your ass so hard you'll be in an old age home before you can afford to get into college!"

"If you'd just let me finish my—"

"I'm phoning your parents, bucko! And the cops! Hell, I'll phone the friggin' *military*! I betcha that's where you stole that tank from. There ain't no way in hell I'm losing my job to a fucking punk who likes to dye his hair ridiculous colours—"

KRAK!

Damian landed a punch to the driver's jaw. He fell like a sack of bricks. Standing over him, Damian said, "For the last fucking time, I said it was a *car*. And I've never even seen hair dye except in TV commercials. This colour is *au naturel*, dickhead!" Then he looked up and noticed he had an audience watching from their cars, all of whom were trapped in the lengthy rows of rush hour. "What are you bitches looking at?"

They immediately turned away from him, avoiding eye contact.

Jeremy's place—Outskirts of North Cloverfield

Someone watched TV on surround sound that could be heard on the street across the scrap yard.

"Alright, boys," the CEO began, leaning dramatically over the boardroom table. "We need to up the ante. Our products aren't selling so well. Fashion and makeup should be making us a ton of money. Now, we need to get on selling. I don't think any of us would want to lose out because of our faggot competition. Who's got some ideas?"

A man in an onyx suit with a red tie raised his hand from the arm of his overstuffed chair. "I do, sir," his voice cut out from the midsection of the table. "Let's introduce a contest that has excellent odds for winning a trip to the Spring Islands. Let's say... a chance of one in every ten people winning, when it'd actually be one in every *hundred*. That oughta sell."

"Excellent!" said the CEO. Then he surveyed the rest of the board members. "Anyone else?"

Another man two seats away from the CEO raised his hand. "I've got one: how about hiring a fresh young star model to represent our product? Someone with sex appeal and an anorexic-thin waist."

"Fantastic!" the CEO exclaimed. He glanced over at a man sitting at the far end of the table, next to the floor-to-ceiling windows. "How about you, Gramston?"

The sound of his name snapped Gramston out of his half-sleep. He found himself staring at the board members. His thoughts raced, and he spoke out the first thing that crossed his mind: "What about a campaign to boost women's self-esteem with phrases like 'Love the flesh you're in,' or 'You're perfect just the way you are'?"

Everyone stared at Gramston.

Then they pushed him out of the fifty-storey window and left him screaming to his death.

The CEO looked around again, acting as if what they'd done was totally normal. Not a single member looked fazed. "Anyone else?"

Another member, who sat across from the late Gramston, said, "Let's make women feel like total disgusting shit. Let's attack their self-esteem directly and make them feel like they would be ugly and totally worthless unless they buy our hair and beauty products. Let's attack the already dwindling confidence and self-respect of women like the Marlsboro Church attacked the gay communities. And let's be equally as subtle about it, too, without sounding like total fucking douchebags." He finished with a broad grin.

The boardroom went silent. Everyone stared at the latest speaker with raised eyebrows.

Then the CEO pointed at him and shouted, "I like it! Give that man a cookie!"

The rest of the board members proceeded to applaud him.

Ktch!

The TV blared from massive speakers installed inside the abnormally huge hangar, accompanied by the loud metallic clangs and clatters ringing out from the interior of a massive aircraft sitting on the roof of the hanger—far too large to be inside. The hangar was a quarter-kilometre in width and half a kilometre in length. A vast mountain range of junk piles, heaps of scrap, and garbage dunes surrounded the hangar.

The aircraft precariously perched on the roof of the hangar was a Copter Ship, and one built with amazing skill. How the hangar managed to support its weight, even with its size and bulk, was beyond Damian and the others' comprehension.

Copter Ships were aircrafts of Dehue origin. They consisted of three floors—the main (which included the lounge, baths, and guest quarters), the second floor (which included the engine room and the cargo hold/hangar), and the third floor at the top (a massive storage area). A row of twenty autocannon gun pods and another row of twenty .50 calibre machine gun pods stuck out both sides of the ship. Solar panels fused with Fate Star metal to prevent any exterior damage coated the body of the ship, strategically placed around the turrets, windows, and the anti-gravitational boosters installed into the belly. A thin layer of Fate Star metal had been smelted into the windows that ran around the drum-like bridge to protect its passengers. The triangle wings that reached over two football fields each had powered rotors mounted on rotating shafts built into the ends of each of them. The rocket boosters in the Copter Ship's rear were huge, taken right out of about four fighter jets and installed into the slick model. The black painted finish gave the Copter Ship a glossy shine in the bright sunlight.

WHAM!

The semi pulled up near the front entrance of the walled-off property—by ramming straight into the brick wall. Damian climbed out, only to lose his footing and fall in the dirt.

Marner got out, tended to him and helped him up to his feet. "Are you okay?"

Damian shrugged her hands off him. "I'm fine," he hissed impatiently. He stumbled toward the sealed gate.

Aria surveyed the scene, unimpressed by the sight. "*This* is your friend's place?"

"Yup."

"Doesn't look like he's home."

"He's home. Usually he lets me right in, though." Damian approached the steel gate, fuming. He glanced over his shoulder at Aria. "Can't you hear the fuckin' TV?" He turned back to the gate and muttered, "Shit."

Aria crossed her arms. "Why don't you take a breather?"

"*You* take a fucking breather, you... you... *fuck*."

Jenny got out of the truck and watched Damian bang his fist against the door twice. After a brief pause, she asked, "You sure he's home?"

"He's home," Damian repeated. "He's a good buddy of mine."

Damian growled angrily and kicked the gate. "Hey, Four-Eyes!" He started pounding his fist against the door again. "Open this fuckin' door, you grease monkey shithead! I know you're in there! Did you get so anti-social you can't even open the goddamn door for old friends?!"

The girls watched him shout various obscenities, insults, and threats whilst kicking the door, maintaining their monotonous expressions. "'Good buddies,'" Jenny said. "Right…"

Damian stopped and scratched the back of his head. "…Maybe his dad's not home…"

Aria spotted something and spoke up: "There's an intercom right over there—"

"Shut up!"

"*You* shut up!"

Damian started kicking the door again. "Jeremy! Open up!"

Kccccchhh!

The intercom buzzed, then a young voice emanated from its crackly speakers, "Damian? Is that you?"

Aria smirked.

Damian stomped toward the intercom and pushed the talk button. "Yes, it's me! Open this damn door!"

"Why were you kicking it when you could have just made contact with this intercom?"

"Because I'm pissed off and I feel like beating the shit out of something!"

"…I thought I made it clear: 'do not destroy my things just because you are in a foul mood.' I hope you fix that wall you previously drove into."

"Fine, fine, whatever, just let us in!"

"Not until you fix that wall."

The girls watched as Damian trembled with fury.

"*You* fix it!" he fired back. "*Pizda*!"

"Swearing in Russian will not help. Also, fixing it myself would be time-consuming and, frankly, rather pointless considering the fact that you have telekinetic abilities that would enable you to repair the damages you just caused to the brick wall my crewmembers have worked *so* hard to build."

"Well… I… *SO*?!"

"So, it took us all two months to build that wall, and I would not so easily allow it to be defiled by the likes of you."

"Do it, or I will surgically enable you to eat with your ass!"

"No."

A light breeze disturbed the dust on the cracked pavement. Damian stared at the intercom, standing with his back to the girls. They knew what was coming, and they had a feeling the boy on the intercom was also aware.

WHAM!

Damian slammed his fists into the wall on either side of the intercom and leaned forward, looming over it like a vicious monster peering through something to spot its prey. "Listen to me, you grease-headed, ass-faced, four-eyed, fuckin' ugly waste of life, space, and air; and you listen good. I have had the *shittiest* of shitty days, and the day isn't even half over. I am in *no* mood to be fucked with, and you know this. For a genius, you're not being very smart, because you know what happens to low-life bitches when they mess with me. So I'll give you one more warning: if you do not open this gate now… *right* now… I'm gonna shank your face and shove it down your fucking neck, and then eviscerate you with a *permanent fucking marker*!"

More silence.

"…I am still not letting you in."

Damian grinded his teeth angrily. He was going to explode. "OH, *REALLY*?! Is that how you wanna play it? I'm so sorry to hear that! Because until you play the role of the courteous host and let us in, I'm not touching a single goddamn brick for that fucking wall, and all you're gonna get is my pistol—"

"Revolver," the intercom voice corrected.

"SHUT THE FUCK UP or I swear to fucking Christ I will fuck you up! …All you're gonna get is my *revolver* shoved up your pretentious ass!"

"If that is the case, then you will fear the wrath of the million or so toasters I have hidden throughout the property."

Damian gasped in horror. His enraged tough-guy act vanished completely. "…You're… you're bluffing! T-that's bullshit! That's a load of bullshit, right?"

"*Is* it?"

"W-why would you have a million toasters?!"

"…Because I own a scrap yard?"

"YOU LIE!"

"Perhaps, and perhaps not. But whether I am lying or speaking the truth is not the question you should be asking yourself. No. The question you *should* be asking is 'why? *Why* does my good friend Jeremy Larson, have over one million toasters stashed within these walls?' The answer is simple and obvious." Jeremy's voice shrank to a menacing half-whisper, "I saved them all just for you, my friend. Every... last... one of them. And they have been waiting an awful long time to finally meet you in a battle to the death. Allow me to correct myself: the question you should not be asking is 'why?' The question you should be asking is '*how*'... as in... 'How will I survive the wrath of Jeremy's toaster nation?' But, my friend, I am not cruel. I will call them off if you fix that wall. I will not touch the remote that controls them all like attack drones. So what will it be, my friend? The choice is yours to make."

You sick son of a bitch.

Damian went stiff. His eyes narrowed, and with a low growl in his voice he said, "You win this round..."

After Damian had repaired the wall, everyone loaded themselves back into the semi, and Damian drove it recklessly up the winding path of the compound, constantly on the lookout for toasters. The five-minute drive to the empty dirt lot that separated the front door of the hangar from the junkyard fence was a tense one. Damian's erratic driving contributed to the sense of danger inside the truck.

Jenny noticed that Damian was almost drenched in sweat, and trembling. His breath—haggard, almost as if he was terrified of driving through the compound. Or... maybe he was terrified of the person they were going to meet.

When the truck pulled through the gate and entered the lot, Damian looked a lot more relieved, even going so far as to breathe a heavy sigh of relief, finishing with a whistle. He had a weary look in his cold blue eyes, like he'd just finished a long day of hard work under the scorching heat of the summer sun.

Jenny turned away from him before he noticed her staring.

When everybody stepped out of the semi, a short boy—about 4.5 feet tall—opened the sliding door of the hangar and stepped out into the open. He wore thick brown goggles over his blank silver eyes, which strapped down a portion of his nest of wild light brown hair that stuck out in greasy spikes. He also wore a loose cotton jacket and baggy pants. Soot, grease, and oil coated his entire body. The first thing that grabbed everyone's attention, however, was the oversized wrench resting on his shoulder; amazingly enough, he was able to wield it with the greatest of ease.

"Now," he said with a scowl, "Damian. I do believe you are quite aware of my intolerance of your stupidity and knack for wreaking havoc. I also do not tolerate your nasty habit of leaving behind a mess in your wake. Therefore, I expect you to clean it up before you commit to some other mundane task. Like throwing a tantrum on my front steps."

"Yeah, well," Damian stomped a pace forward and gave him the finger. "You should know a thing or two about pissing me off when I'm already pissed off!"

"Hmph. Indeed," Jeremy sneered. Then he looked at Jenny, Marner, and Aria each in turn. "And who are these fine young ladies?"

"Ah!" Marner said, tucking a few strands of silver hair behind her ear, stepping forward, and holding out her hand with a humble smile. "I'm sorry. My name is Marner Fraden. It's very nice to meet you!"

Jeremy looked at her hand, then took it in his greasy gloves.

Squish!

A tingle ran up Marner's spine as he shook her hand. "The pleasure is all mine," he said. He passed her, leaving her to stare at her grease-coated hand in silent dismay. He approached Jenny and bowed his head slightly and held out his hand. "A pleasure."

Jenny looked at his blackened glove and said, "Sorry… I don't like shaking hands with people. Nothing personal. My name's Jenny. Jenny Knight."

"Hm?" He glanced at Aria. She shrugged. "I see. Whatever your preference is, then I suppose—"

He took another look at Aria. His eyes went wide. He went slack-jawed and his face beamed like a child seeing new presents under the Christmas tree. He jumped in front of her, took her hands, and shook them both. "My God! I cannot believe I am seeing Aria Knight in the flesh! I am a huge fan of your work! Goodness gracious, your body is even more developed now than it was then! So much more… *womanly* than before!"

Aria blinked. "Wuh…? Thank you…?"

Jeremy stared at her with sparkling eyes. Blushing cheeks. An ecstatic grin. His child-like glee baffled the others.

"What're you talking about?" Aria asked.

"I still have the bonus edition of the forty-fifth issue of *Mechanic's Digest* magazine dating back to August, 2023!"

A pause.

Then a smile crossed Aria's face. "Ahh, the nostalgia."

Jenny looked at her curiously. "'*Mechanic's Digest*'?! Explain!"

Aria chuckled. "Remember Chris? The photographer I was dating back in my wilder years? Yeah, well, he got a job for the magazine, and I nominated myself to pose for his first real photo-shoot experience." She winked at her sister.

Damian yanked Jeremy back by the shoulder. "Enough chitchat. Germ, we need to talk. Inside."

"Alright, alright." With a sigh, Jeremy cocked his head toward the door and headed back inside. "Come along, now. I shall make you all some tea. And don't call me 'Germ.'"

Jeremy led them through the open hangar door. The interior; a massive rectangular space serving as a library for metal shelves loaded with scrap, tools of all kinds, exploration equipment, aircraft parts and incomplete planes and helicopters, research material—huge volumes on machines, mechanics, cars, planes, boats, Copter Ships and countless more—machine parts dangling around the flickering lights, hanging from the trusses running across the arched ceiling; and a disorganized workspace.

And that was just the main level.

To their left was a rickety set of stairs leading up to a wide platform that took up a quarter of the entire hangar. The platform served as a kitchen, a recreation room and a bedroom all in one, with a wide cubical bathroom. The kitchen was at the far end of the platform, resembling an elaborate movie set with its pine cupboards running from one end of the wall to the other above the oven, sink, microwave, and dishwasher; an island counter obscured the view of the utilities from the stairs. A foldout couch and a TV with every video game console ever made sat in a jumbled, tangled mess on the coffee table in the center of the platform. The blinds were pulled down on the windows that stretched down from the ceiling to the floor. Where there weren't windows, there were posters, pin-ups and newspaper/magazine cut-outs of thin, well-built, half naked young women posing suggestively in swimsuits and lingerie, much to Jenny's disgust.

"Whoa," Aria said when they went up the stairs onto the platform. "Quite the collector, aren't ya?"

"Indeed. Make yourselves at home."

Aria surveyed the posters until she found a massive framed poster of her eighteen-year-old self. The poster had her sitting cross-legged in a beach setting, winking and sticking her tongue out at the camera in a provocative manner, dressed in a thin white bikini and thong that appeared to barely contain her. She held two comically large rocket launchers upright with the letters 'F-Bomb' painted on each rocket. "Ah, back in my wild days. My eighteenth year was a crazy one."

Jenny frowned. "Does Zero know about this?"

"Not unless he's a subscriber."

"So what are we doing here?" Marner asked as she sat on the couch.

Dave burst out of the TV in a dramatic explosion of swirling firecrackers. "*NOWHERE*!"

Damian glanced at him hatefully. "If I could kill you, I would."

"Ah, ah, ah!" Dave wagged a stubby hand in his face. "You lose all credibility if you start threatening to kill a ghost."

"That's what pisses me off even more about you," he replied with a snarl. "Someone beat me to it."

Dave spat raspberries at him, fueling his anger.

Marner sighed. "Can you two stop, please?"

"So…" said Jeremy, stroking his chin thoughtfully. "You two can see apparitions, eh? That is very fascinating, indeed."

Damian sat on an armchair on Marner's left and crossed his arms and legs, and pouted. "No, it's not 'very fascinating;' it's a pain in my ass. He pops up everywhere I go. Could be from a TV, the floor, the kitchen sink, the urinal, the toaster... it's annoying"

Jenny snickered. "Glad I don't get stuck with Marner's uncle popping up everywhere I go."

Damian glared at her. "Shut up."

"*You* shut up," she snapped back.

"Do something useful and make us some sandwiches."

"Make your own sandwiches."

Jeremy crossed the living room area and entered the kitchen. "I will prepare the tea and sandwiches if you are hungry."

"Starving," Damian groaned.

"And while I am preparing a snack, perhaps you can shed some light on where in the hell you have been for the past few years."

Damian's shoulders fell, and he groaned again, this time with dismay.

COBALT ROGUE, VOL. 1: THE DEAD BLUE

Episode 005

Escape from Cloverfield

Seth Karma—vice-commander of Systems Corporation; outranked only by Silverstein himself. His white leotard had been blackened by the grenade blast it'd sustained just an hour earlier.

Because of that, his mood had taken a severely dark and shortly fused turn. That fuse was getting shorter with every minute that passed with him squatting in brush under the shadow of Jeremy's perimeter wall.

What a stupid, dead-end job. Seth couldn't believe Silverstein dumped it on him, the second in command.

"You're my most competent asset," Silverstein had said with a hint of mean-spirited amusement in his smirk. "If it were any other tailing mission, I'd send one of our hounds. But this is the Dead Blue, Seth. He demands a higher priority—if not for us, then for his ego. You're perfect for the job."

"Is this punishment for the loss of three of our men under my watch?"

"No."

"What about Aria infiltrating our ranks and blowing me away with a grenade?"

"Of course not." Silverstein wouldn't—or couldn't—hide the upward curl of his dark lips. "I simply find you most qualified for the job."

Seth thought, *More like 'politics and ethics dictate I'm qualified.' Fuck you, Jon.*

He looked at the barbed wire-topped brick wall that boxed in Jeremy's massive scrap yard. "I hate life."

The Hangar

"Hey," Jeremy spoke up as he set a platter of sandwiches on the coffee table, "you mentioned my father when you were at the gate."

"Oh yeah," Damian said. He selected a bologna sandwich

with mayonnaise and bit into it. With his mouth full, he asked, "How's the old fart doin' these days?"

Jeremy offered him a cup of tea. Damian shook his head. Jeremy offered it to Marner, and she gracefully accepted it with a smile. "He is no longer with us."

Damian stopped chewing. He looked up at Jeremy. His eyes followed Jeremy as he went back into the kitchen. "What? When'd he die?"

"The end of the war, after the Fate Star hit… we did not get out in time."

Cloverfield, 2020—The Hangar

A blinding flash had been spreading across the black horizon like the frantic rise of an unnaturally cobalt sun for the past hour. Now, its light pulsated, intensifying with every increasingly erratic beat. Golden rays of light emitted from the base of the strange blue sphere drowned out even the darkest shadows, pouring through every street, building, crack, niche, and crevice like a sparkling tidal wave.

The distant staccato of gunfire had stopped. Now, only the thunderous roar of a prolonged earth-shattering boom could be heard. The hangar trembled to its foundations, shaking loose debris and fixtures out of the ceiling. The vehicles, spare parts, and metal shelves rattled intensely.

Ten-year-old Jeremy struggled to maintain his footing on the shifting floor as he darted through the aisle between shelves fully stocked with books and model airplanes. "Father!" he shouted as he approached a tall man descending the stairs of the platform. "The light is getting brighter! I think it is about to explode! We should have evacuated with the others!"

"No," his father said. "I'm not leaving my life's work behind. If I die, I die with the rest of my life."

Jeremy grabbed him and tugged on his arm. "But what about me!?"

"You're a part of my life, obviously." His father took his hand and led him toward the rug lying in front of the door. He bent down, grabbed the edge, and flipped it aside, revealing a trap door underneath.

And then it happened.

A blinding light poured through the window shades like they weren't even there. It was almost heavenly, digging into the pair's retinas and ripping out their sight.

The loud crack roared through the air as soon as the shockwave hit.

Ka-PPOOOOOOWWWWWWW!

An eruption of hot air burst through the windows, battering their bodies with glass shards and hot debris. All they could see was black, and they could only scream as another explosion obliterated the walls and sent them flying, hands still clung together.

When Jeremy came to, it was morning. He was still clinging to his father's hand. He still couldn't see. The rancid stench of burning death clogged his nostrils and made him cough and gag. He sat up, only to realize something.

His father's hand moved a little too freely with his own movements.

Jeremy shook the hand. Then he ran his fingers over its limp form, stopping at a partially dry, crusted, oozing stump. His heart nearly stopped. "F-father...?"

The hand slipped through his fingers and landed on the floor with a SPLAT. He crawled on all fours across the cracked floor, feeling his way to an overturned desk. He climbed on top of it, felt for the middle handle, and pulled the drawer open once he found it. He fumbled around clumsily for a familiar item, and found it. A pair of goggles. He snatched them up and pulled them on, and flipped the switch behind his right ear.

With a flicker, his vision returned. And the first thing he saw was his father's mangled corpse sprawled under a pile of shattered concrete and melted steel beams. Jeremy stared at the grisly sight; breathless, dumbstruck. His heart turned to ice. "F-father...?" Tears welled up in his eyes. "Father!"

Klink!

Present Day

Jeremy placed his teacup on the saucer resting on the window sill. "The cause of the secondary explosion was a massive chunk of the star crash-landing at the front entrance, just ten paces away. My father shielded me from the blast."

"Shit," said Damian. "Did you at least put that metal to good use?"

"Of course," Jeremy replied bitterly. "The *Scion's Wings* would be nothing without it."

Jenny asked, "That the Copter Ship parked over our heads?"

Jeremy nodded. "Indeed. I have continued my father's work. I was lucky that he had developed these goggles that enable me to see months prior to the war. Originally he had created them with the sole intention of donating them to hospitals and clinics. Without them, his life's work would have been wasted." He took another sip from his tea, wanting to change the subject. "So," he began, "why is there a semi parked in the lot, and how did you convince these fine young women to escort you to my humble abode?"

Damian answered bluntly, "They're my hostages and the semi's full of stuff I demanded as a sort of advanced ransom payment."

Jeremy spat his tea onto the coffee table in disbelief, sputtering, "*WHAT*!?"

Marner, who was reaching for her teacup on the table, slowly withdrew her hand in disgust and disappointment.

Jeremy looked like he was about to smash his teacup over Damian's head. "What did you do *this* time!?"

"Hey, wait a minute!" Damian retorted. "What the fuck makes you think it's *my* fault?!"

"Because it is *never* your fault!" Jeremy replied sarcastically. "You kidnap three teenage girls, steal a truck—because I am doubly sure that vehicle parked outside is not yours, is it?—and bring them *here*?! Now I am an accomplice! What have you done?!"

"Well, I—"

"*EXPLAIN*!"

Damian shrugged. "Well, Systems captured me and imprisoned me after the war. These two got me out." He cocked his head toward Aria. "That one got involved later. Then Silverstein himself came along and tried to crash the party, so I planted a bomb in" —he gestured toward Jenny— "*that* one's stomach, set to go off if something I don't like happens. Oh, and if it explodes, everything within a twenty-kilometre radius goes up. So yeah, I've kinda got the upper hand at this present moment. The cops, Systems Corporation, Division 9, and anyone else who's after us can't do *shit.*"

Jeremy's jaw dropped and his eyes widened. His teacup slipped through his fingers and shattered on the floor. He stared wide-eyed at Damian in disbelief. "I… you… what… This is *insane*! You are *completely* and *utterly* insane! OH GOD! Now they will believe me to be some sort of accomplice in your plan! My life is ruined! My career in Copter Ship design and engineering is over before it has even begun!"

Damian raised his hands. "Whoa. Whoa. Whoa. Whoa. Calm down, man—"

Jeremy raised his giant wrench above his head. "*You* calm down!"

CRASH!

Damian dived out of the chair a split second before Jeremy's wrench split it in half. Damian skidded across the coffee table, knocking everything on it to the floor, and rolled off the edge as Jeremy struck it with the wrench, reducing it to flying splinters.

Marner screamed and curled up on the couch beside Jenny.

Damian drew his energy sword from thin air and blocked a blow from Jeremy. They were frozen for a moment, with Jeremy's wrench grinding against Damian's blade edge. Then Damian pressed the barrel of his revolver against Jeremy's cheekbone and growled, "Jeremy! CALM. THE *FUCK. DOWN.* Or I swear to Christ I will blow you away! Now you know I don't wanna do that, don't you?"

Jeremy trembled. He shuddered, and lowered his wrench. Dropped his head in sullen defeat. "W-why did you come here?"

"I need a ride outta here," said Damian. "The only one I can trust to smuggle me out of the country is you, the guy who just tried to bash my head in with a giant fucking wrench."

"You… you… I cannot believe you would do this to me." Jeremy backed away a few paces and flopped back into his chair wearily, still clutching the wrench. "Using other people's lives to save your own…"

Damian shrugged. "Yeah, basically. Not like I had much of a choice."

Jeremy glared at him. "There is *always* an alternative. There is always another choice."

"Don't you start preaching to me, Jeremy. I'm not in the mood for bullshit sermons."

"Your father would be ashamed."

Damian's ahoge twitched.

"*Whoa*, now," said Aria, butting in. "Let's not get too personal about this."

Damian pointed at Jeremy. "You're my hostage too. That's that. We need a ride outta here, and whatever crew members you've got stashed around."

"The... the crew members? They are running a maintenance check on the *Scion's Wings*."

"You named your ship?"

"If you had created something after years of hard work, would you not give it a name?"

Damian thought about it for a moment. "Hmph. Guess I would."

"Yeah, because you named *me*, after all!"

Everyone's heads turned to the window where a girl's cat-eared head popped into view. She had long pink hair and sparkly pink eyes, and she had a sweet grin on her face.

Screaming, Jeremy bashed her head in with his wrench, much to everyone's surprise.

THWACK!

Damian shouted, "HOLY SHIT! Put that down! Jesus! Why'd you do that for?!"

Jeremy looked at him, terror-stricken. "What would *you* do if a mysterious girl crawled through your window?!"

Damian blinked. "I'd do lots of things to a mysterious girl who just crawled through my window, and braining her with a fucking wrench isn't one of them!"

The girl in the window continued smiling, and stuck her tongue out playfully. "Don't worry, it didn't hurt," she said as blood trickled down her face.

Jeremy stared at her. Then he fainted.

Thump!

Damian sighed and looked at the girl as her blood dripped off her chin. "Mona, you okay?"

Mona crawled through the window and jumped to the floor lightly on all fours, as if she really were an actual cat. She even had a grey tail swishing from side to side behind her. "I'll be fine," she said. "I've been through worse."

Damian smirked and stroked her hair between her ears, which went flat. "Good girl."

"Mmmmmm." She started to purr as he ran his fingers through her hair.

Jenny, Marner, and Aria stared at them, dumbfounded.

"Um," said Jenny. "Who's this?"

Marner said, "I've seen her before… oh!" She pointed at Damian. "I remember seeing her in your photo!"

"Photo?" Damian asked, blinking.

"When we were doing your laundry, we found a photo of a group of Mews in your pants pocket," Marner explained.

Mona nudged her head against Damian's chest. "Aaww, you kept a photo of me! How sweet."

Damian scowled, mildly embarrassed.

Mona nodded, still purring. "Yep. I'm Damian's guardian and servant. It's a pleasure to meet you all. What are your names?"

Damian quickly said, "Forget familiarizing and make me a sandwich."

Mona stood upright and saluted dutifully. "Yes, Master!" she exclaimed eagerly, before dashing into the kitchen to prepare him a sandwich.

Damian turned to the other three girls with his hands in his jacket. "So you guys checked my pockets, huh?"

Marner nodded. "Yes, we checked just in case you had something valuable. I'm sorry."

Damian looked at the sad, guilty expression on her face and noticed Jenny and Aria glaring at him expectantly. He looked at them worriedly. Then he said to Marner, "I-it's not like I was hiding it. I don't care either way..."

"So what's a Mew doing taking your orders?" Jenny asked with disgust.

"As if we hadn't already established that," he said irritably. "She's been my friend since childhood. Her name is Mona Feline. I don't really know where she came from; she just *appeared* during the first battle in the Dehue Extermination Project, and she's never left my side since. She's helped me through quite a load of shit in the past."

"Just 'appeared'?" asked Aria.

Damian nodded. "Yeah, pretty much."

"That doesn't sound the least bit, uh... *convenient* to you?"

Damian shook his head. "Nope."

Jeremy stirred awake, and groaned.

Damian looked at him. "Oh, you're up. Good. Start your ship's engine. I want everything in that semi loaded onto that ship, and I want it ready for take-off in ten minutes."

Jeremy stared at him, slack-jawed and dumbfounded.

Damian blinked. "Um. Now."

When the Copter Ship's loading platform touched down, a member of Jeremy's crew drove the semi onto it. Damian and the others stepped on afterwards, and they ascended into the belly of the *Scion's Wings*. Once they were in the loading bay, Jeremy led them around the semi and a vehicle under a large tarp beside it to the automatic exit. There, they climbed a small set of stairs into a wide corridor and went left up to another set of automatic doors that led to the bridge—the inside of the drum-like portion of the ship.

The girls scanned the clear, circular space of the bridge in awe. Damian gave it a single fleeting look and nudging Jeremy's shoulder. "Alright. Get it up."

"R-right," said Jeremy as he approached an enclosed console board in the cockpit and jumped inside. Jeremy pressed his hand against the palm scanner, and the dashboard lit up in reply. He flipped a few switches and lifted the steering wheel.

Marner looked around the bridge in amazement. "Do you pilot this all by yourself?"

"I have a crew functioning when I require their assistance. Right now, they are warming everything up," he answered. "Activating the anti-gravity boosters."

Vooooooooooooooommmmmmmmmmmmmm!

The belly of the *Scion's Wings* hummed with life, glowing with a dark blue colour. The air rippled under the ship as it steadily levitated off the massive rectangular landing pad that rested on the roof of the hangar. The powered rotors on the rotating shafts in the wings began to spin, whipping up whirlwinds of dust and garbage.

A brief, smooth liftoff.

Damian bit into his bologna-and-mustard sandwich with satisfaction. "Nice take-off, I say. You're a smart guy after all, Germ."

"Do not call me 'Germ,'" Jeremy grumbled under his breath.

Damian tore another chunk out of his sandwich.

Jeremy turned his attention to the three girls. Mona was nowhere to be found. "There is a lounge down the hall. Please, make yourselves at home."

"Thank you," Marner replied humbly.

Damian looked at them. "Yes. Make yourselves comfortable. Hell, you're probably already comfortable, aren't you?"

Jenny said, "Um, I'd probably be more comfortable if you took this bomb out of me."

"Not happening."

"*BOMB*?!" Jeremy shouted with alarm. "*What* bomb?! No one said anything about a *bomb*!"

Damian scowled at Jenny. "Now look what you did."

Jenny frowned and stuck her tongue out.

Damian turned to Jeremy. "I told you about the bomb. Don't act like it's news now."

"I do not recall hearing about a bomb!" Jeremy yelled.

"Well, now you know."

Aria stepped between them. "I hate to break up your guys' cat fight, but you don't happen to have a change of clothes on this heap, do you?"

"Why, yes," Jeremy replied, "in fact we have several changes of clothing in all shapes and sizes. Check any of the closets in the corridor."

"Thanks."

As Aria left the bridge, Jeremy turned back to Damian. "You have a lot of explaining to do."

"Haven't I explained enough?" Damian groaned.

"*NO*! In fact, you have explained *nothing*, except for why we are running away in the first place—because of *you*."

"Okay, okay."

The Square Office—The United States of Troyas

Two tall, narrow windows with red satin drapes were the only source of light in the dark office. A brooding man in a dark suit sat behind a large solid oak desk situated between the windows. In front of the desk lay a giant square carpet made from blood-red silk with a golden lion crouched in the center, ready to pounce. The rest of the chamber's floor, walls, and ceiling were plain black marble, adding another layer of gloom to the chamber's foul mood.

The tall iron doors across the room parted slightly with an eerie creak. A slim, golden ray of light leaked in across the floor, and a dutiful voice pierced the dusty silence as a man poked his head inside. "Mr. President? Sorry to barge in like this... but we have the latest reports from our Cloverfield contacts."

The man leaned forward on the desk, glaring at his visitor with furious green eyes. His neatly-combed black hair somehow stood out in the dark room, and his eyes shimmered with suppressed rage. "Come in."

"U-um… well, the thing is" —the man opened the door fully and approached the desk with a small stack of papers in his hands—"about ninety percent of our contacts and allies in Cloverfield have either severed their ties with us or have been killed by Systems Corporation. More specifically, Jonathon Silverstein. The Dead Bikers gang has pulled out, along with five or six other gangs alone, and the small Yakuza group that live in Eastern Cloverfield, the Zetsubo Clan. Quentin Rodriguez, Shinji Anno and several more crime bosses have withdrawn due to the danger this situation poses. Almost all of the others have been killed off or disbanded. The Lorenzo Family, the vampire mafia, was slaughtered last night. Maria is the only survivor—of course, that's because she's *here*. If you were still considering an invasion, it would be difficult to pinpoint the enemy's exact locations."

Truman's interlocked fingers tightened, his rubber gloves squeaking. "This is most displeasing. So the ones still alive wish to discontinue business, correct?"

"Yes, sir..."

"Hm. Jonathon Silverstein knows how to leave a man blind." Grunt. Truman snarled, "How the hell could he possibly know who and where to attack? It's like the information drops right into his cold, dead, vampiric lap."

"Well, as of today, reports of Jonathon Silverstein's public appearance at a school are all over the news networks."

"*Obviously*, Mr. Informant. Cloverfield Heart led the public to believe that he died six years ago when he was really just lying low, killing off our allies because I didn't fork over the Hell Pentagram. Apparently they *actually* thought the people would believe the lies that the attacks were caused by nostalgic remnants and radical copycats of Systems Corporation." Truman scoffed. "I told more convincing lies during my election campaign. And people ate it up."

"Couldn't you just *give* it to him?"

"Of course not. If I'd given him the Hell Pentagram, he would've used the boy to unleash Diablo, and Diablo would be under his control. That would not bode well for us. And now, he's lost the Dead Blue. He's obviously out searching for him… or he's sending someone else to retrieve him." Truman's permanent frown hardened. "That boy's been an endless source of trouble for us all. If we didn't require his blood, we would all be more than happy to dispose of him. If he can even *be* disposed of."

"So what should we do?"

"A plethora of options have swirled around in my mind. After sitting in this room thinking, I've narrowed it down to these two: either we invade Cloverfield and kill Silverstein, which would put an end to one of our major problems; or we hunt the boy and use him to summon Diablo for ourselves before Silverstein retrieves him. Of course, both are options that could be played out simultaneously, but sending a strike force to obliterate Cloverfield would only complicate the tensions between the World Alliance and our Axis Alliance further. We would need an especially good reason to justify an invasion, and at this current moment, we simply cannot find such a reason."

"What about Silverstein's reputation?" the man asked. "Would that not be…?"

"No," said Truman. "Even though Silverstein is a notorious terrorist and public enemy, a full-scale war against him and his beloved organization full of rapists and warmongers would not be accepted by the World Alliance. They would put the millions of civilian casualties into consideration. They simply could not allow it unless Silverstein—or the Dead Blue—committed an act so extreme it would lead them to rethink their decision. Once Silverstein slips, and we capture the Dead Blue, we could destroy our enemies in one fell swoop.

"Silverstein's acts of genocide will catch up to him soon enough. Before the Dehue Extermination Project, every country in the world faced an over-population crisis. The estimated overall population was around fourteen billion. The population had doubled since the beginning of the 21st Century. There hadn't been a war since the 1974 Viceeper Civil War, not including the decade-long cold war between our alliances. Nearly fifty years later, and the leaders of every nation were scrambling for a breakthrough in human expansion—to build space colonies in the earth's atmosphere, and control as many resources as possible. Little quarrels broke out here and there, but nothing extreme enough to bring the population back down to containable levels.

"Then the war happened. The Dehue Extermination Project." Truman spoke the words as if he felt like the conversation brought back a feeling of nostalgia. "In one year, approximately three quarters of the earth's population was wiped out. The estimated population as of now is 4.6 billion.

"The purpose of this rant is to convey a message, Mr. Informant," Truman said as he stood up, leaning on the desk. "The stakes have just been raised. The Dead Blue's capture should be the primary objective for any Troyan citizen or soldier. I want him found, and I want him found alive. If anyone finds they have the opportunity to kill Jonathon Silverstein, they had better not hesitate to pull the trigger. Call the Elemental Five. We're going to conduct a search."

"A search, Mr. President?"

"I can't risk open war with the World Alliance. Not yet. Not with a shortage in income from our thinning list of allies. My government's budget is already being cut short due to war relief efforts, and covering our tracks from past dealings during the Fate Star Conflicts. Neither side has checkmate; Silverstein has lost the boy. The game escalates from its standstill. Send one of the Elemental Five to find him before anyone else does."

"You just read my mind," said a voice at the door.

Mr. Informant turned to see General Air standing at the door. He had short white hair and silver armour, like a knight from King Arthur's round table. "General Air," said Truman. "Your timing is impeccable."

"I saw the news and was about to make a request to catch the

Dead Blue, so to overhear your conversation is a pleasant surprise."

"I see." Truman sat back down. "Take your brigade and bring the Dead Blue back to me. Alive. If Jonathon Silverstein intervenes, kill him."

"Can Jonathon Silverstein even die?"

"He's immortal, but with a weakness. Just severe his head from his body. There will be no reviving him after that."

Air smiled with cruel anticipation as he leaned against the door with his arms crossed. "Sounds like a plan. I'll take a small brigade with me. That should be enough for one kid."

"Don't underestimate him. He's the—"

"Yeah, yeah, he's the Killer of Twenty Million People. I know the story," he interrupted, waving him off. "You don't need to turn this into a play recital; I know how dangerous the little shithead is. And I'll bring him back, easy as pie."

"See that you do, or there will be hell to pay."

Air snickered as he stepped out of Truman's sight. "I hear ya."

Mr. Informant looked at Truman. "Is it really alright to send him?"

"What do you mean?"

"Well, he failed his other mission… perhaps he's not the wisest choice."

"If he fails, it wouldn't matter. It's the Troyas Brigade I have faith in."

Mr. Informant paused for a moment before nodding in agreement. That made sense. General Air was the weakest of the generals. Even the elite pilots of the Troyas Brigade were stronger in their terrain marchers. "Ah."

"Even if Air fails the simple mission to bring the Dead Blue back, it wouldn't matter."

Mr. Informant noticed the sick, savage anticipation in his voice. Behind Truman's calm and collected exterior resided a ferocious demon hungry for war. Sometimes it even did the thinking for him. "It wouldn't?"

Truman smiled. "No. If he died, Damian Warkowski would have done me a great favour."

Elsewhere

The Copter Ship soared over the city at a quickening pace,

rising weightlessly into the clouds like a vapour. The movement of the ship wasn't rough at all, it was almost soothing.

Jenny stood on the bridge. She knew she wouldn't feel comfortable sharing the lounge with Damian, even if her sister was with her. And so, Jenny looked out the curved Fate Star glass wall at the smoky clouds that rolled around the ship.

Marner was also on the bridge, staring out the window in awe.

"What's this thing's name again?" she asked.

Jeremy looked at her. "I call it the *Scion's Wings*."

"Oh, so you're a Scionian?" she asked.

"Not quite. I was only born in Scionia, but I am a firm believer in the Scionian's way of life." He gently pulled back on the steering wheel, and the bridge tipped upward just as slightly as his movement. It was almost like his shadow the way it smoothly followed his movements. "When I smelted the Fate Star metal that landed in my property and constructed this ship, I gave it its name because the Fate Star metal actually glows when it flies in the sunlight at a certain period, giving it the appearance of a Scion. Like so many of my people believe, I, too, believe that the Fate Star is merely what is left of the armour of Icarizu the Aspirer."

"Icarizu? The god of cobalt and gold?" Jenny said.

"Yes. You know of him?"

"Just the name and the colour scheme, bud."

With a snort, Jeremy said, "His power flows around this ship, giving it an almost... *unnatural* glow in the sun. Like that of an angel."

"A golden angel?" asked Marner, joining in on the conversation.

Jeremy lifted his index finger and gave Marner the same smile a teacher does when his favourite student answers a question exactly how he wanted to hear it. "Precisely. Like a golden angel; it is truly a breathtaking sight."

Aria stepped on the bridge in a new change of clothes: a plain black T-shirt and black loose pants with her usual gloves and bandanna. "I know I am."

That was something that Jeremy noticed quickly. Both Knight Sisters wore black leather gloves. "Not you," he said. "I was talking about how the *Scion's Wings* shines like an angel."

"Ah," she said with an uninterested tone. "So where are we

going?"

Jeremy smiled. "I recall receiving a transmission from an acquaintance of mine in Scionia. It was a crucial message of utter importance."

"What did it say?" asked Jenny.

"As I recall, it was about the… *pandemic* in that country that has been a major outbreak since the end of the Dehue Extermination Project."

"What kind of pandemic?" asked Aria, now interested in the conversation.

Jeremy looked at her with complete dramatic urgency. "Re-animated corpses."

Jenny burst into laughter. "*Zombies*? Really? AHAHAHAHAHAHAHA!"

"It is no laughing matter."

"A real-life zombie pandemic is kinda funny." Aria said. "Lemme guess... that was the result of all the strikes?"

"Exactly."

Aria's smirk disappeared.

Jeremy said, "Of course, no one will do anything about it. The only people who live there are scattered societies of youth. Youth who live by codes of conduct that are... *sketchy*, at best. The laws change when it serves them. They could be gentlemen one minute, and salivating, would-be rapists." Beat. "Like Jonny."

Jenny stared at him with wide eyes, taking a cautionary step away from him. "How…?"

"I am a telepath," he said bluntly.

"I have private things in there!" she yelled, cracking her knuckles.

"Oh, I know," he replied with a sly smirk on his face.

Jenny grinded her teeth angrily, trying to approach him when Marner stepped in front her. "Get outta my way, Marner. I'm gonna replace his nuts with catnip!"

Marner shook her head. "Come on, calm down. He was just fooling around."

Jeremy nodded. "Yes, I respect the privacy of strangers who suddenly take me hostage."

"Hey, *we* didn't take you hostage! *We're* hostages!"

"Hostages can take hostages," he said.

"No they can't!"

"Come on, Jenny! Just ignore him," Marner protested, tugging on her arm.

Jenny looked at her. She scoffed, turned, and stomped toward the windows whilst grumbling angry death threats and profanities. Then she said for everyone to hear, "Why does someone like you have those powers? So stupid…"

"Hm?"

She turned and pointed at him. "What kind of God gives a pervert like you *telepathy*? It's inconceivable!"

Marner didn't feel like listening to the two of them bicker and turned to exit the bridge. Jenny called after her, "Hey, where ya goin'?"

"I'm going to check up on Damian."

"He's not a baby, you know."

"I want his side of the story."

Jenny scratched the back of her head. "*His* side?"

"Of course. There's something else going on, I just know it."

"If we don't know the reason, something tells me it oughta stay that way."

"Maybe it should, but I'm too curious to accept that."

Jenny sighed and followed her through the doorway. "I'm comin' with you, then."

Damian sat in the lounge, cross-legged in the center of the couch, staring at the plasma screen TV that was currently showing a pornographic program. He grinned. "Nice."

"Uhhn! Oooohhhh, baby!" the woman on TV moaned. "It's so big! Oh, God, yes! *YES*!"

"Aw, yeah," the man grunted. "Aw, yeah! You're so tight! Take it, bitch!"

Damian watched intently as the woman started screaming, reaching her limit. "Wow, this is entertaining."

"Oh, God, I'm gonna... I'm gonna...!"

Damian quickly lost interest when the couple's session ended and changed the channel to another adult station, where yet another session was just beginning. But now he was more focused on the TV remote. He wanted to duplicate what he did with the waffle back in Jenny's house, and he wanted to remember how he could do the things he did during the hostage situation on the academy grounds. He felt anger, fear, and an adrenaline rush. It all came so naturally. He didn't even have to think then. It just came to him.

And hell, he knew he could fly, but something told him that every time he would make an attempt, the same phrase would pop into his head: "Try to fly, and all you'll do is *die*."

He set the TV remote down on the floor and glared at it. "Alright. I'm in an impatient mood at the moment. I want you to move. Float off the ground, and change the channel to something other than porn."

The TV remote didn't comply.

"Do it!"

Nothing.

"Do it now!"

Again, nothing.

"Do it, you bitch, do it!"

Nothing. All that could be heard in the room were the grunts and moans and occasional obscenities from the TV.

"...So you wanna play it *that* way, huh?" Damian hissed, crossing his arms.

Just then, Jenny and Marner opened the door and stepped into the lounge. Dave was right behind them. The porn was still going. Damian glanced over his shoulder at them with a scowl.

Silence. Awkward silence.

Marner looked at the TV, gasped, and turned pink. Then bright red. She let out an embarrassed squeal. "Um... um... um... I-I-I'm so sorry! I didn't know you were... uh, busy!"

Jenny heaved an exasperated sigh. "I can see how fun *this* is gonna turn out to be…"

Dave peered at the TV and exploded with excitement. His stubby hands sprouted two thumbs and he gave Damian a double-thumbs-up while shouting, "NICE!"

"Well, that was a little embarrassing..." Jenny said.

Damian looked up at Jenny and Marner, rubbing the spot where Jenny had smacked him with the TV remote. Dave struggled to fight back his laughter in the background.

Damian picked up the remote and flicked to a different channel, where a small group of ragtag survivors fought against a zombie horde that relentlessly closed in on them. Jenny glanced over at the TV as the horde overwhelmed the group and started tearing them apart. Damian replied, "Well, that's your own damn fault."

"H-how's it *my* fault?" Jenny asked defensively

"You just walked in."

"It's the *lounge*! We should be able to walk in here and lounge around. That's the purpose of a lounge!"

"And that's exactly what I was doing," he said. "Just lounging around."

Jenny gave up. There was no sense in trying to argue with him. Nothing would change his mind now.

Marner didn't say anything aloud. *Oh, dear,* she thought, *where did he get this attitude from? I can sort of see why he'd be in a bad mood, but...*

"I see a lot of things've changed since I went to sleep," he said.

"Oh? Yes, it has." Marner snapped out of her thoughts. "I guess the world's changed a lot since then."

"Damn right it has," he scoffed, watching with amusement as a man threw his sputtering chainsaw at a zombie and ran away squealing from the entire undead horde hot on his heels. Unfortunately for the man, the zombies had him surrounded, and the man reached for the sky in vain and shrieked in terror as he sank into a writhing ocean of rotting flesh. "I can't believe how much it's changed. TV, the radio, magazines, books, and the way the city works and looks; it's all different. It's like something straight outta *Blade Runner* without the hot Japanese chicks and the Atari product placement."

He almost sounded upset that the world moved on without him. Jenny and Marner couldn't help but feel sympathy for him. The look on his face was expressionless, but the sadness and disappointment were there.

Marner stared at him sympathetically. *He seems like a completely different person ...*

With a forced chuckle, he said, "I'm surprised the TV networks aren't overloaded with kindergarten-level bullshit nowadays. People were always bitching about how censorship wasn't strict enough before the war."

Jenny scoffed. "Oh, it's gotten stricter. Hardly any R-rated shows on TV anymore. Any network that shows that kind of stuff without a paid subscription gets fined for indecency. It's either one or one hundred with these guys. There is no in between."

Damian shook his head. "That is completely and utterly gay."

"I agree with you there."

Marner stayed silent.

"Anyway, off-topic subject here," Damian began, facing them with a serious, sincere expression on his face, "I'm not going to kill you or hurt you."

The girls stared at him with doubtful frowns.

"Well, unless provoked," he added.

"How can we be so sure?" Jenny asked.

Damian sighed, stood up, and approached her. Alarmed, she took a hesitant step back. He drew his hand back, and then thrust it into her stomach.

Marner gasped in horror and threw her hands over her mouth. Dave's jaw literally hit the floor and his eyeballs popped out of his sunglasses in a cartoonish fashion.

Trembling and gagging, Jenny desperately grabbed Damian's arm. She could feel his hand digging through her insides, moving around and draining her strength from her like an abnormally large parasite.

Then his hand stopped moving, easing the pain a little. Jenny stiffened. The slightest movement sent another scorching pang to her brain.

"Got it," he said. He looked at Marner. "Get something for her to eat. Now."

Marner could only shake violently, watching with wide eyes, in a horrified stupor.

"NOW!" Damian shouted, startling her out of her trance.

Marner darted to the other end of the lounge; on her left was a long rectangular table, and on her right was an island bar counter with a fridge, two sinks, cupboards, a microwave, an oven, and a dishwasher on the other end. The only way into the narrow space was around the bar counter, which was partially obstructed by the fridge. She reached the fridge, opened it, and looked inside: she found a case of Broweiser beer, peanut butter, a loaf of white bread, tomatoes, pears, a couple pitchers of milk, and an electric drill.

Jenny started to moan.

"Shh," said Damian. "Don't worry. The worst hasn't come yet."

"Great," Jenny grumbled. "W-what the hell... are you doing...?"

"Taking the bomb out, unless you want it in your pancreas for the rest of your life."

"N-no thanks... and I thought you put it in my s-stomach?"

"Whatever."

"I'm coming, I'm coming!" Marner yelled urgently with two pears in her hands as she rushed toward them.

Damian looked at Jenny. "Ready?"

"G-get on with it." She retched. "*Ack...*"

Damian ripped his hand out, grasping a glowing blackish-blue orb of energy in his palm. Jenny gasped and hit the floor, grasping her stomach. Damian closed his fingers around the orb until it was reduced to a black vapour cloud that quickly dispersed. "Give her something to eat before she vomits all over the floor," he instructed Marner.

"H-here." Marner knelt down and handed Jenny a pear.

Jenny took it and bit into it hastily, devouring the pear in less than thirty seconds. Then she snatched the other one and ate it at a slightly slower pace as the pain in her stomach began to ease up. Soon enough, the pears were gone, stems included.

Damian smiled. "See? Wasn't so bad, was—"

KRAK!

With a swift uppercut Jenny sent him sprawling on the couch. "You inconsiderate asshole! That fuckin' hurt!"

Damian sat up, massaging his throbbing chin. "...Ow. I think I bit my tongue."

"GOOD!" she shouted before turning on her heel and storming out of the lounge. "Dick!"

Damian couldn't help but smirk as the automatic doors slid shut behind her. "I think she likes me."

Dave laughed. "Dude, you practically *raped* her."

"Did not."

"You *so* did, my friend!"

Damian and Dave looked at Marner. She nervously said, "Um... well... you *did* enter her body without permission, so... Dave is right?"

"Oh, come on!" Damian protested. "It's not rape if I'm taking a bomb out of her liver!"

"Stomach," Marner corrected.

"*WHATEVER*. Look. Do me a favour and don't mention this to anyone else. Hopefully Jenny doesn't spread the word like a disease."

"Why wouldn't she?" Marner asked.

"Pfft. What, you think Jenny became my hostage on purpose?"

"No."

"Then you're an idiot!"

Marner jumped, startled. "W-what?!"

"Jenny and I made a deal. I just pretty much planted a bomb in her spleen—"

"Stomach."

"SHUT *UP*! I planted the bomb in her stomach to ensure our escape." He smirked triumphantly. "Just as planned."

"So… wait, the bomb was a fake?"

"Oh, it was real. I didn't lie about what it could do. *Buuuuuut* it's a good thing I didn't need to use it!"

Marner paused. "…You tricked me. Didn't you?"

"Don't take it personally; I tricked everyone there."

She shook her head. "No, not that."

"What, then?"

"Because I'm special in a lot of ways," he'd said.

"You didn't tell me that you were the Dead Blue," she said. "You lied to me."

"I didn't lie; I just didn't tell you everything."

"You still weren't very honest."

"Well if I was, you probably wouldn't have let me out, now, would you?"

"Well… I… uh…"

"That's what I thought," he said matter-of-factly. "Sure, I tricked you into letting me out, but hell, it's not such a big deal. I only manipulated a few people."

Dave giggled. "You sneaky devil!"

"Get over yourself, Dave," Damian said with a scowl. "You already knew."

"I did?"

"Yes, you did. Moron."

Dave blinked, staring at the wall blankly. "Oh. I forgot. Freak."

"Don't fucking call me a freak!" Damian's angry blue eyes shifted back to Marner. "I didn't lie. I told you I was special in a lot of ways; just didn't put in detail *why* I'm so special."

"But—"

"Don't start. If you want me to leave now, then you're screwed. Tim and Silverstein and God knows what else will look for you and eventually kill you for your association with me. I'm your only hope. You're gonna have to trust me, but I'm not telling you anything about myself that you don't already know."

"You… you killed all those people…"

"Yup. I did. It was easy, too."

"But why?"

"Why?"

Marner nodded.

Damian paused for a few seconds, thinking of a reason. When he finally broke the silence, it startled her, "Because humans are assholes."

"T-that's not a good enough reason!" She froze. She couldn't believe she just shouted her exact thoughts at *him*, of all people.

"Well, too bad," he said. "That's all you're getting. Now get out."

Sensing the hostility in his voice, she quickly left the room and waited for the door to close shut behind her. Dave floated through the door after her. She started stomping her feet on the floor but slowly lightened her footsteps until the noise faded off, moving away from the automatic door. She quietly pressed her ear against the wall and listened intently, hoping she could at least hear *something*.

"What're you doing?" Dave asked in a whisper.

"Shh," she whispered.

"So," said a raspy voice behind the door, "looks like you've got some babysitters now, huh?"

Marner put her hand over her mouth, startled from the new voice.

"Shut up," Damian snapped back. "They're not my babysitters."

"Oh? Then what are they?"

"Leverage. That's it."

Leverage?! She thought, feeling the hairs on her neck prickle.

"Remember our promise?"

"I remember it."

What promise?

"Don't get blinded by their illusion of innocence. They aren't who they say they are. They're different. They want you dead. Just like everybody else. They're going to kill you if you don't watch your back."

"I know, Tyler. I know. I won't forget."

The shadowy figure that stood before Damian looked similar in appearance to him, with the same hairstyle, if a little wilder than Damian's; same facial features save for the colour of the figure's eyes, which were red instead of blue. The figure wore a sinister frown as he stared down at Damian.

""You better not forget," said Tyler. "We have a long way to go."

"I know."

"And what's this I hear about you helping that redheaded bitch find her mother?"

"Heh. Nothing gets past you, huh?" Damian leaned back on the couch with his right leg resting on his left knee. "…It was a lie."

"It *better* have been a lie. And of course, nothing gets past me. *Nothing*. I live in that twisted, manipulative mind of yours, Damian. You can't hide a damn thing from me. And don't you dare forget your promise. It's not something you can just back out on when you feel like it."

"Yeah, yeah, I get it. You don't need to repeat yourself." Damian scratched the back of his head, glanced over at the door, then turned back to Tyler. "So, anyway, has the Fallen Angel said anything? Any updates?"

"None."

"No updates after six years? Really?"

"Pretty much. Everything has been going according to our plan. The Society is making sure that nothing strays off course. The Final Apocalypse's schedule remains unchanged; set for the very second that marks the beginning of January 1st, 2027. Projects

Secret Society is preparing the proxy war as we speak." Tyler blinked, forming a demonic smile. "Does that sound good to you?"

Damian shrugged. "I guess."

"Good. In the off chance you feel any doubts, just remember what the humans did. Remember your hatred for them. Hating is what you do best, after all."

"I'm good at a lot of things; you're not giving me enough credit here."

"Whatever. Just stay on task." Tyler sank backwards into the wall and vanished.

Trembling with fear, Marner slowly backed away from the lounge door. Then she turned and ran down the corridor. *It was a mistake to let him out! I should have known better than to wake him up. I've got to tell the others!*

Splish!

She stumbled, and fell into something cold. Something wet and murky. Shallow, with countless sharp objects under the surface.

Water?

She opened her eyes and found herself staring at a series of dark crimson ripples moving away from her. The pungent odour rising from the thick liquid assaulted her, nearly made her faint.

Blood.

With a horrified gasp and a squeal she jumped back up to her feet and looked around. She wasn't in the corridor anymore. She was somewhere else. Alone. Without Dave. Without anyone. A vast, endless swamp of bones, rotting corpses, and blood surrounded her. She stood knee-deep in it. Lifeless faces bobbed above the surface, all with their glassy eyes fixed on her.

"Where am I? Where am I? Where am I?" she whimpered, shaking violently and splashing around, searching for a way out. "Oh, God! WHERE AM I?!"

"You are in the Abyss."

Raspy, grating, whispering voices spoke in unison behind her. She let out a started yelp and whirled around to find a cloaked figure sitting with its back facing her on a pile of mangled corpses. She could hear chewing noises, like it was eating something juicy.

"W-who…? Who are you?" Marner asked hesitantly.

"No one likes a tattletale, you know," said the voices.

"Especially me."

"Y-you...? Who...?"

The hooded figure glanced over its shoulder at her with an empty eye socket—save for a faint red orb floating inside—that spilled blood down the side of its grinning face profusely. All of the voices poured out of its fanged, grinning mouth when it spoke, "I am he who has fallen from grace."

Then it ripped another chunk of flesh from a severed human arm with its teeth.

Marner kept her petrified stare fixed on the creature before her.

"Can you keep a secret? Just between you and me?"

"...I... I..."

"If you tell on me, I will make sure your time in the afterlife is extremely... unpleasant. Keep quiet and you can avoid a fate that is truly worse than any death. Deal?"

Marner slowly nodded, shaking violently and uncontrollably.

The Fallen Angel bit two fingers off the limp hand and chewed noisily, blood spilling messily from his mouth. "Good girl."

Marner blinked, and the scenery changed completely. She found herself standing in the corridor, staring at the wall, dumbstruck. She broke into a cold sweat, and her stomach turned. With a shuddering breath, she hesitantly looked around the empty corridor, and then darted into the girls' bathroom, entered the nearest stall, and vomited into the toilet.

Dave peered into the stall with a worried expression on his face, watching as she kept her hair from slipping into the toilet bowl as she continued to vomit. "Whoa, what did you see?!"

"N-nothing," Marner sputtered. "I-I don't... I can't tell..."

Cloud HQ, Sky Japan

Kira Cloud looked sullenly at the skyline of the neon metropolis that stretched around his high-rise headquarters. Holographic signage and multi-coloured patterns shimmered on the horizon, overlapped by the golden rays stabbing out from the sunset in the distance.

Ten henchmen were lined up neatly behind him, Uzis strapped to their backs, dressed in black and white suits with their hands clasped in front.

"So… let me get this straight," Kira's grating voice began, "you're telling me that they just *vanished*? You had the entire place surrounded… but yet they *still* got away?"

"Yes, sir," the henchman on the left end of the row said, bowing sincerely. "We're very sorry."

"'Sorry' doesn't find my children," Kira hissed, turning away from the window. His katana clinked on his belt whenever he moved. As he approached the man that spoke, he said, "'Sorry' doesn't excuse the fact that Yuya, Masuko, and Akira are missing. God knows who took them. The Kakashi Clan? The other triads? Cops intent on taking me down? Only God knows. And unfortunately, only God can save you." He slipped his hand inside his dark blue kimono. The golden dragon that wrapped around his body like a snake shimmered. A second later, Kira threw down a small knife on the floor by the henchman's feet. "Pick it up!"

The henchman hesitantly stooped down and lifted the blade off the floor. He looked at the blade, then at Kira in horror.

Kira responded with an angry sneer: "Do it."

The henchman's breathing quickened. He broke into a cold sweat, grasping the handle with both hands, blade pointing at the floor. Then with a final inhale, he raised the blade above his head and plunged it in his stomach. He gasped, wheezed, gritted his teeth as he moved the handle from his left side to his right. Then with a final groan, he doubled over and collapsed at Kira's feet.

Kira stared at the corpse balled up on the floor, then looked at the henchman standing beside it. "What the hell was that?"

"Seppuku, sir."

"No, I know *what* that was. *Why* did he do that?"

"…Sir?"

"I wanted his goddamn *pinkie*, not his *guts*!"

"…Sometimes you give mixed signals, sir."

Kira heaved a deep sigh and returned to the window. "It doesn't matter. I want my children found."

"Father!"

Kira and his men whirled around to see Akira limping toward them from the elevator. Akira was the youngest of Kira's three children, with black hair and attire similar to that of his father, with a katana strapped to his belt. However, despite being only ten years old, Akira was the mature one of the three, and was skilled in many different styles of combat and stealth. And just like his father, Akira had mastered the element of air.

"Akira!" Kira exclaimed as he rushed over to his son. He didn't notice the extent of all the scratches and cuts on his son's body until he got a closer look at him. "...Who did this?"

"I don't know," Akira answered, his voice trembling. "Someone with strong forces. They ambushed us downtown... in large numbers... with gas and poison and stun weapons."

Kira's expression hardened. "Where are Masuko and Yuya?"

"I-I don't know... they took them. I tried to stop it, but..."

"You did your best," Kira interrupted him. "I understand."

"I... I couldn't," Akira sputtered, looking down at his reddened hands.

"You can tell me what happened while we get you patched up." Looking at his son's tattered, blood-soaked clothing, Kira said, "Come. You need medical attention."

COBALT ROGUE, VOL. 1: THE DEAD BLUE

Episode 006

Scionia's Dead Problem

Cloverfield

Elm had managed to escape the academy during Damian's hostage situation, disguising herself as one of Systems Corporation's Elite Infantry at the expense of one of the soldiers Aria had taken down at the main entrance. Luckily, no one had noticed the shattered eye lens in her gas mask helmet when she walked among them. No one noticed her sneak off behind a house at the corner of one of the residential blocks nestled at the base of the academy to ditch the gear in a tool shed and head down the road. Keeping her eyes and ears open for any Systems vehicles that may be passing through, Elm eventually covered about three kilometres and reached the edge of the school district, now entering the city's claustrophobic cluster of grimy towers, holographic advertisements, and overhead LED banners. The city seemed like a menacing fortress compared to the small residential school district.

Upon reaching a small truss bridge that crossed over the narrow canal filled with a steady flow of scummy sewer water, Elm relaxed a little, allowing herself to be seen by pedestrians and the few cars that passed up and down the road. Hands stuffed in the pockets of her long coat, Elm stepped over a homeless man dressed in rags, whose scrawny legs were splayed out across the sidewalk; passed out, clearly drunk, with his back against the rusty bridge railing and his head hanging low. Ironically enough, he slept under a large worn-out sign with faded letters that read: 'NO DRI KING NO SOLI ITI G'. Elm ignored the horrible stench emanating from the man and continued off the bridge. She turned left and walked along the edge of the canal for two blocks before crossing the road; halfway across she spotted a Systems Humvee as it turned off the bridge she'd just crossed, and ducked into a trash-strewn alley. She stumbled over yet another homeless man hugging a wine bottle, hands still in her pockets, and pressed her back against the brick wall, which was covered with old yellowed newspapers and half-shredded wanted posters. Elm snuck a backward glance as the Humvee drove by the alley, its occupants none the wiser.

Safe, she thought.

She turned and headed deeper into the alleyway until there wasn't a soul in sight. She stopped in a small alleyway crossroad, under a canopy of leaky pipes and metal awnings. She stood in the center of the city block.

Elm took out a small radio, similar in appearance to a Bluetooth phone, and pressed it against her ear. She pushed a small button on it, and waited.

Kttcch!

A droning AOL voice answered: "Division 9, Sector Seven, Left Wing Office."

"This is Agent Glasses."

"Voice recognition code confirmed, please hold."

Elm waited for exactly five seconds before a woman's voice cut into her ear: "This is Commander Fish."

Commander Fish, AKA Commander Sigourney Ellen—the head of the secret black ops organization Division 9: Prime Minister John Whitaker's secret police. "Report?"

"I've been compromised. We've got a serious situation."

"The news reports the presence of Systems Corporation at the Cloverfield High Academy, though they don't state why."

"The package," Elm said, "he's out."

"...Which package?"

"Critical. The second is still unaware we're on to him."

"A silver lining, I suppose. But the critical package escaped? That's... unfortunate."

"What are my orders, Commander?"

"Your orders are simple: maintain your position. Put the second package in our custody and be sure he doesn't escape. I'm sure you don't want to lose all your credibility in one day."

"No, ma'am..."

"Good. Then be sure to capture him. Over and out."

Meanwhile...

The Orion Sea passed below the *Scion's Wings*. Crumbling mountains of concrete and debris stabbed up through the water's cyan surface as reminders of a district destroyed and abandoned during and after the Dehue Extermination Project. Crooked utility poles pierced the breeze with loose wires stretching over the flooded ruins like a tattered net. Jenny examined the ruins as the *Scion's Wings* flew over it, pressing her hands and nose against the window. "The old battleground..."

Jeremy nodded, saying nothing.

Aria lingered in the center of the bridge, uninterested in the view. Jenny peered through the glass, trying to spot a single wide crater under the deep blue sparkling water rushing below them, blinking from the sun's sparkling reflections. Realizing it was hopeless, Jenny slipped away from the glass.

Just then, Marner appeared on the bridge, looking paler than usual. Jenny noticed something was off immediately and said, "Hey, you alright?"

"I-I'm fine," Marner answered.

"You don't look fine." Jenny's expression hardened. "Did Damian do something?"

"No, he didn't. I'm just feeling a little sick to my stomach. I guess I get air sick."

Jeremy looked at her. "You 'guess'?"

Marner replied, "Well, I-I've never flown before…"

"Oh, I see."

Both Jenny and Aria remained suspicious.

The *Scion's Wings* tipped upward to avoid jagged spires of debris sticking up from the water. Then the ship penetrated the clouds. It slowed to a hover above them, the wide gap left behind already filling back up in a whirlpool of white fluff.

"We will arrive in Scionia in a few more hours," Jeremy continued. "Do not let Damian provoke you. He loves himself too much to risk anything major right now."

Aria sneered, "That little punk's hiding something."

Jeremy shrugged his left shoulder. "He always was."

"You knew him. What's he like?"

Jeremy inhaled deeply and sputtered as he exhaled, staring forward thoughtfully. "He was always sad."

"Sad?" Jenny said. "Why?"

"Well, no one treated him right. He seemed to be one of the few Dehues in the entire town who was deemed unworthy of respect.

It was almost as if he were condemned since birth."

"Hmph." Jenny crossed her arms and leaned with her back against the window. "Doesn't give him an excuse to be a total asshole."

"I agree."

Aria smirked. "And yet you still aggravated 'im. The gate incident, I mean, with the wall."

"His anger or his traumatic childhood is no excuse for him to just leave my wall with a gaping hole in it. Are you defending him?"

"God, no!" Aria scoffed. "I'm just sayin', you knew all that and *still* went outta your way to piss 'im off. One o' the things I learned from my experiences with that kid is that you gotta keep him as satisfied as possible or stay the hell outta his way. I'm still trying to figure out why he decided to drag us along on his trip. He could've ditched our asses on the ground to fend for ourselves against Systems before he boarded this plane."

"It is not a *plane*," Jeremy said defensively, "it is a Copter Ship. And regarding your previous comment, he most likely 'dragged you along' because you were familiar. After all, the world has changed drastically in the past six years, and he has slept through its transformation. I am not surprised that he seems a little tense and uptight now. Give him time. He will warm up to you eventually."

"Right; I'm gonna love tagging along on this trip," Jenny said sarcastically.

Jeremy said, "I pilot this ship with an open mind and a somewhat optimistic attitude."

"Only a *little* optimistic?" Jenny prodded.

Catching the jab, Jeremy said, "Overly optimistic hostages tend to get killed around Damian."

At the speed the ship was moving, they reached Scionia within the hour. The clouds parted, revealing a thick tangle of tree branches spanning as far as the eye could see, reaching higher than the clouds. The *Scion's Wings* descended on the near-solid patches of leaves coating the abnormally mountainous, apparently solid forest. The gnarled tangle of massive tree roots dived into the water's surface, digging deep into the ocean floor. An eerie mist hovered above the ocean, gently clawing at the edges of the trees. Even the *Scion's*

Wings was greatly dwarfed in comparison to the fantastic forest.

Jenny blinked as she stared out ahead, completely taken aback by the scenery. "Whoa… looks like pissing on trees pays off after all."

"It is a protective shell," said Jeremy. "Matthew's base rests within that forest. Three kilometres in, if I remember correctly."

"In *that*?" Jenny exclaimed, pointing at the forest and looking at Jeremy. "How in the hell do we even get through it?"

Jeremy smiled at her. "Well, I could penetrate it in the *Scion's Wings*. Nothing can break, bend, liquefy, dent, or even leave a mark on refined Fate Star metal. Any attempt to do so would backfire with at least sixty percent interest." There was pride in his voice as he explained.

"So if I tap it, it'll break my finger?" asked Jenny.

Jeremy nodded. "Possibly."

"What if I fired a gun at it?" asked Aria, despite already knowing the answer. "Would the round bounce back at me?"

"Perhaps the thousands of tiny particles will… and they will also rip through your body."

"What if I set it on fire?" Jenny asked with mock excitement.

"Impossible. It would extinguish the flames' heat against it and propel it off in an instant."

"Like a force field?"

Jeremy faltered. "I… guess…"

"What if I shot at it with a tank?"

Marner sighed. Now they were just fooling around, and she wasn't in the mood to hear it. She headed for the doors as Jeremy answered Aria's question.

She looked at Jeremy.

"The room number is on the key. That will be your room until further notice." Jeremy tossed a key at her.

Until further notice? She caught the key in her cupped hands and thanked him before leaving. Jeremy smiled as she left.

"So what about a nuke?"

Jeremy scowled.

Scionia

Matthew Corridian looked up at the thick canopy of leaves and branches above him. The only evidence of the sun's existence was the fact that the large valley hidden within the massive cage of trees and shrubs wasn't drowning in darkness. In that valley was a village, complete with a command center in the middle and thick concrete walls running around the town. Before, it'd been a war base for Dehue resistance fighters during the Dehue Extermination Project, but now it was the home of Matthew's clan of orphans and runaways.

Matthew ran his fingers through his wild dirty blonde hair and blinked his sea green eyes before placing both hands on the concrete rampart and leaning forward, staring hard into the thick forest. He had a long scar over his right eye and raggedy clothes, along with an authentic claymore clipped to his belt, the point of which scraped along the ground wherever he walked.

Huge trees stood firmly on small crags of thick hairy tree roots, forming shallow trenches into the ground that snaked throughout the dirt and cracked boulders.

No sign of them today.

It's already noon, he thought. *Where are they?*

Matthew turned around and looked into the fortified village.

Wires stretched from building to building with clothes and banners hanging over the streets. The market was busy and crowded just like every other day. Artillery guns were mounted along the ramparts; one every thirty feet.

The only sounds that could be heard were the clambers of the village and the rustling of the trees in the wind. This usually meant that *they* would attack sometime in the evening, or late at night.

"Hey, Chief!"

Matthew turned around and saw his short, skinny second-in-command approach him with a piece of paper in his hand. "What is it, Gibbs?"

Gibbs handed him the paper. "Radar team picked up a large object approaching the hidden entrance."

Matthew nodded and followed him off the ramparts and through the winding, bustling streets. They wormed their way through the crowds, past food venders and breastfeeding mothers sitting outside the storefront windows of their shops. Since the Scionians were split into groups during evacuation, children eighteen and under were all stuffed into connected underground shelters. Strangely enough, their shelters were barely touched by the nuclear strike. The oldest in the entire village was twenty-four.

Matthew and Gibbs reached the command center entrance flanked by two soldiers with shotguns, both of whom stood to attention as their leaders entered the building. They descended three flights of stairs and passed through a security gate before entering a dark room. Holographic radar screens hovered above three rows of console boards where operators and technicians sat chattering to each other excitedly. Matthew scowled as he saw the blip approach the centers of the radar screens. "Come on, people. Don't just sit there talking. Patch me through."

His voice startled them, and one of them immediately adjusted the signal into the oncoming object's direction while a single operator picked up a receiver and dialled nine. He set it to speaker, and the ring of the dial tone filled everyone's ears.

The *Scion's Wings*

The phone in the dashboard rang, and Jeremy quickly answered it. "Yes?"

"Unidentified aircraft, please identify yourself or you will be shot down," Matthew ordered sternly, all while thinking, *I know that voice from somewhere...*

"This is Captain Jeremy Larson of the *Scion's Wings*," Jeremy answered, "I have decided to pay you a visit, Matthew."

Matthew blinked. "Oh. Jeremy. Long time, no see." He signalled for the operators to turn the switch on a small dashboard near the front of the room labelled 'Secret entrance'. Then he quickly shook his arms around and whispered, "No!" to a group of operators eagerly gathered around the missile launch panel. The operators' enthusiasm was quickly replaced with heartbreaking disappointment as they tended to other things. Matthew scowled at them before turning back to the radar screens. "We'll open the entrance for you. Welcome back to Scionia, bud. I'll meet you on the landing platform."

"Acknowledged." Jeremy hung up and watched as the trees bent to either side, revealing a hidden tunnel through the thick foliage. Jeremy smiled and gently pushed the steering wheel forward, edging the *Scion's Wings* forward through the tunnel at a gentle, slow pace. The wide rotors on the wings cut through loose hanging branches, whipping up flurries of leaves and twigs in their rotor wash. Despite its size, the Scion's Wings barely even touched the floor, ceiling or walls of the tunnel. Insects and critters crawled around through the thick foliage, hiding from the ship as it passed them. The entrance opened up to the ship like an unfurling rose, and the sight on the other side was one to behold.

The village was huge; building blocks wrapped around the domed command center in a tile pattern and the roads were narrow and golden, peppered with bustling clan members that resembled ants from the bridge's viewpoint. The Scion's Wings descended upon the command center's landing pad.

...Where am I...? It's dark... and it's cold... and it's... familiar...

"Damian! Grab on, you idiot!"

What?

She reached for him. Jenny, of all people to save him from a nightmare, floated above him, reaching for him. Thick liquid filled his lungs as he gravitated toward the crimson sea of blood's dark floor. Everyone he once knew reached for him from the abyss. Rising from the depths. Moaning in agony.

Whispering his name.

What the hell do you want?

Their voices drowned out Jenny's pleas.

"Come back..."

"Join us..."

No, get... get away from me!

"Why would you chase us away?" his mother asked. "Don't go."

"Don't go," the others echoed.

"Don't you care about us anymore?" his siblings asked.

"Don't you care?" they echoed again.

"Come back."

"Son," his mother moaned, "come back, my son."

Get away from me! Stop it! *His pleas only made them speak all at once in a confusing jumble.*

"Why would you abandon us?"

"We were right. You're a failure."

"You're just a loser."

"I hate you."

"Don't talk to me again! Don't ever talk to me again!"

"I don't wanna play with you anymore."

"Piss off!"

"What makes you think I want to talk to you?"

"Get lost."

"BASTARD!"

"Stay away from my son. I don't want you anywhere near him."

"You little prick!"

"I hope you die."

"I WISH YOU WOULD JUST DIE!"

"Leave me alone!"

"What do you want?"

"I HATE YOU!"

"Yet another test you failed to pass."

"Why can't you be more like your brothers and sister?"

"God, I'm embarrassed just by looking at you."

"FUCK OFF!"

"I don't remember promising you anything. I don't even know you."

Liars! You promised! You promised you'd help me...

"No, you promised!"

"Are you going to keep that promise?"

"You need help, alright!"

"He probably won't. He's a liar, after all."

"Never achieves anything; can't keep anything..."

What's that supposed to mean?!

"You couldn't even save us."

"You just let us die."

"You ran away like the little pussy you are."

"Pfft! Can't even fulfill his duty."

"You never could keep anything close to you for very long. They were probably scared of you, and they have every right to be."

"Anything close to you dies."

"Your father would be ashamed."

"You can do better," said his father.

"You're just a failure. A BIG, FAT FAILURE!"

"You don't deserve the role you were given."

STOP IT! SHUT UP! SHUT THE HELL UP!

"Aww, is the baby crying?"

"MORON!" Jenny's yell snapped him out of his terrified trance, motivating him to look up at her again. Like an angel, she steadily dropped further and further down, white light blazing above her. Under the surface; under shifting rays of fiery light. How could she even speak under the surface? Why was she saving him? Why her?

What the hell do you want?

"It's not real!"

Knock, knock!

A rapping at the door caused Damian to stir. The second set of knocks woke him up completely, and he found himself staring at the wall in disbelief, soaked in his own sweat. He bolted upright. His head turned to the door. *What the hell was that?*

Knock, knock!

"W-who is it?"

"It's Aria."

Damian muttered tiredly to himself as he slipped out bed. He was naked, since he couldn't maintain his clothing's form while he slept. His clothes reformed around his body as he approached the door. He opened it and looked up at Aria. "What?" She forced her way into the room, pushed him aside, and closed the door and locked it without a word. "Hey, what the hell!"

"Watch it." Aria snatched a Butterfly knife in her left hand and whirled around to slit his throat.

SPANG!

Damian swung his blade outward, blocking it and snapping it in half in the process. But now he was wide open, and Aria was quick enough to press the barrel of a pistol against his forehead. Damian froze. Aria smirked with the toothpick hanging out the side of her mouth. "Bang," she said.

Damian blinked.

"You've gotten slower," she said. "Probably because of your little nap in the tube for six years, hunh?"

"What the hell is this?" he asked, keeping his eyes fixed on her. "What the fuck's your—"

"I want you to listen, and listen closely." She tapped the muzzle against his forehead. "Keep your dirty hands off of Jenny and Marner. And me too, of course. Got that?"

"Why would I touch them anyway?"

"I'm just giving you a warning ahead of time. Whatever it is you're up to, I've got my suspicions it involves the three of us. So I'm warning you now: if this little 'hostage' situation gets out of hand… I'll kill you. And if I don't kill you, I'm sure Tim or Silverstein will."

"So you don't want me to touch them, huh? Can I talk to them?"

"If you don't they'll get suspicious. Just follow the old saying, 'look, talk, but don't touch.' I guarantee you'll live longer."

"You think you can kill me?" he asked with an arrogant tone. "You couldn't do it before."

Aria smiled. Then she chuckled. "Unlucky for you; I'm more of a cold-hearted bitch than the last time we talked. I've also been killing people and dodging death for as long as you've been asleep, and I can say I've improved more than a little."

"Uh-huh. You still couldn't kill me."

"Just try, Damian. I dare you," she challenged. "And let's not forget the obvious fact that sleeping for so long has made you a lot weaker. You're long past your prime. Your body's already running on a half-empty tank of gas. It's too bad you haven't had much time to recharge those conveniences of yours, huh?"

Damian swatted her gun aside and walked around her. "Whatever. Believe what you will. It's better this way anyway. It'll make the shocked look on your face more hilarious." He unlocked the door.

Aria glanced at him. "Keep talkin' like that and you won't for much longer."

"Why don't you just kill me now?"

"Cuz you've got a bomb in my sister's guts."

Damian snickered. "So basically you're just talkin' big with nothing to back up your claims. Smart. Just accept the fact that I've got the upper hand in this situation, and shut the actual fuck up." He looked at her from over his shoulder. "You're *my* bitch, now."

The toothpick in Aria's mouth snapped in her tightening jaw as she glared at him.

Damian maintained his smirk. "If I say, 'Go to the kitchen and make me a sandwich,' you don't really have any other choice but to—"

WHACK!

She kicked him in the face, shoving the back of his head into the door. Damian whipped out his revolver and pointed it at her, only to find himself staring down the barrel of her pistol again.

"Let's get something straight, schoolboy," she hissed, "if you do manage to kill us all, you don't have any leverage or backup. The world will be pissed off by how you handled things and slaughtered a bunch of teenage kids and a couple adults and set off a bomb in neutral territory. Don't even get me started about the shootout at the school. And of course, there's your reputation that you established in the Dehue Extermination Project. In other words: once you get rid of us, you're about as safe as a rookie cop in the ghetto. It's a lose-lose situation for all of us, I suppose. However, I've got a proposition for ya."

"…What's that?"

"We work together for a while. No secrets. No lies. No back-stabbing. We'll form a little alliance until all of our asses are in the clear. Now, I'm not stupid. I know Jenny wouldn't get caught so easily, even if you are what you are."

"What?"

"What did you tell her to convince her to act as your hostage?"

"What do you mean?"

"Don't play dumb with me. She was obviously acting like a hostage until you planted that bomb in 'er womb."

"Pretty sure it was her stomach," he corrected.

"Screw you. What'd you say?"

Damian gulped. Even he was intimidated by Aria's jet black eyes. "…I told her I'd help her find your mom."

Aria's face twisted in disgust. "Are you fucking serious?" Her finger slowly pulled back on the trigger.

"Hey, whoa, I'm not lying here."

"Enlighten me, you little twerp."

"During my sleep I was able to do that astral projection stuff. I was able to float around town; sneak into strip clubs, watch mob bosses and street gangs fight other mob bosses and street gangs. Hell, I even saw an old lady unleash all sorts of John Woo on a local gang."

"Get on with it," she pressed impatiently.

"Well, during my travels, I saw the woman you had a picture of. Remember the time when we were hiding from Systems in that ruined gymnasium at the school? And that picture fell out of your pocket and you took it from me? You know as well as I do that I never forget a face, so I couldn't be mistaken. I know what I saw, and I swear I saw that same woman. I swear to God it was her, just a year or two ago."

"Where?"

"The Xing Wao Grand Hotel."

Aria paused. "That's in Sky Japan."

"Right."

"You're saying my mother's in Sky Japan."

"Last I saw her."

Aria's eyes narrowed with suspicion. "Why do I not believe you?"

"Because you don't think of me as a trustworthy companion?"

"You're too smart for your own good," she said sarcastically.

Damian's eyes flicked to Aria's gun briefly before he looked back into her eyes. "Also, aren't you gambling your sister's life a little here?"

Aria slowly withdrew her weapon from his forehead, and Damian's revolver vanished. His hand dropped to his side again. "If you're lying," she said, "I'll snuff you with my boobs."

Damian opened the door and stepped out of the room. "Wouldn't be a bad way to go, honestly."

Aria was left standing in the room, trembling with anger. "Goddamn little shit," she muttered.

The *Scion's Wings* touched down on a landing pad between three other parked Copter Ships. Matthew and Gibbs stood by and waited for the engines to die down, the harsh rotor wash dying down.

The ship's loading platform slowly dropped to the landing pad with everyone onboard. When the platform touched the floor Matthew and Gibbs approached them.

Matthew scrutinized each unfamiliar individual as he stepped closer. His eyes stopped when they found Damian. "I see you brought some friends."

Jeremy replied anxiously, "Well, I would not exactly call them 'friends'…"

"Hm? Why not?"

"We took him hostage in order to escape," Jenny said bluntly.

"Well technically *he* did," Aria added just as bluntly, pointing her thumb at Damian.

Gibbs stared at Damian with half-concealed horror. Damian gave him a blank look.

"Oh," Matthew said with raised eyebrows, still staring at Damian. "What're you supposed to be?"

"What?" asked Damian.

"You escape from a comic convention or somethin'?"

"What're you talking about?"

"You're dressed like the Dead Blue. Very nice costume, I might add." Matthew stroked his chin thoughtfully, scrutinizing Damian's appearance with a smirk. "I can tell you put a lot of work into this thing. Looks legit."

Damian scowled. "I *am* legit, you fucking asshole."

"That's what they all say. So, you guys're cosplayers? Who're you runnin' from?"

Aria, Damian, Jenny and Marner exchanged annoyed glances.

Matthew waited patiently for an answer.

Gibbs tapped Matthew's shoulder. "Sir, may I speak with you a moment?"

"Sure."

They turned their backs on the group and huddled together, speaking in whispers, "What if he really is the Dead Blue?"

Matthew scoffed. "Yeah, right. That's impossible; the Dead Blue disappeared almost six years ago."

"Exactly."

"Hunh?"

"What if he reappeared *now*?"

Matthew and Gibbs glanced over their shoulders at Damian. Damian replied with an impatient glare. They turned back around. "Nah, couldn't be true."

"It's *got* to be. He fits the description perfectly."

"Description from whom?"

"From all the interview records from eye witnesses; people who claimed they saw the Dead Blue clearly *and* in action."

"Yeah, 'claimed,' not 'proven.'"

"Oh, come on! We both know it's him! You're just denying

it! Don't you know the description? He's got weird blue hair, cold-blooded blue eyes, emotionless expressions on his face; skinny, broad shouldered, fairly muscular, has a crappy attitude, and when he moves really fast you see blue and black lightning emanate from his body!"

"Hm. I wouldn't know."

"Did you even *read* the text books!?"

"What text books?"

"URGH!"

Damian scowled. "Are you ladies done yet?" He looked at Jeremy. "What was the point of coming here?"

"Ah, yes," Matthew said, whirling around on his heel formally. "Back to my original question: who're you running from?"

"None of your damn business, you giant cock-wielding shithead," said Damian. "What's with all these questions?"

Matthew and Gibbs fell silent, their expressions unchanged. After what seemed like an eternity, with patience evidently falling thin, Matthew and Gibbs turned back around. "Holy crap, I think you're right! It's that undeniable attitude!"

"See? *See*?!" Gibbs said in a shrill whisper. "He's the legendary Killer of Twenty Million People! The Dead Blue!"

Matthew turned back around with a new look of caution. He approached Damian and stuck his thumbs in his belt, deliberately showing off his sheathed claymore. "Tell me something, Damian: are you a cosplayer?"

"For the last time: *no*, I'm not a friggin' cosplayer!"

Matthew nodded, clasping his hands behind his back. "I see. Interesting."

Jenny grew impatient from Matthew's unusual display, as if he were trying to re-enact an interrogation scene from a crime drama.

"Are you a Dehue?"

"Maybe."

"Are you single?"

"Yup."

"Are you running from someone?"

"I prefer to call it professional hide-and-seek."

"What's the difference?"

"I'm not hiding, I'm seeking."

"Seeking what?"

"Hookers."

"Liar."

"Drugs."

"*More* lies."

"Okay, I'm looking for a drinking buddy."

"More lies."

"I can lie if I want."

"You can't lie in an interrogation."

"I just *did*, bitch!"

Jenny groaned exasperatedly. "Hey, you moron, just answer his goddamn questions without the smartass answers. I don't have all day."

Damian snapped, "Excuse me, bitch, but if you have a problem with two men having an intelligent conversation, then feel free to leave. No one's stopping you from fucking off."

Marner slapped her forehead.

Jenny cracked her knuckles. Her eyebrow twitched angrily. "What was that? I'm afraid I'm a bit hard of hearing."

Damian's eyebrows fell. "Clearly you've been outside of the kitchen for too long. Go back where you belong, and make me a sandwich."

"Why?" she asked. "Why are men so incapable of making their own sandwiches that they have to rely on the genius of women instead? God, you guys are so stupid, it makes me sick to my stomach."

"Shut up and make my sandwich already."

Silence.

Marner shook her head. *Did he completely ignore what I told him about her? He's treading on thin ice as it is.*

Jenny was quick to trap Damian in a headlock, making him gasp for air like a beached whale. "MAKE YOUR OWN GODDAMN SANDWICH!"

"Can't... *BREEEEAAAATTHHE*...!" Damian wheezed.

Aria smirked at him. "You had it comin'."

Damian looked at Marner with begging eyes, squeaking like a plush toy when Jenny's hold tightened even more. He even stuck out his bottom lip for added effect.

Marner crossed her arms and watched with half-open eyes that voiced her lack of empathy. "I agree with Aria on this one."

ARE YOU KIDDING ME?!

Matthew stood silently watching the unusual display before glancing over at Gibbs. "Well, I guess questions are going to have to wait."

Gibbs nodded in reply. "It seems we'll have to keep our eyes and ears open from now on, though."

"Good idea. I don't want this clan wiped out by a potential killer. It's even worse considering how much of an asshole he seems to be."

In the background, Damian managed to slip out of Jenny's hold and kick at her head. She caught his raised foot by the ankle and punched him in the crotch. He growled in agony and curled up on the ground, where she relentlessly beat down on him.

"Agreed," said Gibbs. "Those types are the worst of all. Those narcissists always rub it in when they win."

Jeremy joined in on the conversation. "I apologize for my... passengers. If you want to call them that."

"Oh, don't worry about it," said Matthew.

Behind them, Damian's left hook connected with Jenny's jaw, but she stood her ground and countered with a bull thrust that tossed him back several feet. Then she pounced on him.

"It ain't a problem," Matthew continued.

Jeremy nodded, unsure. "I hope not."

"Seriously, old buddy, it's no problem."

"Well, before you consider being hospitable, there are some things that you know—"

"Damian's the Dead Blue, isn't he?"

Jenny punched Damian into a 360-degree spin. Then she wrapped her arms around his waist from behind, bent backwards, and buried his head into the ground, his feet flailing limply in the air. Aria cheered her on while Marner watched with concern from the sidelines.

Jeremy looked at Matthew with surprise. "How... how did you figure it out so quickly?"

Matthew snickered. "Because he's *soooo* menacing."

Damian was sprawled out on the cracked floor, barely conscious, twitching, with Jenny standing over him triumphantly. "Now make *me* a sandwich, *BITCH*!"

Jeremy looked at them, then turned back to Matthew.

"Perhaps we could find a more private place to speak?"

Matthew shrugged. "Alright, then. Gibbs, I want you to supervise the weapons stockpile at the south wall."

Gibbs nodded dutifully and saluted. "Yes, sir." Then he marched toward the stairs.

Matthew turned to Damian and the others and smiled humbly. "As for the rest of you, feel free to browse around town. Make yourselves at home."

Jenny and Aria leaned on the railing at the edge of the command center roof, overlooking the bustling market.

"…So you know why I acted as a hostage, huh?"

Aria nodded. "Yep. Pretty stupid if you ask me."

"Well…! Wouldn't you do anything to see mom again?"

"Maybe. But I wouldn't get my hopes up."

"Why not?"

"This is Damian Warkowski we're talking about here. Just the fact that he put a bomb inside you should tell you just how bad he really is."

Jenny shrugged. "…Maybe he's taking precautions."

"I'm sorry, what?"

"I-I'm not defending him or anything, but that's my guess. 'Course, he really *could* be completely psychotic and hatching a plan to stab us all in the backs and obliterate us. But then again, he could just be taking precautions."

"He's got a funny way of showing his trust."

"Why would he trust us if we don't trust him?"

"Unlike him, we haven't done a damn thing to betray this 'trust' you speak of. *We*, on the other hand, have every right to mistrust him, especially after what happened this morning. He's not even awake for two days, and there's already been public uproar, and four people, minimum, are dead."

Jenny scowled. ***You're** the one who killed those four!* Still, she wanted to tell her sister the truth; that the bomb was gone. But she remembered what Marner had told her about keeping quiet about it shortly before they landed. No one trusted Damian, but Jenny had a feeling that allying themselves with Damian in order to find her mother would be next to impossible if she said something.

All they could do was hope that Damian wouldn't kill them all in their sleep.

"So anyway," Aria continued, "Are you seriously considering his offer?"

"About mom? Yeah."

Aria sighed and chomped down on the end of a toothpick. "You're hopeless."

"Don't you wanna see mom again?"

A pause.

"No," said Aria, much to Jenny's surprise.

"What?! Why not?"

"...My reasons are mine to know," she said. And then she walked away. "I'm gonna get a burger. Catch ya later."

Jenny watched her sister disappear down the stairs with a scowl. *She goes on about trust, and then keeps secrets from her sister. Real mature.*

Matthew's Office

"You wanted to see me?" Matthew was sitting back in his chair with his feet up on his plain wooden desk. Both he and Jeremy were sitting in Matthew's private office. Jeremy made himself comfortable in a chair in front of the desk.

"It's about Damian," he said.

"Ah," Matthew said. "I see. Fun guy."

"'Fun guy'? He is the Killer of Twenty Million People! What exactly is so 'fun' about that?"

"I was talking about his smartass attitude."

"I have known him since I was a young child and I do not recall him being 'fun'! I think you are misunderstanding the point I am trying to make about him."

"Then what *is* the point? Where was he all this time? Did he pull a fast one on us and vanish in an iceberg? Did he... did he fly off into space looking for his home planet's remains? Did he return from the dead?"

"Jenny and Marner awakened him—"

"So he is a zombie."

"No. He was apprehended years ago by Jonathon Silverstein shortly after the war's end. Unfortunately, Jenny and Marner discovered his cryogenic prison and let him out. And now Systems Corporation is pursuing not only him, but *us*."

"Why? Because you woke him up?"

"I did not wake him up."

"You know what I mean," Matthew groaned. "Stop being so damn technical."

Jeremy nodded. "Yes, I have a feeling we are being hunted simply because of our affiliation with Damian."

"I see. Jenny's the redhead, right?"

"...There are two redheads."

Matthew scowled at him.

"Jenny is the younger of the two sisters. Aria is the oldest."

Matthew smiled. "She's sexy as hell. Actually, they both are."

Jeremy sighed and adjusted his goggles.

"Heh-heh, I wouldn't mind sharin' a bed with those girls."

Jeremy gave him a 'be serious' look.

"Even the silver-haired girl's pretty hot. Damn, man, trade Damian for another chick and you've got yourself a harem, you dog!" He chuckled and gave him the thumbs-up.

Clang!

Jeremy lightly smacked him upside the head with a wrench. "Focus."

Matthew rubbed his head with a scowl, as if being beaten over the head with a wrench was like getting punched in the face by a balloon. "Fine. So now, because of Damian, Systems Corporation's after you?"

"That is my assumption. They are an organization of highly-trained terrorists determined to obliterate everything that opposes them. The founding father of Systems Corporation is the very man that pursues us."

"...Whoa, whoa." Matthew blinked, opened his desk drawer, and pulled out a dictionary. "You're lucky I have a dictionary handy."

"Enough with the witticisms."

After slapping the withered dictionary on the desk, Matthew opened another drawer, fished out a water canteen and a glass, and poured water into the glass. "Alright, alright. So what's your big plan to escape this madness?"

"That is one of our primary concerns. There is no plan."

Matthew raised an eyebrow at him. "You mean you went on a

flight to escape certain death and destruction *without* a plan? What a horrible waste of gas."

"Um… the *Scion's Wings* is solar powered."

Matthew corrected himself, "What a horrible waste of solar energy."

"And I did not have much of a choice; they took me hostage. I should probably add that we are all his hostages."

"Why's that? He doesn't look so tough."

"He planted a bomb inside Jenny's colon."

Matthew spat his water on the floor and burst out laughing. "COLON!"

Jeremy pinched the bridge of his nose and sighed.

When Matthew recovered, he sat up straight and poured himself another glass of water with a serious air about him. "As I recall, you owed Damian a favour anyway. Otherwise you would've made their heads explode and that'd be the end of it. So don't give me that crap. Flying with a mass murderer is one thing; flying without a plan is just stupid. Flying with a mass murderer and other hostages and bringing a fuckin' bomb on board without a plan is beyond stupid! Like shit, bro, it's as if you're getting dumber every year. I've seen a lot of stupid shit in my day, believe me, but to see a genius like you get caught in a retarded situation like this… is just… just… *colon*?"

Jeremy blinked several times and shook his head, thrown completely out of the conversation. "What?"

"…Why did Damian plant a bomb in her *colon*? Why her *colon*?! Why?! How? That is a good question too! Just how in the hell did the Killer of Twenty Million People get close enough to a sexy girl like that to surgically plant a bomb in her *colon*?"

"I am not quite sure it was her colon—"

"Then why say 'colon'?!" Matthew laughed. "It makes no sense!"

"I cannot remember *where* he said he planted it, exactly, so I just went with 'colon'."

"That's like taking a shit and saying you threw up, man!"

"Not ex—"

"Just… first you're all technical, and now you're illogical."

"Excuse me if I seem a little flustered. Given the circumstances of this situation…"

Matthew put down his glass and started flipping through the dictionary. "Circumstances… circumstances…"

"Oh, come on!" Jeremy exclaimed. "That is not a hard word!"

"Excuse me if my country's schools were obliterated in the event of a nuclear strike." He added bitterly, "Courtesy of your Jonathon Cockstein."

Jeremy watched impatiently as Matthew read up the word's definition. Then he said, "Are you quite done?"

Matthew slammed the book shut. "Yup. I'm done. Listen, Germ—"

"Don't call me 'Germ'."

"—the fact that you brought a fucking bomb into my town is one thing. Bringing a psychopath with it is another thing. But bringing a fucking bomb with a psychopath into my town while the organization that blew this country to shit in the first place is chasing after you is just plain wrong and really ironic. I'm not a fan of irony, man. Irony is an asshole. I don't want another nuclear strike in my country, man. I hate nuclear strikes! Look..." Matthew said as he got up and went toward the window overlooking the town that sloped up to the south ramparts. "Don't you see what I've got going here? It's peaceful, Germ! It's quiet! I'm the best leader these people have ever had, and that's not ego talking. They said so themselves! ...Most of them. What we've got here is peace, and what we don't need is violence. Hey, I love violence. You know I do. But even a guy like me can appreciate some peace and quiet every once in a while."

KABOOM!

A distant explosion shook the office.

Matthew stumbled, grabbed the window sill for support. He looked around, bewildered, before looking out the window. "What the...?"

Jeremy ran to the window to see a huge column of smoke rising up from a decimated section of the south ramparts. "The wall has been obliterated! There is a large gap in it now!"

Matthew shouted at him, "Fuck you and fuck your irony!" He scrambled to the door, pulling a new shirt on and fastening his claymore to his belt. He looked at his watch and swore again when he saw the time: 6:30 PM. "Damn it! This is what I was talking about, you chaos-bringing asshole! You've brought hell down upon us! Shit, shit, shit! And just look at the time. Oh, ain't that fucking convenient?"

"What?" Jeremy asked, whirling around to face him. "What is it?!"

Matthew looked at him with disdain. "It's almost dark. They'll be waking up soon!"

Damian and Aria were eating burgers from a fast food vender when the south wall exploded. They moved to the middle of the road while the children and teenagers rushed away from the explosion, passing them in a panicked flow whilst shrieking in terror. The explosion was just up the hill at the end of the road, and both of them watched the smoke rise from the wall.

The civil defense siren cried out its long-lasting warning call. Teenage soldiers rushed to the scene with machine guns, axes, and swords.

Damian looked at Aria, chewing his burger. "So… why are they running?"

Aria shrugged. "I don't know."

"Should we run?"

"Why?"

"We are outsiders after all."

"So?"

"So we should run to make it look like we didn't do it."

"But we *didn't* do it, so what's the problem?"

"But they might think differently."

"So?"

"I think we should run."

"You go do that, then."

"I'm not running."

"Why not?"

"Because you're not running."

"You're an idiot; you just said we should run."

"I changed my mind."

"Why?"

"Because then it would look like we did it and we're trying to get out of there."

"You're packin' brains after all."

"I'm always packin'. People just don't look for those qualities anymore."

"I do."

"Okay, besides you, most bitches look for what else I'm packin,' if you know what I mean."

"Ah, must be why you're considered the disappointment of your clan."

Damian paused. He stopped chewing altogether. He even let his burger fall to the ground, as if he'd been completely taken by surprise. Then he turned to her, pointed at her, spat burger bits on her sleeve as he snarled, "Go fuck yourself!"

Aria shuddered and wiped the bits onto the ground with her gloved hand. "Just be quiet."

Damian watched the distant mushroom cloud roll into the canopy of tree branches high above the town. "So what do you think caused the explosion?"

"I don't know."

"And *why*?" he asked dramatically. "Maybe someone wants revenge and is sending someone a message that they're seeking vengeance."

"You're reading too far into it."

"*Graawwllerrrrr…*"

Damian and Aria looked up the hill. "What the hell was that?" Aria asked.

Damian shrugged. "I don't know. Maybe it's a mutant having a seizure."

Finally, they saw a hazy shape rock back and forth in the smoke limply. Whatever it was, it moaned and grumbled like a dying beast.

"I…" said the mysterious voice. Slow, suffering from an incurable agony. "I… want…"

It emerged out of the smoke for them to see a Dehue with rotting grey skin and eyes rolled back in its head. Blood trickled down its face from every pore. Its slouching body swayed back and forth as it groaned, swinging its limp arms with every step. A zombie.

A Dehue zombie.

Damian and Aria stared at it with blank expressions.

"*…B-brrrraaaaaaaaiiiiinnnnnnnsssssss*," it whined.

Aria cleared her throat. "I think it's asking for me."

"Doubtful. It obviously wants my genius. It's hungry for my knowledge."

"What knowledge?"

"*BRAINS*!" the zombie roared.

More muttering and moaning filled the air as a multitude of zombies stumbled and limped out of the thick haze at the top of the jagged, debris-covered slope. "Brains, brains, *brraaaaaiiiinnsss*, brains, *BRAINS*, brains…"

A black energy blade appeared in Damian's hand. He held it readily. "I guess there was no more room in hell."

"No shit, eh?" Aria said as a shotgun sprouted out of her arm. She grasped it with both hands and pumped it with anticipation.

"BRAINS!"

The zombies darted down the hill with shocking speed and ferocity, like a pack of gazelles.

Aria grinned. "So… do ya still have what it takes?"

Damian's maniacal grin widened as he stood in a ready stance. "Do I still got it? Do you still got it?"

Aria put a toothpick in her mouth. "Damn right I do."

POOF!

"Hey, hey!" Dave whooped as he appeared from the smoke in the midst of the oncoming stampede.

Damian watched Dave jog with the zombies, mimicking their cries for brains. "BRAINS! Brains! I want to eat your brains!"

Damian scowled at him. "You never had any to begin with…"

"What?" asked Aria.

Damian shook his head. "Nothing. Let's just kick some undead ass!"

"Sounds good to me!"

They charged forward, and Aria didn't waste any time shooting them down in ones and twos with her shotgun, but when they got too close she disposed of it in favour of two automatic rifles. Her rapid gunfire mowed them down like twin chainsaws cutting through cardboard.

Damian sliced through their bodies, cutting through their shambling ranks like a jagged streak of black lightning. Blood splattered from their dismembered bodies just seconds after his blade passed through them. He ducked as one of them tried to grab him and cleaved it in half.

"BRAINS!" A zombie roared as it lunged at him, arms outstretched like a rotting net.

He kicked it back and stabbed it in the eye, blinking when blood droplets hit his face.

"BRRRAAAINS!" Two more zombies clawed at his left arm. Damian swung his blade through their middles and whirled around to diagonally cut another in two flailing pieces.

He didn't allow himself to get blinded by the thickening shower of blood pouring down on him. Every zombie was like a fountain, squirting and spraying dark crimson into the air.

He split another zombie's face in two, and then cut another's jaw out from under its skull.

They closed in on him, clawing at him, jumping on top of him, pouncing on him, overwhelming him.

Trapped under their weight as they swarmed him, Damian stubbornly continued to stab and slice. He cut off an arm, and a head, and impaled another rotting zombie through its chest, but they just kept coming, compressing him. Every cut and stab only filled the shrinking space with their blood, making it even harder for him to breathe. Luckily for him, they were all too packed together to manage to bite him.

Or so he thought.

He looked up and saw a zombie's open jaws descend upon his head. Thick saliva and blood dribbled out of its throat and off its tongue and grey lips. Damian shoved his Model 500 revolver into its throat and blasted its head off. He lowered his head and groaned in disgust as the zombie's stumpy neck slobbered grey matter and blood all over him.

"Disgusting sons of bitches," he grunted. "Get… the hell… *off of me…*"

They only pressed down harder. His legs started to give. He knew he was still weak from being in the cryogenic capsule for so long, and the sunlight wasn't helping him much, either.

He tried a trigger-happy approach to dealing with the zombies, blasting through their bodies, limbs, and heads with two revolvers, but the swarm only increased in numbers. They reached for him; claws dug into his skin and tore at his clothes, covering him in cuts and blood. He continued shooting whilst struggling to yank himself free from their cold, grimy hands. He kicked and blasted frantically, constantly gasping to maintain his breathing under a never-ending downpour of innards.

Then, the roar of nearby machine gun fire rang out and seemingly lifted the weight of the zombies off his shoulders.

Aria sprayed the dog pile with an M60 machine gun, which she held with her right hand, shredding them and lifting their burden off Damian's shoulders. The M60's ammo belt was strung over her left hand, which also held a flamethrower that she used to incinerate any approaching walkers.

"You alright there?" she asked with a mocking smirk on her face.

"Piss off," he hissed. "I had it under control."

"Well *excuuuuuse* me, princess." Then she turned and continued slicing down zombies with fire and bullets.

Damian could hold his own again. He jumped up and punched a nearby zombie's head off its shoulders. With a single swing of his blade, he lopped the heads off four approaching zombies. With a frustrated shout, he whirled around and punched a zombie's face into its brain. Fragments of the zombie's face popped into Damian's knuckles. "Fuck!"

"BRAINS!"

WOK!

In a swift, fluid motion, Damian whirled around and ripped his blade through another zombie's rotten gut, and then sliced off the top half of its head. Three more charged down the slope with their bleeding fingers outstretched. Damian approached them, cut their hands off with his first swing, sliced their arms off with the second, and beheaded them with the third.

Another zombie grabbed him from behind, wrapping its arm around his neck, opening its yellowed jaws. A foul smell escaped its mouth as its teeth went for his neck.

His blade transformed into a revolver again. "Eat *this*, motherfucker!" Damian quickly shoved the barrel into its mouth, and fired.

BLAM!

Matthew and Jeremy ran through the street, pushing past fleeing civilians and joining a group of defense soldiers no older than they were at an abandoned bar. The soldiers were armed with an assortment of assault rifles and machine guns, wearing crude body armour.

"Guys," Matthew began, "I want to know just what the hell happened down here!"

The captain of the squad approached Matthew and said, "There's a lot of them, Chief! The cause of the explosion in the south wall is unknown, but the gap is huge!"

Matthew gritted his teeth. "Let's hope we don't get overrun by them this time! Who the hell blew up the wall in the first place?!"

"No idea, sir! But I doubt it was an accident!"

"Why?"

The captain stumbled over an abandoned china plate left on the road but regained his footing, still grasping his submachine gun. "The particular section that went off was being stocked with crates of artillery shells and explosives. Not only that, but most of us were told to leave the area before the explosion. We thought something was leaking, but there weren't any fires in the area. Everything just… went off!"

Matthew growled. "So it looks like we have a traitor among us. I want him found and taken in, dead or alive."

"But what about the zombies?!"

They turned the corner onto the main road to see Damian and Aria ascending the hill, cutting them down with their weapons and laughing and yelling various degrading insults at each other as they slaughtered the zombie wave.

Matthew looked at the soldiers. "I think we have it under control."

Then it hit him.

"Where's Gibbs?" he asked.

The soldiers looked at one another. Then, as if hit with the same realization, they all looked up at the smoke rising from the south wall.

Trembling with rage, Matthew drew his claymore and stomped toward the south wall. "That limp-dicked son of a bitch! Come with me, boys! We've got a traitor to catch!"

The soldiers obeyed and marched after him in pairs—ten in total.

WHOOOMMM!

The ground erupted concussively behind them, spraying rubble into the air. Matthew and his soldiers were thrown to the ground, showered with a hot spray of dirt and debris.

"What the…?" Matthew looked up at the south wall to see that several soldiers had turned the artillery guns to the village's direction, shooting the zombies and other soldiers.

BOOM!

The guns' 15-inch barrels belched fire. Matthew shouted, "FUCK! Take cover *now*!"

Matthew and his soldiers scrambled to their feet and dived for cover as the surrounding vendors and buildings exploded.

Jeremy ran in the opposite direction of the south wall, darting under a crumbling cantilever balcony before it collapsed to the ground, just barely missing his ankle.

Matthew sheathed his claymore and yanked out two Browning Hi-Power pistols, and together with his soldiers he returned fire at the soldiers positioned at the south wall. Pecks of concrete and wood rained down on the soldiers as the south soldiers returned fire.

Matthew roared, "It's a freakin' coup!"

A nearby explosion shook the entire building he'd taken shelter in. A large portion of the wood-planked roof collapsed on one of the rear soldiers before he could even scream.

Gibbs stood on the south wall and glanced at Aria and Damian as they progressed up the slope toward his squad of rebels, leaving a mangled road of rotting, twitching corpses in their wake. He whistled to a couple soldiers to get their attention and pointed at Damian and Aria. "Shoot them down! Kill them all!"

A group of soldiers adjusted the nearest artillery gun's position and lowered the barrel, pointing it at the slope.

BOOM!

The artillery shell zipped through the air, ripped a diagonal line through the river of zombies, and exploded between Damian and Aria, knocking them off balance.

Displeased, Gibbs smacked one of the soldiers upside the head. "What the hell am I paying you for?! You missed for God's sake! Reload, and *kill* them this time!"

Damian got up to his feet and cleaved a zombie in half, right down the middle. Then he looked up at the south walls. His ears rang. His head spun. Despite the disorientation, he could still make out what was going on. "What the hell do they think they're shooting at?!"

Aria stood back up and mowed down an approaching group of zombies with her M60. "They aimin' for them or us?!"

"Hey!" Damian shouted at them, waving his hands through the air. "Stop shooting your fucking teammates, you retards!"

Gibbs scoffed and said, "Fire."

BOOM!

With a startled shout, Damian threw himself to the ground. The artillery shell whistled over his head and decimated a nearby shop behind him. He growled angrily as he got back up again. "Well, shit! They're aiming at us! Those sons o' bitches are dead!"

"Damian…"

His eyes widened. He stiffened.

"Damian…"

He slowly turned to see a zombie boy about his age, its black hair falling out and its silver, lifeless eyes staring at him. It took him a few seconds to register what he was seeing, but he knew who he was looking at. He recognized that face, even with its wrinkles and rotten teeth and dead stare. With a shuddering gasp, he said, "C-Carson…?"

"Damian…" it reached for him. "Bro…ther…"

Several years ago

"Brother!"

Damian was nearly pushed to the ground when Carson rammed into his back, and then nearly squeezed to death when he wrapped his arms around him, lifting him off the ground in a constricting hug. "Carson… I can't… breeeaathe!"

"Oh, sorry," Carson laughed, putting him down. "Dad said he wants us to be home in two hours. Just thought I'd tell you."

"Thanks…" he said, gasping for air.

"So what do you wanna do today, bro? Go fishing?"

Damian grinned at him. "Sounds good! Let's try to catch at least one today with our swords!"

Carson scoffed. "HA! Why don't you at least catch one?"

"I've caught plenty, just not when you're around."

"Riiiiiight. Well, let's see if you can prove it today! Whoever

catches five first gets carried home on the loser's back!"

"Oh come on, you know you'll win!"

"You never know until you try."

Three hours later, Damian was carrying Carson down the road on his back.

"Damn," said Carson. "Dad's gonna be pissed."

"Ugh. You're so heavy!"

"That's what you get for cheating."

"I didn't cheat!"

"Dude, you put my fish into your bucket and said 'I win'."

"Oh come on, you only found out because you were trying to steal my fish!"

"So what's your point?"

"You should be carrying me on your back."

"I'll do it tomorrow... if you catch five fish."

"OH, COME ON!"

Carson laughed.

"Brother..."

"Carson, I…"

"Hey… bro…"

Rooted to the spot. Emotions slammed. He couldn't tear his eyes away from the unbelievable sight. Couldn't believe what he was seeing. It was a trick. It had to be a trick. There was no way Carson would let this happen.

No way.

"Damiaaaaaaaan…"

Damian started to tremble, staring into the lifeless eyes of his undead brother. Carson reached for him. Damian hesitantly did the same, as if he were no longer moving by his own accord. "C-Carson…"

BRRRRRTT!

A staccato of gunfire. Damian blinked when something cold hit his face. The next thing he saw was Carson's body collapse in a crumpled heap. "Carson…!"

"Hey!" Aria shouted at him from a few yards away, holding the smoking M60. "What're are you—"

With a furious roar, Damian turned his revolver on her, much to her surprise, and shot her in the chest.

BLAM!

It felt like a bull thrust to the torso, hard enough to throw Aria off her feet. She dropped her machine gun as she fell into the blood-soaked mud, splashing in the spilled innards of the slain undead. She recovered quickly—being immortal and near-indestructible, a single shot to the chest was nothing—and growled angrily as she got back up on her feet. "Little son of a bitch!" She snatched up the M60 and pointed it at Damian.

And stopped.

Damian was on his knees, unarmed, trying to wake up the undead corpse she'd just shot down. The sight struck her as curious.

"Carson! Wake up! C'mon, wake up, wake up! Carson! *CARSON*!"

A sympathetic pang in her chest flared up as Aria lowered the machine gun. She recognized the name. "No..."

"CARSON!" Damian raised his blade above his head. Unbeknownst to him, yet another artillery shell exploded in the ground just a few feet away from him. "YOU BASTARD!" He buried his blade in Carson's face, splitting the skull in half. He hacked Carson's body to bits in a fit of mindless rage and overwhelming sadness, screaming wildly. "You stupid son of a bitch! Why'd you leave me!? *WHY*!? I told you you'd die if you left! I fucking told you! You never fucking listen! Why didn't you listen just this once!? Just ONCE! FUCK! *FUUUUUUCK*!"

Aria stared at him, shocked by his sudden outburst.

Damian burst into tears, still on his knees, soaking in Carson's mutilated remains. He dropped his blade and hung his head as he sobbed. "Why…? You promised me you'd come back… you promised that we'd go fishing again. I practiced while you were gone… before mom and dad and everyone else died. I-I… I got really good at it. You promised you'd come back… and we would catch enough fish that would even give Jesus gas…"

Aria watched as a fresh horde of zombies started to close in on them both. She raised her M60 and gunned down a few of them. Then she turned back to Damian, whose back faced her, and shouted, "Snap out of it, Damian!"

He didn't comply. He was still talking to the corpse, sitting in its remains.

Aria angrily muttered to herself as she blew a cluster of zombies away with the M60. Another artillery shell exploded a few feet away from Damian's spot, filling the air with a fresh hail of burnt flesh and mud. "Idiot's gonna get himself killed!"

"Then we'll have a picnic, brother... until we're sick of fish." The zombies gathered around Damian and reached for him. "I wish you wouldn't go. Don't go, brother. That's stupid. You know Scionia's even worse than this place. All this for some stupid girlfriend you met online. How retarded can you get?" Damian chuckled, staring into his reflection in the crimson pool as if he were looking into another world; another reality...

They closed in on him now. Their gnarled hands latched onto him. But he didn't care. He didn't even notice. He was too busy gathering the remaining portions of his brother's face. "Come back..."

COBALT ROGUE, VOL. 1: THE DEAD BLUE

Episode 007

Scionia Burns

They converged on him, reaching for him, overwhelming him. Damian sat, blankly staring at the mess he'd made of Carson.

"Damian!" A blast from Aria's M60 tore the zombies surrounding him to shreds. She dashed across the slope, slipping once or twice, stumbling over corpses, firing away at the oncoming undead with a never-ending hail of bullets. She felt the tremor of another artillery shell hitting the earth a few yards behind her.

She grabbed him and started forcing him off Carson's corpse.

Damian burst into a hysterical fit and screamed and dug his hands into Carson's remains screaming, "Carson! NO! Don't go! Don't leave me alone again!"

Aria yanked on his arm impatiently. "Let's go, for fuck's sake!" She looked up at the south wall as the rebel soldiers adjusted the artillery gun's position whilst being berated by Gibbs. "I don't have time for this," Aria exclaimed. She dropped Damian onto his knees and hit the back of his head with the butt stock of her M60. She knocked him out cold; before he could keel over she snatched him up and lifted his unconscious body onto her shoulders. "We're getting the hell out of here!"

KABLAM!

Another shell whistled its way into the ground. Rotting flesh and debris went up behind them. A concussive shockwave sent her and Damian flying through the air in an avalanche of debris. They crashed at the foot of the slope, showered by fleshy chunks and clumps of mud.

"Bastard sons of bitches!"

Overcome by his anger, Matthew jumped into the open and charged up the slope with his pistols blazing. He pegged two soldiers in the eyes, and scored another shot in a third's forehead.

The soldiers, having taken cover behind the sandbag barricades, returned fire with their machine guns. Matthew pressed onward; his rage alone made him disregard the bullets that ripped through his body as he dashed up the slope with superhuman speed. When his guns clicked empty, he threw them away and tore his claymore from his belt, roaring like a rabid wolf pursuing its prey.

This was one of those times when Matthew was glad he was an immortal.

With a blind leap, Matthew soared over the sandbag barricade and bisected the nearest soldiers' bodies, separating their chests from their stomachs with ease.

The other soldiers within close proximity immediately unloaded their machine guns into Matthew's body. He didn't falter. He divided the soldiers' bodies into twos and threes. With each swing his path became clearer. Matthew charged over mangled corpses and slipped clumsily in their spilled blood and guts, cutting down soldiers left, right, and center. None escaped his blade.

"*GIIIIIIIIIBBS*!" Matthew roared.

Gibbs' eyes widened when he saw blood and severed limbs being flung into the air from the other end of the trench. He knew what that meant, and immediately ran toward the hatch in the floor in the opposite direction. He glanced over his shoulder and spotted Matthew's soldiers rushing up the slope, firing back at the soldiers behind the barricade. Soldiers collapsed on both sides, sprawling over the barricade or tumbling down the slope.

A severed head flew through the air and bounced off Gibbs' chest, causing him to scream and fall on the ground at the edge of the hatch. One of his soldiers grabbed him and started shoving him down the hatch.

"Get out of here!" the soldier shouted. "We'll handle this!"

Gibbs looked at him. "Are the charges set on the other side?"

"Yes, sir."

Gibbs nodded with approval. "Good. It's been an honour." Then he slid down the ladder of the hatch, entering the underground tunnels.

The soldiers within the barricade abandoned the artillery guns to fend off the advances of Matthew's squad, firing over the barricade wall. Others tried to push Matthew back with riot shields and grenades, but Matthew tore through them as if they were cardboard.

A barricade soldier lunged forward and tackled Matthew to the ground. Another soldier kicked his claymore out of his reach and pinned down his right arm. "Got 'im!"

With his left fist Matthew dislocated Tackle Soldier's jaw. Punched his nose into his brain. Then Matthew kneed Tackle Soldier's gut, throwing him off. The second soldier delivered a swift kick to Matthew's left shoulder, missing his intended mark, loosening his grip on Matthew's right hand in the process. Matthew overpowered him and drove his right fist into the second soldier's face. Then he jumped up, grabbed both sides of his head, and snapped the soldier's neck just as something bounced off his foot.

He looked down as two grenades rolled against his boots.

BOOM!

The ensuing explosion blasted his legs apart and blew the rest of him into the air in a flurry of flaming debris. He landed on the barricade, rolled over the side, and bounced back down the slope. His legs were already growing back, and he knew his soldiers wouldn't help him—they knew he wouldn't allow it. They had a mission, and the mission came first. They were already hopping over the barricade and overwhelming the shrinking force of traitors, most of whom were unsuccessfully retreating to the hatch.

The fighting and the noises of war died down—nothing left but wounded traitors to finish off. By that point, Matthew's legs had rejuvenated, and he had already re-ascended the hill. He stomped over the traitorous leftovers, looking over every corpse on his way to the hatch. When he reached the end of the line, he said to one of his captains, "I didn't see Gibbs among the bodies. The little shit must've escaped."

"Think he's trapped?" the young captain asked.

He shook his head slowly. "...He could easily get out of any entrapment."

"How?"

Matthew clenched his fists and shook them. "The armoury."

The captain's eyes widened. "Oh, shit!"

BAM!

A massive Scionia Army Challenger IV main battle tank barrelled through the shutter door entrance to an underground parking garage and sped up the ramp to ground level. It smashed through the fence gate topped with barbed wire and skidded into the street, screeching across the road and pushing a parked car across the sidewalk and through the storefront window of an abandoned surplus store. Then the tank banked to the right and taxied down the road, facing the north.

Gibbs sat within the tank, watching on the display screens as panicking civilians raced toward the evacuation station in the north end of the town, where several hovercrafts and Copter Ships were located.

Then his scanners picked up something.

He looked closer, and saw Jenny and Marner standing in the middle of the crowd, staring at the tank. With a bitter grumble, he said, "More outsiders."

Jenny nudged Marner's shoulder and said, "Shouldn't that tank be going in the other direction?"

Marner shrugged. "I-I don't know. What should we do? Should we look for the others?"

"Probably a good—"

BOOM!

The tank cannon exploded. Reflexes springing into action, caught in the moment as Marner screamed and hit the ground behind her; Jenny thrust her fist into the fired HESH round. The earth-shattering collision sent a shockwave rippling through the air, and the HESH round exploded a split-second later. Jenny threw her arms out; the flames looped around her arms like snakes slithering around the limbs of their tamers. Jenny shoved her hands forward, hurling the wall of fire into the tank. Flames enveloped the tank completely, forming a massive raging fireball around it like a spherical prison cell.

Jenny shouted angrily, "How d'you like *that*, huh?!"

Inside the tank, Gibbs scowled and turned on the air conditioning.

Jenny continued: "What the hell's the deal?! Watch where you're aiming that—"

She faltered when a putrid smell reached her nostrils. She looked down. All around her were the paralyzed, scorched bodies of the fleeing civilians. Their ages hardly different from her own. Her eyes widened. Her hands started to sweat and shake in her leather gloves. Her heart went cold as ice in her chest. Marner was the only one near her who remained untouched by the explosion or the flames.

"—thing," Jenny finished breathlessly.

Gibbs crossed his arms. Rigid with disappointment. *She's still alive. Is she an immortal… or just another bitch with a superpower?*

Jenny took off her jacket and handed it to Marner. "Marner. Run. Take this and find a safe place to hide."

Marner hesitantly took the jacket, covering her nose and mouth with her free hand and keeping her eyes shut. "W-where?!"

"Anywhere but here. You have your cell phone, right? I'll text you when we're ready to leave this shithole."

"But Jenny...!"

"*Go*," she barked, voice breaking.

"That's a tank!"

"Think I don't know that? I've fought worse. Now get outta here before that tank goes off again! *GO*!"

Brief hesitation. "B-be careful." Without another word, Marner ran out of the street with Jenny's jacket.

Jenny looked over her shoulder as the remainder of the civilians shrank down the road with the exception of a teenage mother wailing over her young son's blackened corpse. "Hey!" Jenny called to her. "I know it stings like hell but you gotta get outta here! *Now*!"

The mother shook her head, cradling her son's burnt form in her arms, as if she could ignore the heat that burned through her skin. "I-I can't… he was all I had… after his father…"

Wrrrrrrrr...

Jenny jerked her head back around, facing the tank.

Another blast of the tank cannon dispersed the fireball around its bulky form like a puff of smoke. Jenny whirled around and dived for the mother.

BOOM!

The ground erupted in front of her, sending Jenny's body flying across the street in a shower of hot debris. She bounced over the curb and rolled across the sidewalk until she hit a phone booth. Ears ringing, Jenny got up to her hands and knees and looked at the burning crater where the mother once was. Only a smoking crater remained. She looked at the tank as it turned its main gun on her. She jumped to her feet and charged toward it screaming, "YOU SON OF A BITCH!"

KABLAM!

Jenny dodged the HESH round, which decimated the phone booth and the sidewalk behind her. She slammed her fist into the glacis plate, puncturing it with a single hit. The engine roared; the tank started to move forward, pushing her onward despite her best efforts to stop it from moving. She dug her heels into the pavement until it cracked and broke apart under the tremendous pressure. She gnashed her teeth and grunted as she pushed against it. Then she dug her fingers into the glacis plate and jerked upward, lifting the entire tank off the road. She could barely hold it up for long, but she only needed to flip it on its top.

BAAAMMMM!

The main gun went off. The road exploded at her heels. The debris and fire raked her backside. The force threw her off balance. She dropped the tank, which landed hard and briefly rattled before it drove over her, crushing her body into the road.

Gibbs chuckled arrogantly. "Sayonara, bitch." But to his surprise...

Jenny lifted the tank off the road again. Her scratched legs wobbled and her bloodied arms shook, but she was too enraged to feel the pain or weakness of her body. Her clothes were shredded and singed. "You think you can just run me over with a tank and get away with it?! You've got another thing comin', *FUCKER*!"

The next step she took shattered the road under her foot. She hurled the tank in the southern direction, causing it to completely flatten a parked truck under its massive bulk. It nearly tipped over, but it didn't, fuelling Jenny's frustration.

The main gun seemed to adjust itself, pointing right at her, and fired.

Jenny leaped into the air and twirled gracefully above the tank. She landed on the hatch and dug her fingers into the creases, and pulled hard. "Dismount the vehicle, asshole!"

The tank jerked into action again, bolting northward at near-full speed. The wind whistled in her ears and through the holes in her clothes, nearly yanking her tube top off. She continued pulling on the hatch. She could feel it loosening, slowly peeling off. She could even hear the air escaping the cockpit with a hiss.

Inside, the alarm wailed deafeningly and the cockpit light blinked black and red. A computer voice repeated, "ALERT.

ALERT." Gibbs sighed, and flicked a switch on his left side. "DEFENSE MECHANISM B1 ENGAGED."

KAZAAAPP!

The surface of the tank exploded with a prolonged lightning burst, sending an electric current through Jenny's body. She screamed in agony as ten thousand volts coursed through her body. All of her muscles burned and convulsed under her skin.

Suck it up! Suck it the hell up!

With an angry shout and a final burst of rage she ripped the hatch door right out and flung it in the opposite direction. The electric pulse stopped abruptly.

"DEFENSE MECHANISM B1 DISENGAGED. WARNING—HATCH BREACHED. NOW SWITCHING TO DEFENSE MECHANISM Y1. USE OF GAS MASK STRONGLY ADVISED. REPEAT: NOW SWITCHING TO..."

"Starting to piss me off, girl." Gibbs hastily opened a large compartment above him and pulled a gas mask helmet over his head. Then, as a greenish fume filled the cockpit, he drew a pistol from the glove compartment, checked the magazine, pulled the slide, and cocked the hammer. He glanced over at the hatch.

Jenny nearly leaped inside the cockpit when a putrid cloud of gas blew up in her face. She nearly fainted immediately from the fumes; her lungs felt like they were being blocked off, and her stinging eyes started to water. She grasped her throat, wheezing, coughing, and crawling away from the hatch as the smoke leaked into the air.

"SECONDARY HATCH ACTIVATED."

A sliding door closed shut at the bottom of the entrance shaft. Once it was sealed, Gibbs flipped the first switch again.

The electric current returned. Jenny jolted and let out a banshee's haunting shriek. Her arms and legs flickered frantically, but she managed to throw herself off the tank before her heart gave out. She skidded to a stop, left behind by the tank, coughing up blood and trembling violently.

Gibbs smirked when he glanced over at Jenny lying on the road in the rear-view screen. His eyes returned to the front screen, where the north wall and the evacuation station grew closer. On the other side of a bridge that crossed over a dried out drainage canal. As he approached the bridge entrance (which was at a crossroad) he adjusted the main gun's aim to the evacuation station, and—

BAM!

Another tank rammed head-long into the left side of Gibbs' tank, shoving it off course. Its main gun fired, blasting a few metallic chunks off of Gibbs' tank.

"GIBBS, YOU GODDAMN PRICK!" Matthew shouted from inside the second tank. "YOU'RE FUCKING DEAD!"

Another shot from Matthew's tank detonated the HEAT missiles from within the left side of Gibbs' tank, creating a fireball that destroyed the main gun, the armoured skirt, and the tracks and road wheels the armoured skirt was built to protect in a fiery conflagration. Matthew's tank forced its way forward, shoving Gibbs' flaming chunk of metal along the side of the drainage trench. Another bridge came up. Gibbs floored the gas, trying to cut loose and careen out of Matthew's path, but Matthew turned with him and pushed him across the bridge lanes.

The tanks burst through the guardrail and plummeted into the drainage trench, grinding down the sloped wall of the trench with Matthew's tank crushing Gibbs' under its weight.

SMASH!

Gibbs' tank was half-buried in the damp white concrete floor. Matthew's tank speared into Gibbs' side, pushing it into the opposite trench wall, lopsided.

Both tanks were decommissioned.

Matthew's hatch popped up, and he emerged from the shaft and skipped to the front of his tank. He hopped onto Gibbs' tank, which belched green and black smoke rising from the gaping holes blasted into it. Matthew climbed onto the burnt tracks, ignoring the heat emanating from them, drew his spare Browning Hi-Power, and peered inside the cockpit.

Gibbs sat bloodied, twisted up, breathing with a raspy wheeze, his blood-soaked head encased in what was left of a shattered gas mask helmet. Gibbs' shredded left arm bled profusely, and a large metal chunk embedded in his ribs was much more noticeable than the smaller bits of shrapnel that stuck into his paling stained red and black skin.

Matthew coughed and waved his hand back and forth until the

green smoke cleared. Then he pointed his Hi-Power at Gibbs and said, "Seems launching coups runs in the family or something. What the fuck were you thinking, Gibbs? If this is about your brother…"

Gibbs wheezed and sputtered, "Hate to burst your… bubble, *sir*… but it is. You son of a bitch… you think you can… just kill my own family… and expect to get away with it? Heh-heh… you're wrong, man… all these years… since that day… three years, and I still remember it like yesterday… how you killed my brother… in cold blood… and threw him in with the zombies… for them to finish him off… now... now he's... he's one of them, damn you. HE'S ONE OF *THEM*!"

"Well, when he turns into a psychopathic murderer that unleashes a zombie horde upon innocent people and launches a coup to establish his own fucked-up government then *yeah*, I expect to kill him and move on! Both of you killed over a hundred people individually, and I'm not gonna take it lying down. I dunno what retardation your family raised you on before the war but I can tell you that we don't kill people for no reason!"

"I'll… kill you for this." Trembling, Gibbs pointed his pistol at Matthew with his right hand. It pained him to even move, since he had to sit upright in his chair (which he was buckled into) to move his arm.

BLAM!

With a single shot, Matthew destroyed Gibbs' pistol (and three of his fingers), causing Gibbs to screech in anguish and flail around in his chair. Matthew holstered his Hi-Power, grabbed Gibbs, and tore him from the seat. He dragged him out of the tank kicking and screaming, and with a steel expression Matthew dragged him up the side of the drainage trench, climbed up onto the road, passed through the evacuation station with many onlookers clearing a path for them, and ascended the set of stairs leading to the ramparts of the north wall.

When he'd reached the ramparts Matthew looked over the side and saw a horde of zombies clawing at the wall and reaching for him, writhing like a pit of snakes. "Brrraaaiiinssss," they moaned. "Brains!"

"Ah," said Matthew as he lifted a silenced Gibbs off the ground. "There's your brother."

Gibbs' eyes widened as he looked down at the zombies.

"What're you…!"

"If you're so bitter about your brother's passing, then I guess I should make it up to you and arrange a fucking family reunion!" Matthew heaved him over the side. "You can *all* rot in hell for all I care!"

Gibbs screamed in terror and latched onto the outer edge with his good hand, kicking at the wall and shrieking, "Please, no! Don't let them get me! Please! Matthew! I'm your friend! W-wouldn't *you* be bitter about *your* family dying?! Wouldn't you!?"

"Oh, sucks to be you right now. I haven't had a family in a *long* time."

"Matthew! MATTHEW! Pull me back up! I'm slipping, I'm slipping! I'm gonna die! Don't kill me, please! I… I was just… please… it's not fair…"

Matthew's expression hardened. "We've been friends for a long time, Gibbs. It's a shame it had to end this way. But then again, it's pretty fitting, isn't it?"

"Please, please, please, *PLEASE* PULL ME BACK UP! I can't hold on much longer! I'm sorry! Please forgive me! Matthew!"

"It's too late for apologies."

"For God's sake, I'm sorry! Don't let me die! Not like this!" Tears streamed down Gibbs' cheeks as he kicked the wall, desperately trying to climb back up. His fingers were sliding further and further over the edge. "Don't kill me!"

"I won't kill you, man. Your brother will. The brother that you were trying to avenge is going to tear you apart and eat your brains. Sibling gratitude at its finest, I say."

"YOU SON OF A BITCH!" Gibbs roared in a surge of terrified rage. "You hypocritical, motherfucking son of a bitch! I'll come back, and I'll kill you! I'll remember this day, even if I'm rotten inside and out!"

"No, you won't," Matthew replied passively. "You're already rotten. And we can't keep rotten things here. It'll stink the place up."

Gibbs was clawing at the wall with his mutilated left hand now, smearing blood on it. He lifted himself off the side for a moment, only to slip and hit the wall with his body again.

Shunk!

The impact shoved the large metal shard deeper into his ribs. Gibbs gasped. The shock of the penetration caused him to let go of the rampart. As he fell, he reached for the ramparts in vain and screamed, "MAAAAATTHEEEWWW!"

Matthew waved at him. "I'll see you in hell if there's still room!"

Gibbs landed right into the zombies' arms, and Matthew watched expressionless as Gibbs struggled and shrieked. The zombies bit into his flesh and slowly, agonizingly tore his limbs off. Gibbs' screams only got louder as he witnessed his own insides being torn from his stomach and chest by hundreds of grey, rigid fingers. He watched as they greedily devoured his intestines and stomach until finally his own zombified brother shattered his skull with its rotting teeth, silencing Gibbs' dying yelps.

Matthew turned in disgust and retreated back down the ramparts. "So long, pal."

The Fraden Residence

A squad of black Humvees screeched to a stop on the curb. Systems Corporation Elite Infantry flanked the front door with their rifles poised in a matter of seconds, awaiting Silverstein's orders. The captain glanced at Silverstein, who stood three feet away from him on the lawn. Silverstein nodded.

The captain lifted his foot, only to be stopped by Silverstein's loud grunt. The captain lowered his leg and looked at Silverstein.

"Use the damn door knob."

The captain grabbed the door knob and pushed it open. The soldiers stormed the place. Penelope Fraden, mother of Zero and Marner, was sitting on the couch watching the cooking channel when the soldiers barged in. She shrieked in terror as infantrymen searched the living room, the dining room, the kitchen, and the bathroom before dashing up the stairs. "WHAT!? W-w-w-w-what's going on!? What is this—"

Silverstein approached her calmly. "Please remain seated, Mrs. Fraden. We mean you no harm."

She screamed in terror at the sight of him. "A VAMPIRE!"

"BE QUIET!" he roared, silencing her instantly.

Penelope remained on the couch, trembling furiously and whimpering in fear of his appearance. "Who... who are you?"

"I am Jonathon Silverstein. One would think you'd know who I am considering my reputation."

Penelope's eyes widened in horror. "I have heard of you... but... this, this is the first time I've *seen* you. Why are you here? What do you want? I haven't done anything; I haven't broken the law. Is Zero in any trouble? What happened to Marner? Did Jenny and Aria break into your headquarters again?! I swear they were just fooling around! They're just kids! I don't have much money. Please don't hurt them! I'll get the money when I can!"

"This isn't a ransom, Mrs. Fraden," Silverstein said patiently. "I do not intend to harm you or your family, unless they interfere with my affairs." He seated himself on the footrest across from her. "No, I'm here to request something from your daughter and her two friends. I believe they were adopted by your son five years ago."

"Why? What did they do?"

"They... unintentionally took someone who is *very* valuable to me, and I'd like to see him returned to me safe and sound."

"S-someone valuable to you...?"

The soldiers gathered around Penelope and Silverstein. "Sir," said the captain, "they aren't here."

Silverstein raised his hand, silencing him. "Yes, someone very valuable to me. Granted, they did it with the best intentions, I'm sure. Unfortunately, the boy they took is also very unstable, and therefore dangerous." He tapped his hat with his index finger. "Mentally."

Penelope gasped.

"Yes, now you see why it's in everybody's best interests to have your girls returned to you, right?" Silverstein smiled. "Do you know where they are?"

"I-I haven't seen them since this morning. B-but I *do* remember Jenny saying something about a boy staying over at her house..."

Silverstein hid his surprise with his regular no-nonsense expression. He looked at the women slicing up onions on the TV program Penelope had on and waited until the TV show host swiped the slices off the cutting board into the cooking pot. "You don't watch the news very much... do you?"

"No," she said.

He stood up and sighed. "Haven't the police stopped by yet?"

"No," she said again. "Why? Has something else happened?"

"Nothing for you to be concerned about." With a sigh, he said, "Did Jenny say anything that you think I would find useful about this boy?"

Penelope paused, recalling what she remembered…

The Flashback to What Jenny Said

Jenny had stopped by for about half an hour when Marner went home, which was shortly after Damian went to sleep.

With a scowl, Jenny bit into an apple and said as she chewed, "I've a got a total douchebag at the house. Just staying over for the night. One night! And already I can't even stand his attitude. I wanted to punch him out and then jump on his face."

Penelope spat her tea into the sink and looked at Jenny in disbelief. "J-JENNY!?"

Jenny shrugged. "What? I said he was an asshole; I didn't say he was ugly."

Penelope blinked. "Nope. Nothing useful. J-just that there was a boy at the house."

"Well, if you see them, or this boy, give me a call. My number's on the back." He handed her a photo of Damian and watched her carefully as she studied it.

"So this is the person who is valuable to you?"

Silverstein nodded. "Correct."

"Alright," she said. "I will call you if I see him. Just... don't hurt them, please. I'm begging you," she whimpered desperately. "They're all the family I have."

"I understand. No one will get hurt. Not if I can help it." He gestured for his soldiers to head out the door. They exited the house in an orderly fashion. Silverstein turned to her and bowed his head slightly before leaving her alone with her thoughts and her fear.

Two Clans Village, December 18th, 2019

"Do you really have to go, Carson?"

Damian and Carson stood in front of their house, out in the snow. Fluffy white flakes lightly descended from the grey sky, fluttering through the bitter cold air. They were both dressed in winter coats and boots and so on, but Carson was the only one with a backpack full of rations, money, and extra clothing, with a sleeping bag strapped to it.

"I'm afraid so, little brother," said Carson. "It's gotten too crappy up here. Everybody's a total dick and I'm getting sick of it."

"What'd dad say about it?"

"He just called me a coward for running away."

"Are you running away?"

Carson scoffed. "Hell no! I've got a girl waiting for me in Scionia. I've known her for years, and we started unofficially going out."

"'Unofficially'?"

"Eh, it's complicated." Carson tousled Damian's head. "Tell you when you're older."

"But why Scionia? It's dangerous out there!"

"So what? Doesn't matter to me, as long as she's there. Relax, when you're older you can come and visit us! I'll send you an email every week, alright?"

Damian started to tear up and sniffled. "You'd better!"

"Just keep practicing with your powers. You'll get it eventually."

"But... who am I gonna play with now?"

Carson's face saddened. Then his expression hardened with determination. He stooped down and whispered, "Listen. Dad would never forgive me for this, but... do you honestly wanna come with me?"

Damian's face lit up. "You really mean it?"

"Yeah, but I have to warn you, we might never see this place again. We might never be forgiven for leaving everyone else behind. To them, we might as well be dead if we both leave. That's why I didn't wanna do this with you here. I knew you'd want to go. I just don't wanna ruin your life, Damian."

Damian stared into his eyes. His serious, trustworthy eyes. His vision blurred from the tears, which were running down his cheeks. Go with Carson, the only sibling who ever treated him nicely and played with him and defended him from bullies? Or stay with everyone else, the people he needed? Damian hesitated.

Then he took a tentative step back.

Guilt and sadness washed over Carson's face, and he nodded with a grave expression. He couldn't hide his disappointment. "...I see."

Damian sniffled and wiped tears from his eyes. His cheeks were already starting to freeze from the relentless cold.

Carson smiled and touched his shoulder. "Hey, don't cry. You need them. I understand." He knelt down and hugged him. "Things'll be fine without me."

"No they won't!" Damian sobbed. "I wanna go with you, but I don't wanna go!"

"Listen, if you change your mind, I'll be at the bus station on the outskirts of town. You know the one. I don't wanna push this on you but you've got an hour if you change your mind and decide to go. Do what you want, not what everybody else wants."

"Okay," Damian sobbed. Watching Carson go was one of the hardest things for him to do.

Damian went back inside, glumly hung up his coat, and put away his mitts, boots, and hat. When he got into the dining room, his father, Jeffery Warkowski, sat at the table reading the newspaper. He took a seat at the table and stared down at it sadly. The room was silent for a while. The only things that could be heard were Jeffery's occasional grunts and the crinkling sounds his newspaper made every time he turned a page.

"...So he's gone?" his father asked.

Damian sniffled. "Yup... he wanted me to come with him."

"Of course he did."

Damian said nothing.

"Did you want to go?"

"Yes..."

"Then why didn't you?"

"Hunh...?"

"You're just a waste of space here," Jeffery grumbled behind the papers. "Go ahead and run away like the little coward you are."

"But dad!" Damian protested.

"What's your problem?"

Damian hesitated. Then he slammed his hands on the table and shouted, "NO! I'm not a little coward!"

Jeffery lowered the newspaper and looked at Damian with surprise.

"I'm a Warkowski, and Warkowskis aren't cowards! I would've gone with him but I didn't wanna leave you and mom and Kayla and Zach behind! I'm staying for my family! Aren't you proud of me?! Aren't you?!"

"Why, you little shit..." Jeffery lurched forward and slapped him across the face. "Why would I be proud of having a coward for a son? You should've gone with him and saved us the trouble."

"But..."

"As far as I'm concerned, you're not welcome here. You underachieve in school, you scare off anyone who could be a potential friend, you slack off in your training, and you can barely move a chair across the room with your telekinesis. I've tried to be patient, Damian, but you're just not worth any more energy than I've already invested in you."

Damian sobbed, rubbing the red mark on his cheek. "Dad—"

"STOP CRYING! For fuck's sake, why can't you be more like your siblings? They never cried about pathetic bullshit like this! You're seven years old; act your age." Jeffery glared at him with steely eyes. These eyes alone insulted everything about Damian until they moved to the beer can sitting nearby. Jeffery snatched it and gulped down its contents. "Go away. I don't want to see you anymore."

Damian ran from the table, darted down the narrow hall on Jeffery's right, and entered his room at the very end and slammed the door shut. He burst into tears and buried his face into his blankets, where he cried and wailed for a good half-hour.

He gasped, nearly falling asleep. He knew what he wanted now. He wanted Carson. Carson never insulted him. Carson never beat him or made fun of his underachievements. Carson was always there to cheer him up, no matter how miserable he was.

Damian rushed out of his bedroom, quickly put on his winter gear, and dashed out the front door. His father was still reading a newspaper at the table, but hadn't uttered a word against him leaving. He just casually turned the page.

Damian ran down the road, slipping through the slushy streets and tripping over items concealed in the snow. He panted heavily as he raced for the bus station, and when the bus station was finally in his sight, sitting just across the street, he ran for it with newfound determination. "I'm coming, Carson!"

Carson was there, waiting at the ninth platform with his ticket and luggage ready. The bus had already arrived, and Carson hadn't noticed Damian.

"Carson!" Damian shouted, running into the street. "Wait for me!"

BEEEEEEEEEEPP!

Damian gasped when white light enveloped him. He turned. Didn't see the car coming—

CRASH!

A crowd had gathered around Damian's broken body as he lay face down in the snow, muttering amongst themselves. Three broken ribs, a punctured organ, a broken right leg, and a broken right arm stopped him from crawling any further.

Carson glanced over at the crowd gathered around Damian, but he still couldn't see what the fuss was about. "Wonder what happened."

"Some dumbass ran out in traffic," said a nearby passenger with a ticket in his hand. "Hit 'n' run. Poor little bastard never saw it comin'."

"Oh," said Carson, before boarding the bus.

Damian managed to roll on his back, crying out in pain. His vision blurred and fading, staring up at all the strange faces that looked down on him, spinning around in circles, saying things that were just faint whispers. He couldn't understand what they were saying. Just a distorted vortex of eyes and noses and mouths spiralling around him. Then he moved his head up, and peered through the forest of bystanders' legs, and saw the upside down image of Carson's bus taxiing onto the road. He screamed Carson's name. Reached for the bus with his good arm. A few bystanders stepped away as he screamed. Others left him alone and continued on their way without a second thought.

He could only watch the bus shrink down the road, vanishing in the shower of snow. His last hope had gone.

Present Day

"Should've gone with him. Should've gone with him.

Should've gone with him," Damian sobbed on Aria's shoulder. "Should've gone... should've gone with him. Shouldn't have said no. Should've come earlier. Damn it Carson, why? Why? Why? Why'd you leave me behind for some bitch? Little bitch wasn't worth it. Took it all away. Took everything away."

"You're awake already? That was fast." Aria was still carrying him, heading toward the command center. She watched the smoke columns rise from the massive circular building, contemplating on whether or not she should go somewhere else.

"Why'd you leave me? Why didn't you wait? You should've talked me outta staying. You should've made me go with you. Shoulda kidnapped me."

Man, he's still babbling. Aria jogged down the empty sidewalk and stepped onto a different road. There, she immediately spotted Jenny in her torn clothes, stumbling down the road with her back to her. "Jenny?!"

Jenny weakly turned around and said, "Hunh?"

"What the hell happened to you?" Aria asked as she approached her wounded sister. She dropped Damian onto the ground, who was still babbling incoherently.

Jenny blinked, staring at her blood-soaked sister. "What the hell happened to *you*?!"

"Zombies. You?"

"Ugh," Jenny groaned as she rubbed her head. "I got run over by a tank."

"A *tank*?"

"Pretty much," Jenny replied with a scowl.

"C'mon, take me with you. Don't go. Don't... don't get on that bus!" Damian said, staring up at the canopy of branches hanging above the town. "Come back!" He reached for the branches, as if trying to take someone's hand. "Don't leave me with them! Fuck!"

Marner slowly approached from a nearby abandoned convenience store with Jenny's jacket in her hands. Her eyes were fixed on Damian the whole time. "What's wrong with him?" she asked.

"I don't know," said Aria, "this is new for me, too. Usually he's the way you guys've seen him." She gave him a sideways glance as he clawed at the air. "I don't know what the hell *this* is, though."

"You bastard, don't go!"

"Looks like he's high on a flashback," said Jenny.

"Maybe all that killing finally got to his head," Aria said. She looked onward at the horde of zombies that were lumbering toward them down the road.

"Don't leave me alone! Please! Carson! Come back!"

"We've got to get him out of here," said Marner.

"I agree. Let's get him back on the ship." Jenny looked around, then looked up at the burning command center. "Where is the ship?"

As if on cue, the *Scion's Wings* descended upon them, hovering just above their heads. The loading platform dropped down for them to hop on with ease, and Jenny and Marner did just that.

But Aria hesitated. She looked at Damian, who was still babbling incomprehensibly. She considered leaving him there, until she remembered one of the conditions that would lead to Jenny exploding. With a surge of frustration, she snatched him up off the ground and jumped onto the loading platform. "You're gonna owe me big time for this one."

The girls entered the bridge of the *Scion's Wings* and immediately moved to the windows. Aria dropped Damian on the floor, which piqued Jeremy's curiosity. "What happened to him?"

Aria shrugged. "Beats the hell outta me. Are we bowing out?"

Jeremy nodded. "There are just too many of them now. The command center has been taken, and apparently Gibbs set up a time bomb in preparations for his coup. This entire village is about to explode."

"Gibbs?!" Marner repeated in disbelief.

"The squirt?!" Jenny exclaimed.

Jeremy nodded again. "Apparently he wanted to avenge his fallen brother, whom had previously started a coup to overthrow Matthew. Instead, Matthew personally threw him over the wall to join his undead brother."

"Hmph," said Aria, crossing her arms. "Poetic justice, I guess."

Damian's eyes bulged as he shouted at the ceiling again,

clawing at the air. "Come back!"

Jeremy looked at him, then looked at Aria. "Perhaps it would be wise to wake him? He appears to be hallucinating."

Aria thought for a moment. "You got a loading bay?"

"Yes?"

"Then just throw 'im in there."

Jeremy gave her a quick look of disgust before taking off. The *Scion's Wings* flew up above the burning village below, which writhed with zombies. Only three more Copter Ships took off from the evacuation station below just as it was overrun, with Matthew's ship (the largest Copter Ship) being the last to lift off.

Cloverfield Dock

The Cloverfield Dock was a complex of warehouses and loading docks that were partially destroyed from the Dehue Extermination Project and left unrepaired. It was eventually forgotten and abandoned by the general public. It overlooked the Orion Sea, about fifty kilometres down the shoreline from Cloverfield Harbour.

It became a gathering point for Systems Corporation, guarded by patrol squads and snipers 24/7. The vast rows of warehouses were completely rundown and stripped of their flaky paint, revealing the dusty red brick beneath.

"Our next assault centers around the Spanios Suburbs," Silverstein stated, pressing his index finger into a small area on a map of the maple leaf-shaped South Cloverfield spread out on the table. Surrounding the table were twenty squad leaders, all of whom were wearing their gas masks. "Once we get in there, we'll take out the leader, Donnie Vanco. He's been laying low in his strip club in the center of the Suburbs. Laying low for him isn't low enough for us, so let's send him lower."

The squad leaders merely nodded in agreement.

He told them the plan, finishing with, "Understood?"

He was answered with a swarm of "yes sir" replies from the crowd.

Silverstein nodded in approval. "Good. We'll attack tomorrow. But I still want the other squads to patrol the city and terminate any other known subordinates of Truman. Dismissed."

Casual chatter filled the room as the squad leaders dispersed. The times when his soldiers were lounging or relaxing or even inside the warehouses (unless to discuss battle plans) were the only times when Silverstein saw their faces without the gas masks. It amazed him just how gentle and cheerful some of them looked, but when he saw the others' rock-hard, battle-scarred faces he felt reassured that he could trust them to do any necessary thing. He thought of it as a perfect balance between harmony and chaos.

"Sir?"

Silverstein looked up from the map to see his least favourite-looking soldier. He had a gentle, boyish face and almost always smiled. It pissed him off. "What do you want, Squad Leader Seven?" he asked in a gruff, uninterested tone.

"What's the point in risking soldiers' lives with attacking Truman's contacts when we could just attack him directly?"

Silverstein smiled. "It's about time someone asked me that question." He placed his hand on the squad leader's shoulder. He could tell it made him uncomfortable. "Son, the reason why we won't attack them head-on is because we don't have enough to overpower him. So we're going to lure him here by killing off his friends and contacts, so that the shady organization the world's leaders are operating behind the scenes will plan a proxy war to try and erase us from the picture. We're ruining their plans.

"Basically, Cloverfield Heart will help us out by reducing President Truman's invading forces. Once that's done, he won't have enough defenses for us when we infiltrate his main base and take what is rightfully mine: the Hell Pentagram. After all, this is all about bringing Diablo back from imprisonment. If that doesn't work, I have other plans, rest assured. But at this present moment, that pentagram's as good as ours. ...We just need to *find* the damn thing."

"But what would that achieve for us?"

Silverstein grinned and put a cigarette in his mouth. "A lot."

Sky Japan—Yuen Kwey's Cyber Sex Shop

Yuen Kwey was a famous sex shop owner, with sixteen outlets scattered throughout Sky Japan, mostly in the Mizu-Shōbai District. His contribution to Sky Japan's sex industry consisted of shops specializing in virtual reality sex simulators. Customers would line up to book a private room to spend an afternoon hooked up to VR machines to live their own sexual fantasies without the limitations of the law. His shops were mostly located in crowded areas near love hotels.

Yuen Kwey considered himself to be a good guy, believing that his VR simulators kept the pedophiles and rapists from acting out their fantasies on real people. His business was able to skirt Sky Japan's laws against prostitution, since technically the sex he was selling didn't even exist, and whatever the customers experienced was for them and only them to know (due to privacy laws).

Kyo Kuma entered the darkly lit shop, flanked by two of his men. Sheathed sword in hand, Kyo made his way around the counter (which was left unattended) and began passing through the narrow corridor lit only by a dim red light. Kyo began his search, sliding open every fusuma door in the corridor to look into each of the private rooms. VR headgear-wearing customers would be lying down on mats or beds, strapped into chairs, or standing up as they performed sexual acts on blank-faced sexroids. These androids had a layer of motion capture technology under their outer layer of skin, similar to what was used for photo-realistic CG animation in films. That way the androids would have the appearance of whatever the VR-immersed customer desired from popular Sky Japanese culture; maids, nurses, schoolgirls, etc.

Kyo only stole brief glimpses into each room and progressed further in disgust until finally he reached one final sliding door at the far end of the corridor. With a grunt, he kicked the door out of its frame and stomped into the room. Five men were in the room; three were sitting on two pink overstuffed couches (the farthest couch had one while the nearest had the other two); two others were bodyguards in black suits standing behind the farthest couch. Kyo's men immediately whipped out their pistols and shot the bodyguards several times, much to the shock and horror of two of the sitters. The third and nearest sitter jumped up and pointed his own pistol at Kyo, standing protectively in front of the other two.

As the two bodyguards slid down the wall on the other side of the room, Yuen Kwey himself began trembling furiously on the farthest couch. He spoke Japanese, as did everyone else, throughout the entire meeting. "What is the meaning of this?!"

The man who had his gun pointed at Kyo wore a brown jacket

with a plain white shirt underneath; faded jeans, construction boots, and a bandana with a stylized eye wrapped around his eyes. For a man who appeared to be blind, he was quick.

Yuen Kwey, middle-aged and wearing a pastel suit, nervously ran his fingers through his greying hair and asked again in his native language, "K-Kyo… what is the meaning of this?"

The youngest of the three men, protected by the third potential shooter, glanced over at Kyo with a confused look on his face. "Mr. Kyo? What's going on?!"

Yuen looked at the youngest, who happened to be his son, and said, "Sit down, Tai."

Tai Kwey sat back down behind the third man.

Yuen looked at the third man and said, "You too, Meiyo."

The man with the bandana wrapped around his eyes, Meiyo, slowly sat back down onto the couch. He took his gun off Kyo, but kept it cocked and ready, finger on the trigger guard.

Yuen glanced up at Kyo, clearly shaken by the noisy entrance. "What's going on?"

Kyo asked, "Where are my children, Yuen?"

Alarmed and confused, Tai looked at his father. So did Meiyo.

Yuen hesitated. "I don't know what you are talking about."

Kyo cocked his head toward the henchman on his left. His henchman immediately popped a round into Tai's stomach. Tai screamed and doubled over, rolling forward off the couch and curling up on his knees.

Yuen bolted upright, eyes wide with disbelief. Meiyo pointed his gun at Kyo again, placing his free hand on Tai's shoulder.

"Lie to me again," Kyo growled, "And I'll ensure your son doesn't leave this room alive."

"A-alright!" Yuen raised his hands in surrender. "Alright! Alright! I… I'll tell you what you want to know!"

"My children came here yesterday. Apparently there was a problem with the bagman, which you reported. They came to sort the mess out, only to have a group of gunmen show up, kill the bag man, and succeed in capturing two of them." Kyo approached Yuen, ignoring Meiyo as he kept his gun trained on his head. "Who took them, and where are they now?"

Tai looked at his father in disbelief. "T-this is a misunderstanding, right Father? Tell them! What have you to hide?"

"If only it were that simple," Kyo said. "If only I were stupid enough to even consider that this was just a freak accident that just happened to be a major coincidence. But it wasn't. Was it, Yuen?"

Yuen lowered his head shamefully. "…No."

Tai's eyes widened.

Meiyo turned his head to Yuen sharply, clearly surprised as well.

Kyo asked, "Why did you do it?"

"…To ensure my business's safety in Multiplier's takeover," Yuen said slowly. "I know that this war will not end well for us unless we switched to the winning side. So I… I made a deal with Boss Kakashi, to provide Multiplier with a means to successfully capture your children."

Kyo's eyes bulged with rage. "WHAT?!"

Meiyo hesitated, then took his gun off Kyo. Then he helped Tai off the floor, slung his arm over his shoulder, and started to head out of the room.

Yuen looked over at Meiyo and shouted, "Where are you going?!"

Meiyo glanced over his shoulder at Yuen and growled, "There is no honour in betrayal. I don't live to serve monsters."

"Tai!" Yuen yelled. "Please!"

Tai glared at his father. "Don't." And with that final stabbing word, Meiyo led Tai out of the shop. Kyo gestured to his men to let them through before turning back to Yuen.

"Alone at least," said Kyo, glowering down at Yuen. "Where are they?"

"Please." Yuen fell on his knees and grovelled at Kyo's feet. "Please, spare me!"

Kyo kicked him back onto the couch in disgust and repeated, "*Where* are they?!"

"Sekigahara District! That's where they are! I-in Multiplier's high-rise! L-look there!"

"You're sure about that?"

"Ninety percent!"

"Thank you." In a blur, Kyo drew his sword from the scabbard and slashed through Yuen's body. Yuen's shrieks rang through the shop as Kyo continued slicing him up.

Kyo was good with his sword. It wouldn't take him long to splatter Yuen all over the walls.

Cloverfield Heart—Zero's Office

BEEP-BEEP-BEEP-BEEP-BONG!

Zero Fraden, now demoted to colonel status and given a desk job in Cloverfield Heart, answered his office phone. "Colonel Fraden's office." No answer. "Hello?"

BEEP-BEEP-BEEP-BEEP-BONG!

He looked at his cell phone and frowned. Muttered, "Gets me every time." Answered his cell. "Hello?"

Penelope's shuddering voice cried on the other end, "Zero, you have to come home!"

Alarmed, Zero asked, "What's wrong, mom? Are you okay?"

"It's terrible... something happened at the school."

"WHAT?!" Zero bolted upright, knocking his chair over. "Are the girls alright?!"

"I don't know; they've been missing for hours! They never came home. And... Jonathon Silverstein came to the house."

Zero's eyes widened. His heart pounded. *Silverstein?!* "Did he hurt you, mom?! What'd he want?"

"He wanted to know where the girls were. He said they took someone important to him and he only wants him back. He said it was all a misunderstanding and that no one would get hurt. He gave me a photo of the person and told me to call him if anything came up."

"Stay right there. I'm on my way. I want to see that photo when I get there. In the meantime, I'll try to get a hold of the girls. Stay safe." He hung up, and after a moment of heavy breathing, he swore and slammed his fists down on the desk.

Cloverfield, Jenny's Place

Zero had stopped at the curb in front of Jenny's place, alarmed by its rugged appearance. The doorway was wide open and splintered, and the second floor window was broken.

The house was even worse on the inside. Everything had been overturned and strewn across the floor. The toaster was blackened and half-melted. The cupboards were stripped bare. And then, the holes in the ceiling...

"What the hell?" Zero stared at the two holes in the ceiling and immediately drew his pistol from the shoulder holster concealed in his jacket. He entered the living room and quickly scanned the mess for any sign of life, stepping on the kicked-in door. He noted the bed unfolded from the couch and cautiously made his way upstairs, pointing his gun forward.

When he reached the second floor, the hallway was empty, but surprisingly the only clean area in the house. He moved to the bathroom and stepped onto the kicked-in door inside. The shower curtains had been ripped off the pole and the cleaning products scattered across the tile floor with the tattered magazines. He entered the bathroom and went straight to the other end, where the small window was sitting above the toilet. He stopped at the toilet.

There was excrement in it. It smelled fresh.

Zero flushed it.

He moved on to the study. The shelves were smashed apart and the manga volumes were dumped on the desk, the door and the floor. They even covered those holes in the floor. The window was smashed open too, from the inside.

He moved to Aria's old room, also finding the door kicked down and the room's contents thrown around and broken. The dresser was stripped of its drawers, and Aria's leftover clothes, underwear, and lingerie covered the pool of DVDs and bed sheets that were thrown off the shelf. The TV was smashed into its stand, and the bed sitting under the window across from the doorway was flipped over. Even her private homemade porn collection was left uncovered, some of which—to Zero's shock and surprise—had her face on them.

He moved on to Jenny's room, which was a little cleaner only because it had less in it. The overturned bed lay a few feet away from the window; the desk beside the doorway had been knocked over, its contents scattered all across the room, mixed with the clothes from her dresser drawer and her closet.

Zero noted that every door in the house had been kicked down, indicating that Silverstein was here. It was practically his infantrymen's calling card—although they rarely left empty houses in such horrific states.

Which meant someone else had been here. Someone completely different. An anonymous addition to the game.

He noticed a book on the floor with the stylized title reading, *Forbidden Teen Love* with two older teenage men smiling and holding each other whilst in their own respective stages of undress. Curious, Zero picked it up and flipped through the pages briefly. He shrieked, "*YAOI*!" and flung the book away as if it contained a dangerous biochemical. He didn't know what disturbed him more—the secret, messy intruder, or his adoptive daughters' secret porn-related lives.

Zero went back into the bathroom. A man has to go when he has to go. He approached the toilet and unzipped his pants.

Ki-ka-clack!

And then he noticed the pair of grenades bouncing toward him. He only had time to raise his eyebrows and yell, "Oh, shit!"

BOOM!

The entire bathroom exploded, tearing the tiles off the walls and decimating the previously cracked mirror. The window was blown out of the wall into the neighbour's yard. Zero had managed to leap in the small space behind the bathtub wall and the other wall, standing on the toilet, covering his ears. Smoke filled the bathroom, and Zero heard rapid footsteps passing the bathroom doorway and stomping down the stairs. He jumped off the toilet and blindly dashed through the smoke into the hallway and cleared the stairs in his pursuit.

BANGBANG!

Zero scrambled back behind the fridge as two bullets hit the wall beside the living room doorway. He brandished his own pistol and returned two shots. Another round glanced off the corner of the fridge. Zero replied with three more shots.

"GAAGHH!"

One hit.

My luck is changing for the better every day!

Zero took the opportunity to curve around the fridge and pounce on his attacker. His attacker, though injured in the left shoulder, managed to kick Zero back.

Zero fell into the pots and cutlery scattered on the floor. His pistol flew out of his hand and clattered by the living room doorway. His attacker also lost balance and collapsed on the plates, shattering them. The attacker's pistol had flown out of his hand right out the front door, probably due to reflex from being shot. They looked at each other for a brief moment. His attacker was blonde, young, around twenty, dressed in a hoodie and jeans and sneakers. Then they jumped to their feet with the first thing they could get their hands on and looked at each other again, brandishing their respective weapons.

Zero had a teaspoon.

His attacker had a large bread knife.

Zero let out a startled gasp: "GUNH!"

His attacker lunged forward with the bread knife and swung it wildly at Zero, who dodged every single attack, progressively backing up to the dining room table. Then he threw the spoon into his attacker's face, smacked the knife out of his hand, and shoved him against the counter. Zero stomped after him, grabbed a handful of hair, and started bashing the man's face off the counter's surface. But his attacker, quick and enduring, snatched the half-melted toaster and hurled it over his shoulder into Zero's jaw. Zero twirled backward and fell to the floor next to an electric knife, and on a pile of forks that dug into his thighs. He growled in pain and snatched the electric knife (with a battery that lasts for hours!), and jumped back up to his feet. "Ha! C'mon, you bastard!"

His attacker reached in the cupboards under the sink and gave Zero a cocky, over-the-shoulder smirk. He turned around to reveal the gas-powered chainsaw in his hands. Zero's heart nearly stopped when he saw it, even faltered hopelessly. The attacker chuckled triumphantly as if he'd already won and said, "Let's cut you down to size, Colonel Fraden."

Why didn't Jenny put that in the tool shed?! Zero asked aloud, "Who the hell are you?"

"Just a man with a license to kill and intent to slaughter."

Zero glared at him. He pushed the button on HI power, and the electric knife roared with anticipation. "Let's carve."

The attacker pulled the cord on the chainsaw. It sputtered. He pulled it again. It shook and sputtered once again. He pulled it a third time; it sputtered, and died.

Zero stared at him. The attacker stared back, with the dumbest look on his face. He pulled it for a fourth time; same result. Zero wasn't about to waste any more time and lunged forward with the electric knife. The attacker blocked with the chainsaw, and pulled the cord again.

RRRRRRRRR!

The chains on the blade ripped the electric knife apart, forcing Zero to throw away the halved knife and leap backward against the wall. The attacker laughed triumphantly with the live chainsaw in his hands. "*Now* we're talking!" He thrust the chainsaw at Zero's body.

Zero dodged it and launched a roundhouse kick to the attacker's face. The attacker flew back, stunned. The chainsaw's grip slipped through his fingers as he fell, flinging it into the air. He hit the pots and pans with a loud crash, and shrieked in terror as the chainsaw came down on him. "NOOOO!"

Zero kicked the chainsaw out the door before it could land on the attacker. The attacker was too stunned to move, granting Zero enough time to pick up his pistol and return beside the attacker with the barrel pressed against his temple. "Who the hell are you?" he asked again.

"Like I said... I'm just a man with a license to kill..."

"What do you mean; like a spy?"

"Maybe."

Zero jabbed the pistol against the attacker's cheekbone. "Don't get smart with me. After this incident, I'm not in the mood to screw around."

The attacker looked at the bullet hole in his shoulder. "Damn... you wounded me."

"So what? You gonna run home crying now?" Zero sneered impatiently.

"Heh... no, but now I can't tell you anything. They'd never let me say a word."

"*Who* won't?"

"That's for me to know... AND TAKE TO MY GRAVE!" The attacker raised a cell phone for Zero to see, revealing that it was dialling a number. Zero thought he was calling for help until the man's stomach beeped.

Beep!

...Wait, what?

He gasped and lifted the man's shirt to see a small light blinking inside his stitched-up stomach. "Now you won't know anything! I'm expendable! And I'm taking you with me, Colonel

Zero Fraden!"

Zero kicked the man in the face to disorient him and raced for the doorway. The man's maniacal laughter followed him out the door until the bomb implant exploded.

BABOOWWWWWWMM!

The entire front of the house blew across the lawn, sending Zero sailing up and over the grass and the curb. He slammed into the side of his sedan.

Instant lights-out.

COBALT ROGUE, VOL. 1: THE DEAD BLUE

Episode 008

Trump Card Trial Run

Warkowski Residence, Two Clans Village, 2019

Damian could finally walk on his own again without needing much help—not that he received much help anyway. His bones healed abnormally fast; he was almost completely healed after only two months of getting hit by that car at the bus station. As his mother put it, he was lucky he got out of that car accident with the wounds he got. May Warkowski, his mother, was a little more caring and gentle than his father. She was also a human. The exchange of human and Dehue DNA mutated her body a little, but not severely. Her hair changed colour from black to dark blue, and her eyes did the same, from green to blue.

Damian went into the bathroom and locked the door behind him. On his left upon entering was the bathtub and shower, and on the right side of him was the closet, the bathroom sink, and on the other side, the toilet. He went over to the sink and looked at himself in the mirror. His face was pale and glistening from the tears that'd dried on his cheeks.

Everybody hates me. What's the point of going on anymore? Carson's gone… the one person who treated me right left me alone… left me to die…

He opened one of the top drawers and fished for a pair of scissors. He took out the scissors and looked at them. ***Why don't I just die? Everybody would be so much happier without me; I'm just a failure. I'm just a waste of space. They really want me to die? I'll give it to them. I'll... fucking... give it to them.*** *He pressed the tip of the scissors against his wrist and took one last look at himself in the mirror.* ***Just a waste of space.***

"Is that all?" his reflection asked.

"GAHH!" Damian screamed in terror and jumped away from the mirror, stumbling over the side of the tub and falling into it. Chest heaving, eyes glued to the mirror. He whimpered and shook

uncontrollably. He held the scissors defensively and gulped. He hesitated, and slowly climbed out of the tub, keeping his eyes on the mirror without a single blink. His legs gave out and he fell to the tiled floor, startling himself. He whimpered and broke into a cold sweat, grasping the scissors tightly. "I don't wanna die," he muttered to himself. "I don't wanna die, I don't wanna die, I don't wanna die, I don't wanna die, I don't wanna die, I don't wanna die, I don't wanna die, I don't wanna die, I don't wanna die, I don't wanna die—"

"Then what's with the scissors?" the voice above the sink asked.

Damian ducked and clamped his eyes shut. "I don't wanna die, I don't wanna die, I don't wanna die, I don't wanna die..."

"Hey! You listening to me?"

Tears ran down Damian's face. "I DON'T WANNA DIE, I DON'T WANNA DIE, I DON'T WANNA DIE, I DON'T WANNA DIE, I DON'T WANNA DIE..."

A hand grabbed him by the hair and yanked him off the floor, causing him to scream in terror. The hand slammed his head against the counter and a fierce voice roared, "SHUT UP!"

Damian bit his lip and whimpered.

"You're contradicting yourself, Damian," said the voice, just a few inches from his face. Damian's eyes looked up at the mirror, and saw that a hand with jet black skin protruded from the reflection in the mirror, holding him down. He sobbed and shut his eyes again. "First you're trying to kill yourself, and now you're saying you wanna live. Which is it?"

"Please don't kill me... please don't kill me... please don't kill me... please don't kill me. I don't wanna die. I don't wanna die. I don't wanna die."

"Pathetic." Another hand snatched the scissors from Damian's hand and held them to his throat. "Why shouldn't I kill you? Hunh? Why not? Why don't you grow some balls and make a decision already?"

"Everybody wants me dead..."

"Hah! Is that what you think?"

"I know *it. Everybody wants me dead. They don't want me around. They don't play with me. They don't help me. Everybody... everybody makes fun of me. They call me a freak. They act like I*

don't exist. So... so maybe I shouldn't exist, right? Isn't that the point of dying?"

"You think dying's the answer? Are you a man, or are you just an over-emotional pussy?"

"I... I..."

"You're a man, aren't you?"

"Y-y-yeah..."

"Prove it." Damian felt the hand loosen its grip on him and he quickly jumped away from the counter and watched the hand sink back into the mirror. His reflection was different; it had jet black skin, red eyes and narrow pupils, and longer, wilder hair.

Damian dropped the scissors. The terrifying sight struck him near-senseless. He asked in shallow breaths, "W-What are you?"

The reflection smiled. "You can call me Tyler."

"Are you... like a split personality? Or a dark half or something?"

"Something like that."

"Oh, God... Am... Am I going crazy...?"

"Maybe."

"Where did you come from?"

The reflection—Tyler—grinned and pointed at him, through the mirror. The glass rippled around his arm. "I came from you."

"Me...?"

"You see, when you hurt, I hurt. I'm like your subconscious. I hear all of your thoughts... I feel all of your feelings... I know what you know. I know everything about you, Damian, because you and I are two sides of the same personality living in the same body. Basically. We're like a coin. You're heads and I'm tails."

Damian didn't say anything. He was too terrified to move, but not too terrified to listen.

"When Carson left us alone, that was the last straw. I'm a little more impatient than you are, Damian, and you aren't a very patient kid, so that's saying something. I couldn't take the verbal abuse, the physical abuse, the psychological abuse anymore. They're saying we're weak and helpless and worthless. I'm getting sick of it. How could someone as special as you put up with that shit? Why don't you prove them different? Why don't we show them what we can do?" His smile grew fiercer. Wilder. "They don't have the right to treat us like that. They don't realize just how

powerful we really are, and deep down, you know that's true. So... why don't we put 'em in their place?"

Damian liked the sound of that. Now Tyler had his full attention. The thought of his father and siblings acknowledging him for his abilities and praising him made him smile. The thought of his classmates finally respecting him and being his friends instead of beating down on him with their fists and insults made him giggle with glee. "...How?"

Tyler grinned. "Follow my instructions from now on. And I mean don't ask any questions, no matter what I tell you. Show Dad that we aren't worthless and pathetic. Show him that we've got guts. Let's show him and everybody else that we can do anything. *We'll* make *them respect us."*

"Yes..." Damian breathed.

"Let's change their perspective about us. We'll show them! We'll show them all! Even if we have to kill those miserable fuckers for hurting us!"

"Yes!"

"Then we can make the world see us for who we really are! Let's change the world! Let's make them accept us!"

"You're a genius!"

"We're *geniuses! This is your plan as much as it is mine!"*

Tears of happiness streamed down Damian's face. "That's right. We're geniuses... you and me."

"You and I."

"I and you."

They spoke as one: "Us."

Damian stepped out of the bathroom feeling refreshed and relieved. Now he had someone he could trust. Somebody he could turn to. He couldn't believe he didn't realize it sooner.

All he needed was himself, or some sort of figure in his own imagination.

"Hey, shithead!" his oldest brother, Zach, approached him. Zach was three feet taller than Damian was, towering over him like a giant. Zach had black hair with blue streaks, blue eyes, and wore jeans and a grey T-shirt. "Where the hell's my CD?"

"How should I know?" Damian replied. "I-it's your CD."

Whack!

Zach smacked him upside the head. "Don't get snippy with me, you little bitch! Where the fuck is it?"

Hit him back.

Without hesitation, Damian buried his fist into Zach's stomach. Taken by surprise, Zach stumbled. "What the—"

Hit him again.

Damian punched him in the stomach again. The rush got to him. Damian roared savagely and dived into Zach's middle, causing him to fall on his back. Damian mounted him and drove his fists into Zach's face repeatedly. He threw all of his rage into each blow. "I don't have your fucking CD! Leave me alone! LEAVE ME ALONE!"

YES! Hit him again! Hit him again!

Krak! Smack! Pow!

Damian didn't stop. His rage fuelled him. Zach's face got bloody. Then, pulpy. The element of surprise served Damian well. Damian didn't stop hitting him, even when his knuckles ached and bruised, or when they started to bleed. Pounding Zach's skull into the floor. He felt the bastard's teeth pop against his knuckles. Felt—

"What in God's name is going on?" Jeffery voice shouted from the far end of the hallway. Damian could hear his footsteps stomping into the hall, but he ignored it. Jeffery stopped at the end of the hall, watching with surprise as Damian pounded down on his brother's face. May and Kayla appeared from the living room behind him, equally shocked by the sight. Jeffery's face tensed up. He said, "Damian."

Damian gasped, and stopped. Then he turned and looked at Jeffery with blood droplets on his face. His eyes were wide. He was in for it now. "Dad...?"

"What... the hell... have you done?"

"I-I'm sorry, dad, I... I..."

Jeffery approached him. Damian shut his eyes and braced himself. He knew he was going to get beaten and scolded for screwing up. Jeffery grabbed his shoulder and lifted him off Zach and examined his bloody knuckles. "Hm." Jeffery looked at Zach, who moaned in agony. "You see that, Zach? That's why you never let your guard down, even with a gentle, clumsy puppy. Kick the puppy all you like, and enjoy it while it lasts, because some day that puppy will bite back."

Damian trembled, awaiting his punishment.

Jeffery turned to Damian and led him back into the bathroom. And he did something Damian never thought he'd ever see directed toward him.

His father smiled. *Pride. Approval. Not a single sign of the usual shame or anger showed. "Let's get you washed up, son."*

The shock hit Damian like a train running at full speed. That was the first time since his birth that Jeffery had ever been gentle or kind to him. Now Damian knew what he had to do. It should have been clear before, but the fact that it wasn't didn't matter now. Now... he was his father's son, and not some disgraceful outcast. He had a purpose. And it was all thanks to Tyler; his other half, his mysterious saviour.

They were starting to acknowledge him.

Two Clans Village, 2019

It didn't seem real. Only three months ago, Damian had met Tyler. Since then, Jeffery, his father, was training him for combat.

Now, things were beginning to culminate.

New Years Eve, 2019

The perfect final test seemed to fall right into Jeffery's lap: a hostage situation in a police station—forty-two hostages; thirty-eight cops and four civilians held captive by fifty-seven prisoners that had managed to break out of their holding cells. Three more hostages had already been killed, sent running from the front entrance only to be gunned down in front of a large crowd that had formed a wide semi-circle around the place, cordoned off by police barricades.

It was ten in the evening. As soon as Jeffery saw the news report, he took Damian and rushed to the scene and immediately took control of the situation, using his status as military commander to gain the upper hand over the police officers. Once the technicalities were over and done with, Jeffery immediately sent Damian in to save the hostages with nothing but a radio transmitter to receive Jeffery's orders and instructions. But Damian hesitated, and didn't cross over the barricade until Jeffery's orders escalated to shouting. When Jeffery started yelling, Damian quickly hopped the barricade into the open, into the view of a large group of wide-

eyed civilians that looked on in shock and disbelief.

A young boy walking into an inferno.

"Remember your training," Jeffery said over the radio.

Remember the training.

Damian took a deep breath and approached the building, stepping over the three dead hostage demonstrations sprawled out on the road.

Brrrrtttaaataatatttattaat!

And that's when the windows lit up, as if New Years was being celebrated a few hours early. Damian raised his hands, maintaining a blank expression on his face. The bullets bounced off the transparent shell that enclosed itself around him, following his movements as he pressed forward.

Shelter from the rain.

Damian made a pushing motion; an invisible force slammed the front doors inward off their hinges. Still maintaining his steady pace, Damian lumbered up the concrete stairs and entered the station.

Watch out for snakes.

A blur in the corner of his eye. Damian whirled around, caught a knife-wielding hand in his grip. An energy blade appeared in his free hand. He severed the arm from his attacker. The attacker shrieked as he fell back, blood spurting from the stump in his shoulder.

Always be on the lookout for falling trees or hidden predators.

A giant figure pounced. Damian nimbly dodged a wooden plank, which smacked against the floor. Then he thrust his blade into the tall, hulking figure and swung in an upward arc. More blood showered the ceiling. A severed head rolled through the air. Six and a half feet of hard muscle and thick limbs crashed to the floor.

He turned back to the first attacker, who was sitting with his back against the wall next to the double door entrance, and pointed his index finger at him, thumb raised.

Pew.

His thumb bent down on his fist. The tip of his index finger flashed for a moment. The attacker's legs buckled, then the portion of his head that wasn't just burned to nothing lolled forward.

Damian whirled around and dashed through the lobby, which narrowed into a corridor with closed doors on either side.

"Remember to watch your surroundings."

Thanks, dad.

Damian approached the first door on his right. He stared at the door. He gripped his sword tightly in a sweaty fist.

If you can't see the enemy, they're fleeing, in hiding, or preparing to strike. Get in their head. Where are they running? Where are they hiding? When are they going to—

CRASH!

The door splintered. Something huge fell through it and collapsed on top of Damian, pinning him to the floor. It was heavy and pudgy and its breath stank like a shit-eating wild animal as it held him down with a thick, hairy arm. Damian panicked, pushing his own arms up against the hand that was slowly bringing the tip of the knife closer to his face.

Disorient the tiger…

BLAMBLAMBLAM!

An energy pistol appeared in Damian's hand and he quickly drilled three tunnels through his attacker's gut. The attacker jolted, then his arm slackened.

…then disable its claws…

Damian shifted his head to the side, twisted his arm up, and fired another shot through the attacker's wrist, decimating the knife-wielding hand. The knife clacked against the concrete floor a few inches from his face.

…then break its teeth.

CRACK!

Damian quickly pressed his knees against his chest and launched his feet up into the attacker's jaw. He could hear the jawbone shattering and he could see a flurry of cracked teeth in the air as the attacker arced backwards.

Damian got up and kicked down the next door and found the room empty. The next three rooms were empty offices. The fourth room wasn't as empty. Two inmates were crouched behind the desk, blasting the door apart with their shotguns. Pumping and firing, pumping and firing; pellets and smoke sprayed out of the doorway. Damian pressed his back against the wall beside the door, waiting for the stream of pellets to end.

Clickclickclickclick!

Damian leaped into the open with two energy pistols in his hands, and opened up on the desk. Papers and pens and sparks and a computer flew up. The window behind the desk shattered and the blinds hanging over it were torn up and blown outside. Energy pellets punctured large holes through the desk as blood sprayed up from behind it. A headless body tumbled into view, sprawled out beside the overturned office chair. A pained shout rang out. The second gunner jumped into view, screaming as he clutched his bleeding hand, which only had his pinkie and his thumb still attached.

BLAM!

Crimson mist exploded from the second man's chest as he fell backwards through the tattered window blinds.

Don't leave a single stone unturned when searching for prey.

Damian moved to the next door and fired his twin pistols through it nonstop. He didn't even bother trying to open it. The window in the door shattered; the door itself crumbled into flying splinters and flakes of paint.

No need to reload. That's the beauty of telekinetic guns. You don't have to reload and you don't need to cock them or pull the slides. Best of all, they don't jam and there's no recoil to worry about. Even the heaviest cannon is light as a feather. It's all energy; expendable little bursts of energy.

Damian didn't stop shooting until the door was a pile of wood chips and the doorway was a gaping hole. The office itself was just as torn up as the door, with a single shredded body draped over the window sill, his blood dribbling down the wall. Damian moved on. Compared to what he'd seen in countries like Malawsian and Viceeper, this was nothing.

The last two offices were empty.

The corridor expanded to a larger room with a staircase leading to the second floor and the holding cells below. He went up the stairs, stopping on the landing to listen for any sounds before continuing his ascent to the second floor.

BRRRAAACKAAACCKKKAACCKKAAAKK!

The entire second floor erupted with the thunderous staccato of gunfire and muzzle flashes. Damian dived back to the landing, terror-struck by the sudden noise. Pecks of concrete and glass rained down on him as the rattle of machine guns roared in his ears.

If you can't reach them, smoke them out.

A ball of energy appeared in Damian's hands. He got up on one knee and hurled it at the top of the stairs. It vanished in the spray of bullets. Then a dark blue flash lit up the second floor, followed by a cacophonous BOOM.

The window strip across the second floor exploded. Civilians screamed and instinctively ducked, shielding themselves with their arms. Some people ran away. Police officers took cover behind their cruisers as flaming bits of inmates and debris showered the lot, but Jeffery stood his ground, watching the explosion behind dark sunglasses.

The side of his mouth curled upward slightly. He was pleased with the results so far.

Damian heard screaming when he opened his eyes. He aimed an energy assault rifle at the top of the stairs in his shaking hands.

He saw movement. A figure enveloped in black flames, wailing in agony, arms flailing. The man continued screaming even as he tumbled down the stairs. Damian jumped out of his path, and a second later the man fell on the landing and started flinging his arms and legs around, rolling back and forth like a turtle that had been flipped on its shell. He kept screaming as the flames devoured his body, melted through his flesh, clawed through his insides. He begged for it to stop, tried to vainly roll to put the flames out. Damian could only look on as the man rolled about, struggling to bat the flames away.

Then, like a spring, Damian leaped down the stairs. The man's screams and pleas followed him all the way into the basement. He tried to block it out. Tried to ignore it. But it was like the man's dying shrieks were stalking him, clinging to him like a horrendous odour. Even in the basement, he could hear it.

Remember to cook your kills thoroughly for a healthy meal.

Damian shook his head. No. This is different. It's a human, not an animal.

What's the difference?

Big *difference.*

Is there?

I think so…

They're all the same. Humans kill to survive. Animals kill to survive. It's all the same. Humans are just as monstrous as the monsters they live to kill. Is being human really different from being an animal?

It has to be. That's why human and Dehue lives are so precious. That's why it's hard to kill them. That's why it's so terrifying.

What makes them different?

What makes them human?

What* is *human?

The stairs dropped down to a dark, narrow corridor. Damian stumbled down the corridor, hugging his assault rifle like it was the only thing that protected him. He couldn't stop himself from shaking. The screaming upstairs continued echoing through the police station.

"Dad, I'm scared…"

"Keep going. You're not finished yet."

"But… I can't. I can't…!"

"Yes, you can. Remember your training."

"I remember it, but…"

"Or are you just a coward?"

Damian froze.

"You can do better than that. I didn't waste three months training you for you to run away from a fight. Keep going until all of them are dead."

Tears welled up in his eyes. "I… I… I don't… want to…"

"Don't embarrass me, Damian."

Damian gulped, sliding down the wall to the floor. Then he looked at his gun and started to sob hopelessly.

"This is your chance. This is your time. This is your moment of truth. On this day, you can prove to them all that you are not the cowardly, disgusting failure you were three months ago. Forget about your dog. Forget about your traitorous brother. Forget about those who abandoned you. You need not concern yourself with them. You must only remember the one person who didn't give up on you when everyone else did. Don't disappoint him. Don't throw away the opportunity."

Opportunity?

"...What... opportunity?" Damian asked.

"This is your chance to truly make me proud. Make your father proud, Damian Warkowski."

Damian's tearful eyes widened.

"My son."

Damian trembled. Then he got back up to his feet and pressed further down the corridor.

He turned the corner and kicked down the door of the holding room. There was a corridor with ten holding cells in total. Five hostage takers and one restrained hostage, a cop, stood in the corridor. A few light bulbs dangled from the ceiling.

Act fast. Riddle the jungle with bullets.

BANGBANGBANGBANG!

They fired at Damian with their Uzis and pistols. Something inside him snapped. It all happened too fast for him to completely register. His assault rifle exploded. He screamed, releasing all of his terror and rage in that one scream. Bits of flesh and gallons of blood splashed in every direction. Severed limbs twirled through the air and bounced across the blood-spattered floor. The room, once lit with white light, was now drenched in red light. Blood had gotten on the three light bulbs that swung loosely from the ceiling, saturating the room's light crimson.

Don't leave any prey alive.

Damian blinked. It was over in an instant. The place looked like a sausage factory dumped a days' worth of leftovers onto the floor.

Damian took one look and vomited his dinner. He gagged and coughed, falling on his hands and knees and sputtering over the expanding blood pond. The hostages in the holding cells looked on in disgust and horror.

When he was finished for sure, panting heavily, Damian concentrated on the cell doors. The bars of the holding cells glowed black and slid open. The hostages hesitantly filed out into the aisle. They sloshed through the gory mess Damian had made with panicked haste and rushed past him in an orderly fashion, disappearing down the corridor. Damian could hear their rapid footsteps clambering up the stairs.

Except for one.

Damian looked up—

BLAM!

--and was blown back from a bone-shattering punch in the shoulder.

Damian's shoulder was numb for a few seconds. One of the hostage cops kept his smoking pistol fixed on him.

Damian rolled onto his side just as the throbbing pain kicked in. He clutched his bleeding shoulder and curled up in the fetal position and cried out. The pain intensified, becoming even more unbearable than before. Tears streamed down his face as he yelled from the stabbing pain.

The cop's hands and pants were covered in blood, and his gun, a Heckler & Koch P7M8, glistened with a dark red coating. "You fucking little shit," the cop said bitterly, his voice cracking like glass. "Do you realize what you've done?"

Damian's body shook violently as he stared at the gun. Completely petrified. He could barely breathe. Couldn't even move.

"You just... rushed it... and shot them all down. My... my best friend was...! Didn't you see him before you started shooting into this room like some fucking amateur? Didn't you fucking see him?"

Damian breathed heavily, still staring at the gun with wide eyes.

The cop raised a black leather square. Then he opened it up with his thumb, revealing a police ID inside with the dead hostage's profile. Then the cop flicked the badge at Damian. The badge bounced off Damian's chest and flopped open. "You killed him as if he were one of them. My only friend... killed by a freak Dehue bastard little shit!"

BLAM!

The cop squeezed off another shot. Damian's right kneecap shattered. This time he felt the pain right away, threw his head back and let out an agonized howl at the top of his lungs.

"What's a boy doing here anyway?" the cop continued through gritted teeth. "Who in their right mind would send a kid *to save hostages?! Jesus. The world really is turning to shit."*

BLAMBLAM!

His stomach burned. He couldn't even scream anymore. Damian knew he was dying. He didn't want to but he was. The idea of fading away from life; fading into another world that the living can't see... terrified him

Chak!

The cop looked at the gun. The slide had locked back. "Shit," he muttered.

Enemy is confused. Now's the time.

Damian rolled so that both shoulders touched the wall behind him. Then he lurched forward on his hands and his good knee and pounced on the cop.

Tackle the enemy to the ground. Keep them from struggling.

The cop stumbled back, slipped on some gore, and fell into the murky human remains with a splash. Damian crawled on top of him and cupped his hands around his energy blade, raised it high above his head—

Stop 'em dead.

SPACCKK!

—and plunged it into the cop's stomach. And twisted it. And pushed it further and further up, slowly splitting the cop's chest open through the middle. A gurgling sound came out of the cop's open mouth as the blade sawed through his ribs. Blood spurted from the gash in his body, spattering against Damian's face and shirt.

Fillet it like a fish. Approximate cooking time: one hour. I hear salmon is nice this time of year.

Dinner is served.

Damian remembered sitting in his room, listening to a couple voices arguing angrily in the foyer. The argument lasted for about half an hour before Damian heard the front door slam shut. A minute later, Jeffery opened the door and entered the bedroom, finding Damian curled up on the far corner of his bed.

Jeffery closed the door without saying a word and sat on the edge of the bed and made a tent with his fingers. He stood his elbows up on his knees, still keeping his index fingers connected, and sighed wearily.

Damian was still curled up on the bed, his face burrowed in his knees.

Jeffery broke the minute-long silence, "That was the police chief in charge of the situation."

Damian didn't respond.

"He had quite a lot to say."

Damian still said nothing.

"How are your wounds? Already healed?"

"Yeah..."

"No point in my asking, I suppose."

Damian didn't reply.

"The police chief especially had a lot to say about those two cops in the holding cells."

"...I didn't mean to."

Jeffery glanced over his shoulder at Damian.

"I was just... just trying to save them... I didn't mean to."

Jeffery turned back to the bedroom door and stared at it as if it'd just insulted his intelligence. "It doesn't matter. They were just humans. Their deaths weren't a very significant loss anyway."

Damian looked at him in disbelief. "What...?"

"Humans are monsters. The less of them that exist, the better."

Damian eyebrows went up. "But..."

"Listen, son. Today was a test. Your final test. These past three months have been tough, I know... but I had to prepare you for the near future."

"What do you mean?"

Jeffery disconnected his fingers and reached into his jacket pocket. "The world you're so familiar with is going to end in a short matter of time. Things are going to change rapidly. You may feel as though you won't make it, won't survive, but trust me... you will. You have to live. You have to live for all of us, Damian."

"What's going to happen?"

"I don't know for sure." Jeffery took his hand from his pocket, hiding whatever it was he took out from Damian. "All I know is that there are very bad people looking to steal something crucial to our survival." Jeffery held up a large syringe filled with some sort of black liquid for Damian to see.

Damian reeled back from the horrific-looking syringe. "W-what's that for?"

"It's for you," Jeffery answered glumly, his eyes fixed on the syringe.

Damian started to tremble. "But why?!"

"It's necessary."

"How?!"

"The original formula is over a hundred years old. In fact, it was in development even before our own world fell apart and landed in this world. Do you know what it is?"

"N-no," Damian said.

"This is the work of countless generations in the Warkowski bloodline. Countless hours... days... weeks... months... years... generation after generation. And finally, after such a long, agonizing wait, it has reached perfection—no... it's become perfection *itself.*

"The Black Icarus project," he said as he turned toward Damian with the needle raised. "A power that no human—or vampire—can control. The power of a god." There was an ominous glimmer in Jeffery's eyes as he studied the syringe.

Damian blinked.

Jeffery looked at him again. "And now it's yours."

Present Day—The Scion's Wings

Damian opened his eyes and found himself staring up at a driver's license hanging over him. He blinked, staring at the profile of the man whose semi he'd stolen on the highway several hours earlier. The cab was dark and filled with the musty smell of beer and stale potato chips. A light blue blanket had been draped over him. He realized that he was naked under it.

Figures, he thought. *I ought to at least wear some regular boxers.* He groaned and sat up in the drivers' seat. His knee bumped the horn.

HONK!

He jumped at the sound. Something else jolted in front of him. He looked up and saw Jenny sitting on the cab's hood, peering through the windshield. He stared at her with raised eyebrows, surprised to see her. She looked equally as surprised, obviously startled by the sudden noise.

Her expression softened with a relieved smile. "So... you're finally awake. Had us goin' there for a while."

He scowled at her. "What're you talking about?"

"Your little stroke back there."

"Hunh? Stroke? I had a stroke?"

"You had *something*." Damian had just noticed that she had a beer can in her hand. She took a sip from it before continuing, "Kept going on about going with somebody or something. Flashbacks, I guess?"

It came back to him. He felt like he was trapped in the memory of being left behind by Carson. Seeing his dead brother in Scionia was like a shotgun blast to the chest. "*Tebya ne ebut, ti ne podmakhivai,*" he snapped.

"What?"

He grimaced. *Right.* "I said, 'mind your own fucking business.'"

Jenny drew away slightly, taken aback by his reply. "Don't need to be a dick about it, you know."

"Well, it's none of your fucking business," he repeated. "What're you doing here, anyway?"

"I felt like hanging around. Maybe offer you a beer." She held up a spare unopened beer and curved her hand around the windshield, handing him the beer through the driver's window. Damian looked at it and took it, and Jenny withdrew her hand. She was still staring at him, taking a few sips, watching him pull the tab and guzzle down the soft, foamy liquid. Surprisingly it was still cool.

"How long've you been here?"

"Not long. 'Bout fifteen minutes, maybe."

Damian paused. Then he asked, "How long have *I* been out?"

"Three or four hours. Another half-hour an' it'll be midnight."

Damian's eyes narrowed with suspicion. "Why're you being so nice to me all of a sudden?"

"'All of a sudden,' he says." Jenny scoffed. "Like offering you a place to stay despite your suspicious qualities is an act of aggression or something."

Damian rolled his eyes, but he knew she had a point there. "Alright, fine. Thanks, I guess. But wait… did you look under this blanket or something? Maybe *that's* why you're even nicer than before…"

"*NO,*" she said. Her face turned red. "*Hell* no! I mean, it was kinda hard *not* to see anything, considering how your clothes sorta just… *poofed* away and stuff… in the middle of the bridge." She turned away with embarrassment. "Aria put a blanket on you and threw you in here after that. You nearly gave Marner a heart attack."

"And what about you?" he asked with a half-smile, stealing

another sip from his beer.

"That's none of your business," she said quickly.

"Seen my package twice now and you've just started to get to know me. I dare you to critique it."

"Yeeeaaahhh, no. Not gonna happen." She scowled at him. "Don't think that just because I threatened your dick with a pair of scissors and gave you a beer, I'm gonna sleep with you."

Damian raised an eyebrow. "...Wait, *are* you?"

"NO!"

"Oh." He sounded disappointed and she caught it.

"Why in the hell would I do that? You're a pervert!"

Damian snickered. "Can't blame me for trying."

"What?"

Damian opened the door and threw the blanket off. Jenny turned away, though looked back when she noticed that Damian's clothes had already materialized. She hopped off the hood and followed him to the back of the trailer. "Where're you going?"

"Getting a snack," he answered as he reached the back and telekinetically threw the doors open. Inside was a glorious mountain of waffle boxes, maple syrup, chip bags, and 24-packs of Broweiser beer. Damian imagined a heavenly choir singing in his head. "Just lookit that. It's glorious."

Jenny glanced inside and smirked.

Damian noticed and asked, "What?"

"This isn't a refrigerated trailer," she said. "Those waffles are probably bad now. And all that beer is most likely warm."

Damian clambered into the trailer and replied, "That's bullshit. No way that'll happen."

"Why not?"

"My waffles aren't allowed to get soiled until I shit them out."

Jenny scoffed and rolled her eyes. She crossed her arms and watched as he crawled on his hands and knees toward the pile. "You're lookin' kinda pathetic right now."

"Shut up."

"Just saying."

Damian sifted through the waffle boxes and chip bags and syrup bottles. He picked up a box of waffles and stared at it. Then he threw it at the wall and swore.

The side of Jenny's mouth curled upward before she took

another gulp from her beer. "Toldja."

"I said shut up, goddamn it." His head drooped low as he released a heavy sigh. "Damn."

"Well at least the syrup, beer, and chips are still good."

Damian's narrow, agitated eyes turned to her, looking over his shoulder. He stared at her for a few moments of silence. Jenny could just barely make out the rest of his exhausted scowl behind his shoulder. "Fuck you," he said.

Jenny shrugged her left shoulder and took another sip. Damian turned back to the pile and grabbed a bag of dill pickle-flavoured nachos. "Don't throw another tantrum" she said calmly.

"I'm too tired to blow you up right now."

"I guess you forgot that you took the bomb out of my stomach, too."

He twisted his head toward her with alarm. "I did?"

"Um, yeah."

"Fuck." He turned back around.

"You're really out of it right now, aren't you?"

Damian ripped open the chip bag and started munching away, his back still facing her.

"Uh," Jenny stuttered. She cleared her throat and asked, "Hey, can you pass me a four-cheese flavour?"

Damian didn't reply. He just continued munching away.

Jenny frowned. "HEY!"

"*What*?" Damian asked irritably. "I'm eating."

"Chips. Four-cheese flavour. Please and thank you. Now."

Damian sighed. A black orb glowed faintly in the trailer as it floated toward Jenny. When it reached her, it vanished and a bag of four-cheese flavoured nachos fell into her hands. "Satisfied?" he asked.

Jenny climbed into the trailer and sat against the wall, her leg dangling over the side. She ripped the bag open, the fresh smell of marble cheese and tortilla blew into her face like a soft breeze. She looked at his back. He sat cross-legged on the floor, eating his nachos in silence, but Jenny knew he was tense and vigilant, as if he was expecting her to attack him. The walls of the trailer rang with the crunching sounds of him eating. "What was your life like before the war?"

Damian stopped chewing and bristled. Beat. Jenny thought

she'd struck a nerve.

"What?" he asked over his shoulder.

"What was your life like before all of this shit?"

"None of your business," he snapped.

"Okay." Jenny scowled. "Don't need to be a prick about it."

"Word of advice, Jenny." He stood up and approached the trailer exit, stopping right in front of her. She tucked her feet closer to her chest, staring at him. "We don't need people like you shoving their noses where they don't belong."

"Who's 'we'?" she asked with a raised eyebrow.

Damian blinked, eyes wide. "I… I meant, like… you know, everybody onboard."

"Most of the crew members were already friends to begin with. Well, sorta…"

"Shut up."

"What're you hidin'?"

"Nothin'. Don't worry about it."

"No, I think I will."

"Fine. Go ahead and worry—"

"What'd you do to Marner?"

Damian looked at her again. She casually took a sip from her can. "Marner? What?"

"She left the lounge lookin' pretty pale. I thought I heard her throwing up, too."

"I didn't do a damn thing to her."

"Sure you didn't."

"I didn't!"

"Riiiiiight. You did *something* to her. What'd you tell her?"

"I didn't say anything that would make her throw up, nor did I *do* anything to make her throw up. She probably ate some rotten fruit for breakfast or something!"

Jenny stood up, glaring at him, dropping the bag of chips. "One thing you should know, Damian: don't fuck with me, and I won't fuck with you. The same thing applies to my friends—"

"Yeah, yeah, I've heard that one before."

"I'm telling you not to fuck with me or my friends!"

"I know that!" he shouted. "And I'm telling you I didn't do a goddamn thing to her!"

"If you're lying—"

"I'm not lying. If I did something I would've already told you, and then I would've told you to leave me the fuck alone."

"I know you did *something*! So spill it!"

In a surge of anger Damian grabbed her jacket by the collar and slammed her back against the wall. Her beer can fell out of the trailer and bounced across the hanger floor, spilling beer through the grated tiles. She froze, looking at him with startled eyes, unsure whether she should be feeling fear or maintaining her defiance. Damian moved his face close, just inches away from her, his cold eyes boring into hers like icicles. And he said in a low, threatening tone, "Listen real close, and listen good: I didn't do anything to Marner. Maybe you've forgotten—but seeing as how you're her best friend and have known her for six years, you shouldn't have—but she is a ghost whisperer. She and I have that much in common. We see dead people. We see things people shouldn't be able to see. Did you even stop to consider for a fuckin' second that maybe, just *maybe*, she saw something else that had *nothing* to do with me at all that made her react like that?"

Jenny trembled, both hands grasping the strong arm that pinned her to the wall.

"People are always blaming me for every little thing," he growled. "'Oh, there are starving children in third world countries! It must be the Dead Blue's fault!' 'Damian caused me to miss the asteroid that destroyed my fleet!' 'I spilled my fucking beer all over my trousers because Damian nudged my shoulder.' 'I missed the toilet because I heard Damian masturbating in the next stall and it distracted me.' *Which*, by the way, is *not* true!

"But it's really starting to piss me off. And I'd appreciate it if you just kept you mouth shut. I said I didn't do it. I *didn't do it*." His voice escalated to a yell, making her jump, "Stop fucking pestering me about it!"

Get a hold of yourself, Jenny.

Jenny took a deep breath. Then she swatted his arm away and glared at him with newfound defiance. "Don't bully me."

"Or else what? What're you gonna do?"

"I'm gonna kick your ass, is what."

"Ooooohhhh, I'm shaking in my comfortable telekinetic leather war boots."

Jenny smirked. "You don't scare me."

"That's a lie."

"No it isn't."

"Yes it is. I know I scare you because *I* scare me and *I'm* not afraid of anything."

Jenny raised an eyebrow. "What?"

Damian grinned. "You heard me."

Jenny knitted her eyebrows and continued her defiant stare.

K-chak!

Damian's eyebrows went up. Then he looked down at the Jericho pistol she had pressed against his crotch. "What the—"

"Back off," she barked. "Or I'll blast you a new vagina."

Damian stared at her, blinking a couple times, the surprise frozen on his face. Then he burst into a fit of laughter and stumbled against the opposite wall. "Jesus Christ! Now that is priceless! I like that line. Mind if I steal it?"

Jenny, who still had her gun trained on Damian, shrugged and said, "Go ahead."

"Where'd you get that gun anyway? Have you had it all this time, or…?"

"Picked it up off the sidewalk in Scionia and smuggled it onboard."

"Nice, nice." Damian chuckled and slipped out of the trailer, landing lightly on the grated floor. "Heehee… *that's* funny." He curled up the top of his chip bag and looked up at her with a smug grin. "You have a talent for talking your way outta shitty situations."

Jenny maintained her angry glare. She pushed the hammer back into the Jericho with her thumb, which she held at her side. "Yeah, thanks, I guess."

"Sorry. Guess I'm just a little tense right now." Damian half-saluted, half waved as he walked out of her sight. "Be seein' you."

When she knew he was gone, Jenny breathed a sigh of relief. *Jesus...* that *wasn't intimidating at all...*

As Damian walked away, he shuddered. *That bitch is fucking scary.*

Sky Japan

On the other side of the world, a vast island hovered in the night sky, detached from the surface of the earth. Resting on the floating landmass, or 'sky island,' as its type has been dubbed, was a city. The multi-coloured skyscrapers penetrated the thick canopy of rainclouds like an endless concrete jungle of light and noise.

The city of Sky Japan.

It was a world where neon-coloured signs written in the traditional Japanese kanji mixed with English hung at every corner and lit every street. It was a world of its own, with its flashing lights pulsing through to its core and causing the endless downpour of rain that crashed down on the thick rivers of cars and pedestrians to shimmer like a billion overlapping rainbows.

A fine example of deceitful beauty.

The Sekigahara District was one of the many areas consisting of mainly upper class penthouse suites, casinos, bath houses, mansions, grand hotels, and corporate buildings and commercial outlets.

One of the penthouse suites on the top floor had few lights on. The city's bright reflections shimmered off the tall windows of the suite. Most of the silk curtains were drawn, and a cantilever balcony was wrapped around three quarters of the suite.

Within its windows, a group of men socialized tensely in the living room. Five of them had suits, and stood around a nervous-looking man seated on one of the couches. The nervous man selected a biscuit off a plate on a rectangular glass coffee table, which stood in between his couch and its twin. Two trembling girls and one boy lay sprawled on the opposite couch, breathing weakly and drenched in sweat, struggling to maintain consciousness.

The pleasurable moans and yells of a girl rang out faintly through the suite from behind the closed door of the bedroom. Rhythmic thumping and squeaking could be heard, but the guards in black maintained their hardened expressions, keeping their sinister eyes on their nervous guest.

The moans got louder, and the girl screamed a variety of words and obscenities for a good minute or so. Shortly after, the thumping, moaning, and squeaking quickly died down, and all was silent. The nervous man started to shake. His teacup rattled on the saucer when he lifted it up to his mouth. He spilled some tea on his shirt, and slurped half of his tea before clumsily placing it back on the saucer on the coffee table.

The lock of the shoji door to the bedroom *clicked*, and the door slid open behind the guest's couch. A tall, broad-shouldered man in a yellow bathrobe exited the room and walked around the couch until his back faced the windows. His long shadow interrupted the multi-coloured patterns that danced across the living room floor and walls.

The man in the robe fixed his sadistic red eyes on his guest. He pointed at one of the children lying on the couch. He spoke in English, and nothing but. "Explain this, Mr. Takahashi."

The guest, Takahashi, looked at the sweating, panting children, then turned back to his host. He immediately broke into a cold sweat and replied in Japanese, "Multiplier, I… well, they're drugged."

"I see that, Mr. Takahashi," Multiplier replied coolly. "My question is: why? Why the fuck are you drugging my merchandise? Throughout the south side, there're more o' these kids getting fucked up on heroin and meth than I care to admit. My love hotels aren't making as much money down there, either. Are my kids getting uglier, or are you rippin' me off? Or both? You have two minutes to explain why." He jabbed a hostile forefinger at him. "Go."

"W-well, you see, sir, I-I just thought drugging them would reduce the risk of any kids attempting to escape or fight back. This way, we can keep our merchandise. They would be too screwed up to do anything we wouldn't want!"

Multiplier glanced over at the children, and then returned his gaze to Takahashi. "Do you know what drugs do to kids, Mr. Takahashi? They fuck kids up. And when they fuck kids up, they spread to fuck *more* kids up. And when they spread and fuck even more kids up, the *good* cops get involved. And when the good cops get involved, there's loss of business, income, and kids. And when there's loss of business, income, and kids, I get fucked. In short, Mr. Takahashi—" Multiplier took a step forward, drawing a cigarette from the breast pocket of his robe between his middle and index fingers, and shouted, "—I. Get. *fucked*! Do you understand me!? I want my kids to get out there and make me some money, not get addicted to this shit! Hell, some customers love it when they fight back. It makes the fight for dominance that much more satisfying. But now they might as well be fucking a backpack or a... a pair of socks! Why? Because of the crack you're giving them! Do you understand?! YOU STUPID ASSHOLE! The wrong people are getting fucked in this situation, Takahashi, and I don't fucking appreciate it!"

"Mr. Multiplier, I swear to you, I am forever loyal to you and you alone! I would never purposefully jeopardise your business! Never! I had the best intentions; I never thought—"

BLAM!

Multiplier whipped out a golden Desert Eagle and obliterated the drugged girl's skullcap with a single shot. Multiplier looked at Takahashi, who was totally horrified and slack-jawed, staring at the dead child slumped on the opposite couch in horror. The other two children weren't even aware of the act. "Oh, I'm sorry; did I break your concentration? Well, too goddamn bad. Your time is up. See these junkies stinkin' up my sofa here? They could've made me money. Unfortunately, they got their attractiveness and innocence sucked outta them by your so-called 'insurance.' How many more o' my kids've you fucked up with this shit?"

"T-twenty-five. Just the most… most rebellious-looking ones. Including the ones on this… c-couch."

Multiplier ran his fingers through his hair and exhaled through his nose sharply. "That's twenty-five kids I'm gonna have to throw in the gutter because of your retardation. You just took the homes of twenty-five kids away from them. You just completely fucked up twenty-five of my precious children's lives. How does that make you feel?"

Takahashi gulped and stuttered, "N-not very good…"

"NOT GOOD ENOUGH!" he shouted, making Takahashi jump. "You should be feeling like total shit right now! Total! Shit! You cost me money, man, and everybody knows that I don't like losing money." He cocked his head toward his bedroom, whistled sharply, and called out, "Annabelle!"

"Coming, Master!" A naked girl with her brown hair pinned back in a ponytail pranced out of the room and pressed her small, sickly thin body against Multiplier, moaning seductively.

Multiplier tousled her hair, stroked her cheek lovingly, and said, "Annabelle, have I ever given you drugs?"

"No, Master."

"And you've never thought about running away or starting shit, have you?"

"Not since Annabelle understood that she was born to be

yours." She ran her tongue up and down his arm.

"And when was that?" he asked with a perverted smile.

"Three months after Annabelle was brought here."

"And how do you feel now?"

"Annabelle's always hungry for Master. Mmmmm, Annabelle always touches herself thinking of you, Master."

'That's good, isn't it? Is there a place you'd rather be right now?"

"No, Master."

Multiplier looked at Takahashi and pointed at her. "See that? It's called progress. You don't need meth or heroin or that new Spiral Suicide shit to control a little bitch or a rebellious bastard you snatch from their room or a parked car or the sidewalk, or even the school. You just gotta show patience and understanding." He pushed Annabelle aside and said, "Go put some clothes on, you fucking little slut."

"Right away, Master!" She disappeared back into the room, and didn't even bother to close the door.

As Multiplier watched her dress herself, Takahashi said, "Mr. Multiplier, please… I've been working for you in this business for five years now. This… this is only my first mistake! Please!" Takahashi threw himself off the couch and bowed before Multiplier, just inches away from his feet. "Please forgive my foolishness!"

Multiplier twirled his gun around thoughtfully. "First mistake... last mistake."

BLAMBLAMBLAMBLAM!

Multiplier emptied his pistol on the last two children on the sofa. Takahashi shrieked in terror and bolted for the door, pushing through the security guards. He didn't get far; they hooked onto his arms and held him firmly as he struggled and screamed.

Multiplier sighed and tossed his empty Desert Eagle on the coffee table. He gestured toward the dead children lying on the bloodied sofa. "Take this trash out, gentlemen." He approached Takahashi, whom the guards turned around so he could look him in the eye. "As for this guy… hm… the butcher shop, maybe? No, no. I got it." With a smirk, he said, "I think we owe the Chop Suey Sisters another night of fun." He winked at the nearest bodyguard and snickered. Then he took a drag from his cigarette and said, "You know what to do. Get this sick, twisted motherfucker out of my goddamn sight."

Takahashi's screams escalated as the bodyguards dragged him to the door. "No! *NO*! You can't do this to me! Please! Multiplier! *MULTIPLIEEEERRR*!"

Multiplier continued to inhale the cigarette's toxic smoke. "Bye, now!"

Outside, a small, lone figure had perched himself on the rooftop ledge above the windows with an audio surveillance device hooked up to a waterproof headset. An electronic visor over his eyes translated all of the English words into his own language. The sleet of heavy rain dribbled over his dark blue kimono; the golden dragon ripping across his back shimmered, bathed in neon. He clutched tightly a sheathed katana in his hands, readying himself for an attack.

"No," Kira's voice ordered in the headset. "Wait, my son. We must know if he has our family with him. This is strictly a surveillance mission."

"Understood," Akira replied quietly.

Multiplier snatched his cell phone out of his pocket and dialled a number. He flopped on the couch Takahashi had been sitting on with the phone to his ear, patiently listening to the call being patched through. He exhaled cigarette smoke from his lungs and propped his feet up on the table.

Click!

Kyo answered in Japanese, "Hello? Who is this?"

Multiplier responded in Japanese, "Hello, Kyo Kuma."

"…Multiplier…"

"Guess what I have?"

"…What?"

"I found three beautiful-looking children in a sex shop downtown the other day. They kind of looked like yours. Unfortunately, one of them got away before we had our fun with him, but at least we got the other two safe and sound. I hear you killed Yuen Kwey earlier today at his shop. Tsk, tsk. Yes, Kwey played a key role in the kidnapping, but damn, you really tore him a new asshole. Guess the little one told all, huh?" After a brief period of silence, Multiplier continued, "Anyway, they looked lonely so I thought I'd… well, you know…"

Kyo exploded with rage, "You bastard…! Tell me where they are, before I—"

"Ah, ah, ah! You're in no position to make threats or demands. I'm seriously considering auctioning your eldest daughter and son off to Boss Kakashi, as a little tribute. Unless, of course, you can persuade me to act differently…"

"…What do you want?"

"Fifty billion yen in cold, hard cash."

"T-that's preposterous!"

Multiplier chuckled. "Well, unfortunately I found Yuya and Masuko when some stupid redhead bitch decided to try and run my business into the ground while I was just beginning my expansion, so I'm afraid I need the money to compensate. Yours should do fine."

"You… you…!"

"Of course, if you are unable to pay, I'm sure I'll get more than a few pretty pennies for your beloved heirs."

"How dare you…! Do you know what you are doing!? Interfering in a war like this!?"

"Oh, quite aware. Too bad there isn't a damn thing you can do to stop me. It's only fifty billion yen. I expect it in a week. Save this number in your contacts or whatever the fuck you do to keep in touch with people and call me in exactly one week with the location you'd prefer the deal to go down. And don't forget the money. Bring along any allies or cops, though, and I'll see to it that you never see your children again."

Click!

The boy on the roof started to chew his bottom lip in frustration. "What now, father?"

Silence. The boy listened to the pitter-patter of the rain, patiently awaiting his father's answer.

"…I hear a certain someone is out making trouble again these days. We will recruit the one man who may be able to help us… for a price. But I feel that he may need some drastic convincing."

"No... you can't mean..."

"…Yes... we will recruit the Dead Blue."

COBALT ROGUE, VOL. 1: THE DEAD BLUE

Episode 009

Hot Spring Visitation

Saturday, October 3rd, 2026

Only two Copter Ships drifted across the midnight clouds. The rest of Matthew's clan had retreated to a different location, but Matthew, claiming he still owed Jeremy a debt, decided to go along with Jeremy and the others. He was too stubborn to accept any other option.

Damian lounged on the roof of the *Scion's Wings* with a can of Broweiser beer in his hand, looking up at the dark clouds passing over him in silence. He enjoyed the feeling of the cold night breeze brushing through his hair. He enjoyed being alone now. Before the war, he couldn't stand the thought of being alone for a second. But now, Tyler was all he needed.

Him and his saviour.

Creak!

Damian glanced over his shoulder to see Jenny's head poking out of the hatch. She looked straight at him and said, "Hey."

"Hey," he replied, turning back around. *You again?*

"This spot taken?"

"Yeah, scram."

"What're you doin'?"

"Drinking lots of beer."

"Oh."

"Yeah, something you couldn't handle."

"You're being funny, hunh?"

CLATTER!

Damian flinched when she dropped a full 24-pack of Broweiser beside him. Then she sat down on the other side of the case and took a can for herself, pulled the tab, and—much to Damian's surprise—chugged down the whole can in five seconds flat. She finished with a satisfied sigh and tossed the empty can over her shoulder. She looked at him smugly and wiped her mouth on her jacket sleeve. "You look surprised."

Damian looked away from her, back up at the clouds, and took another gulp. "I'm not surprised," he lied. "I am Jack's complete lack of surprise."

Jenny doggedly replied, "Sure, sure. Hate to break it to you, but nowadays most ten-year-olds can out-drink their grandparents. While you were busy sleeping in that thing, I was busy partying and punching out perverts who tried to take advantage of me whenever I got drunk."

"I see. Partying, huh?"

"Yup."

"No wonder you dress like a slut."

"Pfft. That's not it at all."

"Oh, really? You don't have a particular reason why you're dressed like that?"

She gave him a mockingly seductive smile, leaned back, and playfully shook her well-endowed chest back and forth.

Damian was surprised by her suddenly acting like this. Then he remembered she was already drinking when he woke up. "You're drunk, aren't you?" he asked.

"Eh. Well, that might be one reason why I dress like this. To pick up guys, I mean."

"Any luck?" He slurped his beer, sneaking a sideways glance at her chest. *And yet she goes on about hating perverted guys… with a chest like* that *it's no wonder…*

She shrugged. "Only perverts who wanna get in my pants. All they wanted were one-night stands and nothin' else."

"…So, from my understanding, Tim was one of the exceptions?"

"Tim wasn't a douche at first. It's just… when we… well, you know… did it, he sort of turned into a man-whore."

"Oh?"

"…Yeah. Came home one day and found him in bed with my best friend—"

"Who the fuck? Marner?"

"*No*, not Marner. Marner wouldn't do that. Some bitch named Sharon. She was one of Aria's business partners before she died last year." She took another can and pulled the tab, listening to the air hiss from the can. "So what was with your little spaz attack today?"

"*That* again?"

"You went crazy all of a sudden and started babbling about going with someone."

He looked at her. She took a gulp from her can, keeping her curious eyes fixed on him. He glanced forward again. "Like I said before; it's none of your business."

"Fine, whatever."

"Why do you wanna know?"

"Are you kidding? After an outburst like *that* who wouldn't wanna know?"

Damian sighed. "Good point." He took another mouthful from the can.

"…So… you gonna tell me? Or keep it bottled up?"

"Nosy, aren't we?"

"I prefer the term 'curious'."

"Well be]curious' elsewhere."

"I know everybody else. Well, except Jeremy, but he didn't kill off so many people way back then."

"I don't particularly enjoy being reminded of that," he said.

"Oh." More silence. She finished her second can, and took yet another one. "Zero called today."

Damian looked at her.

She noticed the recognition in his eyes. "Oh, you know 'im, do you?"

"Zero Fraden? The general?"

"Well, he's not a general anymore. He got demoted. But yeah, you're thinking of the right guy. He adopted Aria and I after the war… took us in… gave us a home and a school and friends to talk to. We owe him our lives."

"Sounds like Zero," he said. "He saved me once."

She stared at him, waiting for his story.

Instead, he asked, "So what'd he want?"

With a disappointed sigh, she said, "Well, he just wanted to know what happened."

"Did you tell him about the bomb?"

"I hate that I had to lie to him and tell him I've still got it."

Damian burst into a snickering fit, spilling some beer on the rooftop.

"What's so funny?"

He looked at her with a purposefully creepy, wide-eyed grin.

"I'm inside you. PFFFT—"

She smacked the back of his head. "Knock it off, you perv."

He frowned and rubbed the back of his head.

Jenny glanced at him curiously. "So what's it like?"

"What's *what* like?" he asked with a little annoyance.

"Being awake after six years. It's exhausting, right?"

"Not really. It's like waking up from a long nap. I've noticed though that my powers need recharging. And taking their sweet time doing it. It sucks. One would think that six years was long enough."

"Ah," she said, opening her fourth beer for the evening.

"You're gonna get sick if you keep drinking that so fast."

"Oh, do I sense a hint of concern?" She chuckled. "Relax. Only pussies get sick from drinking beer so fast."

Damian scowled. He didn't particularly enjoy being talked down to by anyone; especially a girl. She was on her—at least—fourth can and he hadn't even finished his second.

Bothered by the thought, he gulped down the last half of his beer in two swigs and quickly grabbed another one.

"Do you hate being alone?"

"…No. Why do you ask?"

"I hate being alone. I guess war just affects us differently."

"'Us'?"

"Yeah, 'us'. We all went through the same thing—"

"No we didn't. You never went through what I went through. Don't ever say you've got it all bad, when you don't. Start complaining, and I'm gonna have to share some nasty stories that will make you lose a few nights of sleep."

She stared at him. "You. Have. Issues."

He picked up another can and snapped the tab off. "Right… and you don't?"

"Of course I do. Everybody has their own issues. I'm not the judgmental type."

"That's a laugh. A teenage girl who isn't judgmental."

"Hey—"

"I have a question for *you* now."

"Hm?"

"Why are you suddenly so talkative?"

"No reason whatsoever." She looked at her can. "Buzzed...?"

Damian gulped down a mouthful. "You didn't talk this much

before with everyone else around. Why're you talking to me?" His eyes narrowed. "Wasn't that interrogation enough for you?"

"I just figured you wanted to talk to someone."

"Sounds pretty fuckin' fishy to me."

"Yeah, well, you're paranoid as hell."

Damian turned away from her, still sipping his beer. "Is that all?"

"Nope. Also wanted to know more about you."

"I didn't realize I was so intriguing to you people."

Jenny scoffed. "Of course you're not. Get your head out of your ass. I just don't wanna be flying in the sky with a lunatic."

"I'm sticking with the penis theory."

"We're not bringing that up again."

"Fine, whatever."

"Answer my question."

"I'll tell you something: I'm an amazing person who shouldn't be fucked with."

"We all know you're a narcissist."

"Lies."

"Deny it all you want."

"I shall."

Brief, sweet silence.

"So *are* you a lunatic?" she asked.

"What?"

"A lunatic," she repeated patiently.

"Maybe I am, maybe I'm not. I guess you won't really know until you wake up one night with my gun barrel shoved down your throat."

"So you're gonna be a smartass about it now, huh?" Her eyes narrowed. "*Which* gun barrel are you referring to?"

"Not the rapey kind, I'm telling you that right fuckin' now." He continued drinking at his leisure until the can was empty. Then he tossed it over his shoulder and grabbed another one, amazed by how long Jenny was quietly doing the same.

Now on her—supposedly—fifth can, Jenny looked at him and said, "What's your beef with Tim?"

Sure doesn't stay on one topic long, does she? "He's an asshole."

"I already knew that… I dated him for a while, remember?"

"He and I had a… *disagreement* in the middle of the war."

"Wow, you guys knew each other *that* long?"

"Sort of. We weren't close, like brothers or anything. We just knew each other, until everything went to hell and we ended up fighting."

"How'd everything go to hell?"

Damian shook his head and took a swig from his can. "Forget it."

"No, tell me." Damian looked at her with uncertainty. She realized she was a little too pushy, and she looked ahead and said, "Sorry. It's none of my business."

"It's fine. I forgive you."

You act like I had *to apologize,* she thought, glancing sideways at him. "So what do you wanna talk about?"

"…You're not gonna leave until we're something like friends, are you?"

"Nope."

"I thought you didn't trust guys."

"I don't. That's why I'm asking so many questions."

"Oh, *now* I get it. …Something like friends, huh?"

"We're not gonna be friends with benefits. I'm telling you that right now."

Damian blinked, giving her an oblivious, innocent stare.

"Don't give me that look, Damian Warkowski. I could see it in those pervy blue eyes." There was a playful note in her voice and a knowing smile on her face.

"Whatever. Think what you like. You know you want me."

Her eyes moved from his feet to his face a couple times, then she turned away from him and sipped her beer. "Not interested in you in that way."

"I don't care anyway."

"Good. What's your favourite movie?"

"What?"

"Your favourite movie?" she repeated.

"Hmmm. I've only seen a handful of movies in my childhood," he replied. "*Hard-Boiled*, maybe. That John Woo movie. Or *First Blood Part II*."

She snorted and burst into laughter. "WHAT?!"

"They're two-hour movies, but about an hour and a half of

them are all gunfights. Coolest movies ever." He knew she wasn't going to be satisfied until he threw the question back at her. He did, to make his life a little easier, "What's yours?"

"*True Romance*. You know, that movie with that call girl and her comic book store clerk lover... guy? And like, they get this suitcase thinking it's the call girl's stuff, but it's actually heroin, and Christopher Walken gets pissed off and sends a bunch of guys after them."

"Uh-huh."

"It's a good movie."

"Right."

"I love movies. I have a huge collection at home."

"Really? What, like a big movie fanatic? What do they call them? Cinephiles?" He took another swig from his beer. "Movie otakus?"

"I don't really go by a term… but if I did it wouldn't be 'cinephile.'"

"Why not?"

"Because it makes me sound like a movie rapist."

Damian shrugged his left shoulder. "Fair enough."

"You have a favourite band?"

It's like she rehearses these freaking questions. "No," he answered out loud.

"Favourite movie star?" she asked, talking a sip of beer.

"Only porn stars. Ashley Brooklyn."

She spat out her beer, coughed and wheezed, "Wrong… windpipe! *Hack*!"

"Haha."

"That's not funny."

"It is for me."

"Whatever, you dick."

"I was kidding."

"Yeah, right."

Damian looked at her hands. "So why do you always wear gloves? Come to think of it, your sister wears them, too." Jenny paused for a brief moment, and looked at her hands with a solemn look on her face, as if she'd remembered something she wanted to forget. Damian knew he triggered something. *Whoa, I finally shut her up.*

When she finally answered, she said, “No reason. Don’t worry about it. What’s with that hair?”

“What about my hair?” he asked defensively.

What’s he all defensive about?! It’s just hair! “Well,” she said aloud, “it just looks unique so I thought I’d comment on it.”

“Comment on it *how*?”

Jenny hesitated and thought quickly and carefully before she answered. “On... how... awesome it looks. Seriously, it kicks ass.”

“Good,” said Damian, oblivious to her sarcasm. “My hair looks even better after a shower, although even *that* much zombie blood couldn’t possibly ruin my appearance. After taking two showers, then sitting up here with some beer and a light breeze, I feel refreshed.”

“Would it ruin mine?”

“Would what ruin what?”

“Do you think zombie blood would ruin my hair?”

“Of course it would,” he said bluntly. Then, taking the deadpan misogynist approach, Damian added, “The only things you’ve got going for you are your body and your pretty face. So if you don’t take care of them you’ll just be acknowledged as a skank who’s both annoying and ugly.” *Now leave. Leave in disgust, and don’t ever talk to me again.*

Well aren’t you the biggest asshole ever. Jenny was starting to get agitated by his replies. “That was more than a little uncalled for.”

“Oh.”

“Don’t you look for personality in a girl?”

“I’ve only known you for a day or so. So far there isn’t much to know.”

“Well…! You never ask about the good stuff.”

Damian looked at her chest again. His eyes quickly jumped up to her scowl. “You mean there’s something *good* inside as well?”

“*Yes*, you jerk!”

He shrugged his right shoulder. “Fine, then. What… um… you know what, you start explaining. I hate asking questions when it doesn’t involve asking people if they want to live.”

“Alright, then.” She cleared her throat. “My favourite movie—well, you already know that. I lack self-respect. I’m very honest for the most part. This jacket used to be my dad’s. It was one of the only things that came back from his involvement in the war. I always wear it. I'm... um... a masochist, I guess." She turned away, knowing that her cheeks were reddening.

"What the hell's a masochist?" he asked, oblivious.

"Never you fucking mind. Anyway, my favourite food is pizza. My, um... favourite drink? Uuuh, cream soda. I have a shitty temper; especially towards boys."

"Why is that?"

"I'm not telling you that, either. It's kind of, um... kind of a touchy subject."

"'Touchy' how?" Damian paused. "Did you get raped or something?"

She went stiff. Damian thought he literally heard something *snap*. She glared at him. "You know what? Fuck you. You might be cute an' all, but you've got waaayyy too much baggage."

Damian blinked, once again surprised by her swinging temperament.

"Not to mention, you are *fucked* in the head, asshole!"

"Oh, *I'm* fucked, huh?" Damian snapped back. "At least I'm not a little cunt who wants to bang every handsome guy she meets!"

"I'm not a cunt, you dick waffle freak! And I don't want to fuck every guy I meet! I don't even wanna fuck *you*, you fucking... fucking... SHIT-FACED DICK-SWALLOWING *FUCK*!"

"Keep 'em comin', *sooka*!"

"In fact I just wanted to be your friend, or you know—"

"'*Something* like it,'" Damian interrupted. "Right?!"

"Shut up," she barked. "Freak!"

He stood up and loomed over her menacingly, grabbing her by the jacket. "I'm a *freak* now, huh?!"

"Yeah, your chance is gone, dipshit!"

"Do you realize how much freakin' shit I'm about to beat out of you?! Do you have any fucking idea!?"

She jumped up to her feet. Their foreheads collided, sending Damian stumbling backward. "Bring it, you freakish bitch!"

Damian regained his footing quicker than she'd expected. His temper exploded. "You... fucking cunt!" He lunged forward and punched her in the face. Then he grabbed her by the hair and slammed her head down on the Fate Star tile. She bounced, then rolled on her back and drove her foot into his stomach.

"OOFF!" He landed on his back. Hard.

With a furious shout she pounced on him and started pounding his face against the tiled roof with her fists. It felt like someone was beating his face with a sledgehammer; he was completely shocked by her strength. "FUUUUUUUCK!" he roared. "STOP HITTING ME!"

He grabbed her wrists and squeezed. She struggled to get free and slammed her forehead into his left eye. They rolled across the deck—punching, kicking, scratching, and swearing—until they hit the side of an outdoor air conditioning unit with Damian on top of Jenny. His hands wrapped around her throat, his thumbs pushing inward. She choked and struggled.

WHACK!

She slammed her fists against his ears. Felt like she cracked his skull. He recoiled; his ears rang at a deafening pitch. She kicked him off of her, rolled backwards onto her hands and knees, and took a few seconds to gasp for air. She looked up.

SMASH!

Damian threw the case of beer down on her, slamming her to the floor. The cardboard box broke apart and beer sprayed out everywhere as ruptured tin cans spilled onto the Fate Star tiles. Then he kicked her against the air conditioning unit, denting it. He kicked her in the face. Then in the stomach; she vomited flecks of blood onto the deck. He swung his leg for another kick, but she caught him by the ankle with her teeth and bit down through his pants, breaking skin.

"*OW*, goddamn it!" Damian yelped and jumped back. "Fuck!"

Jenny wiped blood from her lips and stood upright. Then she spat more blood to her left and wiped her mouth again, glaring at him with fierce blue eyes. Chests heaving, readying themselves for another round. "Whatsamatter?" she asked. "You surprised that a girl is kicking your ass?"

"Pfft. *I'm* kicking *your* ass," he replied with an angry sneer. His head was still spinning. Blood kept filling his mouth and trickled down his chin.

"Yeah, right," she replied mockingly. "I can almost see real bullshit coming out of your mouth."

"I don't eat shit, bitch."

"Then what's spilling all over the deck?"

Damian's eyebrows fell. "You think you're funny?"

"I *am* funny," she said with a snarky giggle. "Sometimes I just crack myself up."

Damian gave her a menacing grin. There was a hint of maniacal sadism in his eyes as he cracked his knuckles. "How 'bout I crack the rest of you up?"

She raised her fists. Her middle fingers popped up, and she shook them around. "Oooohh, I'm *so* scared! What'cha gonna do, freak show? Bitch me to death?"

"THAT'S IT!" He charged at her.

"BRING IT, YOU COBALT WHORE!"

He became a blur; next thing she noticed was his fist in her stomach, then an uppercut that sent her reeling. She quickly recovered, vision faded slightly, imbalanced. She saw him charging toward her like a raging bull. She dodged and grappled him in an underhook. He jabbed her ribs numerous times, but she didn't break. She kneed him in the face, spun him around, and slammed him to the ground. He rolled into a crouch, but Jenny tackled him again before he could act.

Like a repeat of before, they rolled aft across the deck. They broke up. Damian kicked her on her stomach and started bashing her face into the deck three times before she countered with a backwards elbow to the throat. "GUCK!" Then she whirled around, face bloody and bruised, and cracked her knuckles across his jaw, snapping his head back. Damian staggered, spat blood to the side. "You fucking little bitch—"

WHACK!

Her fist caught him in the face. He twirled, stumbled in a half-dive. She snatched the back of his jacket, pulled, and threw him to the deck. Then she stomped on his chest, and then his face, and raised her foot again. Damian blocked the third drop of her foot, grabbed it, and twisted it. With a surprised shout, she fell on top of him. He reached for her face.

She pinned both his hands to the deck with her foot and her right hand and started choking him with her left hand. She was leaning forward, crouched on his wrists. It felt like her shoe was flattening his left ankle. She squeezed his right hand. Crouched awkwardly, trying to put all her weight on the hand that had his neck. Her balance was anything but sturdy.

His knee jammed into her spine, causing her to yelp and fall forward. Her left leg slipped and her head—

"MMMPH?!"

Shockingly enough, their lips touched. They bristled, staring into each other's wide eyes in disbelief, but their lips didn't part just yet.

She separated from him and raised her head. Her jaw remained slack. Eyes wide. Heart pounding like a war drum. Flustered, she wiped a bit of blood and saliva off her chin and placed her hand over her mouth. "Umm…"

Damian sat up abruptly and kissed her again. She didn't fight him. Didn't want to. Instead she draped her arms over his shoulders and pressed her body against his chest. She tightened her legs around him. He wrapped his right arm around the small of her back and held her close as their kissing escalated heatedly. His left hand glided up her waist, her ribs, her breast...

"You fucker," she breathed.

He broke off for a moment, looking at her.

She frowned. "I didn't tell you to stop."

They kissed again.

She let him slip his hands under her top, and she released a soft moan when he started squeezing her breasts roughly. Her breathing grew heavy and ragged as she ran her fingers through his hair. Her fingers clenched when his thumbs toyed with her nipples. "Ah..."

Then he pushed her on the floor and climbed on top of her, pinning her down and lifting her top, all while she kept her legs wrapped tightly around his waist, squeezing him, constricting him.

"Wait." Damian stopped and sat up, stared at her with uncertainty.

"What's wrong?" she panted, still lying on the floor with her arms spread out. She didn't even make an attempt to cover her exposed breasts, which were touched by a few droplets of blood from his face. Her own face looked like it had been assaulted with a glass bottle.

"We're drunk or some shit." He wiped blood off his forehead with his sleeve and looked at it with scrunched-together eyebrows.

"So? Are you gonna go on about how drunkenness affects our thinking? I hope not. All this fighting's got me too hot for thinking straight."

"Weren't you the one bitching about guys getting in your pants?" He smirked. "And here I thought you were much more sensible than that."

"Do I *look* like a sensible person to you?"

"No."

"What, you don't wanna...?"

"No, no. I think I figured out what a masochist is just now."

Jenny smiled, nearly laughed. "Shut up and fuck me."

He touched her breasts again and pushed down lightly. She moaned; it was a tiny, pleasurable squeak. Then she smiled again with rosy cheeks. It was more than enough to set him off. "Don't need to tell me twice."

And then he went down on her.

That escalated quickly...

"No shit," she said.

"Stop doing that."

Spring Islands, Later that October 3rd Morning

The Spring Islands were a small cluster of tropical islands located in the South Gomai Sea, veined by canals and connected by a simple system of bridges. The small fishing port called Rain Harbour took up three quarters of the Spring Islands. The rest of the tropical habitat was left untouched, with the exception of a Kyoko-style hot spring resort called the Palm Tree Onsen, which resembled a Chinese castle from the Feudal Age.

The two ships arrived at ten in the morning, with a designated co-pilot landing *The Spartan* in a grassy field. The *Scion's Wings* landed nearby in the cover of the dense tropical foliage.

Matthew's clan members gathered with him and his crew to discuss how things would go for them. Jeremy's crew ran maintenance checks on the ship, while Aria, Marner, and Jeremy sat in the lounge eating their breakfast.

"Say," said Aria as she bit into a piece of toast, "where's Jenny?"

Jenny moaned and turned over on the deck. Golden rays of sunlight shone down on her, causing her skin to shine radiantly. Her clothes were loosened up and her hair was a jumbled mess. She only had one shoe on; one of her pant legs were rolled up above her knee and her belt buckle was undone, her pants were unzipped and pulled down to her thighs, revealing her pinkish strawberry panties (which were on crooked). Her top twisted around her collar, her well-endowed chest exposed to the sky. She only had one arm in her jacket and she was unwittingly clutching her other shoe in the hand that wasn't poking out of her jacket sleeve.

"Mmmm…"

She rolled over again and hit something. She cracked her right eye open and found herself staring at Damian's closed eyelids and catching a whiff of his breath, which smelled like beer. A throbbing pang in her head welcomed her back into the real world. She groaned and turned over again. "*Unnnnghhh…* Shit. Shit. Shit. Shit."

She froze, now realizing that something was very *wrong*.

She quickly turned back over and stared at Damian. He lay on his side. His clothes were nowhere to be found. He muttered things that she preferred to ignore for the most part.

Oh God, don't tell me I... I... NONONONONONOOOOO. She pulled her top down and readjusted the rest of her clothing post-haste. With her index finger, she poked his cheek. Then she poked him again. His face twitched slightly and he mumbled something in Russian: "*Poshol na... khui,*" was what she'd heard. She poked him again. He muttered something. She poked him again. He shuddered a little, and exhaled deeply, still asleep. She moved in for another poke.

"Fuck off," he growled in English.

She quickly withdrew her finger as he opened his eyes in narrow slits and glared at her. She stared back into his eyes and turned around. Her face was more than a little flushed. "S-sorry."

He grumbled, sat up and ran his fingers through his messy hair. "What time is it?" he groaned sleepily.

She cleared her throat. "No clue." She stole one last glance at him before asking, "Put some clothes on."

As Damian's usual clothes returned, he asked, "Think anyone will know?"

"…'Bout what?"

He gave her a mischievous smirk. "You know…"

Her face got even redder. "Uh, well… I… hope not."

"Everybody's gonna think you're a slut if they did."

She scowled at him. "Thanks for the support, dickhead."

"Just saying."

"Yeah? Well if Aria found out—"

Aria's voice interrupted her. "AHA! *There* you are!"

Startled, Damian and Jenny glanced over their shoulders at Aria, whose head poked up out of the hatch.

Aria's eyebrows fell when she got a good look at them. Then she glanced over at the smashed up beer case and the tattered cans scattered all over the deck. Her suspicions were immediately aroused when she saw how flustered and disoriented they looked. "Now wait just a damn minute…"

The pair watched her climb up onto the deck and approach them. Their hearts started to race. They hoped they wouldn't break into a nervous sweat.

"What were you two doing up here?" Aria asked with her hands on her hips, leaning forward, glaring at them.

Damian quickly said, "We got into a fight. I kicked her ass eventually."

Damian, you quick-thinking son of a bitch! Jenny was grateful that he at least had that talent. She would have been left stuttering, and the secret would have been out. "I knocked his ass out cold, though."

"I totally won, though."

"No, you didn't. I did."

Damian snickered. "Aw, don't let your pride get too damaged. Admit it. I beat your tight ass and mopped this deck with your face."

Jenny's eyebrow twitched with irritation. "And I made your asshole wider with my foot!"

"Did not—"

"It still hurts, doesn't it!?"

"*NO*, because it never happened—"

"Getting defensive, aren't we, shithead?"

"You want a rematch, you redheaded skank!?"

"Bring it, bitch!"

"*Yob tvoyu mat*!"

Aria stepped in. "Whoa, whoa, whoa, whoa. Why'd you too start fighting last night?"

Jenny's glare moved to her sister. "Because I was getting sick and tired of this douchebag constantly telling me to make him a sandwich! Seriously! It's starting to piss me off!"

Aria turned to Damian. "Damian?"

Damian shrugged. "I like sandwiches."

Aria raised an eyebrow.

"And they're less hazardous to make than waffles."

Jenny chuckled mockingly. "Yeah, because *you're* scared shitless of toasters."

"Nah," he said, "those fucking things just always know how to catch me off guard, is all."

"Don't lie. You're afraid of toasters."

"No, I'm not!"

"Yes you are! Say it!"

"What?!"

"Say you're afraid of toasters!"

"NEVER!"

"SAY IT, YOU BITCH, SAY IT!"

Aria curtly barked, "Knock it off, you two." She put a toothpick in her mouth and sighed with exasperation. "Jeez, is there no end to all this bickering? I swear, I could separate you two so each of you is either in the front of this ship or the back and you'd still be bitching."

She turned around and headed back down the shaft. "Anyway, we're gonna get off the ship, soon. I suggest you guys eat breakfast or something."

They waited until Aria closed the hatch door before looking at each other.

Damian said, "I just remembered something."

"What?"

"Guess you earned it. The reason I had that little attack yesterday… I found out my only good brother was a zombie. Laugh or don't laugh; it's pretty ironic how he ran off to Scionia to start a new life."

"Why?" *And why tell me this now?*

"He met a girl online. They were dating for three years—if you can fucking call it that. I remember Carson used to jump on the computer every day after school or work and he'd talk with her for hours. But somehow he still made time for me, unlike everybody else in the house. He was the only one who hung out with me. We'd go fishing, and play tag, or hide-and-seek... sometimes we'd even make forts in the junkyard and fight territorial wars with the other kids." His head tilted to the side, and he scowled. "'Course, I saved his ass most o' the time."

She stared at him, amazed by the fact that she'd just heard a heart-warming story from the most unlikely of the *Scion's Wings*' temporary crewmembers. "Wow."

"One time, we caught so much fish you'd swear Jesus would've gotten gas if he ate it all in one sitting." He stood up and stared off into the shifting canopy of palm trees. Pacific Gulls cried out in the sunny sky, where a few white clouds floated on by. In the distance, a mountainous structure with overlapping angular rooftops stood up above the palm forest, lined with red clay tiles and solar panels, with classic grey brickwork in its foundation and white cement walls running up the massive tower.

"Sounds charming," said Jenny. She was still staring at him with half-concealed astonishment. She saw a sort of childish nostalgic side of him she'd never seen before. Of course, she only knew him for two days and three nights, but this was the first time since he first woke up that his manner wasn't the same old 'I'm better than you and I'm gonna kill all of you bitches someday' attitude. He had a harmless, childlike aura about him right now.

"So where the fuck are we?"

And now that childlike aura was gone, butchered by his regular crude, juvenile approach to just about everything.

Jenny scowled. "I dunno for sure. Can we get outta this sun? My head's killing me."

He turned and walked toward the hatch. "Sure—"

"Hold up." She grabbed the back of his jacket.

He nearly fell off his feet. The sudden jolt sent a surge of pain rushing to his head. He yelped and grasped the sides of his head. "Aggghhhh… *pizda*, *govnyuk*, shit, OW, *FUCK*!"

"Sorry," she said, taken aback by his outburst. "But listen." She got up and pushed her foot into her other shoe. "Last night was an accident."

He raised an eyebrow and cocked his head toward her. "What?"

"Hey, I didn't mean to… you know… not that I have anything

against you… which I do… but, you know…"

"No, I don't. You're not making any sense for me to know a damn thing."

She blushed. Her eyes strayed away from his face. "The… thing we did last night… it just didn't happen."

"Why not?"

"…Because, I… I can't control myself when I get like that, okay!?"

Damian scowled. "Wow. You are so uptight right now. It was just sex."

"I don't know how you were raised on the subject, but I was taught that sex should only be shared between people who share a mutual love and understanding for each other, where each one is special in the other's eyes—"

"Yeeeaaaahhh, because Tim is one *special* motherfucker," Damian said sarcastically.

"I…! Well…!" She frowned. "You win that round. I was stupid back then."

"No shit, you were."

"Hey, *you're* not exactly genius material, either! Surely you've done something stupid that you regret!"

"Fucking you was pretty stupid, but I don't regret it."

That reply surprised her. She was speechless for a moment. "R-really…?"

"Are you kidding me? It felt like I just had sex with a supermodel I'd been idolizing in a porn magazine all my life! And if Richard is satisfied, I'm satisfied."

She blinked. "Who's Richard?"

With an 'are you serious' frown, he turned and pointed at his crotch.

Jenny said, "O-oh! Okay…"

"And don't call me Shirley."

Jenny frowned. *Are you fucking kidding me?*

"No, I'm not."

She gasped. He grinned.

Damian stumbled into the lounge groggily, groaning and rubbing his aching head. Everyone in the lounge stopped eating and watched him stagger to the bar counter and climb up onto one of the stools, and flop on the counter. For a moment, they thought he'd fallen asleep on the counter until he raised his arm lazily. The fridge turned black. The freezer door opened. A small, black rectangular box floated out of the freezer and fell on the counter against the wall opposite the island counter. The box split open, and several round objects wrapped in black energy rose out of the box and fell into the toaster. The black energy vanished, revealing the objects to be waffles.

Damian groaned impatiently as he waited for them to pop out of the toaster. "Shiiiiiit..."

"Rough night?" Aria taunted.

"Shut up," he snapped.

As she sat down with her breakfast, Jenny spoke her idea, "If you have a headache, why don't you go to the Palm Tree Onsen?"

"Shut the—what?" he turned around and looked at her inquisitively. "Palm Tree Onsen?"

"Yeah, that building," she said. "I just remembered what it was called. It's a Kyoko-style bathhouse. I hear it's one of the greatest bathhouses in half the world. The steam might help your hangover. …And mine."

"Hunh." While Damian contemplated his decision, the waffles popped out the toaster and startled him. Dismayed, he muttered something in Russian and manipulated the waffles onto a plate and positioned the plate in front of him.

Jenny chuckled. "Ah, toasters."

"Get back to the onsen thing. What's 'onsen' even mean?"

"It's Kyokonese for 'bath'. You didn't know that?"

"Yeeaaahhh; while you were getting finger-banged by Tim's squiggly fingers in school, I was locked up in an Antarctic boob tube. 'Member? Or did that slip your mind?" The fridge door opened and a black bottle of syrup approached Damian and dropped into his hand. Once in his grasp, a quarter of it was dumped on his waffles. "Christ, it feels like a grenade went off in my skull…"

Marner encouraged Jenny's idea before she felt any dissuasion from Damian's constant condescension. "I think it's a great idea! Why don't we all go to the resort?"

"Suuuuure," said Aria, leaning back in her chair with a toothpick in her mouth. "I could use a good soak."

"As could I," said Jeremy, standing up to take his empty plate to the dishwasher. When he put the plate and fork in the dishwasher and closed it up, he added, "I will ask Matthew if he or any of his clan would like to come along. I doubt Jonathon Silverstein will find us out here."

"They shouldn't," said Damian with a smirk. "He wouldn't risk jeopardizing the safety of Jenny's life."

The lounge fell silent. Damian could feel them all staring at him. He stuffed a waffle into his mouth and said with his mouth full, "Food for thought."

Cloverfield, Fraden Residence

Zero opened his eyes and stared up at the familiar white ceiling hanging over his bed. He sat up slowly and looked around to find himself in his old room. He could faintly hear the TV playing downstairs and got up to investigate. His mother must have brought him into his room after the explosion, which, while seemingly odd, was the only explanation he could give himself.

He stepped out of bed, surprised to still find himself in his day clothes. He opened the door, entered the hallway, and walked downstairs into the open area of the living room, dining room, and kitchen. He turned to the couch, which had its back to him, and saw Silverstein sitting on the couch sipping tea from a teacup and watching a live broadcast on how to prepare 'the greatest, juiciest, tastiest steak of all time.'

Jonathon Silverstein—the *Jonathon Silverstein... is in my house.*

Zero's heart nearly stopped at the sight of him. He froze completely, hoping Silverstein hadn't noticed him yet.

Silverstein *did* notice, without even turning around. "Good morning, Colonel."

"W-what the hell are you doing here?" Zero asked, looking around quietly for his gun.

"Don't bother looking for your pathetic firearm. I've got it sitting right here, next to my biscuits." He turned, smiling with approval, and raised the teacup for Penelope to see. Penelope stood in the kitchen in the far corner of the open area. "This tea is lovely, by the way."

"Why, thank you," Penelope replied with a smile.

Zero looked at her in disbelief.

"And to answer your question, Colonel, I'm here because you saw something and killed someone you shouldn't have."

"Who? One of your captains?"

"That's a thing of the past."

"Oh, just like how the Dehue Extermination Project was a thing of the past?!" he snapped. "I'm sure you're 'oh so sorry' about *that*, too."

"*Listen*," Silverstein hissed, "and listen closely: I did what I had to. I just approached the situation in a more extreme—but necessary—way. We could discuss my reasons for nearly wiping out all life on the planet for the greater good… or we can discuss why I'm here."

Tough question, Zero thought. "Alright. Why are you here?"

"First off: sit. Have some tea."

"I'd rather stand."

"I wasn't asking."

"I won't comply."

"That's too bad. This is good tea."

"I know. I drink it."

"Then have some."

"Just *get to the point*."

Silverstein took another sip and set the teacup down on the saucer on the coffee table. "Yesterday, I believe you found your adoptive daughters' house in shambles. Everything was scattered all over the place. Am I right so far?"

"...Go on."

"So then, you were ambushed by an agent of some sort who tried to kill you. After a brief scuffle, you wounded him, and he suddenly exploded, tossing you out of the house as a result. Grade my accuracy." He glanced at Zero over his shoulder.

Zero stared at him with surprise, knowing that Silverstein knew something valuable. "Are you trying to tell me you know who attacked me last night?"

"Well, it sure as hell wasn't me."

"How can I trust that statement from *you*?"

"First of all: I wouldn't have left a big mess behind. The doors would be the exception, since my men seem to have made that sort of thing an odd tradition. Second of all, I wouldn't have left someone behind. And another thing: what benefit would I get from killing *you*?" He took his teacup and sipped the rest of its light brown contents elegantly. "Nothing. I have nothing against you, or Jennifer, or Marner, or Mrs. Fraden."

"Uh, it's 'Miss,' actually," Penelope corrected.

"Oh. Sorry."

Zero added bitterly, "*He* died in *your* war. With my brother."

Silverstein acknowledged with a grunt.

"What about Aria?" Zero asked. "You have something against her?"

"Aria is one of the reasons why my campaign failed. Not to mention, during the war, she released Damian when I finally had him incarcerated, costing the world another fifteen million lives to add to the number of casualties caused by his previous rampage. Other than that, I don't have any issues with her that would inspire me to seek revenge. Besides, she's probably one of the very few people in this world who *could* actually succeed in killing me."

"By that logic, you should hate Jenny and Marner."

"What Jenny and Marner did was an accident. Aria did it on purpose."

Zero was surprised to hear Silverstein say something like that so admittedly. But his curiosity nagged him to return to the previous topic. "So who attacked me last night?"

Silverstein looked at him, dead serious. "Have you ever heard of the secret organization called... Projects Secret Society?"

"No."

"You most likely wouldn't. They're a secret society that control and manipulate every event that occurs all around the world."

"You mean like... illuminati?"

"Precisely. Illuminati. And they emphasize on the word 'secret' by assassinating anyone who learns of their existence beyond theory. You've seen one of their agents, which is why I have some of my men guarding your property. Think of it as an apology for getting your kids dragged into this mess with Damian." He leaned forward and took another sip from his teacup.

"But why the hell would an agent go through their house?"

"Jenny and Marner were the ones who woke Damian up. Clearly, they were after Damian. If your girls were there, they'd probably be dead."

"They aren't weaklings. I doubt they could be killed by an agent like the one I killed last night."

"Don't underestimate the Society. You're damn lucky to have survived that agent." He stood up and drifted toward the door like a shadow in flickering firelight. "Now, I'd love to stay and chat, but I've got business to attend to. Thank you for the tea."

"One more thing," Zero said, following him to the door. "The agent killed himself. Why?"

"Why do you think? The society can't have their agents running their mouths off about their secrets, can they? As soon as a serious injury is inflicted on the body, the bomb surgically implanted in the stomach goes off. It's a precaution in case the agent is being tortured for information. That's their one weakness. But I advise you two to move to a secret location with my squad. Don't trust anyone outside of the squad. And don't get any ideas about this, either. I'm only apologizing. I don't necessarily enjoy having numerous unwanted casualties in my missions, you know."

Zero scoffed. "That's news to me."

"Well, you have two choices," Silverstein began, "you can have my protection, or you can allow the Society to kill you and leave behind those three young girls. Your choice."

"So you've started a movement against them like you did against the Dehues?"

"No. Unlike the Dehues with their tails, members of the Society have no features that we can distinguish them from everyone else with. They're as good as invisible. Wiping them all out would be impossible."

"Then who have you been killing all this time?"

"That's none of your concern. I strongly advise that you don't get yourself involved too deeply in all this. You're not much of a threat because you don't know much. Keep it that way, and you'll stay alive."

"So it's like that..."

"It's *always* been like that," Silverstein replied.

Good point, Zero thought.

"I'm just warning you," Silverstein continued. "There's a storm coming, and when it hits it'll hit like a typhoon of fire. That's why you need to leave. Get out of the country. Go to a neutral zone. It won't be totally safe, but it *should* be safer than any soil grown under an alliance flag. You've been warned." He bowed his head toward Penelope. "Thank you for the tea. It was delicious."

COBALT ROGUE, VOL. 1: THE DEAD BLUE

Episode 010

Hot Spring Standoff

Spring Islands, Palm Tree Onsen

The Palm Tree Onsen was a huge resort with three attached buildings on the property: the main building with the check-in lobby, the rectangular bathhouse with a fan-sloping stone base which walled in the hot springs and divided them in half for both genders, and the four-storey hotel with the restaurant added in. The slanted, slightly curved overlapping rooftops had opaque steam vents built in above the baths, but the rest was pure solid clay running up to thin spires where gold palm trees were perched. The palm tree forest surrounding the Kyokonese-style bathhouse served as an odd contrast to the building's eastern roots. Below the bathhouse was a wide cantilever parking lot that stretched out over the water connected to the freeway overpass extending over the canal from the edge of Palm Tree Island to Rain Harbour.

The restaurant was fairly spacious, with three dining rooms attached to either side of a classy, upscale bar. The kitchen was on the northeast side of the bar counter, separated by a half-glass partition. The entire restaurant was coated in yellow tile, and framed pictures that captured highlighted moments in the restaurant's seventy-five-year history were hung up on every pillar. There was an extended balcony over each dining area, providing twice the space for patrons to sit. The sun shone through frosted skylights, and the dining areas beneath the balconies were divided by half-glass partition walls. The dining areas themselves occupied every other corner that the kitchen did not, with the double door exit located between the southeast and southwest dining areas.

Damian sat on a stool leaning over the counter with a cup of saké in his hands. Mona was right beside him struggling to open a bottle for herself with her teeth, and hissing at it whenever she failed to pry the cap off. Dave floated over the stool beside her, watching with silent amusement. The bartender was also watching Mona's struggle with a raised eyebrow. "You want some help with that?" he asked her.

She hugged the bottle defensively and hissed at him in response. He recoiled.

Damian smirked at the sight as he took another sip. "That's all you're gonna get, bartender."

"Is she, um... uh, well, you know..."

"Is she retarded?" Damian asked. "Is that what you're asking?"

"Uh, yes," the bartender said, scratching the back of his head. "No offense..."

"None taken," Damian said. "You don't need to act like such a sensitive pussy."

The bartender frowned.

Damian looked at Mona as she smacked the bottle neck against the edge of the counter repeatedly, like a baby with a plastic mallet. "She's got a few screws loose, I'd imagine."

"So... she's a Mew, huh? First I've ever seen one o' those in person."

Damian didn't say anything. He gave the bartender a fleeting look, then glanced at a shady group of customers whispering in a booth in the farthest corner of the third dining room over his shoulder.

Whap!

Something hit him in the shoulder. Damian's eyes shot upward to see—

Matthew. Cocky smirk and all. "This seat taken?"

Damian frowned and turned back to his cup of saké. "Yeah. Take a walk."

"Taken by whom?"

"My slave there." Damian jutted his thumb at Mona, who had resorted to unscrewing the bottle cap with her teeth.

Matthew stole a glance in her direction, then looked at Damian and said, "She's on *that* side, though."

"Doesn't matter," Damian said.

Matthew chuckled as he unbuckled his claymore, set it against the counter, and pulled up the stool on Damian's right. As he sat down, he ordered himself a cup of saké.

The bartender sighed. "You kids even old enough—"

"Just serve the fucking drinks," Matthew snarled.

Damian raised an eyebrow at Matthew's hostility, but didn't turn away from his own cup, which he took another slurp from.

"I felt the need to talk to you, anyway," Matthew said. He thanked the bartender when he got his drink.

"What's your reason?" Damian asked with an annoyed groan.

Matthew shrugged. "I just want something cleared up, man. I'm not lookin' to make friends or enemies or whatever it is you'd call 'in between.' I'm just looking for some answers."

"Another interrogation? Fucking great."

"Bro, I hate interrogations. I wouldn't do that to someone I just got to know."

"Sure didn't stop you when we first landed in your village." Damian paused, then turned to face him and said, "I bet you blame *me* for the zombie apocalypse, don't you? C'mon, let's hear it. Get it over with, already."

"That wasn't it at all. In fact, from what I saw, I'd almost commend you."

Damian blinked. "Uh... what?"

"See, it wasn't you that caused that, and I'm well aware of it. My second-in-command was totally responsible. He had it out for me. You prob'ly already knew that, but hey, I'm just lettin' you know that I know that."

"So what the hell are you wasting my time for?"

Matthew chuckled impatiently. "Don't."

"'Don't' what?" Damian asked, sensing the clear challenge.

"I controlled an entire clan full of know-it-all, violence-prone teenagers in the wilderness, surrounded by zombies, in a deserted military base where the Scionian Army kept its ordnance supplies... for over five years. I've heard it all, seen it all. If my clan existed in the eighties and we made international headlines, we would've been the prime inspiration for the marines in like... every James Cameron movie ever made. Your macho bullshit doesn't get to me. Like I said before: I just want one thing cleared up."

"And that would be?"

"Whose side are you on?"

Pop!

Mona hollered a triumphant cheer as the cap flew off her saké bottle. She danced on her stool, shouting, "YAY! Yay! Yay! Yaaaaaaayyy!"

The bartender clapped, congratulating her and thanking his lucky stars the cap Mona had sent flying only grazed his left ear.

The other patrons in all three dining rooms momentarily stopped what they were doing to look at the oddball sight of Mona prancing around with joy on her stool.

Damian ignored her, focusing on Matthew's question as he stared into his cup.

"Well?" Matthew asked impatiently.

"Define 'side,'" Damian said.

"Good guys, bad guys; our team, their team—whatever."

Damian smirked. "Right, because we're the 'good guys' here. There're too many teams in this game."

"There are?"

"*Way* too many."

"Go with the 'good guy/bad guy' routine, then."

"That line's so blurred I'd have better luck passing an eye exam after diving into a vat of acid without my goggles."

Matthew squinted at the analogy, taking a sip from his cup.

"There aren't any good guys, Matt. It's just us and them, then, now, and there; all stuck in a sick game of cat and mouse. Our only problem is figuring out which are the cats, and which are the mice, and which are in between—the rats."

"Which're you?"

"I'm a mouse since I'm running from Silverstein and all those other groups that want me for one reason or another. ...But I'm also a cat... because I'm looking for someone."

"Who?"

"That's none of your goddamn business."

"Fair enough. But you're both, so does that make you a rat?"

"No, no. You don't get it. The rats are the traitors. The slimy motherfuckers who'd sell out their own Jewish people in the attic so that the Nazis don't kill them, too. I'm not a rat and I never will be. Only the worst, bottom-of-the-barrel, limp-dicked cunts are rats."

"I get it now."

"Which one are you?"

"I'm the same as you, I guess. We're all looking for that special someone we'd rather not talk about. So I guess we're both on the same page."

"If you mean that we're both mice eluding a horde of cats

while looking for the cheese, then yeah, I guess we are."

"So what d'you say we form a partnership?"

Damian emptied his cup, put it down, and gestured for the bartender to refill it. As the bartender did so, he asked Matthew, "What *kind* of partnership?"

"A sort of… 'I scratch your back, you scratch mine' kinda deal," he said. "Cover each other's asses when the going gets tough."

"Friendship?" Damian scoffed.

"Nah," Matthew said. "I don't need friends. I need *allies*. Get me, bro?"

"I see what you mean."

"It'd just make things easier for both of us. Better to help each other out with the little things to make our separate journeys all the more pleasant."

"Little things can go a long way."

"Exactly. So?"

Damian thought about it, ignoring Mona as she rolled across the counter chugging down the contents of her newly opened bottle. "…I don't see why not."

Matthew offered him his hand. Damian shook it. "Alright."

Damian turned back to his cup and said discreetly, "If we wanted to start this now, I've got news for you."

"What's that?"

Damian gave him a suspicious sideways glance. "We're not alone."

Matthew paused. Then he went back to drinking his saké, maintaining his casual posture, but keeping his eyes keen. "Oh yeah?"

"The few 'patrons' in all of the dining areas… well, they aren't patrons. Be casual if you're going to look. You'll see that they're all sitting in places that'd give them the upper hand. On the balconies, in corners, behind pillars… name it. These motherfuckers're everywhere."

"Jeremy mentioned Systems Corporation—"

"It's not them."

"It's not? Then who are they?"

"I dunno yet, but they sure as hell aren't Systems. If they were Systems, they'd be a lot harder to spot."

"So what the hell are they waiting for?"

"Dunno. In the meantime, I'm gonna go bathe while I still can. Maybe pay a visit to one of the girls."

"Aria?" Matthew chuckled.

"The other one."

"Oh. Makes more sense. Also slightly less creepy. Not that I'm one to judge."

Damian got up from his stool and turned to leave. "Her sister's gonna kill me."

The bartender was quick to grab his shoulder from behind the counter. "Hey! You gonna pay for that?"

Damian turned back around and leaned over the counter, getting right in the bartender's face. "You got a family, bartender?"

The bartender's expression became distorted with anger. "Are you threatening my family?"

"No. I'm *warning* you. Answer the question."

The bartender hesitated. Then he said, "A-a wife… and daughter."

"There's gonna be shit flying real soon. I suggest you get the fuck outta here and run home to your wife and daughter," Damian said. "Consider the drinks your 'thank-you' card."

"Hey, you can't just tell me—"

The bartender froze when he saw Damian's revolver pointing at him, concealed from the 'patrons'.

"I wasn't telling you to do anything," Damian hissed. "I'm warning you to take your sorry ass and get the fuck off this island. Or else you'll never see your wife an' kid again. And the little missy gets to grow up without a daddy. Do I make myself clear, jerkoff?"

The bartender's eyes widened. He quickly threw his apron aside and fled into the kitchen. Damian watched him exit the back door through the window in the partition. When he was clear, Damian smacked Matthew on the shoulder and said, "I'll send Aria your way."

"Why?"

"You're gonna need some guns."

"I have a sword and two guns."

"A sword isn't gonna do shit. And two guns won't be enough unless you're in a John Woo movie."

"Well, I dunno about that."

"Distract her a bit for me anyway, will ya?"

"But—"

Damian looked over his shoulder at him. "You scratch my back, I scratch yours."

And with that, he left the restaurant.

Aria was walking in the halls, leaving the spa after a back massage that was more than a little satisfying. She bumped into Damian on her way to the bath and said, "What're you up to?"

Damian stopped and looked at her, his expression blank. Aria thought he dozed off with his eyes fluttering open and shut before he said, "Matt wanted to see you."

"The chief guy? Why?"

"How in the actual fuck should I know? He just told me he's at the bar."

"Sounds suspicious," she said, eyes narrowed. "What's he want with me?"

"I just told you, I don't know."

Aria crossed her arms. "Are you hiding something?"

"Christ, can't I relay a simple message without someone giving me the eye?! Fuck, man!"

"Alright, alright," she said. *Maybe I'm being just a little too harsh there.* "Where's the bar?"

"In the restaurant."

"Where's the *restaurant*?" she asked impatiently.

Damian pointed down the hall he'd come from. "That way. Take a right when you reach the end."

"You're sure you don't know what he…?" She was stopped short by his agitated scowl. "I guess you really don't. Alright, I'll check it out."

"What's with the scrutiny?"

"Hey, don't blame me. You're not exactly 'trustworthy' material after these past few days."

He shrugged. "Guess not."

"The bar, right?"

"Can't miss it."

Damian watched her head off in the direction he pointed, and smirked mischievously as she disappeared around the corner.

*

Jenny was the first one in the hot springs, soaking in the steaming water reaching up to her shoulders. Her arms rested on top of the hot rock she leaned against, and the heat of the water soaking into her skin was the best thing she'd felt in a long time. She heaved a long, content sigh and mumbled to herself, "Finally, some peace and quiet..."

Sploosh!

She opened her eyes and stared at the ripples spreading from a distant spot in the water. "What the…?"

She kicked her foot in the direction of the ripples, and hit something.

"BWAAAGGGHHHH!" Jonny screamed as his head flew up out of the water with Jenny's footprint on his face. He fell into the water on his back, and then floated up to the surface.

Jenny's eyes widened. "…Jonny? *JONNY*?!" She grabbed him by the neck and shook him wildly. "ARE YOU FUCKING KIDDING ME!? HOW?! *WHY*!? How do you *always* find out where I am!?"

She stopped shaking him. He stared at her with wide eyes. "Jenny, is that you?"

"*Yes*, it's me, dipshit! Don't think I'm stupid enough to fall for your little 'innocent' game. I know what you're like! What the hell are you doing out here?!"

"W-well, I set out to save you from the evil clutches of the Dead Blue! And then bring you home… and maybe woo you under silk sheets and moonlight… and then marry you… and stuff." He blushed and gave her a nervous chuckle. "Not in that particular order. But honest to God, I didn't know I'd find you here. I just felt like taking a break."

"…In the women's bath?" she asked sternly, with a vicious scowl on her face.

Jonny's eyes moved downward; his face reddened. "…I'd say this is the best reunion ever."

CRACK!

She slammed his face into the nearest rock, knocking him out cold. "DAMN IT! How dare he!"

"Yeah!" Damian exclaimed, perched on a nearby rock with his arms crossed, with only a towel around his waist. "How *dare* he show such nerve!"

Jenny looked at him for a moment before turning back to Jonny's limp form floating face down in the water. "Like, what's his problem!? I was hoping—"

She snapped her head back around.

Damian grinned. "Helloooo."

"What're *you* doing here!?"

"Hey, wasn't that guy at your school?" he asked.

"Don't ignore me!"

"I think he was…"

"DAMIAN!"

"What?" he asked with irritation, looking at her. "You do realize you still haven't covered up, right?"

"YIPE!" Jenny dropped down into the water, crouching, covering herself up. Her face was bright red. "Damn it…"

"Anyway, I just thought I'd drop by. Seeing as how you're alone and we're both—"

"Don't even go there! I told you to forget about what happened!"

Damian slid down the rock and splashed into the water beside her. He smirked. "Why forget when we can benefit from it?"

She stared at him with half open eyes. "You're horny, aren't you?"

"…A little."

"Well it's not happening. Not that it wasn't fun, but no. We're not doing it. Look, you gotta get into your own bath; my sister'll be in here any second now!"

"Yeah, right. I sent her off to the bar. She shouldn't be back for a while. We've got all the time in the world."

"The time, sure, but I don't have the freaking patience, Damian."

Damian smirked, resting his elbows on the rock. "I think you're just shy."

She glared at him, her face redder than a stop sign. "Damian, I swear to God…"

"What's God gotta do with my penis?"

"Nothing, I just—"

"Are you ashamed or something?"

Jenny sank and blew bubbles under the water, her eyes lingering just above the surface. Damian stared at her. "You're acting weird."

She went up until the water reached her shoulders and said, "*You're* the one being pushy. Do you know how uncomfortable this is?"

"…You're not gonna throw that feminazi 'oppression' crap at me, are you?"

"No, I just don't wanna have this conversation with you right now, especially when anyone could just walk in here at any moment."

"I just told you I took care of Aria—"

"Yeah? What about Marner?"

Damian paused, staring off into space. Then he said, "I forgot about Marner."

"Thought so."

He shrugged. "We could make it quick, you know."

"*Or* you could treat me with some fucking respect and get the fuck out!"

He looked at her again, barely able to make out the outline of her curves in the water, which she covered up with her arms. "Dunno if 'respect' is the word I'm looking for…"

"That's too damn bad, Damian. I'm not talking to you until you show me some."

"Some what?"

"Respect, dipshit."

"Do you know how self-contradictory you sound?"

"I don't care," she said icily.

"Oh," he said with mock surprise.

"I'm not a sex toy you can just jump on whenever you feel like it, and the sooner you get that through your thick skull, the better. I might be a hyb… hyb… hybrid? Hybrid Bristol…? I DON'T FUCKING KNOW THE WORD! But I'm… I'm… I'm s-sexually attracted to people I consider psychopaths, okay?!"

"Right, okay—"

"Do I have to get the scissors?"

He stopped and stared at her. He remembered her interrogation all too well. He glared at her defiantly. "You wouldn't…"

"Fucking *try* me."

"You love *it* too much."

"I can find someone else who's just as big and three times more decent."

Damian faltered as he tried to think up a snappy comeback.

Jenny cut him off. "I don't care if it was a one-time thing or not. On my part, it was a total accident, and it was irresponsible, and stupid, and… and…"

"A fluke?" he suggested.

"Yeah, a fluke! A big, fat, giant, horribly regretful fluke and I wish I could go back to last night and bitch-slap myself out of it before I hopped onto you so that we wouldn't be having this stupid fucking conversation!"

"Wow. Cold."

"Is a little respect too much to ask?!"

"…How little?"

"Don't be a sarcastic dick."

"Oh, it was rhetorical."

"I just want to be seen as equal, you know?" She looked at him.

He looked back at her, blank-faced.

Her expectant look turned into another glare.

"…Rhetorical?" he asked.

"No!"

"Oh. I see."

She went on with her rant: "Seriously, every guy I've spoken to seems to only want me for my goddamn body! It's like I'm a fucking... friggin'... misogynist magnet! You, Jonny, Tim, and all of those douchebags who kept trying to rape me because I was drunk and 'wouldn't know the difference,' and just once, just *once* I'd like to talk to a guy who isn't all over me for the size of my tits or the roundness of my ass!"

Jonny managed to slip back into consciousness to comment: "I think your tits are lovely—"

KRAK!

Her fist bounced his skull against a nearby rock. With a pleasurable moan, he slid limply underwater, and Jenny continued, "See? Like that! *That's* what I'm talking about! That's all they're after! That's all they're *all* after! Not my personality or the fact that I've got feelings and needs too. It's just 'pussy' this and 'boobs' that, and every time I complain everybody tells me that I shouldn't dress like such a fucking slut AND IT'S JUST FUCKING PISSING ME OFF! WHY DON'T I JUST TAKE A GUN OVER THERE AND BLAST THEIR FUCKING BRAINS OUT?!"

"Whoa," Damian said, eyes wide.

"Oh wait! I forgot that *they can't die* because they're fucking immortal because God's got a fucked-up sense of humour and he's a FUCKING ASSHOLE AND I HOPE HE DIES A SHITTY DEATH FOR GIVING LONG LIFESPANS TO ALL THE WRONG FUCKING PEOPLE!"

"Jesus Christ," Damian said, eyes growing wider.

"But *noooooooo*! I forgot, I can't talk like that! I have to be a girl! I have to bow down and kiss their asses. I have to wear makeup. I have to *dress* a certain way. I have to *act* a certain way. I can't *just* be friends with someone. It's *my* fault I'm fucked up. It's *my* fault I can't do the things I can't do. It's *my* fault when I'm robbed, or beaten, or ridiculed on the internet, or raped." To Damian's shock, Jenny broke down and cried on a nearby boulder. "Fuck, maaaaan...!"

"Um... that escalated... *way* too quickly," Damian said.

"You wanted to see me?" Aria asked as she took a seat at the bar next to Matthew, watching Mona roll around on the countertop with her saké bottle as if she had a ball of yarn.

"Yeah, sort of, I guess."

"What's up?" She scanned the bar, and peered through the window to the kitchen. Then she asked, "Where're all the servers?"

"The ones who aren't hostiles are gone," Matthew said.

Alarmed, Aria immediately switched to 'inconspicuous mode' and stooped over the counter to grab a bottle from the shelf below the register, discreetly scanning the area as she did so. "Oh, I see. Interesting. Know who it is? They don't look like Systems."

"How would you know?"

"They'd be a lot harder to spot."

Matthew scowled and took a sip from his cup. *Right...*

She sat back down on her stool and popped the cap with her thumb. "Want some guns in case the shit hits the fan?"

"You aren't worried?"

"Nah."

"Neither am I. 'Sides, I've got a claymore."

"That sword? You brought a sword to a gunfight?"

"I fight better with a sword. Especially in these close quarters."

"Sure, if you like to call spacious two-storey dining areas 'close quarters.' Suit yourself. I'm gonna go check something out."

"Check *what* out?"

"If this infestation is exclusive to this area or if it's spread throughout the entire facility."

"Oh. Good plan."

"You stay here an' keep watch with Damian's servant, or whatever the hell she is."

"Sure, whatever."

"If the situation doesn't escalate before then, I'm gonna go get naked and take the bath I came here for."

Matthew's heart skipped. He looked at her with surprise. "Seriously? With this going on?"

"Yep."

"B-but..."

"If these guys wanted something, they would've done it already. Which means they're waiting. If they didn't act when Damian was in here, then I guess that still gives us a little while to enjoy our short vacation." Aria placed a small radio on the counter beside him. "Enjoy it while it lasts." She got up and took her freshly opened saké bottle with her into the hall. She stopped at the entrance as the double doors swung shut behind her, glancing both ways before choosing to go left. She made her way down the empty corridor, footsteps echoing.

Then she rounded the corner and headed down to the maintenance area. She figured it'd be the best place to look, since customers wouldn't—or shouldn't—think to go down there and look for anything out of the ordinary. She figured right.

Because when she finally reached the janitor's closet and 'discreetly'—as in, she made sure no one was around—kicked the door down, she discovered the corpses of the original bartender, the masseuses, the servers, and the manager of the bathhouse piled up in the corner.

"Ah, shit."

Jenny was still sobbing on the rock. Damian watched her,

unsure of what to do. He was quiet for several minutes, hoping her crying would die down, but with every passing minute, the feeling of hopelessness became more intrusive.

"Um... sorry?"

"Fuck you," she snapped.

"...Well, I can't offer you my sympathy, but at least I get it."

"Get what?"

"You know, the... the thing."

She looked at him, wiping tears from her eyes. "What thing?"

Damian scowled at her. "I'm not explaining every freaking thing I say—"

"*What* thing?" she pressed.

Damian got up and trudged through the bathwater toward the change room. "Nah, moment's gone. I'm out."

"Damian!" she called, following him, still covering herself with her arms. "Get back here!"

"Pfft. Why?"

"Because... I... um... Wait a second. Those're the *female* change rooms, damn it!"

"So? I doubt anyone's in 'em—"

Shunk!

The door slid open, revealing Marner in a towel.

Damian stopped, standing on the edge of the platform, staring at Marner.

Jenny stopped dead in her tracks, her eyes bulging with shock. "Shit."

Marner was stiffer than a statue, gripping the edge of the door with one hand and clutching the knot in her towel with the other. Her eyes, which usually seemed greyed-out and blank, were now wide with shock and horror.

"Uh," Damian said, "I'd say 'it's not what it looks like' but I don't think you can even hear me right now."

She squeaked, then fainted.

"See?"

Jenny slapped her forehead. "How the hell am I gonna explain this when she wakes up?"

Damian breathed a heavy sigh and laughed with relief. "Well, at least she didn't scream and alert your sister—"

Shunk!

The door to the hall flew open. Aria stopped when she saw Damian, toothpick hanging out of her mouth, eyebrow cocked.

Damian and Jenny bristled, gaping at her for her impeccably-timed entrance. Aria simply stood there, hands on her hips.

"Uh," Damian said, "It's not what it looks like?"

Aria didn't look amused. She stepped into the change room, swinging the door shut behind her. Damian could only watch with increasing dread as she walked between the lockers.

Then, unexpectedly, she lifted her shirt off and tossed it aside, and then proceeded to strip down in front of them.

Jenny's jaw dropped. Damian's surprise intensified.

"ARIA!" Jenny shouted.

Aria stopped pulling her pants down, which were just below the panty line, and looked at her sister. "What?"

"I—YOU—HE," she stuttered, unable to form a proper sentence at first. Her heartrate a mile a minute. "WHAT THE FUCK ARE YOU DOING?!"

"What does it *look* like I'm doing?" she asked casually. "I'm getting ready to take a bath."

"Do you not *see* Damian standing right there?!"

She looked at Damian, whose dumbfounded expression amused her. And he was still naked. She scrutinized him for a moment, then looked back at her sister and said, "I don't care."

Jenny was at a loss for words.

She dropped her pants to the floor and kicked them beside Marner, who was still passed out on the floor. "Besides, why do you two get to be naked and I don't? Ya little hypocrites."

"T-that's not the point!" Jenny exclaimed. "I didn't ask him to be here!"

"Neither did I but you don't see *me* complainin'." Aria hooked her thumbs into her panties and started to—

"Don't even think about it!"

Aria stopped. "Think about what?"

Jenny pointed at her and said, "Don't you dare take those panties off."

Aria chuckled. "Oh, Sis. So insecure."

"N-no I'm not!"

"Yes you are."

"No I'm not!"

"C'mon, I'm sure there's nothing here Damian hasn't seen already."

Jenny looked at Damian, who was staring at Aria's breasts with his usual emotionless expression. "Damian!"

No response.

"Damian!"

He still didn't respond.

"*DAMIAN*!"

"*WHAT*?!" he shouted, turning to face her.

"Stop staring at my sister and put on a goddamn towel!"

He gave her a challenging glare. "Make me."

Aria laughed. "See? He doesn't even care. Let 'im watch if he wants."

"Aria, I swear to God…"

"God doesn't care, either."

"Come on! You can't do this, it's… it's *wrong*."

"How? I don't care if he sees. *He* doesn't care if he sees. Not to mention nudity's about as natural as breathing."

"He's… he's… he's underage!"

Aria said to Damian, "How old're you again?"

"Sixteen," he said.

Aria smirked at Jenny. "Age of consent's fifteen over here. So ha."

Jenny seethed with rage, still pointing at her sister.

"Someone's jealous," Damian mumbled.

"WHAT WAS THAT?!"

"Nothing," he said. "You know what's funny, though? Marner's unconscious on the floor, Jonny's sprawled out on a rock over there with his head split open, I've been standing here getting shrivelled from this slightly cool damp air, and yet you're bitching about your sister getting naked for the bath." Damian chuckled and crossed his arms, still making no effort to cover up. "Irony."

"I don't think that's irony," Aria said.

"It totally *is* irony."

"I dunno, seems like you're talking about double standards rather than irony."

"It's ironic somehow."

"No. It's not."

"Yes it is!"

"No, it's a double standard, because she's not making a big deal out of you being naked, but when *I* start stripping down, *that's* a whole other ball park."

"Weird, though. Usually it's the other way around," Damian said, giving Jenny a roguish smirk.

"Shut up," she hissed. "And stop gawking at my sister."

"Someone's jealous," he said. "Eh, Aria?"

"Agreed, squirt."

"Don't call me 'squirt.'"

Aria winked teasingly at him, sliding her panties down a little farther, still managing to hide everything from view. "Still wanna see, big boy?"

Damian looked at Jenny, who glared fiercely at him. It was almost intimidating. Almost.

He looked back at Aria, who had managed to slip out of her socks, and was now only in panties. He knew Aria didn't mind him—or anybody, in fact—staring at her well-endowed chest, which must have been bigger than Jenny's by a significant amount (not that he was measuring or anything). But his main problem was Jenny. Even since the interrogation with the scissors, Damian knew that Jenny was capable of making his life hell. He was starting to think that maybe, just *maybe*, his own hostages might be as or slightly more unhinged than he cared to admit. And that worried him.

Big time.

"Uh," he said, shifting unnerved glances between the sisters. His mind raced. He sure as hell wanted to see, but his primary thought kept repeating itself: *DODGE THE BULLET! DODGE THE BULLET! DODGE THE BULLET! DODGE THE BULLET!*

Then it hit him.

"Hey, what're we gonna do about those undercover soldiers in the restaurant? W-we should prob'ly take care of 'em before we get too comfortable. Right?" He looked at the two of them again, his head swivelling back and forth. "Right?"

"WHAT?!" Jenny exclaimed. "We've got soldiers in the restaurant!?"

Aria sighed and straightened up, crossing her arms, clearly discouraged by the change in subject. "Yeah, I kinda found the bodies of the real faculty stuffed in the janitor's closet. And most of the stand-ins are gathered in the restaurant."

"*WHAT*?!" Jenny shouted. "And your first thought was to take a bath instead!?"

Damian and Aria looked at each other. Then they shrugged and said in unison, "Yeah."

"I don't believe this shit! Did Systems catch up to us already? How'd they find us?"

"It's not Systems," Aria said.

"How do you know?"

"They'd be a lot harder to spot," Damian said. "Duh."

"Great," Jenny said. "So we don't even know who the hell we're up against? That's just fucking *great*!"

Damian smiled and looked at Jenny's chest, which she was still covering up. "You'll stunt your growth with all that shouting."

"FUCK YOU!"

Aria laughed. "Lighten up, Sis. Geez, you're acting weird today."

"Whatever, just tell me what you guys've thought up," Jenny said.

"Huh?" Damian asked.

"Tell me how you guys plan to deal with those soldiers," she said impatiently.

Damian and Aria stared at her. Then, somehow in perfect sync, they tilted their heads to the side and asked, "Huh?"

Jenny's jaw dropped with disbelief. "YOU HAVEN'T THOUGHT UP A PLAN?!"

"No, actually, we were pretty much just gonna wait for something to happen," Damian said.

Aria nodded in agreement. "Pretty much."

"They're soldiers!"

"Oh, please. It's just a worthless scout party awaiting the arrival of the bigger group," Aria said. "Why waste our energy on two fights when we can just wait for the whole package to show up? That way, we'll not only get to open the action figure, but *also* the accessories—all in one go."

"That doesn't make any—" Jenny paused as her sister's explanation registered. "...Actually, that *does* make a little sense. In your guys' weird sort of way."

"See?" Damian said with a smirk.

"Shut up, Damian."

He frowned.

Jenny thought it over for a few seconds. Then she said, "But if we wait for them all to show up, we'll be even *more* outnumbered than we already are, and then we'll have *two* armies to deal with because we were too lazy to pick them off separately!"

Damian said, "See, now *that* sort of thinking is what got us in this mess in the first place!"

"What? No it didn't!"

"Yes it did!"

"Oh, so Marner waking you up from cryosleep, which led to you going on a rampage through my school and taking us hostage to escape the country, only for us to end up here to get surrounded by nameless soldiers is my fault?!"

Damian stared at her, maintaining his serious scowl. "Yes."

"HOW?!"

"It just is."

"That's not a good excuse, goddamn it!"

"You know, I read somewhere that every time you shout, you cancel out half a millimetre of growth as your body continues to develop through the—"

"Bullshit!"

"See, like that. Your boobs would probably be bigger than Aria's if—"

"Stop talking!"

Aria looked at Jenny and said, "He's got a point."

Jenny got out of the bath and quickly wrapped a towel around her body. "No he doesn't." She threw Damian a towel. It landed in a heap at his feet. "Put that on."

Damian looked at it, then at her. "You serious?"

"Yes, dickhead, put the damn towel on."

"I'd rather enjoy this brisk, steamy air that's currently caressing my exposed genitals."

"Okay... first of all: ew. Second of all: I'm not comfortable continuing this conversation with you in the nude."

"What's wrong? Don't like my natural side? Should I cover it in makeup and buy it a skimpy outfit first?"

"I hear full-on latex harness outfits are 50% off on Amabay.com," Aria said.

"I dunno, I'm curious about those shirts with the bras built into them..."

"Knock it off!" Jenny glowered at Damian, seething with anger. "Damian, I swear to God. Put on the fucking towel."

"You're not my supervisor."

"I don't care! I'm getting tired of your shit!"

"*I'm* not tired of it, though."

"Of course you're not. But I don't care. Just put the towel on."

"Make me."

"Do I have to get the scissors?"

Aria looked at the two of them, watching their intense stare-down with slight amusement. "I had to be there, didn't I?"

"I wish *someone* was there," Damian said, keeping his eyes fixed on Jenny.

"Ah, I see."

Damian said to Jenny, "If you want this towel on me so bad, you're gonna have to put it on me yourself."

Jenny's face turned red. Completely taken aback by his reply. "W-what?!"

Damian crossed his arms triumphantly. "You heard me."

"As *if* I'd do that!"

"Then stop bitching."

"I—"

"It's *my* penis; I should be allowed to do whatever I want with it! Swing it or wield it, I have the privilege to holster it or leave it out in the sun."

Jenny looked to Aria for help. All Aria did was snicker. "Aren't you gonna say something?!"

"What's to say?" Aria asked. "You're blowing it out of proportion."

"Really? And you're gonna let 'im talk smack like that?!"

Aria shrugged. "Not like *you're* being a saint."

"Yeah, you feminazi."

Then Jenny said, "I am *so* done," and stomped behind the wall of lockers that divided the change room to get dressed.

"Hey, guys?" Matthew's voice came up on the radio.

Aria snatched it off the bench and said, "What's up, punk?"

"I think our friends are getting agitated."

"How agitated?" she asked. "Are they getting restless in their seats?"

Matthew looked around at the two dozen submachine guns that surrounded him on his stool. The soldiers holding those guns maintained their thousand-yard stares as their companions carried munitions crates into every dining area, and even the kitchen.

"They're not even *in* their seats," Matthew said. Then he turned to one of the soldiers standing behind the bar counter and handed him his empty cup. "Mind refilling that for me?"

The soldier smashed the cup with his fist, then racked his submachine gun threateningly.

"They're not very friendly, either," Matthew added, frowning at the soldier.

"What d'you mean?"

"They kinda took me as their hostage. And they're multiplying by the minute."

"Do they know you're immortal?" Aria asked as Jenny rounded the locker wall fully dressed, and urging Damian to 'conjure up his clothing.'

"No, they don't know that."

"Know what?" one of the soldiers snarled.

Matthew looked at him and quickly answered with the first thing that sprang to mind: "This week's winning lottery numbers are 11-34-62-78-50-43 bonus 62."

"Goddamn it!" someone shouted from the kitchen. "Off by *one* freaking digit!"

"So yeah," Matthew said, "they've kinda got me by the balls—figuratively, of course—and apparently they were waiting for whom they perceived to be their weakest asset to end up alone." He chuckled. "They think *I'm* the weakest asset."

"Well, the actual weakest is passed out on the floor over here... why'd they think it was you?"

Matthew looked at the captain of the squad—a burly soldier with his uniform sleeves rolled just above his elbows, narrow brown eyes, and a black moustache cutting across his face, deformed from a multitude of jagged scars running every which way. "Why'd you think I was the weakest again?"

The captain rapped the countertop with his bulky twelve-shooter revolver, obviously gesturing toward the claymore leaning on the counter beside Matthew. The captain chuckled and said, "You brought a sword to a gunfight."

"Told you so," Aria said.

Matthew scowled. "We'll see who's laughing later on..."

"Think you can distract 'em long enough before we get there?" Aria asked.

"They don't need distractions; they're legit *waiting* for you guys to show."

"Oh."

"Yeah," he said.

"We'll bring Jeremy along for the ride."

"Hurry up. These guys're impatient."

"Got it."

Click!

Matthew put the radio down. Then he looked at the captain and said, "Alright, guess we've got some time to kill before they get here."

"How long?" the captain asked, his gruff voice like boulders slowly crushing broken glass.

Matthew shrugged. "Maybe fifteen minutes?"

The captain popped the cylinder of his twelve-shooter and took out eleven random slugs. Then he spun the cylinder, and before it could stop on its own he slapped the cylinder into place and put the gun down on the countertop between them. "How 'bout some Russian roulette?"

Matthew looked at the gun, then at the captain. "How many bullets?"

"Just one. Explosive rounds. Sure to blow your head clean off," the captain said with a sly grin.

Matthew blinked. "Oh, joy."

Damian, Jenny and Aria went into the men's change room to get Jeremy and inform him of the situation. Much to Jenny and Jeremy's annoyance, neither Damian nor Aria bothered to put any clothes on during the briefing. Damian was eventually convinced to put on his regular telekinetic clothing, but Aria remained in panties only, with a towel over her shoulder like a scarf, which barely concealed her breasts.

"So now what?" Damian asked. "We go in there guns

blazing?"

"No," Jenny said. "It might be smart to try an' talk to them first. You know, to find out what they want."

"Since when did *you* stop and listen to someone else?" Damian asked, laughing at her.

Jenny scowled. "Don't start with—"

"Moving on," Aria cut them off casually, smirking when she noticed Jeremy staring at her partially exposed chest. "I kind of agree with Jenny on this one. We go in, see if we can negotiate something, and hopefully get out scot-free—or at least, in a way that'll end up with us in that hot spring."

"Still thinking about the bath?" Jenny asked.

"Hell yes. Those baths look *so* good."

Damian's revolvers appeared in his hands. He examined them closely as he said, "If the shit hits the fan, at least we'll be prepared."

"Yeah, as if *they* will not be prepared," Jeremy replied, rolling his eyes.

"Well *of course* they're gonna be prepared, dipshit," Damian said. "They're trained soldiers with weapons of every calibre stuffed up their asses, on a mission (most likely) to capture *me*, the one guy everybody seems to be afraid of right now."

"Justifiably so," Jeremy added.

"Still. They're prepared for a showdown. Their purpose is to save the main group some time and hopefully get me early. They wouldn't be crazy enough to risk the outcome of their mission over some pointless bullshit. I mean c'mon. That's like... basic training."

SNAPT!

The hammer slammed into an empty chamber. The twelve-shooter, which the captain held against his own head, didn't go off. He breathed a sigh of relief and let out a jittery snicker as he slammed the gun on the countertop, and pushed it toward Matthew.

The soldiers passed along lost bets to the opposing team—an exchange that was brief but rowdy, with shouting and cheering.

Matthew lifted the revolver. One of the soldiers yelled, "Place your bets!" as Matthew put the gun to his temple and cocked the hammer. He waited for the soldiers to place their bets, which gave him enough time to collect himself. Beads of sweat trickled down his forehead when the soldier yelled, "Bets closed!"

Matthew said, maintaining a superficial grin to hide his anxiety. “Ah, hell.”

Then he pulled the trigger.

COBALT ROGUE, VOL. 1: THE DEAD BLUE

Episode 011

Hot Spring Roulette

Five minutes since Aria received Matthew's call, she had distributed a big load of firearms and grenades to Jenny and Jeremy thanks to her unusual ability to sprout items from her hands. Damian already had his telekinesis to rely on, and the four of them were all set to go out like the Wild Bunch in a blaze of glory. Now they were going down the hall in standing two-by-two formation—Damian and Aria in front, Jeremy and Jenny in the back.

A thought crossed Jenny's mind on their way. "Jeremy, you're trained for this sorta thing, right? I mean, you've been in shootouts... right?"

Jeremy looked up from his M16 rifle and said, "Yes, I have done this before."

"What kinda mechanic gets into gunfights, though?"

"The kind that does not like it when hooligans trespass onto his private property to try and steal his modified cars."

Jenny blinked, trying to picture Jeremy as a gun-toting badass machine-gunning hapless carjackers in the middle of the night, even at one point glancing at the Hawk MM1 grenade launcher in her hands as if it had the image projected on the side. "Nope. Can't see that."

"Looks can be deceiving," Jeremy said.

Damian said, "I can vouch for him on that one. The guy's a maniac if you touch his shit in the middle of the night."

"You would know," Jeremy said with a snicker.

Damian frowned. "That toaster bomb was not funny."

Jenny snorted. "What the hell is a toaster bomb?"

"That would be because you did not have the detonator in your hand," Jeremy said, ignoring Jenny as she laughed alongside him.

Damian glanced over his left shoulder at Jeremy. "No, and even if I did, I *still* wouldn't have laughed." He looked over his right shoulder at Jenny and added, "Seriously though: he's reliable in a gunfight. Best mechanic ever."

Aria cleared her throat. She still only wore panties with either end of a small towel draped over her shoulders and partially obscuring her breasts. She dual-wielded two full-sized Uzis. "Don't forget me now. You've got two of 'em in the group, you know."

Damian looked at her. "You're a mechanic now?"

"Yep. It's my day job, actually."

"I didn't know that. Get many customers?"

"Mostly just Max. He drives a real piece of shit."

"So why keep it?"

"Because the back seat is comfortable as hell and it doesn't hurt my knees."

Damian looked ahead of them for a few moments in silence. Then: "You'd know."

"My garage is probably destroyed now, though..."

"Why?"

"Because of you."

"Hey, I didn't burn it down."

"Systems probably raided the shit out of it. That's what I mean."

"Oh. In that case, you're probably right."

"Uh-huh," Aria grunted.

"...The 'destroyed' part, not the part where it's my fault."

"Right," she replied, frowning.

Without warning or hesitation, they approached the restaurant entrance. Damian kicked the double door entrance down and shouted, "Trick or treat, you fuckin' dickheads!" to announce their arrival, interrupting Matthew and the captain's game of Russian roulette and (not unexpectedly) finding themselves in a Mexican standoff with the enemy squad. With guns pointed at them from every direction, even from the balconies and possibly through the skylights, Damian and the others slowly made their way to the bar. Soldiers cleared a path for them.

When they reached the bar, Matthew put down the twelve-shooter and said, "You're just in time. Gun only had two shots left."

Damian looked at the captain and said, "Who the hell are you?"

The captain smiled and replied, "I am Captain Chucky Davis of the 7th Division of the Troyas Brigade. To put it bluntly, I'm here to retrieve you and take you back to Troyas."

"Oh, so you're with Troyas, huh?" Damian said, stealing a suspicious glance toward Aria. *The plot thickens.* "And what do you want with me?"

"That's classified information."

"I don't give a flying fuck."

"All I can say is: 'cooperate, please, or come back with us by force.'"

"Yeah, like *that'll* happen."

"How about a deal, then?"

"What kind of deal?"

"Are you a betting man, Mr. Dead Blue?"

Damian paused. Then: "Depends on the circumstances, I guess."

Captain Davis tapped the twelve-shooter with his forefinger and said, "A game. You win; you get a thirty-minute head start before we come after you."

"Sir," one of the soldiers protested, "We can't do—"

Davis raised his hand sharply, cutting him off. He continued, "I win... you come with us, and you give us your full cooperation."

"This's got something to do with that pentagram, doesn't it?" Damian asked.

"Yes, it does. I think you can guess what'll happen from there."

"What makes you think I'll cooperate?"

"If you lose?"

"I'm a pretty sore loser."

"You won't have much of a say in the matter. See, the slug that's chambered in this gun is enough to blow any normal person's head off. But *you're* not normal, are you? It'll take you out for a couple of hours, but you'll be back. You're one of those special cases that can't die from just a close-range shot to the head. But when that slug decimates half your skull, it'll give us all the time we need to do what we've gotta do."

Damian nodded thoughtfully, running through it again in his mind. "You really thought that one through."

"And don't worry about your friends—"

"Hostages."

Jenny rolled her eyes.

Davis continued, "...Hostages... they're of no consequence to us. They're free to go. Getting them involved would only complicate things."

"We're *already* involved," Jenny hissed.

"Jenny," Aria said quickly, grabbing her shoulder and shaking her head. "Don't."

"I meant *more* involved. You can do whatever you want. We're only after Damian. Once we have him, you're no longer in this ridiculous extended chase sequence. You can go home."

Aria didn't bother asking what they were going to do with Damian, or how he fit into all of this in the first place. She figured they'd just go along with their 'classified' bullshit again. Just the thought of it made her scowl bitterly.

Damian gave it some thought. He surveyed the area, seeing the dozens of armed soldiers behind partition walls and crouched behind glass banisters on the balconies. They filled up every dining area, and some of them were even in the kitchen. Starting a gunfight now wouldn't be a very smart move. They'd be cut down in an instant, and all bets would be off. "Alright," he said. "So if I play your little game, and I win, doesn't that mean you'll die?"

"Let me worry about that."

"Suit yourself."

"Deal?" Davis stretched out his hand.

Damian looked at Jeremy, Jenny and Aria in turn, then swivelled back around and took Davis' hand. Davis probably thought of this as a 'shake hands with the devil' kind of situation. Damian couldn't help but smirk at the thought. *You have no idea.* "Deal."

Davis gestured toward Matthew and said, "Have a seat and we can begin."

Damian looked at Matthew. Matthew looked back at him and said, "Get your own seat."

"Okay," Damian said. Then he shoved Matthew to the floor and propped himself on the stool.

"The fuck, man!" Matthew exclaimed as he picked himself up off the floor and grabbed his claymore. He barely picked the sword up before Damian had his own revolver in his face.

"Don't," Damian said. "Now's not the time, man."

Matthew growled at him, "Maybe not now... but someday..."

As Matthew retrieved his claymore and joined the others, Damian turned back to Davis and picked up the twelve-shooter. "Whoa, this brings back memories."

"You've played Russian roulette before?" Davis asked, eyebrows cocked.

"Yeah, well, when you're dying of starvation during the war with five other kids and only one waffle box to split, you tend to learn a few things."

Back then...

Ten-year-old Damian sat with the Model 500 in his hand. A tattered box of waffles he'd discovered sat in the middle of the group. He looked at the five dead children splayed out in a circle around the waffle box, lying in pools of their own blood and brains.

Then he said, "Guess it's my turn." He put the gun to his head, clamped his eyes shut, tensed up, and pulled the trigger.

Click!

Relieved, Damian grabbed the waffle box and pulled it closer.

Then stopped.

"Wait a minute." He popped the revolver's cylinder open and looked at the five spent shells in their chambers. "...Oh."

Present Day

"...Huh," Davis said. "I don't know what I should say to that."

"Yeah, this brings back memories." Damian snapped the cylinder open and looked at the one slug loaded in it. He took it out, studied it closely, and put it back in. Then he spun the cylinder and slapped it back into place. He cocked the hammer and said, "Alright, you guys wanna make bets, make 'em now."

"Place your bets!" one of the soldiers yelled.

The soldiers placed their bets in a rowdy ten seconds, much to Jenny and Jeremy's disbelief.

"This is disgusting," Jeremy said.

"Hey, easy money," Aria said.

Damian looked at them. "Aren't you guys betting?"

"Hell no!" Jenny exclaimed.

When the soldiers placed their bets, Damian put the gun to his head.

"Bets closed!" one of the soldiers called.

"Be careful, Damian," Jenny said.

"Since when were *you* worried for my safety and well-being?"

Jenny stole a quick glance at Aria, who raised an eyebrow. Then she snapped, "N-never! I was just... like... you know, uh—"

"Do I sense a little 'Bonnie and Clyde syndrome' there?" Aria asked with a slightly concerned sideways glance.

"NO!" Jenny exclaimed. "I was just saying! *GOD*!"

"Pfft," Damian said. "Relax. My chances of losing are one-in-six." He pulled the trigger.

Snapt!

Damian blinked. Everyone else jumped. The gun didn't go off. Damian smirked and put the gun down on the countertop. "One-in-five. The odds are stacked in my favour."

Captain Davis picked up the gun and slowly put it to his head. He cocked the hammer and wrapped his finger around the trigger. The soldiers held their breaths. The tension seemed to be at its thickest when—

Snapt!

The hammer clicked.

The soldiers exhaled all at once, as if a cold draft had swept through the room. Then the soldiers got rowdy again as they exchanged bills of money.

Davis put the gun down and slid it across the countertop toward Damian, who promptly lifted it to his temple and pulled the hammer back.

"Place your bets!"

The soldiers went about their usual calls, with several betting against their own captain.

"Bets closed!"

Damian tensed up, as did everyone else. Then he pulled the trigger.

Snapt!

More exhaled breaths hissed through the air as Damian slammed the gun on the countertop and pushed it under Davis' raised hand. Davis picked it up, and before anyone could react, he'd put the gun to his head and fired.

Snapt!

Davis laughed—it was the laugh of a man who had let go of any ideas of surviving to see the sunset. Damian didn't know if he'd given up on living, or if he was just relieved to have survived the second round. Having seen so many soldiers act similarly during the war, it was hard to distinguish one from the other.

The soldiers got loud and rough again as Davis slammed the revolver on the counter and twirled it like a spin top. Some of them forked over money while others greedily snatched up lost bets. It wasn't too long before they quieted down again, anxiously awaiting the beginning of the third round.

Round three began.

"Place your bets!"

The soldiers became an angry mob again, shouting their bets and perceived odds on how the third round would go.

"Forty on the Dead Blue!"

"Sixty on the Captain!"

"Fifty-fifty odds, eh?! I think I'll stick with the Cap'n on this one!"

Almost half done. Odds of blasting half my face off... one-in-four. Now things're starting to get interesting, Damian thought as he took the gun and lifted it to his head.

"Damian, wait," Jenny said. "Just do something else."

"Shut up, Jenny."

"This is insane," she continued, "what if that's the loaded chamber?! Just put the gun down a-and we can figure something else out!"

"Shut *up*, Jenny."

"You shut up! I'm trying to be the voice of reason here!"

"I don't *need* your voice of reason!"

"Don't you see how crazy this is?!"

"Don't you know when to shut the fuck up?!"

Jenny's heart skipped when she saw him thumb the hammer. "C'mon, p-put the gun down..."

"If I do that, then I lose automatically."

"So what's a loss or two?!"

"In the center of an angry mob full of soldiers? Probably everything."

"He is correct," Jeremy said.

"Yeah, you idiot."

Jenny looked at him. "You too?"

Jeremy nodded, the grim expression on his face practically

telling Jenny exactly what he thought about the situation. "If he forfeits, all bets are off. Our odds would not be high, because they have us surrounded—in case you have not noticed—and only two of us are immortal—"

"Make that three," Matthew said.

"*Three* of us are immortal. The rest of us are not so fortunate."

"Damn. Well… can't we negotiate with them some more and come up with something else?"

Davis chimed in, "No, little lady, you can't. Negotiations are as good as done."

"But—"

"Little lady," Davis said, cutting her off with a fierce glare, "the contract is final. The terms must be met. Don't try to deprive me of the simple pleasures of this game. It's my favourite game, after all, and to play it with the Dead Blue has been an ultimate… *personal* goal of mine; something I never dreamed would actually come true until today. So leave it be."

Jenny and Davis stared at one other; Jenny with intimidation from his glare, and Davis with vicious annoyance to her pleas.

"Bets closed!"

Damian glanced over his shoulder at her. "If it bugs you so much, leave the fucking room. Maybe Marner would like some company if she happens to wake up before we get back." His impatient glare shifted toward Aria. "Christ, control your sister."

"She's not a dog. I can't tell her to sit, Damian," she snapped back.

"Well you can't *now*. Should've started when she was younger," Damian said.

"Yeah, right; I'm gonna train my younger sister to sit and be quiet when I tell her to, you jackass."

"…Goddamn it," he hissed. "You'd swear she was wet for me or something."

Jenny was quick to retort, "Hey, just because I'm concerned doesn't mean—"

"FUCK'S SAKE, JENNY!" Damian yelled. "SHUT! The *fuck*—" He pulled the trigger.

SNAPT!

"—UP!" he finished, slamming the twelve-shooter down between him and Davis.

Jenny's eyes widened. "Oh my God…"

"Jenny," Aria said, "stop."

Jenny looked at her sister in disbelief. "Y-you can't be serious…!"

"I get it," Damian said. "You're worried. I get it. But I don't need your shit right now. This is tense enough without your constant whining."

"Agreed on that one," Davis said with a chuckle. "We're almost half over and neither of us has bitten it yet. My men are running out of money." He put the gun to his head. "I'm running out of patience, too." He inhaled sharply, and—

SNAPT!

Davis breathed a sigh of relief. *Leave it all to chance.* He put the gun down and reached under the counter. Aria tensed up and fingered the triggers of her Uzis until he brought up a bottle of saké. "How about one last drink?"

Damian blinked, surprised by Davis' casual attitude. "Uh… sure?"

The soldiers once again started yelling and shooting angry insults and obscenities at each other as they exchanged lost bets. A fight broke out in the southwest dining room, with numerous onlookers cheering them on as they slammed each other through tables. One of the participants splintered a booth table in half with his companion's face, right before his companion wrenched himself free of his grip and shattered a whisky bottle over his head and kicked him through a glass partition wall.

"I bet you sixty an' paid up!" the companion yelled. "You bet forty on the Captain, and gave me ten! Goddamn son of a bitch owes me another thirty!"

"Just wait till next round, fucker!" the other soldier responded as he lunged through the hole in the partition wall and tackled his companion to the floor. "*You'll* be the one to pay up!" He drew a Bowie knife from his belt. "You'll pay, alright!"

The other soldiers quickly intervened, separating and restraining the two brawlers as they continued to swing their fists and shout death threats.

"Shit," Damian said, watching the spectacle from his stool. "Someone's not turtley enough for the Turtle Club."

Matthew glared at Damian and said, "I should kill you for that reference."

"Bite me, fuckface."

"No thanks," Matthew fired back, "I'd probably catch 'asshole disease.'"

"Can't catch what you already have."

"Fuck you."

"You're not my type."

Matthew started to growl angrily, arms rigid. He was ready to strangle him from behind. "I fucking *dare* you to say that again."

Aria stepped between them. "Hey, hey. Knock it off. We don't need this right now."

Matthew pouted. Damian smirked, figuring he'd won the argument.

"Now, then," Davis said as he poured saké into two cups and passed one on to Damian. "Shall we continue?" He raised his cup. "To winning."

Damian didn't know what to think of Davis' casual attitude at first, but when Davis raised his cup for a toast, Damian couldn't help but feel a little respect for the man, primarily due to his supposed fearlessness. Whether he'd fully go through with it was a different story that Damian was eager to see to the end. *Hopefully he doesn't turn out to be a pussy pulling wool over my eyes. I'd kill him right there and then.*

Davis maintained his competitive glare as Damian lifted his cup at face level. *I hope you're not all talk, Mr. Dead Blue. I'd be... very disappointed.*

Damian tapped his cup against Davis' and said, "To dodging bullets." The restaurant quieted down as the two competitors chugged their drinks, and smashed their empty cups on the countertop with fire in their eyes.

"Place your bets!" the self-appointed bet caller yelled, igniting another rowdy series of bet placing from the anxious soldiers. It lasted a minute before the bet caller yelled, "Bets closed!"

Damian snatched the twelve-shooter and put it to his head. He shot Davis a cocky grin in an attempt to conceal his nervousness. Davis seemed to be understanding. Damian could see it in his eyes—it wasn't condescension, but acknowledgement. *Heh... bastard sure knows how to throw a party.* He cocked the hammer. Only then—to his surprise—did his hands start trembling. His forefinger curved around the trigger and started to pull it back. Then—

"One last thing," Davis said, making Damian jump. "In case this is the last shot to be fired, I want to know something."

Damian sighed, easing up on the trigger. "What?"

"Your name. What is it?"

"Don't your records or whatever tell you that?"

"I'm just a grunt. They only refer to you by the popular name, 'The Dead Blue.' Never once have I ever found out your real name. And I'd like to know before you—or I—meet the bullet."

Damian stared at him, still trying to stop the shaking in his hands. The gun seemed to rattle in his ear. "It's Warkowski. Damian Warkowski."

Davis smiled. "Damian Warkowski. That's a nice name, actually."

"Better be; it's the only one I've got."

The captain chuckled. "Maintaining a sense of humour in the face of death, eh? Very sportsmanlike. That'd make a good story."

If these were going to be his final words for the next few hours, Damian wouldn't have had a problem with that: "It would, wouldn't it?" He pulled the trigger.

Jenny gasped. Jeremy flinched. Aria and Matthew simply blinked, while the majority of the soldiers inhaled sharply.

SNAPT!

The sound of the hammer hitting an empty chamber lifted some of the tension from the room, only for it to shoot back up when Damian handed the gun to Davis.

Davis accepted it graciously and put it to his head. Cocked the hammer. And fired.

SNAPT!

Davis exhaled deeply, as did everyone else, Damian included. He placed the gun down on the countertop as the soldiers went wild.

"I don't believe it! There's gonna be a *sixth* round?!"

"This's gotta be the first time a game's lasted this long!"

"Jesus goddamn Christ, I don't believe this shit either!"

As the soldiers continued yelling and throwing money at each other in bouts of rage and frustration, Damian calmly tapped the countertop with his forefinger. "Mind passing me another bottle of that stuff?"

"Certainly," Davis said as he reached down and got another bottle, and handed it to Damian.

Damian unscrewed the cap and started downing the entire bottle. Davis gawked at him before shrugging and doing the same with the half-empty bottle in his own hand. The restaurant quieted down again as the spectators witnessed Damian and Davis emptying their bottles, and then smashing them into the countertop at the exact same time. "Let's do this!" Damian shouted as he grabbed the revolver and put it to his head. "It's either you or me this time. No more copouts. No more time. No more options."

"50/50," Davis said, gripping his end of the counter with his fists, actually managing to crack the wood. "All or nothing."

"Place your bets!" the caller roared excitedly.

The soldiers were louder than ever. A quarter of them voted for Damian while the rest bet on their captain.

Aria laughed excitedly, more out of anxiety than entertainment. "This's getting intense!"

Jeremy shook uncontrollably beside Jenny, gnawing at his bottom lip until it bled.

"Bets closed!"

The soldiers didn't stop this time. They started yelling, chanting for the final round, stabbing the air with sweaty fists and loaded guns as they screamed their support for both competitors.

Jenny lost her nerve. She brushed past Aria and pushed her way through the mob to get out. Aria watched her leave with sympathy, knowing it was bound to happen, which also confirmed her worst fears. *She's got a thing for him. ...Shit.*

Damian cocked the hammer. This was it. He stared into Davis' eyes—the eyes of death. The last pair of eyes he may ever see before he's used as a weapon of mass destruction, to serve the goals of humans. Humans… he hated them. Most of them. Or all of them. He wasn't quite sure. But he knew for a fact he hated the people who were after him. The stinking politicians and world leaders that wanted to achieve the status of godhood with his blood. The rotten bastards, who exterminated his race on the basis of a wild rumour, spread by the one man he hated most—who wasn't even human—Jonathon Silverstein. *Fucker's gotta pay,* his thoughts raced. *I can't go down yet. Not yet. Not yet!*

Davis grabbed another bottle from under the counter with

hands that shook so violently that when he tried to unscrew the cap he ended up snapping off the bottle neck. His eyes never left Damian's for a second.

Damian's heart raced. It pounded with the force of a grenade exploding inside his chest. The gun kept sliding away from his temple, causing him more frustration as he fought to keep his hand level. *Do it, fucking do it you fucking pussy. Fuck! Do it! DO IT! DO IT!*

"Gimme that fucking bottle!" Damian shouted, snatching the broken bottle from Davis and chugging down half a litre before dumping the rest of the saké and broken glass over his head. He felt a few chunks of glass cutting his cheeks and scraping across his teeth. He chewed them up and spat them up onto the countertop. He didn't lower the gun even for a split second, drenched in sweat and saké, spitting blood and glass to the side. His hands were going numb. The gun was slipping, until he started to clench on the trigger. It seemed like all the blood in his body rushed to his face as he started screaming, "Fuck! Fuck! Fuck! I can fucking do this! FUUUUUUUUCK!" He smashed the bottle on the counter, splattering glass shards and saké all over the place and cutting his hand, which he balled into a fist and frequently slammed into the counter. Glass slashed his rigid fingers, but he didn't care.

The crowd went mad, jumping up and down, cheering them on. Their roars deafening. Their ears ringing. This was it. Either I win, or that goddamn bullet tunnels through my skull and blasts my fucking head off!

And to everyone's shock, Damian started to laugh. Then Davis started to laugh. The crowd was still going crazy, even as the two combatants on either side of the counter laughed in each other's faces, obliterating the restraints they maintained on their own insanity, even for just this moment.

"GONNA DO IT! GONNA DO IT, GODDAMN IT, I'M GONNA… LIVE! I'M GONNA LIIIIIVE! HERE GOES FUCKIN' NOTHIIIIIIIIING—" Finally, Damian clamped his eyes shut, gritted his teeth, and squeezed the trigger.

SNAPT!

The gun didn't go off. Damian was still screaming even as he jumped off his stool and slammed the gun into the countertop, cracking the wood and smashing the glass shards that covered it.

"FUUUUUUCK!"

The room went dead silent.

Damian was practically dry-heaving over the counter, gasping right in his adversary's face. "Fuck yeah! That's what I'm fuckin' talking about! VICTORY, BITCH!" He slumped onto his stool, panting.

Davis stared back at him with an equal amount of exhaustion.

Then Davis picked up the gun and put it to his head. "Well, then…"

Damian blinked. "What… what the hell are you…?"

"Seeing my game through to the finish."

"Why?!"

"It wouldn't be very sportsmanlike if I didn't."

The soldiers started to desperately swarm around their captain, reaching for the gun all at once and shoving Damian's companions/hostages aside. "Sir, don't!"

"It was an honour playing with you, Damian Warkowski."

BANG!

Episode 012

Hot Spring Shootout

Bang!

The gunshot made Jenny drop her grenade launcher and slap her hands over her mouth, fearing the absolute worst. *Damian had the chambered bullet. Oh God... he had the bullet... please tell me that wasn't him.* Each heartbeat was like a painful, burning throb that sent a hot rush flowing through her chest.

She couldn't explain why her perspective of him was suddenly changing, but she had a few guesses, all of which she perceived to be one form of weakness or another. *Snap out of it, you stupid bitch.* If she were standing in front of a mirror with no one around, she would have said it aloud. *This is stupid. I mean... if he's the one who died, then... then everything would be over, right?*

...Right?

The last thing Damian saw before Davis splattered his head all over his soldiers' uniforms was the satisfied grin on his face. In a flash, it was gone, leaving the crowd in shocked silence, watching as Davis' headless body tumbled off the stool and hit the floor in a crumpled heap. Damian stared at the spot where Davis' face was just a few seconds ago, before leaning over the countertop and looking down at the corpse to make sure what just happened really just happened.

The body was there; blood was pooling from under Davis' corpse, and Damian and his companions/hostages were still surrounded by soldiers. Damian gulped. "That was… unexpected." He turned to Aria, whose eyes bulged. "Did you see that coming?"

She shook her head back and forth slowly.

"Because *I* didn't see it coming! Jesus Christ! Why the fuck did he shoot himself?!"

"Eh," one of the soldiers said as he wiped his dead superior's brains off his vest with disdain. "He always *did* say he hated his job."

Damian looked at him.

"Kept rambling on about 'the perfect opponent' in his stupid Russian roulette games and how he hoped to lose at one point."

Damian's narrowed his eyes. "Why even *give* him a gun, then?!"

"...Because he's a military captain and we never took him seriously?"

Damian squinted at the obvious contradictions in the soldier's answer, shaking his head slowly. "Your government isn't the shiniest keg in the larder, is it?"

"Hey!" the soldier growled. "How dare someone like you make such a heinous mockery of our God-fearing, freedom-loving democracy!"

Flabbergasted, Damian cocked his head to side. "Uh... what?"

"You see the nerve of this little shithead, boys?" the soldier yelled for all to hear. "He kills our captain and then has the nerve to make fun of our democratic government and insult our beloved President Truman!"

Angry murmurs surfaced from the crowd.

Aria glanced around worriedly as the soldiers started to converge on them like a pack of wolves. "Oooh shit."

"This is not good," Jeremy said, gripping his M16 tightly.

"No shit, Captain Obvious," Matthew said.

"Hey, *I* didn't kill your captain," Damian said. "And I only asked a simple question. You'd swear I just threatened to kill everyone or something!"

"Jesus goddamn Christ!" the soldier screamed. "He just threatened to obliterate our country with... with... terror threats against our people and our Constitutional freedom! That's more than enough justification to act with full-on hostility! Rack 'em up, boys!"

The soldiers trained their guns on Damian and his hostages. Damian pointed his revolver at the soldier who started this, while the rest of his tag-along crew poised their guns defensively, standing back-to-back with each other.

"Wait just one fucking minute," Damian said. "I didn't do *anything*. And we made a deal with your captain—"

"Exactly!" the soldier said. "Your deal was between you and the captain, not *us*."

Damian blinked, then scowled and muttered, "Goddamn it."

The soldier gasped in horror. "You spreadin' hate speech about Christians, boy?! I oughta drop you like the rotten piece of freakish Dehue shit that you are."

Aria noticed it right away. The twinge that would spark absolute chaos. "Damian..."

"What the fuck did you just say?" Damian asked with an undertone of barely subdued anger.

"Damian," Aria said again.

The soldier smirked, clearly unfazed by the telekinetic revolver pointed at his head, and leaned forward to whisper it mockingly, "I'll repeat it slower so that you can understand: I..."

"*Damian*," Aria said, louder this time.

"Ought..."

Damian's glare intensified. *Why'd he have to go and use that fucking word?*

"To..."

Go ahead—say that again.

"Drop..."

"Damian," Aria said. He wasn't listening. Aria turned to Matthew and Jeremy. "Get ready to duck."

"Um... why?" Matthew asked incredulously.

"You... like... a..."

He paused. Everyone in the room stiffened, as if everyone—not just Aria and Jeremy—knew that something big was about to happen.

Then the soldier leaned even closer, getting in Damian's face, the muzzle of his energy revolver touching his forehead. Threatening him. Challenging him. "FREA—"

KAPOW!

Damian blew the soldier's head off and continued ripping holes through his body with a rapid succession of shots, all while turning a second revolver on two others, blasting one in the stomach before drilling a cavity in the other's chest.

Jeremy and Aria squatted, guns blazing, cutting down a score of soldiers before they could react. Matthew lunged into the group of soldiers gathered behind Damian, swinging his claymore through their bodies and sending their top halves spiralling through the air in a wild blood spray. One of his victims flew into a framed picture on a nearby pillar, shattering it.

The rest of the soldiers opened up with a deafening roar that shook the place to its roots. The bar stools splintered as Damian and Jeremy dived behind the counter. Matthew was a deadly blur of silver and red, shredding through bodies like a buzz saw, spinning toward the staircase leading up to the balcony.

Aria didn't make an effort to dodge them or take cover, grunting when bullets pelted her back. Then she whirled around and blasted soldiers through the half-glass partition with her Uzis. Her bullets tore across the southwest dining area; punching frosted glass out of wooden frames and ripping her way through a platoon.

Soldiers on the balconies delivered a hail of blazing lead onto the bar and the area around it. Aria darted toward the southwest dining area, bullets chasing her across the clearing. She hopped onto a table and vaulted over the partition wall, her Uzis tearing up the nearest group of soldiers gathered on the other side as she soared through the air.

She landed on another table and rolled to the other end, all while enemy bullets ripped up the ornaments and the furniture. The table flipped over as she squatted and darted across the dining area. A tsunami of hot lead obliterated everything in plain sight as Aria dashed between tables with her head down. The soldiers trudged through the area in pursuit, kicking over tables and chairs, their bullets skipping across tabletops and cutlery.

KABOOM!

A fireball erupted from under the southeast balcony, curling up between two pillars, across the clearing from the bar. Soldiers and splintered booths blew across the restaurant as another explosion ripped the tiles off the pillars it rolled between, blasting more carcasses and debris in the bar's direction, shattering the half-glass partition wall.

Jenny made her way down the hall, launching grenades through the walls and flinching when the walls disintegrated from the subsequent explosions. Soldiers bounced across the corridor as she headed toward the restaurant entrance, her volley of grenades blowing up the northeast dining area as if they were cannonballs zipping through straw houses.

The tables and wall tiles were reduced to plumes of burning

fragments that pelted the fleeing soldiers like hailstones. Fireballs blossomed from every impact point, launching bodies into the ceiling or through bullet-torn booths. By the time Jenny had blasted the main entrance inward, flames had swelled through the pillars, devouring the furniture and the soldiers trapped within its shattered confines.

Damian and Jeremy were crouched behind the bar counter, shooting at the soldiers on the southeast balcony with stubborn resilience, even as enemy fire sprayed the countertop and the shelf behind them. Saké bottles burst above their heads. Glass particles rained down from the skylights.

Damian noticed Jenny making her way across the room and the two locked eyes. Relief flashed across her face and she gave him a quick smile before she went back to work.

Jeremy flinched as an overhead shotgun blasted bits of saké bottles out from under the counter into his face. "Goddamn it, Damian," he growled as he ducked down to wipe saké from his eyes.

"Whoa, now," Damian said as he turned to see a soldier emerge from the kitchen doorway. He splattered him against the wall. "Do your parents know you use that kind of language?"

"Very funny, you inbred son of a bitch," Jeremy hissed as he straightened and opened up on the southeast balcony.

"What the fuck's your problem?" Damian fired a shot through the skylight, rewarded by a soldier's body pivoting through it and crashing down on the bar counter in a shower of glass.

"Our situation has escalated from 'bad' to 'worse'!" Jeremy said as he retreated behind the counter to reload. "All because you wanted to play Russian roulette with the highest-ranking officer in the enemy scout troupe!"

"Well, first of all: that's not what made the situation worse. It was that soldier who decided to be a douchebag and twist my words around." Damian blinked as enemy bullets shredded the corpse that had fallen from the skylight, splattering his innards all over the place like a blender without a lid. "Second of all: before you go with the whole 'this would not have happened if you had stayed in the cryogenic capsule' argument, know that if you *do* try to use that, I won't hesitate to kneecap you. Third of all: I kept my end of the bargain and played that captain's stupid game to the finish, so don't blame me if his subordinates aren't happy with that! And *fourth* of all: *I'm* the only one who can state when the situation escalates! That's my thing! Also, fifth of all—" he paused to hurl a saké bottle across the room. It shattered against an infantryman's helmet. The infantryman turned to face Damian and immediately took an energy bullet in the face. "—I didn't want to play Russian roulette with the highest-ranking officer in the enemy scout troupe, so don't go around saying I did like some chirpy bitch."

Jeremy slapped in a new magazine and started shooting over the mulched corpse of the skylight sniper, which had just lost its head to a shotgun blast. "Oh, stop acting so childish."

"Says the one who just threw all the blame on me! You're a fantastic friend, you goggle-eyed, Copter Ship exhaust pipe-sucking asshole!"

From the burning wreckage below the southeast balcony, a soldier leaped up and made a charge for the bar, waving his fighting knife around like a lunatic until a shot from Damian's revolver caught him in the face. The soldier's legs buckled, then he fell forward, headless shoulders hitting the front of the counter.

"Copter Ships do not have exhaust pipes!"

"Whatever!" Damian stood upright and fired through the window into the kitchen, scoring a soldier who had just pulled the pin on a grenade. The soldier rotated, arms rigid, energy bullets ripping through his torso, grenade slipping through his outstretched fingers. "Stop acting like this sort of thing is new, Germ! Also, duck." Damian grabbed him and yanked him to the floor just before a plume of flaming shrapnel hurled the soldier through the window. Jeremy jumped smartly when the soldier landed awkwardly between them.

"Do *not* call me 'Germ'!" Jeremy snapped as he ejected an empty clip and shoved a new one into his assault rifle. "Move aside!" Still in a crouch, he pushed his way past Damian toward the kitchen entrance.

"Where're you going?" Damian asked irritably.

"Taking the kitchen," Jeremy answered before rounding the corner and hosing the kitchen interior with bullets, cutting down four soldiers that stood near the back door.

"Fix me a snack while you're in there."

"Have I not done enough?!"

Another soldier burst through the back door, only to be blown away by Jeremy's assault rifle.

"It's a snack, not a fucking blowjob!"

A sniper crouched behind the railing on the southeast balcony peered through the scope of his rifle, waiting for Damian's head to pop into view. "C'mon, ya little shit. C'mon. I got three bullets left—"

SHWACK!

Matthew's claymore swung through his scope and chopped the sniper's head in two. The impact slammed his body through a table.

Matthew cocked his claymore back for another swing—only then did the other soldiers notice his presence. Before they could properly react, Matthew had already plunged his blade through another soldier's skull. The soldiers screamed as their assailant became nothing but a shadow. A bright flash, a powerful strike, a sickening crack, and the next thing the soldiers at the far end of the balcony saw were the flailing body parts of their seven companions splattering all over the walls and tabletops, and even the ceiling. Matthew stood under a downpour of shredded flesh dripping from the ceiling, staring at them with crazed eyes like a being from their worst nightmares.

They were next.

"OH MY *GOD*!" one of them screamed as Matthew approached them.

"OPEN FIRE! OPEN FIRE!"

BRRACCK!

The soldiers' guns exploded. A wall of bullets slammed into Matthew, but all he did was stumble. He was still approaching them, convulsing from every bullet that ripped through him. He smiled, laughed at their futile attempts to bring him down, the edge of his sword scraping across the crimson puddles on the floor. "You guys're so fucked." His free hand drew a Browning Hi-Power from the back of his pants. "So, *so* fucked."

And then he charged forward, pistol popping bullets through skulls, claymore ripping through flesh and bone. Brains splattered, limbs spiralled through the air; a soldier flipped over the railing, his screams cut short by the table he landed on. The survivors of Matthew's initial charge retreated toward the southwest balcony, adjoined with the southeast.

"Pull back! Pull back!"

Matthew sliced through a fleeing soldier's Achilles' heel, causing him to scream in agony and twirl to the floor. All the soldier could do was roll onto his back and shoot at his attacker. Matthew sliced his submachine gun in two and blasted the soldier's head into a red mist with his Hi-Power.

Another retreating soldier's skull splintered under Matthew's claymore. "Where're you cowards going, huh?" Matthew roared as he shot at the rest of them. "The fuck you runnin' to?"

In the southwest dining area, Aria was crouched behind a booth, which was in the process of being disintegrated by relentless enemy fire. She waited it out, listening to the staccato of gunfire, which was getting louder as they converged on her location. *Wait for it... wait for it...*

"Reloading!"

Bingo. Aria popped into view, inspiring another hail of bullets that at worst skimmed her arms and cheeks. She had a rocket launcher on her shoulder, pointed right at the terrified soldiers. She smirked when they screamed and scrambled for the opposite end of the dining room. Some of them dropped their guns. Others dived under tables or behind booths and pillars. A handful of them tried to climb through the shattered partition windows into the northwest dining area, which Jenny was in the process of destroying. The rest of them trampled each other in a vain attempt to escape, knocking over furniture and pushing each other aside.

Aria snickered. *Gets 'em every time.*

Then she fired. The rocket screeched through the air, smacking ornaments and lights out of the ceiling, and finally colliding with a table in the center of the room.

KAPOOWWW!

Aria ducked back down as a flaming gale enveloped soldiers and splintered booths. Fireballs stripped the pillars of their tiles, all while decimating the partition walls and blasting Troyan corpses out from under the balconies. Their screams reverberated through the restaurant as the flames swept them away. The balconies shook violently from the impact, shattering the rest of the outer partition walls. The intense explosion flattened the outer fusuma walls and spilled into the empty parking lot.

When the explosion died down, Aria stood back up to admire her handiwork. Everything had been scorched. Nothing but the odd weapon or table leg scattered here and there could be identified.

Jenny stormed the northwest dining area with her grenade launcher and a MAC-10, cutting down soldiers with fire and lead. The explosion that Aria caused had weakened the enemy's numbers greatly. Aria was quick to join her sister in the slaughter, blowing them away with countless grenades that tore the dining area asunder. Before the soldiers on the ground level dining area were completely dealt with, Aria clapped her sister on the back, said, "I'll deal with the shit up above," and then bolted up the stairs to the balcony, which wasn't attached to either of the south balconies.

Aria was surprised by how little resistance she'd received. There were only two handfuls of soldiers cowering behind booths and pillars, but Aria had no qualms against levelling the furniture with a heavy machine gun to get to them.

The area was clear enough from Damian's vantage point for him to no longer require the bar counter as a protective bunker. The northeast dining room was a blazing pit. Matthew slaughtered the platoon stationed on the balcony above it. Just about everything else had been cleared out, with the exceptions of the northwest dining area that Jenny and Aria were sweeping through, and the soldiers that were cornered in the far end of the southwest balcony, which Matthew approached.

Damian ran into the kitchen to assist Jeremy, who stood in the corner shooting a backup pistol through the back door. "How many?"

"Lots!" Jeremy exclaimed as he withdrew to avoid the enemy's return fire.

The doorway was the only entrance to a narrow rear corridor clogged by a small platoon. Across from it was the pantry door battered relentlessly by enemy fire.

Damian yanked Jeremy aside to steal a quick peek, retracting his head in time to avoid a shotgun blast. "Wow, they're really stuck in there."

"No," Jeremy replied sarcastically.

"Now's not the time to be a little bitch," Damian replied as he surveyed the kitchen for anything that would grab his attention. "Find something to flush these bastards out with."

Jeremy looked around the room. His eyes settled on the propane tank tucked away in the corner. He holstered his backup pistol and snatched the propane tank, dragged the heavy tank across the floor, and then tapped Damian's shoulder to take his attention away from the soldiers. "This should do."

Damian's eyes lit up when he saw the propane tank. "Oh, *fuck the hell yes*!" He lifted the tank with one hand, his superhuman strength allowing him to heave the tank down the narrow corridor. It bounced toward the platoon. The soldiers in the front line stopped firing and immediately turned to run, held back by their oblivious companions.

"Hey, why the fuck you runnin'—"

Damian fired his revolver into the corridor blindly as Jeremy ran for cover behind the single pillar that stood in the middle of the kitchen.

Sixth shot hit the tank.

BAWHOOOOMMM!

A brilliant flash-fire charged through both ends of the corridor, enveloping the platoon before they could even scream. The rear wall of the kitchen blew outward. Damian deployed a telekinetic shield around himself just as a fiery wave of debris and utensils ripped through the kitchen. A fireball sent a stove flying across the floor, and the refrigerator cart-wheeled over an overturned table and slammed into the pillar Jeremy squatted behind.

On the other end of the corridor, flames rushed out into the rear storage room of the resort where several more soldiers were gathered. The soldiers could only scream as fireballs cascaded through the storage room. The entire storage building went up in a fiery conflagration, hurling chunks of clay and melting palm tree ornaments into the surrounding jungle.

Aria had finished off the soldiers on the balcony, razing everything to the ground, leaving not so much as a framed picture on the walls—mostly because there were barely any walls left to speak of.

Jenny had finished before Aria reached the top of the staircase.

All of her victims lay burning under a thick blanket of flaming debris. The stench of burning flesh pervaded the air. She almost gagged.

Matthew was finishing off the soldiers in the southwest corner. They were all huddled together gripping their empty machine guns with sweaty hands, whimpering with fear as he approached them with his sword in one hand and Hi-Power in the other. "C'mon, little piggies. I'm gonna carve some nice, crisp bacon strips outta you!"

In an instant, he was upon them, pistol blazing, claymore dismembering, all the way through to the last member of the group, who squealed in terror, hugging the severed head of a fallen comrade. "Shit! Shit! Oh Jesus, oh shit!"

Matthew aimed his pistol and fired.

Click!

He looked at it, frowning. Then he holstered it and turned back to the sole survivor of the group, shrugging. "Guess it's the sword with you."

"Fuck that!" The soldier whipped out a pistol of his own and shot himself dead.

Matthew blinked, and sheathed his claymore with a disappointed grunt. "Pussy."

Damian and Jeremy stumbled out of the smoke-filled kitchen and walked into the middle of the restaurant. Jenny and Aria joined them. Matthew was the last to regroup with them. All of them looked like they'd managed to crawl through a meat grinder. They looked around awkwardly, occasionally stealing glances at each other, unsure of what to do, how else to react.

Finally, Damian shrugged and said, "Now what?"

Episode 013

Hot Spring Relaxation

"Now we wait," Aria said with a long sigh as she sank into the hot bath water. "Aaaaahhh. I'm in heaven..."

Jenny stared at her in disbelief, sitting with her back against a stone slab a few feet away, the water reaching up to her collar. "I don't believe this shit."

"What's to believe?" Mona asked as she spread herself out on top of a nearby stone bank, enjoying the steamy air of the bathhouse.

"More like 'what's *not* to believe,'" Jenny said, "and that'd be this. We're sitting here, after killing dozens of soldiers in a scout party, enjoying a bath as if we didn't just slaughter a scout party, and waiting for the main army to arrive instead of hauling ass out of here!"

Aria spread a damp cloth over her forehead and propped her arms up on the back of a smooth half-submerged stone bench. She closed her eyes as if she were ready to take a nap.

"Don't ignore me," Jenny hissed.

"I'm not ignoring you."

"Yes, you are."

"No, Jenny, I'm just willing to spend the rest of the afternoon relaxing until the rest of them get over here."

"That's my point, though!" Jenny exclaimed. "Why can't we just leave now and avoid the rest of them?"

"Why can't you take your tampon out and just relax?"

"My tampon isn't even—"

PHONE CAAAAAAAAAAAA—

Beep!

Damian, who sat on the other side of the stone bank in their blind spot, answered the radio with, "*Dā*?"

Jenny stiffened. Aria smirked. Mona giggled.

Damian listened for a response, ignoring Jenny as she clambered over the rock bank and looked at him in disbelief. Mona sat up beside her, her tail whipping back and forth playfully.

"Hello...?" he said again.

General Air finally answered, "...Who the fuck is this?"

Jenny said, "Damian, where did you get that?"

"Took it from the captain's body," Damian answered without looking up.

"Answer my question!" Air barked from the phone.

Damian said, "This is Damian Warkowski, otherwise known as the great fucking Dead Blue. Who the hell are you?"

No answer.

"Hello?"

"*The* fucking Dead Blue?" Air asked hesitantly.

"Any *other* fucking Dead Blues out there?" Damian asked.

"So then... my scout party is dead."

"Yes it is."

"...Fuck!"

"I know right? That prob'ly pisses you off."

"You're goddamn right it pisses me off! Did you kill *all* of them?!"

"Uh... I think so."

"You... you... holy shit!"

"Well not just me. My hostages kinda helped me out with them."

"Son of a bitch!"

"I know, right?!" Damian laughed.

"Alright, you little shit. Enough games. You're going to surrender to me, and we're gonna go back to Troyas and finally end this!"

Damian scoffed. "You're welcome to try. We'll be sitting here waiting for you."

"Oh, I'll—wait, what?"

"Yeah, we're all sitting in the bathhouse, enjoying the bath water." He looked up at Jenny. "*And* the nudity."

Jenny's face turned red as she slowly retreated to her side of the stone slab.

"...That doesn't make any sense. You killed my scout party, and your first thought is to relax in the exact spot where you killed my scout party?"

"Yep."

"...What the fuck?"

"We came here to relax, dipshit, and that's what we're gonna do."

"I see... well then. We should be there in the next hour. Think you can stick around that long?"

"Probably. Maybe. Depends."

"On what?"

"Huh?"

"On *what*?"

"What do you mean 'on what'?"

"*What* does it depend on?!" Air shouted impatiently.

"I don't know. It was a figure of speech. But I guess if I had to decide on what it depends on, I'd say..." he looked at the six empty saké bottles bobbing up and down in front of him. "...'it depends on how much alcohol I have left.'"

"I see..."

"Yep."

"So... how much is that, exactly?"

Damian looked at the five unopened bottles propped up on a nearby slab. "A lot," he said.

"You've got a lotta balls, kid."

"Just two, actually."

"Whatever. Just, uh... stay in touch."

Click!

"Pfft." Damian tossed the phone into the water. "'Stay in touch,' he says." He grabbed another bottle of saké. "'Got a lotta balls,' he says." He squeezed the bottle neck and popped the cap off with his thumb. "Nothin' like a good negotiation to make you thirsty," he said before guzzling down a quarter of the bottle.

Jenny looked over the stone bank again, scowling at him. "So, Damian..."

"What?"

"Why're you here?"

"What does it look like? I'm bathing."

"In the women's bath?"

"It's where the alcohol is."

"Uh-huh. Why don't you just take it with you over there?"

He looked up at her. Then he lowered his head and stared off at the change room doors, taking another swig from his bottle. "Nah."

"I wasn't asking."

"Huh?"

"It wasn't a question!" she snapped impatiently. "It was an order!"

"Sounded like there was a question mark placed at the end of that order," Damian replied. "Plus, who died and made you chief?"

"I swear to God, Damian—"

"Aw, leave 'im alone," Aria said. "It's not like he's hurting anybody. Besides, he's sitting out of our view. Shouldn't you be worried about the *actual* peeping Tom?"

Jenny whirled around to face her sister. "Peeping Tom?" Her eyes narrowed with suspicion. "Where's Jonny?"

Aria shrugged. "Dunno, don't care."

Jenny looked around vigilantly, scanning the area for any sign of Jonny. "I bet he's watching us right now..."

"So what if he is—"

Crash!

Everyone looked up as one of the skylights shattered, dropping a screaming flailing body into the women's bath. Even Aria was interested enough to lift the damp cloth from her eyes to watch Jonny plummet down to the waters below. He was yelling, "I HAVE NO REGRETS—"

SMACK!

Damp stone broke his fall. He landed on his front, just a foot away from Mona, who flinched. The sickening packing sound of flesh and bone shattering against the top of the stone bank bounced off the walls. Jenny and Aria stared at his body with raised eyebrows, knowing all too well that this didn't mean the end of him. Mona leaned over his carcass, poking the back of his head, which was covered in clumps of silver and red hair. "Ew, it's mushy," she said as she continued poking him.

"Well," Damian said, taking another swig from his bottle, "that *de*-escalated quickly."

Jenny scowled, watching Mona continue to poke at Jonny's shattered head. "Wow. Just… *wow*. It's like he's got nothing better to do."

"I know, right?" Aria said, laughing. "The man's got some mad determination."

"More like desperation," Jenny said.

"Agreed with Jenny on that one," Damian said.

"Thank you," Jenny said sarcastically.

"You're welcome."

Aria snickered as Jonny's brains started to slither through the cracks in his skull, undergoing the rejuvenation process. "Ah, reminds me of the good ol' days."

"*What* good old days?" Jenny asked with a frown.

"The days when I'd catch some pervert looking through the bathroom window when I'm taking a bath. Guess what I did."

"Why do I have to guess?" Jenny asked.

Damian was already on it: "You did nothing."

"Oh, come on," Jenny replied to his comment. "She's not *that* lenient." She turned to Aria. "Did you shoot him with a rifle? Or did you let loose a cloud of tear gas, or something?"

Aria blinked. "I was gonna say 'I gave him a show and invited him in,' but whatever."

"…Did you at least make him pay for it?"

"No."

"Why not?!"

"He was hot, horny, and single!"

Jenny paused. "…This actually sounds familiar. Who the hell are we talking about here?"

Aria gave her a mischievous smirk. "Remember Chris?"

Jenny's eyebrows fell. "Oh, for God's sake."

"And *that's* how my camera days started."

"He had a camera, too?!"

"I think I still have some DVDs stashed at the house—"

"OH MY GOD!" Jenny shouted. "That's disgusting!"

Damian's voice from the other side: "Aren't you worried about your growth?"

"SHUT THE FUCK UP!"

"Just saying."

Aria said, "I don't think that's disgusting. I actually thought it was sweet when he showed me the camera."

"The—the…?" Jenny stuttered, at a loss for words.

"I think you found that stash at one point and thought they were music CDs. "'Member?"

Jenny could recall finding a stack of discs in Aria's closet and trying one in her CD player, but when it didn't work, she figured it was a defective disc and dropped it in the trash. Jenny slapped her forehead. "I can't believe I *touched* one of them."

Damian laughed.

"Quiet, you!" she snapped.

"Make me!"

"You know," Aria said, "you're not exactly using your indoor voice either."

Point taken, Jenny thought. "Still," she said aloud. "He's not even supposed to be in here." She looked over the stone bank again and asked, "Why the hell are you in here?!"

Damian looked up at her and shrugged. "I don't know. Because I felt like it?"

Her eyes narrowed. "Perverted reasons, I bet."

Damian chuckled. "Said by the one who's been climbing over the wall and looking at me while I'm bathing and minding my own business. Yes, Jenny. *I'm* the pervert."

She blushed and quickly turned away, knowing that not even she could argue against that.

Aria snickered at her newfound shyness. "He got ya there, Sis."

"S-shut up," she said as she sank into the water on her side, staring flustered at the boulder sitting across from her and blowing bubbles in the water.

"I get he's an asshole," Aria began.

"Hey!" Damian exclaimed from the other side.

"Oh, shut up," Aria said, before continuing, "but seriously, in this case, what's the big deal? It's not like he's lookin' for a fight."

"More like *waiting* for a fight, am I right?"

"Shut up, Damian," Aria said. "If 'e wants to sit in the women's bath, who're we to complain about it, right?"

Damian could sense the sarcasm in her voice. "Is that a rhetorical question?"

"Yes, Damian," Jenny said with a scowl, "yes it is."

"Thought so."

Aria slapped the cloth over her eyes again and leaned her head back with a relaxed sigh. "Let 'im do what he wants. It'll make things so much easier."

"Um, that's why we're here in the first place!" Jenny yelled.

"Wasn't *my* idea to go to a hot spring," Damian said as he

finished off his current bottle and placed it beside the rest of the empty bottles.

"Why us, Damian?"

"I didn't pick you guys; I picked Marner, who's… strangely absent right now."

"Probably still passed out on the bench," Aria said.

"Why Marner? What's wrong with the rest of the ghost whisperers?" Jenny asked. "You could've picked *anyone* else in the whole world."

"Exactly," Damian said. "I could've stumbled upon someone else. But that's not the case here, is it? I found Marner, because Dave found me and felt sympathetic to my problem. Besides, with all the weird distortions in the Spirit Core, not too many whisperers could be found."

"Hold up," Aria said, pulling the cloth off her face. "What do you mean by that?"

"Marner was the only one near my location that was available and reliable, so—"

"Not that. I meant the weird distortions," Aria said patiently. "*What* weird distortions?"

"Oh," Damian said as a fresh bottle approached him in a telekinetic bubble. "Uh… I guess, 'distortions,' like… I don't know how to explain it but it's gotten really weird. Like it's getting darker or something."

"'Darker'?"

"Yeah, something that didn't really feel right. It got stronger every day, and it seemed to be scaring off ghosts and ghost whisperers." Damian chuckled. "I thought I was gonna be stuck in there for a lot longer than I ended up."

"That doesn't answer my question," Jenny said. "You knew a lot, even if you knew Aria and Zero during the war. How'd you know about our mother?"

"I had lots of spare time in that space, that's how. For every whisperer I found, I'd do this thing like background checks where I'd look back through their history and see where they go or whatever. It's like supernatural time travel. It's fucking sweet."

"Okay, so…?"

"So when I found Marner, Marner's history was pretty dull for the most part, but she seemed reliable when it came to helping spirits and astral projections. Through her, I found you two. I knew Aria, I knew Zero, so that led to my eventual discovery of your mother. And boom. Spotted her in Sky Japan… maybe about a year ago?"

Aria scrunched her eyebrows together. "So your intel is a year old?"

"Pretty much."

"And you didn't think to look further?"

"I wasn't looking for her," Damian said, "I told you already; I was looking for a way out."

Jenny felt the frustration start to boil up. "Can't you just project yourself again?!"

Damian scoffed. "Sure, if I was stuck in a fucking tube again! I can't do it from out here, and I'm not going back to that school basement to find out."

"Shit," Aria said with a heavy sigh. "So Sky Japan is our only option for now. What a drag."

Jenny bit her bottom lip. "That can't be it. There has to be *something*."

"Not that I know of," Damian said. "Someone in Sky Japan prob'ly knows where she is. I bet she's still there. The hotel is the perfect place to start looking."

"Unless you were in a coma," Jenny said.

"Sure, if—" Alarmed, Damian looked up to see Jenny standing over him with a towel wrapped around her body, lifting a boulder over her head. "WHAT THE FU—"

SMASH!

Jenny threw it down on him. Damian leaped forward just before the boulder crushed the empty bottles with a giant splash. The boulder shattered.

"Jesus Christ, Jenny, what the *fuck*!" Damian yelled before dodging another boulder. "Are you trying to fucking kill me?!"

"No, of course not!" Jenny replied as she tore a chunk out of the stone bank and hurled it at him. "Just hold still!"

Damian squatted; the chunk of rock flew over his head and broke into small pieces against a different bank. "'Hold still'?! WHY WOULD I DO THAT?!"

"I've read the text books," Jenny said as she picked up a much smaller rock. "Being in cryostasis is like being in a coma, except with your body being preserved like a fossil."

"SO?!"

Jenny cocked her arm back, ready to throw. "So all's you gotta do is get into a coma to find out where our mother really is. I sure as hell don't want to go to Sky Japan unless I've got no other choice."

"So your first thought is to brain me with a giant rock?!" Damian exclaimed.

"Pretty much."

"Aria, control your sister!"

Aria shrugged, still sitting comfortably in her spot. "Hey, she's got a point, Damian."

"Thanks, Sis," Jenny said before throwing the rock at Damian, who dodged it. "Come on, stop moving!"

"Make me!"

"I would if you'd let me hit you!"

"Yeah, because *that's* going to happen!"

Jenny lifted another boulder that was twice her size over her head. "HOLD… STILL!"

Damian whipped out his revolver and pointed at her. She froze. "Drop it!" he shouted. "Do it! Do it now!"

Jenny glared at him. "You've got a lot of nerve to point that at *me*."

"Drop it, you bitch, drop it!"

Mona sat crossed-legged between Jenny and Jonny, staring up at Jenny with newfound admiration. "Ooohh… you're so strong!"

Jenny looked at her awkwardly, still holding up the boulder. "Um… thank you?"

"Towel theft!" Mona screamed. She snatched Jenny's towel off her and ran away with it, laughing like a lunatic.

"HEY! GIVE THAT BACK!" Jenny screamed, unable to drop the boulder. Her face turned redder than a stop sign as she turned back to Damian, who was staring right at her. "S-stop looking at me, you pervert!"

Damian smirked, maintaining his stare. "Not like I'm wearing a towel and I'm perfectly fine. Mona." He looked at Mona, who was perched on a boulder on the other side of the bathhouse now, waving Jenny's towel over her head like a flag. "Good job."

"Thank you, Master!" she said, beaming.

Jenny started to tremble with embarrassment. "I'm going to

kill you when this is over…"

"Bitch, please," Damian said as he turned back to her. "I know embarrassment is one of your turn-ons."

"Not like *this*, you jackass!"

"Ugh," Jonny said as he lifted his face off the boulder. "My head… how long was I out?"

Aria stifled a laugh at Jonny's impeccable timing.

Mona whistled the Cloverfield national anthem whilst waving Jenny's towel around.

Jenny gasped in horror as Jonny's eyes turned on her. "Oh… shit."

Jonny's eyes were glued to her body. His blushing intensified. He started shaking. He could barely got the words out. "Aw… aw… awww…! AWESO—"

SMASH!

Jenny slammed the boulder down on him, pancaking him under half a ton of rock and breaking the stone bank in the process. "FUUUUUUUUUUUCK!" she screamed loud enough to make Damian wince.

"Jesus! Remember your growth, woman!" he shouted.

Jenny turned to him and started throwing chunks of the boulder at him. "GET THE FUCK OUT OF HERE!"

Damian bounded toward the far wall opposite Mona, dodging most of Jenny's projectiles, and swearing when a few of them actually managed to hit him.

"And take this dipshit with you!" she screamed as she grabbed Jonny by the hair and hurled him at Damian. Jonny cart-wheeled through the air and collided with Damian, sending them both phasing through the wall in a tumble, disappearing like shadows without leaving any damage in the wall. Jenny fumed, wheezing with every deep, heavy gasp. "FUCKING ASSHOLES!"

"Breathe, Jenny," Aria said calmly. "Don't forget to breathe."

"How'd they even *do* that?!"

"What?"

"The ghost-phasing thing!"

"Damian can pass through walls, you know."

"HE CAN?!"

"Um… yeah?"

"Fantastic!" Jenny shouted. "Yet another reason why he's so

fucking creepy!"

Aria shrugged. The corner of her mouth curled upward as she placed the damp cloth over her eyes again, and cozied up against the rock. "Ah, the good ol' days."

Jenny whirled around and pointed a hostile forefinger at Mona. "And you! Gimme back my towel, you little bitch!"

Splish!

Damian and Jonny fell into the water in a crumpled heap. A second later, Damian's head resurfaced. He moved toward the nearest hazy figure that sat in the steam, rubbing a spot on his left side where a chunk of boulder hit him. With a sigh, he sat on the rock beside the figure and said, "So, Jeremy, what've you been up to since—"

The steam cleared just enough to reveal the actual person sitting beside him—and it wasn't Jeremy or Matthew.

Tim stared at him with wide eyes. Damian froze. Both of them bristled, gaping at one another in shock. Neither of them said a word for a full minute, until the situation registered.

CLANG!

In an instant they locked energy blades. Sparks flew as the edges grinded together; both of them struggling to overpower the other. Damian grinned sinisterly as he said, "Well look what the cat shit out—IT'S A FUCKING PUSSY!"

Tim shouted, "*You're* one to talk, you freak!"

"What the fuck're you doing in here, ruining my vacation?"

"I said I needed a vacation. So here I am. On vacation. Figures you gotta ruin *this* day off, too! Just like everything else!"

"Vacation, eh?!" Damian leaned forward, forcing more of his weight on Tim's blade, still grinning like a crazed maniac. "You have some nerve climbing into my pool."

"This is a goddamn public bathhouse, you piece of shit!"

"Not right now, it isn't! Right now it's *my* bathhouse and you and your artificially flavoured, microscopic dick aren't invited!"

Tim grinded his teeth in a surge of fury. "You have *so* gotta die, and I don't give a shit what Silverstein says about it! You are *fucked*!"

"Bitch, please! You couldn't get a refund on a tuna fish sandwich, much less kill me!"

"What's the fuck's up with your obsession with sandwiches?! You like your meat between someone else's buns?!"

"Yeah, your ex-girlfriend's!" Damian barked.

Shunk!

Matthew and Jeremy opened the change room fusuma doors and stopped when they saw Damian and Tim locked in their stance.

Matthew said, "What the hell's goin' on here?"

Jeremy scratched the back of his head. "Damian, who is this person you have become… ah, 'acquainted' with?"

"'Acquaintance' is the most *inaccurate* description of this son of a whore I've ever heard!" Damian snarled. "His family was too broke to abort him! That's a secret, though." Damian put his finger to his lips. "Shhh!"

"In your dreams, asshole!" Tim replied angrily. He pushed Damian away from him and drew a red energy pistol.

In his backwards stumble, Damian drew his revolver and pointed it at Tim.

They froze, pointing their guns at one another, swords at their sides, murder in their eyes.

Tim glanced at Matthew and Jeremy and said, "You guys are idiots."

"Why's that?" Matthew hissed. "Want me to kick your ass all up and down this bathhouse?"

"You don't know who you're travelling with. This guy's a psycho. He'll be your friend now, but sooner or later he'll stab you in the back. He'll ruin your lives. I promise that if you stick around with him, that's what's gonna happen. You can't *possibly* be stupid enough to help him out! No one's *that* stupid!"

Matthew looked at Damian. Damian didn't even bat an eyelid.

Jeremy said, "I have known him since we were little. Damian may be a lot of bad things, but he would never betray his true friends."

"Well said," Damian yelled, "dunno if a motivational speech was what we needed right now, but whatever. Well said!"

Tim scoffed. "Wow, apparently idiots like you really *do* exist! That's what I thought, too! What has he done to earn your respect? Or your trust!? He's just a murderer without a cause! All he wants is for humanity to suffer the same thing the Dehues went through! He should've died with the rest of those freaks!"

Damian snarled at him, "How much longer are you gonna keep going? Shut the fuck up!"

Tim trained his gun on Damian's head. "I don't know what you did to get these poor bastards under your thumb, but it ends now."

"Does it?"

"I've had enough of your shit."

"The feeling's mutual."

Jeremy nudged Matthew and said, "We should depart…"

"Right," said Matthew as they slowly backed into the changing room. "Back to the ships."

Damian cleared his throat. "Looks like we've got ourselves a little Mexican standoff, eh?"

"I guess so," said Tim. "Even if I die, you'll be goin' with me."

"I'm not so sure about that, so why're you? Just how far up your ass did your head get to?"

"I dug two graves, and I expect to fill them with the bodies that match the names on the gravestones."

"Wow, you went that far? You're one prepared son of a bitch. Got it all figured out? I hope you wrote 'This is Tim's ass' on one gravestone and 'This is the rest of him' on the other because bitch, you came in one piece and you'll be leaving in *pieces*."

SPLASSSHH!

With a bloodcurdling battlecry, Jonny burst out of the water behind Damian with a blade of ice raised above his head. Startled, Damian whirled around, swung his blade through Jonny's stomach, then blasted an energy bullet through his chest.

Tim took his chance and fired his pistol.

Two shots rang out.

Jonny's body slammed against the wall with two fresh holes blown through his body. Damian crouched in the water with a new graze wound across his left cheek. His gun pointed at Tim. Tim had a split second to react—

BLAM!

Tim ducked. The top of the rock behind him crackled. He fired three shots. Damian dashed to the left, firing more energy projectiles at Tim. Tim leaped to the right, shooting frantically in retaliation.

Damian hurled his blade at Tim. It traced a wide arc through the air like a Frisbee, leaving a bluish trail curving behind it. Tim gasped and jumped backwards into the water, still firing at Damian.

The blade just barely skimmed Tim's nose and penetrated a rock. He didn't have time to celebrate the close call. The blade's glow intensified and the low hum emanating from it escalated into a rhythmic roar. Damian was still shooting at the water where Tim fell. Tim launched himself into Damian's view and dived over a nearby rock bank.

Then the blade went off like a bomb.

BOOOOMMMM!

A massive black-cobalt fireball erupted from the rocks, hurling Tim through a hail of rock chunks and a flying sheet of bathwater, shielding his face with his crossed arms. His back cracked the wall upon impact. Then he splashed into the water like a ragdoll.

Damian perched himself on a fat rock and peered into the smoke. He watched intently as dark blue smoke spread through the bath, rolling upward in a mushroom cloud.

Matthew poked his head out of the changing room, fully dressed. "Is 'e dead?"

"I dunno," Damian replied. His eyes didn't move from the smoke.

WHOOSH!

Tim jetted through the smoke like a rocket, spearing Damian's chest. Both of them tumbled off the rock Damian had perched himself on. Their bodies slammed against another rock face. Tim's feet splashed into the water, but Damian was still pinned against the rock. Tim seized the opportunity and started pummelling Damian's body with his fists until Damian interlocked his own fists in a ball above his head and smashed it down on Tim's spine. Tim grunted and doubled over just before Damian kneed him in the face, sending him sprawling against another rock.

Jenny, Marner (who'd joined them shortly after Jenny had calmed down), and Aria jolted upright at the sudden rumble of the explosion from the other side of the wall. The water vibrated as the entire building trembled. The explosion from Damian's blade had disturbed their quiet, 'peaceful' morning of soaking in the bathwater.

"What the hell was *that*?" Jenny asked as she looked at the wall.

Aria shrugged. "Probably just the boys foolin' around. You know how they are."

Marner sighed. "I wish they'd all just get along…"

"Relax, Marner," Aria said with a smirk. "It's probably just a harmless little tussle."

WHACK! WHACK! WHACK! WHACK!

Damian kept smashing Tim's head against a rock, painting it red with his blood and cracking it with his face. Tim started to go limp. Losing consciousness. He couldn't die here. He couldn't lose again.

So he desperately lashed out one last time.

"AGH!" Damian shouted, stumbling away. His stomach burned; the searing pain shot up to his brain. He looked down and saw a wide, jagged slash running across his stomach from the left side of his waist to his bottom-right rib. Blood ran down his front like a waterfall. Furious, Damian looked at the small crimson energy dagger in Tim's right hand. He noted the serrated edge on the blade. "*Ebanatyi pidaraz*." He whipped out two revolvers and pointed them at Tim, but—

Shunk!

Tim's dagger-wielding hand blurred. Something burned inside Damian's stomach, but the biting pain that should've only lasted a moment never left. He looked down again at the energy dagger stuck in his stomach.

"Ow…"

Damian's guns vanished as he stumbled backwards against the rock bank. His hands pressed against his bloody stomach. "Goddamn it." He glared at Tim. "You stabbed me, YOU—"

Vmmvmmmvmmmmmmvmmmmmvmmmmmmmmmmm…

Alarmed, Damian looked at the blade as it started to glow. That familiar hum filled the bath again. Its glow intensified, as did the hum.

VmmmvmmmmmmvmmmmVMMMMMMVMMMMMMMMM!

"SHITTING FUCK!" Damian ripped the energy dagger out and—

Tim was already unleashing a hail of energy pellets from his pistols, pegging Damian a few times and transforming the rocks around him into a fountain of chunks. To his shock and surprise, Damian gripped the bloody dagger in his hand and charged straight into Tim's oncoming fire. The blade was almost ready to go off.

"BANZAAAIIII!" Damian lunged at Tim, dagger raised over his head. Tim's pistols were still going off, though Damian's unexpected suicide-lunge caught him off guard. All he could do was shoot at his oncoming enemy.

Jonny regained conscious at the last second, and the last thing he saw was Damian seemingly hovering above him and Tim in slow motion, glowing dagger raised. *What the—*

On the other side, the girls savoured the water's comforting warmth. Marner slunk down so that the water reached up to her neck, partly due to shyness. She could feel herself sweating in the steam vapours, but that didn't matter to her. All she cared about at that moment was the smooth rock she leaned on and the heavenly feeling of the bathwater.

Jenny sat a few metres away from her, against a square-shaped rock that tilted back like a crude reclining chair. The water reached up to her shoulders, though she was sinking deeper and deeper into it with a pleasurable moan. "I take it back—I don't think I'll ever wanna leave."

"Agreed," said Aria, her eyes hidden under the small wet cloth. She leaned against a rock bank with her elbows propped against it and the tops of her breasts glistened with sweat and bathwater just above the water's surface. "This is what I needed. I think we're agreed that this is what we all needed. Am I right?"

Mona, previously sitting behind Aria's rock bank, now leaned over with her fingernails scraping against the ledge, just a foot away from Aria's head. "Oh, I think so, too."

Aria smirked. "I don't think we've been properly acquainted. I'm Aria."

"Mona," she replied with a friendly smile. "I'm Damian's servant."

"That must suck," Jenny said with disdain.

"Oh, no, not at all. I enjoy it, actually." She blushed. "Sometimes he even rewards me."

"Ugh," Jenny hissed. "Sounds like a shitty way to live your life."

Aria thought she sensed a hint of jealousy.

"Doesn't really matter anyway," said Mona. "I've been alive for over a thousand years, and I've only served Damian for about six of those years. Besides, he's *definitely* one of my favourite masters."

"I'm sure he is," Jenny replied curtly.

Mona's tail waggled back and forth. Her face was still beaming. "Ooh, someone's jealous."

Jenny's head snapped in her direction. Her eyebrows went up. "What? Jealous? That's a load of bullshit if I ever—"

KAPPPOOOOOOOOOOOOOOOWWWWWW!

In a thunderous roar, the wall shattered. An avalanche of debris cascaded violently into the bath. The lights flickered furiously as thrashing bodies and smashed rock flurried. Marner screamed and ducked behind her rock. Jenny dipped into the water. Aria and Mona didn't move from their spots, though Aria lifted her cloth to see what was causing such a commotion. She and Mona identified Tim and Jonny's flailing forms soaring above their heads. Jonny hit a rock and splashed into the water. Tim skipped across the water's surface a few times before his back slammed into a stone bank; he then sunk beneath the bubbling water's surface. The scattered remains of the wall that separated the men's bath from the women's pelted the water briefly before letting up.

Thick smoke clouded the bath; it seemed to merge with the steam and rise from the bathwater. For a moment, there was silence.

Jenny hesitantly resurfaced from the water, and she looked around cautiously until her eyes found Aria and Mona. Both of them were still sitting quietly with passive looks on their faces. "What the hell was *that*?!"

Aria shrugged. "Guess their little tussle got outta hand."

Tim's body jumped out of the water and flopped heavily against a small rock only a few feet away from Jenny, clambering onto the rocks with his back to her, but she recognized him immediately.

"*TIM*!?" Jenny exclaimed in disbelief. "What the hell are *you* doing here?"

"Urgh," Tim grunted in reply. "Shut up…"

"NO!" she shouted angrily. "What the fuck are you doing here?!" She covered her breasts with her arm. She hugged herself protectively and yelled, "If *you're* here, that means your boss is here, too! Oh, shit! Aria—"

"Silverstein isn't here," Tim growled. "I came alone."

"Bullshit, as if we're supposed to *believe* that!"

Tim glared at her. "What *I* don't believe is how you assholes can ruin not just my life, but my *vacation*, too!"

Aria raised an eyebrow. "You came all the way out here for a vacation?"

"What's with the surprise? *You* came all the way out here to ruin *my* vacation!"

Clack!

All heads turned to the gaping hole in the wall where a hazy silhouette lumbered through the smoke atop a mountain of debris. As the smoke cleared, Damian's mangled form became clearer. Hunched over, covered in blood and cuts with chips of rock protruding from his skin. His left eye was closed with blood streaming over it. Three of his fingers on his left hand were broken, bent backwards, though somehow he still clutched his revolver, pointed down to the rock pile he stood on. His entire left arm appeared to be broken; shredded from the explosion, hanging loosely from his shoulder. Blood leaked from the sides of his half-open mouth and dribbled down his jaw and his neck, while the rest dripped off his chin. Red flames ate away at his shoulders, arms, and thighs, slashing the air like whips.

Jenny and Marner gasped, shocked by Damian's appearance.

Open with a joke.

"Nobody move," Damian said, his grating voice like broken glass being grinded against concrete. "Name's Nixon. I'm a tax collector."

Bitches love comic book references.

Tim's pistols reappeared in his hands. "For Christ's sake!" Tim shouted. "Just stay dead!"

Damian stumbled down the jagged slope of debris, his gun dangling back and forth with every step. He looked even worse than the zombies in Scionia.

"You *will* die, you son of a bitch!"

"Come and get it, *suka*," Damian replied. His voice sounded exhausted and hollow. He was broken, smashed up, shredded, bloody and covered in a sheet of fire, but somehow he still managed to walk on his own. Jenny and Marner stared at him, wide-eyed with shock. Aria's eyebrows went up. Mona flicked her tail, but otherwise her smile remained, as if she found the entire situation amusing.

"Wow," Aria said. "You look like shit."

"Thanks," Damian said. "I feel like shit."

"How the hell aren't you dead yet…?" Jenny asked.

"I'm fucking invincible."

COBALT ROGUE, VOL. 1: THE DEAD BLUE

Episode 014

Hot Spring Chaos

THOOMMM!

The entire bathhouse shuddered.

THOOMMMM!

The lights flickered. Everyone looked up at the ceiling as it rattled to the rhythm.

THHHOOOOOMMTHOOMMTHOOMMMTHOOOM!

Giant footsteps. The building shook violently as the thunderous stomps intensified. The bathwater splashed back and forth like a storm without the hurricane winds.

SMMAAAAASSSSSSHHHH!

A giant metal fist plunged through the ceiling, dumping a thick blanket of debris into the water. Damian stumbled backward, shielding himself with a telekinetic bubble. Now everyone scattered. Jenny and Marner ran to the changing room for cover. Aria leaped out of the water after the girls. Tim hopped from rock to rock, dodging falling debris. Jonny screamed just two seconds before an air vent lid bounced off his head and knocked him unconscious. Mona dived inside Damian's bubble and quickly patted his shoulders to put the fires out.

Another giant metal hand appeared, and both hands tore the ceiling asunder. Debris showered the bathwater, creating massive waves that crashed into Damian's shield, but Damian didn't budge. The violent waves poured through the changing rooms, sweeping everyone in both change rooms out into the corridors. The hands parted the steel beams, the rows of lights, the solar panels and clay, revealing a massive round silver helmet with two crimson eye slits.

Damian stared up at the massive Terrain Marcher Class 04 looming over him. His expression was that of pure awe and surprise. "*Ni… khuya… sebe…*"

"Master, you're hurt!" Mona had managed to put the fires out and was licking Damian's wounds.

Damian scowled when she licked the cuts on his chest, then

gave an agitated yelp when she started to move lower and pushed her away. "Not now, goddamn it!" His wounds were already starting to heal.

The booming voice of the Terrain Marcher's pilot exploded from the giant speakers in the robot's helmet, which extended from its coil-like neck, causing the room to vibrate from its every word. "DAMIAN WARKOWSKI! SURRENDER NOW, OR BE... BE..."

"Destroyed?" Damian asked.

"NO, I NEED YOU ALIVE!"

Damian blinked. "Who's in there?"

"I AM GENERAL AIR, THE SECOND GENERAL OF THE U.S.T.'s ELEMENTAL FIVE. SURRENDER TO THE POWER OF TROYAS, AND EVERYTHING WILL COME TO A QUICK AND PLEASANT END."

"Yeeeeaaaaaaah, I'm gonna go with 'no'."

"SO BE IT." Air's Terrain Marcher reached inside to grab Damian with its massive right hand, but Damian leaped into the air at the last possible second just before the hand smashed into the pile of debris. He landed on the hand, dashed over its studded knuckles and quickly worked his way up its right arm with his sword and revolver held outward. When Air's right arm jerked, Damian flattened himself on it and buried his blade into its elbow joint.

CRASH!

The right arm swung through the roof, scattering debris in every direction, but Damian still held on. Fragments of clay and brick tore at his body. Flames roared out of the large nozzle built into its wrist, dousing the upper levels of the Palm Tree Onsen with flames like a garden hose. Air stumbled backwards into the path he'd made upon his arrival consisting of massive craters and crushed trees. Air threw his right arm up, flinging Damian into the sky. Damian flew over its head, aiming his Model 500 at its eyes, and fired.

Both glowing eye slits exploded, causing Air further confusion. Two massive Gatling gun barrels jumped out of the automaton's wrist compartments and started firing blindly into the sky.

Still in the air, Damian hurled his blade into one of the smoking holes where the slit used to be, and a few seconds later, a large portion of the automaton's round head was blown to pieces.

"Shit, what the hell's up with that!?" Air shrieked inside the cockpit. The speakers were damaged; no one could hear him now. "This is coming out of my paycheck, you little bastard! Stop damaging my goddamn robot!"

With a deafening metallic groan the automaton lurched forward and slammed into the building. Its enormous bulk reduced most of the building to burning splinters, demolishing it like a wrecking ball through a matchstick house.

Bathwater burst through the fusuma walls and flooded the main lobby of the resort, sweeping Damian's barely-dressed 'hostages' over the side of the balcony. A squad of soldiers lingered on the staircase leading down to the lobby. Jenny and Aria grabbed the balcony railing. Marner squealed past them, only for Aria to catch her wrist, fighting against the strong current. Matthew and Jeremy clung to the railing on the other side of the staircase. The Troyas platoon gathered at the bottom of the stairs could only shout with surprise before the bathwater tsunami swept them out of the building and strewed them across the parking lot.

Chunks of the ceiling came crashing down all around Damian's 'hostages' as the resort's trembling intensified. A huge portion of the second floor collapsed on the reception area. A pillar teetered out of place and split the staircase right down the middle, causing the railings to fall out and drop the group off the edge of the balcony. The balcony then broke apart. Marner and Jeremy screamed as they fell five feet to the partially flooded marble floor.

Aria looked at Marner, who cried out when she landed awkwardly. "You okay?"

"I-I think I sprained my ankle!"

"Terrific. Jenny?"

"I'm fine," Jenny said.

The balcony's supports shattered; Aria picked up Marner and slung her over her shoulder, and raced for the exit with Jenny in hot pursuit. Matthew and Jeremy dived out from under a collapsing pillar and scrambled for the exit, joining the girls in their flight as five storeys of concrete and clay pancaked above their heads. The whole ceiling was coming down; the entrance just barely within reach.

KA-SMASH!

The entire resort came down. The 'hostages' got out just in time; air rushing out from under the collapsed resort sent them flying over the hill that sloped down to the parking lot. They tuck-and-rolled at the bottom of the hill in a hailstorm of debris.

Aria was the first to get up. She saw the Troyas soldiers recovering from being flushed out of the lobby. Aria turned to a nearby Troyas Jeep and saw that it was unmanned. She quickly lifted Jenny and Marner to their feet and said, "Get in the Jeep! Hurry up!"

"Ugh… what?" Jenny said, staggering as Aria practically dragged her to the Jeep.

"You two!" Aria yelled, turning toward Matthew and Jeremy. "Move your asses!"

One of the soldiers got up to his feet and rounded the Jeep with a shotgun. "You ain't goin' nowhere—"

BANG!

Aria shot him between the eyes with a pistol before gently—but hastily—loading Marner into the back seat. "C'mon, get goin'."

Matthew and Jeremy rushed toward the Jeep. Jeremy climbed into the back seat and Matthew jumped into the front passenger seat and crawled behind the wheel.

Jenny lingered behind, giving her sister a worried look. "What about you?"

"I'll be fine," Aria said. "You ought to know that. Now haul ass!"

The soldiers had come to, circling the back of the Jeep. "They're stealing our car!"

"Hey, goddamn it!" another soldier roared. "That's Troyas property!"

Jenny gave them the finger. "Eat me!"

They opened fire in response. Jenny dived into the Jeep as Aria fired an assault rifle at the soldiers, standing her ground. Marner and Jeremy hunkered down in the back seat as bullets ripped across the windshield. By the time Jenny got into the front passenger seat, Matthew was almost done hotwiring the Jeep.

Matthew glared at her. "Way to piss them off, you stupid bitch."

"Shut the fuck up and drive!" Jenny fired back.

The wires sparked. The engine roared to life. Matthew shifted gears and floored the gas. Tires screeched. The Jeep lurched across the parking lot as bullets shattered the rear window.

Now crouched behind a lamppost, Aria glanced over her shoulder as the Jeep zoomed toward the jungle. Then she turned back to the platoon as the soldiers went scrambling for their armoured Humvees and Jeeps scattered about the parking lot, and started shooting at them again.

Something moved in the corner of her eye. Aria turned to see a fighter jet hovering over the edge of the parking lot, locked onto her. "Oh, shit!" she yelled, just before the jet launched a rocket straight for her. She barely reached ten feet before a fireball concussively ripped across her back and hurled her into the side of an abandoned Jeep.

Rain Harbour

The Supreme Chief of the Spring Islands Police Department, Oxford Grand, noticed the fire in the distance right away. He knew something was amiss before. From the rooftop of the police station by the riverbank of Rain Harbour, he peered through his binoculars to see the bathhouse set ablaze and torn down by Air's Terrain Marcher 04 from across the river.

"There's trouble over there, and it's big," he grumbled to himself. He snatched his radio off his uniform strap and spoke into it with the utmost urgency, "Calling all units, calling all units. We have a code red situation at the Palm Tree Onsen…"

The Palm Tree Onsen

Damian landed on the slanted rooftop of the highest level of the burning building, noting that it was coming down fast. He found himself sliding to the edge as the top two storeys hung precariously above what remained of the men's bath. The roof gave out under his feet, dropping him into a thick downpour of flaming debris. "Fuuuuuuck!"

BOOM!

A stack of falling rubble suddenly exploded near Damian. He shielded himself as he fell, temporarily blinded by a red flash.

BOOM!

Another explosion went off directly under him. Damian dropped through the searing hot crimson smoke and opened his eyes, immediately spotting Tim, who stood on a rock with a telekinetic shotgun in his hands. Damian saw him launch another energy ball at him, and twisted his body, just barely dodging it, and turned over as it exploded above him. He drew his revolver and returned fire.

Tim leaped from rock to rock under the hail of black fire and blazing debris coming down around him.

"You can fly, right?" Tyler's voice asked him.

Damian blinked. *Hey, I can, right? I remember flying, I just don't remember how!*

"Concentrate, you moron!"

What?

"FLY!"

Damian spread his arms out. *Flying... flying...!* He tried flapping his arms.

CRASH!

The debris crashed down on the baths, riling up a violent tidal wave that rolled over the rocks and flooded the men's and women's baths. The brick foundation didn't budge an inch; instead it acted as a rectangular bowl with the changing rooms operating as a drain.

Damian regained his balance in a midair back flip and landed clumsily on his feet on a small portion of what remained of the women's bath rooftop with his blade in his hand. He balanced himself out on the jagged truss protruding above the water and pointed his blade at Tim, who climbed out of the men's bath. Then he looked up to see a Troyas anti-gravity hovercraft suspended above them. The hovercraft was huge, casting a large shadow over the entire burning resort, hanging just above the height of Air's Terrain Marcher.

"What the hell?" Damian looked down at Tim as he stepped toward him. He took a ready stance; one foot back, a blade in his left hand and his revolver in his right. "Well, *this* has turned out to be a lovely day."

Troyas soldiers rappelled out of the hovercraft like fish bait. They had submachine guns in their hands and their armoured battle uniforms were coloured blue. They fired at both Damian and Tim in their descent. Damian and Tim moved like lightning, returning fire and dodging bullets from the soldiers and each other.

Damian zigzagged across the rooftop shooting holes through random soldiers as they landed on the roof. Clay tiles popped and exploded like little firecrackers under their corpses.

Damian dashed across the rooftop and stopped when a soldier landed in front of him. “Stop, or—”

Damian zipped by him, leaving behind a trail of fading blue light. Seconds later, the soldier’s stomach separated from his waist and both halves of his body spilled his innards all over the roof.

Most of the soldiers had landed on the rooftop, shooting frantically at Damian and Tim.

Damian punched another soldier in the face, twisting his head at a 360-degree angle, and then dropped into a crouch and ran his blade through a soldier that stood behind him. He withdrew the blade from the gasping soldier’s body and beheaded three more with a single sideways slash.

They converged. Damian swung his blade frenetically and—with his gun—mowed down a cluster of soldiers. He buried his blade into the chest a soldier that approached him from the side. Then he yanked it out, whirled around, and beheaded yet another.

A soldier made some distance between him and the chaotic fray, standing on the highest point of the rooftop, and fired his gun at Damian. He let out a maniacal roar and pelted Damian’s body with bullets.

Damian stumbled backward, slipped on some blood coursing down the rooftop, and fell on a soldier’s mangled corpse. The bullets didn’t rip him apart, surprisingly; they bounced off—but they hurt like hell.

Click! Click!

The soldier’s magazine clicked empty. Damian growled and shot the soldier in the face, scattering his brains all over the other side of the slanted rooftop. He noticed something on the rooftop, picked it up between his index finger and thumb, and bent it as he examined it. “Rubber bullets, what the fuck?”

Tim sliced through two soldiers’ bodies and charged toward Damian with a red Micro Uzi blazing in his hand. Damian dived forward; the spot where he stood exploded a split second later. He returned fire in mid-dive, and then rolled across the roof, Tim’s explosive fire chasing him.

Damian sliced through a soldier’s legs, grabbed him by the back of the collar and raised him like a shield. The soldier’s gurgled shrieks only got louder as Tim’s gunfire ate away at his body.

Damian shot at Tim over the disintegrating man's shoulder, forcing Tim to dash to the side and convert his Micro Uzi to a grenade launcher. Tim's launcher released a huge energy ball at Damian, traced an arc through the air. Reacting to the oncoming energy grenade, Damian quickly abandoned his Troyas meat shield and leaped over the side of the rooftop.

BOOM!

The remainder of the rooftop blew apart. The few leftover trusses and support beams gave out beneath layers of clay and human gore as the resort's five floors pancaked on each other.

"SSSHIIIIIIIIIIIIIT!" Damian screamed as he plummeted into the women's bath. He shielded his face from the red flames and spray of debris with his crossed arms as he fell.

The River

Supreme Chief Oxford Grand had an army of police officers with him on the river water. Over two hundred motorboats roared across the river toward the island on both sides of the bridge. On the bridge were twenty police cruisers and tactical force Humvees charging straight for the island with their sirens wailing and their guns ready.

General Air watched from inside the cockpit of the fallen Terrain Marcher 04 as the law enforcement army crossed the river on the bridge and the water. He immediately got back up and said into the private channel he shared with his hovercraft crew, "Focus on capturing the Dead Blue alive. I'm going to deal with these idiotic policemen. Don't lose him, Captain, or I'll put you in front of a firing squad!"

The captain replied on the radio, "Yes, sir."

Veeeeemmm!

A Gatling gun barrel snapped out of each of the Terrain Marcher 04's wrists. Air turned them to the bridge and fired. The Gatling guns took a few seconds to rotate, but once they reached their full speed they spewed giant explosive rounds from point A to point B, obliterating the bridge and everything on it. The remains of the bridge and the police Humvees poured into the river.

Oxford Grand watched in horror as the bridge disappeared beneath the water's surface. He looked up at the Terrain Marcher 04 as it turned its guns on the motorboats.

"Evasive manoeuvres!" Grand shouted into his radio. "*NOW*!"

The Gatling guns spat more explosive rounds into the river, walking a giant parade of waterspouts across the surface and through the motorboats that desperately attempted to careen to safety. Two intertwining walls of water shot up from the surface, hurling debris and human shreds into the air. The explosives on the motorboats popped like firecrackers. Screaming bodies were flung into the raging waters. Oxford Grand himself abandoned his boat just a second before an explosive round blasted it to splinters.

The Jungle

The Jeep bounced through the thick vegetation, tearing through bushes and leaping off hills. Matthew fought the wheel back and forth to avoid just about everything in sight. As the Jeep weaved through the jungle, Jenny glanced into the rear-view mirror on the door—about a second before a tree branch ripped it off.

She knew what she saw, and peered through the rear window to confirm it. Sure enough, Troyas Humvees were in hot pursuit of them, closing the gap between them. "Um, we've got company."

"Well thank Christ for that," Matthew said sarcastically. "I was starting to get lonely!"

A machine gunner mounted on the back of the lead Humvee opened fire. Jenny screamed, "DOWN!" as .50 calibre rounds zipped through the Jeep and punched holes into the windshield.

"Holy fuck!" Matthew yelled, ducking as the headrest on his seat burst apart. He jerked the wheel; the Jeep skimmed between two palm trees and started up a grassy knoll. Marner screamed as more enemy fire punctured the roof. Jenny flinched as a hole appeared in the dashboard.

"They're coming!" a Troyas infantryman yelled as he ran down the knoll to join his group, all of whom stood under a canopy of coconut palm trees. "Here they come!"

"Get ready, men!" another infantryman said as the rest of them racked their machine guns. "They'll be comin' fast!"

The Jeep reached the top and vaulted through a cluster of coconuts and tree branches. Then it landed hard and barrelled through the group of infantrymen, tossing two of them on the hood.

Matthew and Jenny shouted, "WHOA!" when gore splattered across the windshield.

"What the fuck did you hit?!" Jenny yelled.

"Mosquitoes!" Matthew said, laughing as he turned on the windshield wipers. "They're everywhere!"

"Whatever, just give me a gun," Jenny said as another wave of .50 calibre rounds ripped through the Jeep.

"What the hell makes you think I'd do that?! You women can't aim for shit!" Matthew drew one of his Hi-Powers and blew out the blood-spattered windshield to see where he was going.

"Did you not see me in the restaurant?!"

"You had a grenade launcher against guys with semi-automatics. That's cheating! Grenade launchers don't require aiming!"

"Oh yeah?! Watch me!" Jenny yelled as she snatched Matthew's other Hi-Power from his shoulder holster.

"Hey!" he snarled.

Jenny knocked the window out with her elbow and said, "Keep this goddamn thing steady."

The Jeep went off another hill and knocked down a small tree, bouncing uncontrollably across a shallow marsh. "Easier said than done," Matthew grumbled.

Exiting the marsh with a splash, the Jeep hit a clearing. Jenny saw her chance and climbed out of the window. She sat on the door and aimed her newly acquired pistol at the pursuing Humvee in the lead. She narrowed her eyes, concentrating, heart pounding, gun arm shaking. The Jeep bounced again, nearly tossing her out, but she managed to grab onto the roof rack to steady herself. Wind and tree branches brushed through her hair. *C'mon, c'mon...*

The machine gunner let loose another volley, which tore up the roof rack and nearly hit her hand. Jenny fired three rounds in response, right through the windshield on the driver's side.

The Humvee slammed into a rock and flipped, flinging the machine gunner forward like a ragdoll.

The following Humvee collided with the leader and spun out of control, right into the path of a third Troyas vehicle, which plowed into the second, causing them both to explode.

Any follow-ups were quick to avoid the wreckage, continuing

their pursuit.

"FUCK YEAH!" Jenny banged her fist against the roof, celebrating her success as she ducked back down into her seat. "Did you see that?!"

Matthew rolled his eyes, twisting to avoid another tree. "Colour me impressed. Where'd you learn to do that?"

"…Did you not see my sister in the restaurant?"

"It can't run in the blood. No way."

"You're questioning how I just caused a military pile-up with only three bullets, but I don't remember anyone asking how I wrestled a fucking tank and *lived*!"

"*Lived…*" Matthew said, straight-faced, "...but didn't *win*."

Jenny scowled.

Jeremy found a box at the foot of his seat and snapped the clasps open. Looking inside, he found a fully-assembled assault rifle, an attachable grenade launcher, several magazines and a large number of grenades. "This ought to be interesting," he said as he equipped the launcher to the assault rifle and fully loaded his new weapon. He spotted a loaded pistol at the bottom of the case and handed it to Marner. "Here!"

Marner hesitated, then took it and handed it to Jenny over the seat. "Here, Jenny."

"That was for you," Jeremy hissed as he racked his assault rifle.

"I don't kill people," Marner said.

"This is not the time for moral limitations," Jeremy snapped.

"If we don't have boundaries then what does that make us?"

"Survivors!" Jeremy spotted another Humvee approaching them on either side, and smashed the window on his side with the butt of his rifle. As the Humvee dodged a tree, Jeremy fired a five-round burst at the machine gunner. When that didn't work, he blasted the Humvee with a grenade, sending it twirling off its wheels and crashing into a palm tree.

Jenny reached over her seat, took Marner's pistol and said, "Thanks, buddy. I get it."

Marner was discouraged nonetheless. "I know…"

More machine gun fire stuttered behind them as a group of enemy Jeeps started to flank them, two on each side, not including the Humvee that already approached Jenny and Marner's side.

Jenny turned her two pistols on the driver of the nearest Humvee and fired both of them through the side window until a patch of red sprayed out from the inside. The Humvee ran free with a panicking passenger and a screaming machine gunner in the back clinging to his mounted M60 for dear life.

And then… the landscape suddenly dropped.

Everyone screamed as the Jeep lifted off the ground, sailing over the steep mountainside between trees and shrubs. The grass and shrubs whipped at the Jeep as it traced an arc over the cliff. Their pursuers were also airborne, their tires skimming across rocks and bushes. The driverless Humvee on Jenny's side sprang off the ground and flipped over, pounding the machine gunner into the earth as it cart-wheeled down the mountainside. Marner held her breath, her heart jumping in her throat. Jeremy aimed the assault rifle out the window and launched another grenade into the side of a flying Jeep.

BOOM!

The enemy Jeep exploded in midair and twirled in a flaming spiral over the slope, flinging one of its flaming passengers into the forest as it descended into the ground.

WHAM!

The teens' Jeep touched down. The back tires leaped up into the air; the Jeep lurched violently. Jenny and the others thought they were going to flip over. Every bump they hit sent them back up into the air.

The seven remaining enemy pursuers landed. One of the Jeeps collided with a tree, shattering the windshield and hurling the machine gunner further down the steep slope.

Jeremy broke open the grenade launcher, let the empty casing slip out, and then shoved a new grenade into it—all while maintaining his balance and keeping his head from smacking off the ceiling.

"We're hitting a jump!" Matthew shouted.

"A jump, *what*?!" Jenny yelled.

RATATATATATATATATAT!

Machine guns roared behind them. Another volley of .50 calibre rounds ripped through the Jeep and tore the roof to shreds. Everyone ducked their heads down. The stereo system burst.

Jenny and Matthew looked at the stereo system in horror, then at each other.

Matthew slammed his foot on the gas. The Jeep hugged the slope as it sped up, tires shredding through shrubberies and dead branches, straight for the ditch at the foot of the slope. And then...

WHOOSH!

The Jeep flipped forward, rear tires in the air, front bumper scraping across the ditch floor. Then all tires hit the floor as the Jeep pitched off the other side of the ditch like a ramp, and sprang up over a jagged ravine full of rocks and weeds. Marner screamed as the Jeep burst through a canopy of coconuts. Then, finally, the Jeep hit the ground and skidded onto a paved road.

Their pursuers took the same jump. One of them smashed into the ditch wall. Another one fell short of the road, crashing into the rocky ravine and exploding.

The last four made it to the road and swerved into the correct line, knocking a civilian vehicle off the road. Now they were right behind their prey.

Jenny turned around in her half-destroyed seat, said, "Give me that fucking thing!" snatched the assault rifle from Jeremy's hands. Then she stood up, aimed, and blasted a grenade through the windshield of the leading enemy Jeep. The explosion blew the roof off the Jeep and sent the soldiers flying onto the road from either side to get run over by their companions.

Three more, and the machine gunners weren't alone in their barrage—all of the soldiers started shooting from every window.

Marner and Jeremy huddled down on the floor again. Jenny, standing fearlessly on her seat in the enemy's line of fire, broke the launcher open and let the casing slip out and bounce off Jeremy's head. "Ow!" Ignoring him, she shoved another grenade in, and sent it flying under a Humvee that took to the wrong side of the road.

BOOM!

The Humvee capsized into the air. The machine gunner shrieked in terror as the road rose up to meet him, and in the next instant he was crushed under the overturned Humvee.

Jenny dropped the empty casing, and grabbed a fresh grenade when a .50 calibre round burned a deep groove across her left shoulder. She screamed, dropped the round, nearly falling backwards from the impact. "FUCK! FUCK!" she yelled, her left arm hanging limp at her side. Then, with her good hand, she raised the M16 and sprayed the second-last Humvee with bullets. "FUCKERS!"

The soldiers in the front seats ducked down as bullets raked the hood and shattered the windshield. Several rounds pelted the Humvee, eventually skating across the rooftop and hitting the machine gunner in the chest. The machine gunner gasped as he stumbled out of the turret and landed on the hood of the last Jeep, much to the chagrin of its passengers.

The machine gunner, still alive, gripped by fear, trying desperately not to fall off the hood and blocking the passengers' view in the process. The passenger yelled, "Get out of the way!"

But the machine gunner was too scared to comply. He simply gripped the sides of the hood, holding on as the Jeep swerved back and forth in an attempt to shake him. When that didn't work, the passenger cocked his shotgun and blasted the machine gunner through the windshield. First shot blew his head off. Second shot sent the rest of him flying under the Jeep's tires.

The leading Humvee moved to the opposite lane and caught up with the 'hostages' Jeep, flying down the road side-by-side. Then it swerved, slamming into Matthew's side. The Jeep bounced back and hit the Humvee. Matthew grunted with frustration as the passenger looked him in the eyes and then fired a pistol at him. Matthew and Jenny kept their heads down, with Matthew jerking on the wheel and ramming the Jeep against the Humvee again. The enemy passenger's gun ran out of ammo.

A semi barreled down the road toward them. Jenny and Matthew promptly drew their Hi-Powers and blasted the passenger side of the Humvee, tearing the passenger's face off and slashing the driver's forehead, distracting him long enough for him to not notice the semi until it was already on him, its driver honking the horn furiously.

SMASH!

The vehicles collided head-on. The shattered Humvee disappeared from sight as the trailer screamed by the Jeep.

Jenny loaded a fresh round into the grenade launcher and handed it back to Jeremy. "Here."

"Suddenly I am needed again?" Jeremy asked sardonically as he took the assault rifle.

"My arm's fucked; I can't aim that thing with just one arm in a moving Jeep, smartass."

"You seemed to be doing fine earlier."

"Just blow them up before they reload!"

Without looking back, Jeremy fired the grenade over the back seat. The last enemy Jeep burst into flames and rolled off the road, confirming his hit. "There," he said with agitation as he handed her the assault rifle. "Satisfied?"

Jenny scowled and propped the rifle on the seat beside her.

Matthew took the next turn onto a dirt road through the jungle. "We're almost there," he said, looking at Jenny. "Can I have my gun back now?"

The Parking Lot

Air's automaton shook the ground with every step as it stormed the beach, tearing up the police forces that tried to cross the river. Its heavy footfalls eventually tore the parking lot asunder, transforming it into a mountain range of fissures and jagged cliffs that shifted around like gravel, forming crumbling islands. Soldiers that stayed behind instead of taking part in the jungle pursuit did everything they could to keep from falling into the fissures. Some didn't succeed, while others maintained their balance or jumped to safer sections that weren't breaking apart.

Aria hopped from island to island, avoiding bullets and rockets from the fighter jet as it struggled to get a bead on her. Soldiers that had survived the earthquake caused by the automaton opened fire on her to make things even more difficult.

Aria dived over a trench, gunning down a row of soldiers with her Uzis in midair. Riddled soldiers fell over the edge of their island and disappeared into the underground piping system as Aria landed gracefully on the other side. One of the survivors in the firing squad squatted at the edge of his island and sprayed her with bullets, slamming her against the wall of an elevated mass of concrete. She took the bullets with a pained grimace, and then tore up the last soldier with her Uzis until his corpse rolled out of sight.

The fighter jet floated around the bend until its target came into view. Its miniguns rattled. Aria leaped up, latched onto the edge of a higher platform, and pulled herself up to the top of a towering block of concrete. With no time to stop, Aria bolted across the top, chased by the jet's bullets, and a loosed rocket whistled after her like a bird swooping down to catch its prey.

Aria reached the edge and jumped. The rocket dove into the tower's top and exploded. The fireball curled into the sky; the force of the shockwave propelled Aria over the fissure, toward a squad of soldiers gathered on the other side.

She barely made the jump and reeled into the middle of the squad. The fighter jet's miniguns cut the squad members down without distinction, following Aria as she rolled down the sloping island with the soldiers turning into splatters around her. Then she reached the other side of the island, right at the edge, and stood upright with a cylinder shotgun in her hands, pointed right at the fighter jet. "Time to check out," she quipped.

And fired an explosive round right at the jet.

The pilot gasped.

The co-pilot screamed, "Wasted paintjob—"

KABOOM!

The jet's left wing splintered, its rockets exploding prematurely in the silos. Then the rest of the fighter jet disintegrated in a giant fireball that scattered its remains across the sky.

From a short distance away, just out of Aria's sight, a Troyan lieutenant peeked over the top of a concrete mound, watching as the skeletal remains of the fighter jet plummeted flaming into a ravine. "We need backup, ASAP. These people are fucking insane; I just saw a topless redhead blast one of our jets out of the sky like in some Andy Sidaris movie!"

"No!" a captain on the other end yelled in dismay, "Not Sidaris!"

"Sidaris, sir!"

"Goddamn it! We're doomed!"

"What should I do, sir?"

"Retreat! Our top priority is the Dead Blue. Why the hell're we even wasting men on those unimportant psychopaths?"

"I don't know, sir! I don't give the orders, sir!"

"Don't get smart with me, private—"

"Lieutenant, sir!"

"WHATEVER! Report back to the bathhouse!"

"Yes, sir!"

*

The Palm Tree Onsen

Damian groaned as he resurfaced from the hot bathwater, swearing and muttering in Russian and in English. He trudged through the water with his shoulders slouched and his head lowered, ignoring the downpour of burning rubble.

KABRASH!

Tim burst through the ceiling and fell into the women's bathwater with a splash, landing on his feet just a few paces away from Damian. Damian leaped away from him and fired his dual revolvers at him.

Tim bounded toward him with his blade drawn, deflecting Damian's energy blasts with lightning speed and precision, approaching his foe with his blade drawn back. "Time to die!"

"STOP RIGHT THERE, BITCHES!" Damian and Tim turned to see Jonny aiming two submachine guns at them. "Not another freakin' step!" Jonny shouted. "I've had enough of this shit. I'm taking Jenny home. Out of this… this…"

Damian scowled. "You're a fucking idiot. You think you can just run out of this situation you're in? I bet you're one of those 'love conquers all' faggots, aren't you?"

"No, I'm not," Jonny snapped, glaring at Damian. "I *do* love her, but you know what? I'm not here just because of that."

"Then why else are you here?"

"I'm going to kill you."

Damian laughed. "Good luck with that!"

Tim barked at Jonny: "Hey, he's mine, Jonny, you bastard!"

"Yeah, get in line," Damian said. "And pitch a tent. It's a long line."

Poink! Poink!

Something fell in the water. Something small; one near Jonny, and one in front of Tim. Tim looked up at the hovercraft and saw another cluster of Troyas soldiers hanging from cables like a colony of spiders. "Oh, SHIT—"

BABBOOOOMMM!

Water erupted, sending a tidal wave hurtling toward Damian, burying him under the surface.

Troyas soldiers dropped into the women's bath and pelted Damian with rubber bullets as he struggled to fend them off with a telekinetic shield and his guns. He couldn't concentrate when he was constantly being bombarded by the enemy's gunfire. They forced him to his knees and consequently under the surface of the hot bathwater. He could feel the aching pain in his bruises somehow drain his energy from him. He could barely move. He didn't even have the strength to hold his breath. He could only silently panic as water filled his lungs and pulled him deeper and deeper into an unwanted sleep. What the hell's going on, he thought. Why am I so useless…?

Into the abyss.

He cracked his eyes open and found himself staring down into a black, writhing void with wide, lifeless eyes staring back up at him. Thousands of eyes and clawed hands and bony arms rose up to meet him like shadowy tendrils.

"Come to us, Damian."

"Come back..."

"Join us..."

"You know you want to..."

No…

"What?"

"Why not, Damian?"

"Are you scared?"

Stay away from me! I don't want anything to do with you!

"Still a whiner."

"Failure."

"You won't abandon us again!"

"You traitor!"

"Get back here!"

They grabbed him, one by one. They got his arms first. Then as they yanked him down, they gripped his legs and body, and starting squeezing their hands around his throat.

"YOU'RE NOT GOING ANYWHERE!"

He found himself staring face to face with a girl he once knew. Here she was, sobbing, her face just inches from his. Her half-open face, with a jagged crack splitting her head down the middle. "Come back to me!" she cried with a voice almost as distorted as her darkened face and red eyes. "Don't leave! DON'T YOU DARE LEAVE ME!"

Just then, something wrapped itself around his stomach and yanked him upward, pulling him out of the grasps of his ghostly visions.

"Got 'im!"

One of the Troyas soldiers had him draped over his shoulder, carrying him like a sack of potatoes as the line clipped to his belt lifted him back up out of the water, reeling him into the hovercraft. "Alright, we're outta here, boys!"

"What the hell got into 'im?" one of the soldiers asked.

As the remaining soldiers boarded the hovercraft via ramp extended from the loading bay, the man that carried Damian explained: "Clearly you weren't listenin' to our Captain's orders, Mac. We were s'posed to coat our rubber bullets with traces o' Spiral Suicide. Wouldn't be enough to force 'im to kill 'imself or give 'im an adrenaline boost, but it'd be enough to disable 'im with hallucinations an' shit."

"What do you think he hallucinates?"

"Jackson, I don't think I wanna know."

"Think the punk dreams o' killing everyone, Mark?"

Mark, the man that carried Damian on his shoulder, crossed the ramp and entered the loading bay. Shortly after entry, he dropped Damian on a steel bench. "Like I said; I don't wanna know what this punk's dreamin' 'bout. Could be dreamin' 'bout killin' ev'ry las' sucker on th' planet, or he could be dreamin' 'bout butterflies 'n tooth fairies. I seriously doubt that, though. Just lookit 'im. I can't even sit beside 'im without checking t' make sure 'e's still sleepin' ev'ry five seconds. Goddamn brat gives me th' creeps."

"Hard ta believe that *he* is the Dead Blue everyone's talking about. Hell, he's just a kid. I mean, *look* at him. Looks like a baby the way he's all passed out on the bench there," another soldier said with a chuckle. "The Killer of Twenty Million People… unbelievable."

"Looks can deceive, Jarvis."

All of the soldiers were on the loading bay, and as the doors closed up, blocking any outside light, the soldiers grouped around the bench Damian lay sprawled on, their nervous eyes fixed on him. His eyes were wide open, staring blankly at the ceiling, which only added to their edginess. When the doors were fully shut, a red light came on.

"We're off!"

"'Bout fuckin' time."

"Let's just get back as quickly as possible. I don't like lookin' at this little shit. Goddamn little bastard's more trouble'n he's worth. And will somebody close his eyes?! It's givin' me the creeps, for Christ's sake!"

"No way, man. I ain't goin' near 'im."

"Pussy."

"Ha! Sez you!"

"They abandoned us. They crossed the road before we could. They left us behind to suffer in this war."

"No... they wouldn't!"

"Didn't you notice?"

"Notice what?"

"They didn't want you. You were too different. Too special. Sure, dad gave us that extra power with that seal on your... our *back, but that was because he was* supposed *to."*

"What do you mean?" Damian asked.

"That was his job all along. Don't you understand yet?"

Thunder rumbled over the grey clouds. Rain poured down on Damian's head. "Understand what?"

"That nobody loved you."

The walk signal flashed.

Other people taking shelter under their umbrellas pushed past Damian to cross the street. He stood completely still as they moved by him like robots going about the motions they were programmed to do. The rain pattered hard against their umbrellas.

"Let me take over."

"What? How?"

"Give me control, and I'll bring us closer to changing this miserable world. And then we'll never suffer again. Nobody will be able to hurt us anymore."

Damian liked the sound of that. No war. No pain. No more suffering. No more hiding from anyone. It sounded like pure, unadulterated paradise. Damian couldn't help but smile at the thought.

No.

It wasn't a thought. It was his fantasy.

"Yeah," he finally said. "Let's change the world... Tyler."

The stop signal flashed.

"Why do you persist?" Tyler asked.

What do you mean?

"What's the point in promising those stupid little bitches that you'll help them find their mother?"

Sure, it might sound stupid. But why shouldn't they be...?

"We lost everything, *Damian."*

I know...

"Who took everything from us, Damian?"

...Humans did.

"Humans did what, *Damian?"*

He sighed. Humans took everything from us.

"So why would you help them?"

I... well...

"You never listen to me."

You're not my mom or my dad. Why should I?

"No. They're gone. I'm the only person with a shred of common sense in his head."

Ironically, that's my *head.*

"Shut up. Ditch these humans. You can do better."

"You can do better, son," said Jeffery. "You can do better than that."

Brief, hesitant silence.

I... I don't know...

"It's because you slept with that girl, isn't it? Is it because of her?"

Well, I...

"Pathetic. You *of all people should know... you should understand the manipulation humans are capable of. You're falling right into their hands, letting them attach the strings to your arms and legs. Soon you'll just be their puppet. But you can't. You can't fall for it. I'm disappointed, Damian. Always allowing yourself to get easily attached to such pathetic things like morality and love, and puppies and girls. You have a goal. Don't let some stupid girl ruin everything! If you don't keep your promise, I swear..."*

I won't, I won't!

"Won't what?"

I won't break my promise.

"Better not. What is she to you?"

What?

"The girl. What is she to you?"

...I don't know, really. A friend, maybe?

"A 'friend.' Someone like you, 'friends' *with a human like that? Friends don't do what you two did last night. Utterly disgusting of you to do such things with a human."*

Last night was an accident.

"Sure it was. Just don't forget what you're supposed to do."

Don't worry about it. I'm not gonna forget, and I'm not gonna go back on my word.

Their conversation went quiet.

Ring, ring!

Damian looked up at the payphone across the street from the grungy bus stop shelter he sat under. He stood up off the bench and approached the edge of the sidewalk, staring at the payphone that hung within the confines of the hard plastic booth, which was scratched up, broken, and covered with vulgar graffiti.

Ring, ring!

He looked both ways down the empty street before taking a hesitant step out from under the shelter.

Ring, ring!

He hurried across the street, entered the phone booth, and answered the phone. "Hello?"

"Damian Warkowski," a thousand raspy whispers replied in unison on the other end. The sound nearly made Damian drop the phone, almost made his heart stop.

"W-who is this?"

"Just a friendly neighbour from the Spirit Abyss. I'm a big fan of your work."

"...Who are you?"

"You already know who I am."

He hesitated. "You're that... Fallen Angel guy?"

"Correct."

"What do you want with me?"

"You're a special boy, Damian. But you already know *that, don't you?"*

"...How'd you know?"

"I've been watching you. I've had my eye on you for quite some time."

"Yeah? That's pretty creepy, man."

"Creepy or not, I have to say I'm impressed."

"Why? What do you see in me? Just a special weapon, right?"

"Why do you say that?"

"That's what everyone wants. They just wanna use me for some stupid bullshit."

"I see you more as a partner."

"Oh, really?"

"Yes. Oh, yesss. I do need you for something. After all, I can't do this alone, and it's in your and your brother's best interests if we work together. We all have the same goal, more or less."

"And what might that be—"

"Damian?"

He whirled around and saw Jenny standing just a few feet away from him with a grave look on her face. "What the hell are you *doing here?!" he gasped.*

She stepped closer, holding up her hand. "What are you doing? Who are you talking to?"

"None of your damn business," he said, keeping the receiver out of her reach. "Go away. Leave me alone."

"What are you doing?"

The Fallen Angel: "Who is that?"

"I don't know," said Damian before turning his back on Jenny again. "Go away, Jenny."

"There's another way, you know."

"What?"

"You can't just kill everyone."

"FUCK OFF!" he shouted, whirling around and backhanding her across the face. He grabbed her by the hair and threw her inside the booth. "Where the fuck did you come from, anyway?! Why are you always showing up in my dreams?! Why are you always there!? GET OUT!" He relentlessly stomped his feet down on her. "GET OUT GET OUT GET OUT! Get the fuck out of my head!"

She stared at him with saddened eyes. Then she closed her fingers on the hook. The dial tone rang in Damian's ear, causing him to angrily shout, "FUCK!" He threw the receiver at her. "Agh! Why're you getting in the way?" he asked. "WHY!?"

She looked at him and said, "...Maybe it's because you liked me from the start?"

"Don't give me that bullshit."

"It's true, isn't it?" She approached him. "You like me, huh? You don't think it's right, do you?"

"She's manipulating you, brother."

BLAM!

Jenny flew backwards into the phone booth with a gaping hole in her stomach. She looked at it and coughed, and sputtered, and sobbed. "Damian..." she whimpered as she slid to the floor, leaving crimson smears on the walls of the booth and the payphone.

Damian held his gun in his shaking hands. "It's not true! She's lying!"

BLAMBLAM!

"LIAR!" he screamed as he fired repeatedly into the booth.

BLAMBLAM!

"FUCKING LIAR!"

***BLAM!** Click! Click! Click! Click! Click! Click!*

"All... a fucking lie..."

The phone booth's interior ran red with blood. Holes punctured the translucent walls of the phone booth. Jenny was sprawled on the floor with her legs stretching out of the entrance. Her blood oozed out onto the road. Six gaping holes in her body; two in the stomach, three in the chest, one in the face, and one in the right shoulder. Her head hung forward over her maimed corpse.

Damian panted heavily, staring at her and keeping his gun level. His arm quivered. "It's all just... another lie"

Her left index finger twitched. He stiffened as she raised her head. His eyes widened in horror.

She looked up at him with her right eye wide open, and a bloody socket where her left eye used to be. Blood gushed from the hole in her face and dripped off her chin into her lap. A small red orb glowed dimly in the center of the socket. "Damian," she moaned. Her voice echoed inside his head; every syllable was like a hot pang sent directly to his brain. "Don't make promises you can't keep. Please... help..."

"I don't help liars."

BLAM!

"I hate liars." He started shooting her again, endlessly squeezing the trigger, blasting her to a pulpy mass. "And I hate *humans! Why the fuck should I help you?! What makes you think you deserve it, hunh?! You fucking bitch! You're probably just trying to trick me into helping you! Trying to seduce me, eh? Well fuck you! Fuck you, fuck your mother, and fuck all of humanity! You're* nothing*! You had your chance and you blew it! You all blew it! Humans don't deserve to live anymore!"*

"…All humans… must *die*."

The remaining Troyas soldiers were huddled in a corner staring at Damian as he stood over the bloodied corpses of their fellow soldiers with two smoking revolvers in his hands. The loading bay walls were coated with blood and punctured with sizzling bullet holes, and even the floor was flooded with three inches of dark glistening red. Severed limbs and heads and torn corpses were strewn about the floor and benches and even nailed to the walls with energy blades.

Damian stared at the far wall with distant, glowing red eyes, standing with his back facing the few horror-struck survivors that remained.

"Fuck this," one of them shouted, grabbing his shotgun. "I'm usin' *real* bullets!"

"NO!" another soldier shouted, knocking the gun out of his hands. "His life is top priority!"

The first one hit his shoulder and shouted, "Fuck his life! I ain't dyin' for this little shit!"

"Shut up," said Damian.

BLAM!

The first soldier's head exploded. The five remaining soldiers shrieked and scurried away from the first soldier. One of them fired his submachine gun at Damian. Sparks flew as bullets bounced off the walls, floor, and ceiling, punctured one of the soldiers' eyes and chest, and ripped the right pinky finger off another soldier's hand.

Damian chuckled, unharmed by the spray of submachine gunfire. He raised his guns, pointing them at the soldiers, and splattered their bodies with a fusillade of cobalt energy. By the time he finished, they looked like someone had spilled pasta into a dirty heap of laundry.

The alarm wailed. Damian ignored it, grinning sadistically as he gloated over the corpses. His anger was at boiling point, but he couldn't stop himself from smiling with satisfaction at what he'd done.

BOOMMMMM!

The loading bay shuddered violently, nearly throwing him off his feet. He leaned against the blood-soaked wall for support as a high-pitched hum overpowered the wailing alarm siren. The loading bay jerked around and tilted to the left, slamming Damian into the wall.

The *Scion's Wings* and *The Spartan* circled the Troyan hovercraft with their minigun pods blazing, sticking out of the main bodies of the ships, hurling explosive rounds into the hull of the anti-gravity hovercraft. One of the rotary engines of the hovercraft burned up and was rendered useless by cannon fire. The hovercraft spiralled out of control, belching flames, knocking down any lingering debris that jutted out of the burning bathhouse.

Jenny and Marner stood on the bridge of the *Scion's Wings*, watching the burning hovercraft spin around uncontrollably. With a freshly bandaged arm, Jenny maintained a bitter expression, keeping her arms crossed as she watched the explosive rounds slowly eat away at the hovercraft's bulk. "Can't believe these assholes ruined our little vacation," she muttered. "This is bullshit!"

"Quite," Jeremy replied from the cockpit. "Although I agree, I do not see the point in repeating yourself five times, Ms. Knight."

"Well it's fucking bullshit!"

"I know, but I do not see the—"

BLLAAAMMM!

Marner screamed and fell on the floor as the windows lit up and the bridge shook. Jenny stumbled away from the windows and collapsed beside Marner.

Outside, General Air's Terrain Marcher 04 sprayed the Copter Ships with fire and explosive rounds, doing astonishingly little damage to their exteriors, though causing them to bank in the opposite direction. "Fucking little bastards!" Air roared within the cockpit, "Stop interfering with my mission!"

BOOM!

The Troyas hovercraft suddenly groaned. It expanded from the middle, growing wider and wider. Then, to Air's shock and horror, it burst like a giant metallic balloon, blasting metal and human bits in every direction. Damian hovered within a ball of writhing black chains and blue flames, almost as if he were floating underwater. He appeared to be staring at the ground with an energy blade in one hand and his revolver in the other. Both flaming halves of the hovercraft plummeted to the palm tree forest below and exploded like ignited propane tanks, launching massive fireballs and chunks of dirt, debris, and tree branches into the air.

Jenny's eyes widened as the spectacle unfolded before her eyes. She pressed her nose and hands up against the glass, watching Damian from afar with newfound fear and curiosity.

Damian turned to the automaton and aimed his revolver at it.

Air spotted him on one of the monitors and gasped, "Shit!"

BLAM!

Damian's black energy projectile whistled through the air, leaving a spiral-patterned trail behind, and exploded upon impact with the Terrain Marcher 04's right shoulder joint, reducing it to flying bits. The right arm went limp, dangling from a few loose wires that clung to its socket and the giant ammunition belt linked to its 'backpack'. Its spiked knuckles dragged through the forest as the bulky robot reeled from the impact.

BLAM!

The left elbow popped, severing half of the automaton's arm, flattened a cluster of trees in its fall.

Air watched in horror as Damian adjusted his aim. He aimed his revolver directly at Air, like he could see him through the cockpit, his sinister red eyes boring deep into his soul. "Shit! Shit! *SHIT*!" He withdrew his hands from the motion-sensitive glove controls and yanked the lever on the side of his chair up. His chair jumped up the shaft and nestled itself within the battered, half-demolished head of the Terrain Marcher 04.

BLAM!

A bolt of black lightning impaled the automaton's body, lighting up the tanks and ammo packs stuffed into the 'backpack.' Small explosions started to tear up the interior of the Terrain

Marcher 04, causing it to shake violently and fall on its knees.

Drenched in sweat, Air hastily entered the coordinates into the dashboard and pounded the EJECT button.

KAAABWWHOOOOOMMMMMMM!

The explosions flared out from the pack, consuming the automaton, dissolving it in a massive blinding fireball that expanded rapidly, engulfing everything within a half-kilometre radius. Everyone standing on the bridges of the Copter Ships shielded their eyes from the blast as the ships tossed and turned in the violent shockwave. The palm trees and the burning remains of the Palm Tree Onsen disintegrated instantly. Tim put up a force shield to protect himself just as the energy poured over him and tore the ground out from beneath him. Seth, who had been observing from his own hovercraft several kilometres away, held onto the guardrail as the shockwave plowed through the jungle and rammed the side of his ship.

The fireball dissipated, revealing a massive column of red and black smoke rising from the center of a black crater. A huge portion of the island had been vaporized. Ocean water rushed to fill the gap.

Jenny turned back around and saw Damian, who continued to hover above the crater unscathed. Her heart skipped a beat when he glanced over at her with his blood red eyes and jet black face. Somehow his skin had transformed from the regular pale peach colour to night black. The sight shocked her, rendering her completely speechless. She could only stare at him through the fluttering red embers dancing from the wreckage below.

He smirked and pointed his gun at her. "Time to die."

POW!

Jenny stiffened, clamping her eyes shut. Something made her open them—curiosity, maybe? Disbelief?

To her surprise, Damian's limp body was plummeting into the crater, disappearing in the smoke. She mumbled something, quivering uncontrollably as she stared at the spot where he vanished. "What was that…?"

A fully clothed Aria stood in the crater with a sniper rifle in her hands and a gas mask over her face. She jogged her way through the thick shroud of smoke until she found Damian's unconscious body, now reverted back to normal. She sighed with relief, hissing through her gas mask, as she stood over him. "Nobody threatens my family, you son of a bitch."

The *Scion's Wings*

An hour later, Damian lay in the infirmary, unconscious and snoring. Mona sat beside him with her feet tucked up on the chair and her chin resting on her knee. Standing at the foot of the bed was a teenage girl in a white nurse outfit with blonde hair pinned back in a ponytail and circular glasses over her green eyes. She held a clipboard and pen firmly in her hands as she watched Damian intently. She had a surgical mask pulled over her mouth and nose, and her outfit had a few dark stains on it.

"I've never seen anything like this before," the nurse named Katherine (everyone called her Nurse Kat) said. "He reverted back to normal all on his own. No sign of any wounds, either. Can you explain that?"

Mona smiled at her and said, "He'll be fine. Just give him a few hours."

"Can't you tell me anything? Anything to go on?"

"Nah," Mona said. Her tail wagged back and forth. "It's best if you don't know."

"Why's that?"

Mona leaned over the bed and purred as she nuzzled her cheek against his. "Trust me."

The group had gathered on the bridge of the *Scion's Wings* for a meeting.

Jenny slammed her hand on the cockpit dashboard. Jeremy winced as if she'd smacked him instead. "Alright, let's get some exposition dialogue going on here! No more bullshit!" she exclaimed agitatedly. "Starting with why he pointed a gun at *us*. We're supposed to be on the same team, right? So what the fuck was that?"

"I—"

Before Jeremy could start, Jenny cut him off with a loud shout, raised her index finger. "Actually... no... let's start with the most important question first." She pointed at Jonny, who stood a few feet away from her "Why the fuck is *he* tagging along?!" She turned to Jonny and yelled, "How did you even survive that explosion?!"

"I ducked," Jonny said. Then he looked at everyone else, grinned, and waved. "Hi, there. For those of you who don't know, my name's Jonny Kyle."

Jeremy cocked his head toward him. "Jeremy Larson. A pleasure." He looked at Jenny. "Also, it would be wise to let someone answer your first question before you ask them another question. People tend to get confused."

"Shut up!" she growled, still pointing at Jonny. "You don't get it! He's a lecherous pervert! He's like a rapist-in-training! Why'd you let him onboard?!" She turned to Jonny. "Why the hell are you onboard?!"

"I'm so glad you asked, my sweet!" Jonny replied, adopting a standoffish pose and brushing his white hair back with an air of exaggerated heroism. "I came to show you my true worth and potential while saving you from the evil clutches of the—"

KRAK!

She punched him in the face, sent him twirling into the window. As his unconscious body slithered down to the floor, Jenny turned back to Jeremy and said, "See?! *SEE*!? He's an idiot! How many idiots are you prepared to handle in one trip?! You gotta kick him off! Let's all throw him overboard! It's not like he'll drown to death! He can't even die!"

"Calm down." Jeremy adjusted his goggles and sighed, leaning back in his chair, crossing his arms. He calmly replied, "Might I add that whatever alliance we have established is a very unstable one?"

"Don't give me that bullshit!" she continued to shout.

"Indoor voice, please, Ms. Knight."

"What's with this?!" she shouted again, completely ignoring his request. "You're letting Jonny fly with us and you're hiding information about Damian from us!" She threw her hands down on the dashboard, looming over Jeremy menacingly. "Now *TALK*!"

"I will not give you a cooperative response until you agree to keep your voice level at a minimum indoor volume."

"Whatever! Now tell us what the fuck happened out there!"

"Watch your language, Sis," said Aria, who had her back against one of the windows. She was chewing on a toothpick that hung out the side of her mouth. "I've heard enough uses of the word 'fuck' for one day from the blue-haired squirt."

"Why ask me?" asked Jeremy.

"Because *you* knew him since childhood! I *know* you know something we don't know!"

"Would it not be more sufficient to ask the Mew girl?" Jeremy asked.

"Don't worry, I'll be asking *her* some questions soon enough."

Marner sat huddled in a corner, watching the scene with a troubled expression.

Jeremy scratched the back of his head. "Well... I *do* know him; you are correct."

"So why'd he try to shoot us?"

"He didn't—"

"*Yes* he did! I *saw* him point the gun *right* at us!"

"And *I* am telling *you* that *it was not him*!" Jeremy yelled impatiently.

Jenny faltered, taken aback by Jeremy's sudden outburst. "If it wasn't him, then…"

"It was his brother."

Aria gave Jeremy a sideways glance.

Marner looked up, confused. "What?"

"His *brother*…? What the hell are you talking about?" Jenny asked with a bewildered look. "That was *him*, though…"

"Are you aware of the defensive form of the Dehue?" he asked.

"Yeah, it's uhh... that protective shell thing that coats their skin to prevent them from getting seriously injured, or something. Right? That's the only 'defensive form' that I learned about in school."

"That is precisely the mechanism I mean. Their appearance changes; their skin turns black, and even their eyes are coated with a thin—but strongly effective—shield that gives the pupils an illusionary red colour. However, Damian's defense mechanism is… different."

"What d'you mean?" Jenny asked, narrowing her eyes and leaning forward on the dashboard.

Jeremy nervously looked at her cleavage hanging in front of his face and turned away. "Do you mind…?"

With a scowl, Jenny straightened and zipped up her jacket.

"Damian had a big family. Before him, the Warkowski family consisted of a mother, father, one daughter, and two boys. For a while, his father was a depressed alcoholic. I suppose being the commander of the Dehue military at the time was not very rewarding, considering the many discriminations they faced. But he tried his best to support his young children."

Jonny slipped back into consciousness. When he realized Jeremy was in the middle of his explanation he sat quietly next to Marner and listened, only mildly interested, staring at Jenny's backside.

"Imagine his shock when he found out his wife was expecting twins. The news bothered him for several days… weeks… months. It always lingered in the back of his mind. How was he going to fend for seven people, including himself? How were they going to survive? These questions, I'm assuming, never stopped haunting him. But one day, he came home drunk. Their plight enraged him and, after a brief period of conflict with his wife—"

He scratched the back of his head and glanced up at Jenny and the others and said with a sickened glare in his blind eyes: "—he threw her down four storeys' worth of stairs."

Marner placed her hands over her mouth.

Jonny blinked. "What the hell…?"

Jenny stayed silent.

Jeremy continued: "One of the children died. It was a miracle that even *one* of them survived the fall. Hell, it was a miracle that his *wife* survived. But something unusual happened. Apparently the stillborn fetus of Damian's twin merged with him… body and soul. Now, it seems as though both of their souls are struggling for control over one vessel. His brother—whom he and Damian have unanimously named 'Tyler'—seems to have complete control over the defensive form, or 'demon half' as many call it."

"That's creepy," Jonny said.

"That sounds like bullshit," Jenny said.

"Aria can vouch for me."

Jenny, Jonny and Marner glanced over at Aria. Aria shrugged and said, "Kid's got it right."

Jenny's eyebrows went up. Then she approached Aria and jabbed her sister's chest with her index finger. "You *knew*?"

"Sure," Aria said.

"...You fucking *knew*?"

Aria's eyebrows scrunched together. "Yeah, I knew."

"And you didn't think it *might* be helpful if you told us?!"

Jeremy said, "She has a point there."

Jenny whirled around, pointed at him. "*You* aren't one to talk, jackass!"

"Cool down, Sis," Aria said. "You know what the doctor said about getting too frantic."

Jenny retorted, "You *still* could've told us! It'd be helpful to know! Like, say, over the phone, or... or sometime during the six-year period after the war! Or *maybe* before we got onto this fucking voyage with him! That would've been just fucking *great*!"

"Hey, I didn't think I'd see Damian again. And secondly, I was kinda busy thinking about how we're gonna get out of the mess you got us into!"

"ME!? This is *my* fault now?!"

"*You're* the one who let him out and let him sleep over at your house, you little slut!"

"Hey, *I* wasn't the one who discovered him, alright! I was just being courteous!"

"That's a load o' bullshit! You were horny! We all know it!"

Marner spoke up, "No, she's right."

Everyone looked at Marner.

Marner's voice was filled with regret. "I-I was the one who found him. I told Jenny about it and made her come along with me to help wake him up. I didn't know it'd turn out like this. If I knew, I swear I wouldn't have...!"

Jeremy raised his voice, interrupting them. "Enough bickering! Jenny, you wanted to know what is going on, so I suggest you be quiet and listen! Marner, you did not know, therefore you are not to blame. ...Well, not entirely." And Aria, if you please... explain it!"

Jenny drew back against the window, muttering angrily under her breath.

Aria stole one last annoyed scowl at Jenny before explaining: "Just for future reference: that demon half thing's got a weakness. He might be pretty freakin' strong, but there *is* a way to stop 'im dead in his tracks. Hit that weakness and he'll switch back in a flash. None of you might've noticed at the bathhouse, but Damian's got some weird tattoos on his back. They look like angel wings (not that they symbolize his charming personality or anything), and shooting right between those wings, right in the spine, will disable his brother. That's the only way to switch him back to the better half of him. I got 'im with my trusty Remington out there. Like bird hunting."

"That's just… weird," Jenny said, recalling the tattoos she'd seen on his back during her interrogation a few nights earlier. *He said he didn't know… but if that's true, how the hell does Aria know?*

"That is the truth, take it or leave it," said Jeremy.

"Did Damian tell you this?"

"No, our mothers were close. My mother told me shortly before she died."

"How'd *she* know?" Jenny asked.

"I do not know," Jeremy replied.

"That's messed up," said Jonny. "But it won't stop me. I also still think he's a dick."

Jenny whirled around to face him and snarled, "I don't need saving from anybody. And he *is* a dick, by the way. I'll give you that one. But *you're* the last person whom I'd ever ask to save me."

Jonny scowled. "Fine, whatever. But if he's unconscious, and a dick, why're you guys hanging around him? Can't we just tie a weight around his ankles and drop him in the ocean?"

Jonny's question silenced everyone in the room for a brief period.

"No," said Aria, breaking the awkward silence.

"Why?" Jonny asked with disbelief. "Why keep him around?!"

"Because we feel like it."

Jonny raised an eyebrow in her direction. "Isn't that a little stupid?"

"No, no, no, no," Aria replied. Then she winked at him mischievously. "It's adventurous, little boy. Don'tcha like adventurous things?"

Jonny blinked. Then he said, "Depends on what they are."

"Good, because we're going on another one right now," she said.

"What?" Jeremy said. "Where?"

She turned to him and answered: "We're going to Sky Japan."

Almost everyone looked at Aria with concern and confusion.

They weren't about to question her decision about where they would dock next. Most of them knew that Sky Japan was the place they wanted to go. Jeremy started to enter the coordinates for Sky Japan into his computer. The famous neon metropolis floating in the sky may be their final destination in their search for Jenny and Aria's mother, Alexandria Knight. Jenny wasn't looking forward to it, and Marner, who had been informed of the situation before General Air's attack, was hoping that their search wouldn't lead to a dead end.

Then Jonny asked, "Why?"

The Office of President Truman

Truman sat quietly at his desk, hidden in the shade between the two tall narrow windows as the red light of the afternoon sun crept across his office floor. He'd become an insomniac, having slept only two hours or less each night for the past few months. He was always tired. He was no longer able to fully comprehend whether or not he was sleeping or awake. He felt like he was always dreaming, always walking the grassy plains of the Spirit Core. In there, everything seemed to make sense. Out here, nothing felt real anymore.

CRASH!

One of the windows exploded, hurling glass inward. Something smashed through, taking part of the wall with it as it dived into the floor, digging into the ground. The furthest wall from Truman was all but decimated; the strange, massive object that hurtled its way into the office had mostly entered the next room over, and it scraped the ceiling, slowly grinding to a halt.

Truman stared unfazed at the round object as sparks spewed from its shredded exterior, his fingers still interlocked in front of his face. *This is too surreal...*

Click! Clatter! Whack!

Whatever was in there made quite a racket.

Plonk!

A sheet of metal fell off and General Air tumbled out onto the floor after it, covered in blood.

Truman was instantly discouraged. He knew exactly what'd happened. Or got the basic idea of it. "I see you've returned to me empty-handed, General," he said. "Where is the Dead Blue?"

"That little... bastard destroyed my air navy... took us all down!" Air sputtered, struggling to pick himself up off the floor. "All my men... my ship… my fuckin' robot!"

"Your mission was to capture the Dead Blue alive and kill anyone who stood in your way. How is it that you've been defeated by a mere group of children, even *if* the Dead Blue stood among them? Your brigade is all but gone; you've cost the Troyas government millions of valuable dollars that we do not have."

"You never told me I'd be hunting a fucking monster!" Air shouted.

"Don't give me that. You knew what you were getting into—or at least… you *should* have had a good idea. Clearly this is a case of failure due to underestimation. Let's not forget the fact that you tore up a neutral zone with that Terrain Marcher. I'm sure I will enjoy explaining that one to the press."

Truman's guards pounded at the office doors, yelling and trying to beat the door down.

"Mr. President! Are you alright?!"

"Goddammit, it's jammed!"

Truman called out, "I'm alright. Nothing to be concerned about."

Air: "Mr. President, I'm... only doing my best to... serve my country!" Air said.

"No! Becoming a major setback for the Divine Gift Project is the only purpose you serve now, and it's a purpose that must end." Truman stood up, brandishing his pistol—a CZ-75B—and pointing it at Air.

Air gasped, staring at the gun in disbelief, rooted to the spot. He raised his hand as if he could catch the bullet. "Sir, please... put the gun away! C'mon. I know I failed numerous times but I can still accomplish really important tasks! I-I can still be a commander worthy of the Elemental Five! I can endure any mission you put me through!"

"That's what I'm afraid of," Truman said as he flicked the safety off.

Air scrambled backwards toward the door, breathing heavily. "Please, sir. Please don't pull that trigger. I barely managed to get back. They almost killed me, but I survived. I can still be a soldier! I *am* a soldier! Give me one more chance, Mr. President. I won't disappoint you again. I won't fail my next mission. I swear! I'll succeed next time!"

"Allowing you to leave this room with your life would only prolong your death." Truman cocked the hammer.

"C'mon… c'mon…!" Air started to sob. "Please… you don't have another soldier that can replace me…"

"I'll look in Kyoko or Sky Japan. That's where I found you, after all. There are plenty of individuals there who can manipulate the weather. With people like that around, who accomplish the tasks they set out to do, who needs someone as lowly as you?"

Air slid up the door to his feet, staring down the barrel of Truman's gun. "You… you can't. You can't! You're the president! If this gets out, you're fucked! It'll be one of the biggest political scandals in U.S.T. history!"

"You needn't concern yourself with any of that, Air. This won't get out. Of all the things I've suppressed from public knowledge, do you honestly think one little murder will change anything?"

Air's fingernails scraped against the door, his arms rigid.

"You went rogue. Went against orders. Your goal was to gain some sort of superiority and/or promotion for attempting to capture the Dead Blue yourself. However… there were no survivors. The Dead Blue killed everyone, and you disappeared without a trace soon after." Truman couldn't help but smirk at the look of terror on Air's face. "Your death will not be remembered, nor will you be missed."

"HOLD IT! Hold it. Hold it. Hold on a second." Air drew his pistol from his shoulder holster and aimed it at Truman. "You wait one goddamn minute! Don't shoot, you son of a bitch, or I swear to God, I'll paint that flag behind you with your brains!"

The guards behind the door started shouting again.

Air kicked the door and yelled, "SHUT UP!"

The guards continued shouting and kicking against the door.

BANG!

Air's fingers—and consequently his gun—exploded out of his hand. Shocked, he looked at Truman, who shot him again in the stomach, right shoulder, left side of his head, chest twice, and then the right eye. The last shot splattered the contents of Air's skull against the door; a dark red smear left behind as his body slid to the floor.

Brriinnngg!

Truman placed his smoking gun on the desk and pushed the speaker button on his office phone. "President Truman speaking."

"Donnie Vanco has been killed. Jonathon Silverstein got him."

"That is unfortunate," he replied bitterly, glancing up at Air's body briefly.

"Are we going to pursue any course of action?"

"Jonathon Silverstein wants a war. My reply to his actions will be unmerciful. General Aqua and General Steel will assemble the majority of our forces to invade Cloverfield. General Stone will continue the mission for the Dead Blue's capture alive, effective immediately."

"Are you sure an invasion is wise, sir?"

"My informant in the Council has notified me of the Council's plans to use me as a proxy. I'm fine with that, honestly. They don't know about the Hell Pentagram in my possession. Quite ironic that this alliance is keeping secrets from its allies as well, and then treats me as if I can't be trusted. All we need is a plausible reason to justify an attack. It's Silverstein's move. Once he moves further across the board the invasion can begin, and Cloverfield will fall."

"What about the search for the Dead Blue? Has General Air returned?"

"General Air has been… *decommissioned.* It seems he had his own private agenda that involved my assassination. I'm fine; I shot him first."

"…Yes, sir. But there is another thing that you'll be interested in..."

"What is it?"

"The World Alliance Council has gotten suspicious of our activities. They even went so far as to send a spy to investigate."

"A spy?" Truman repeated with slight surprise. "They are willing to go that far based on assumptions alone?"

"Apparently they sent a Division 9 agent."

"How can you be so sure?"

"Suspicious activities had been reported in the Southeast Nathan District in Cloverfield, including a murder," his informant said as he flipped through photographs of an elderly man's body lying face down in an alleyway with a cell phone in his hand. The informant stood in a room full of technicians working on several computer consoles in four rows of five. "We tapped into the victim's phone records and his last call was made right before he died to someone named Ericka. We are currently tracking Ericka's whereabouts. She's also in Cloverfield."

"She may know too much. Send someone untraceable to take care of her. As for the spy: find out who he is, and what Division 9's true objectives are."

"Yes, sir."

"Anything else?"

"No, sir."

"What about the shipments? Are the solar energy panels and towers installed yet?"

"Just about; they're in the final stage."

Truman voiced his approval. "Good. What's the status on the Divine Gift?"

"The Divine Gift is progressing well, but if it's activated now, it'll cause a widespread blackout in several power grids. Half the country could experience widespread power failure if it's turned on. Since the solar panels haven't been activated yet, it's just a theory, so those results could be a little inaccurate when the Divine Gift is connected to them. Installation should take another four hours. We still need a reliable subject for testing, though. Someone who's worth the risk, but not the loss."

"So other than General Air's mishap, the Dead Blue's elusiveness, and Jonathon Silverstein's continuous assaults against my dwindling list of informants and allies… and the spy, everything is moving according to plan... this is excellent news. Find a reliable subject for the Divine Gift. Anything else?"

"No, sir."

"Good."

BAM!

The office doors flew open, knocking Air's body near the carpet as Truman's bodyguards poured in with their submachine guns, looking around frantically. They spotted Air's body and gathered around it, expressing their disgust and surprise in murmurs.

"Stand to attention, men," a tall woman barked formally as she marched into the room with her machine gun resting on her right shoulder. She was dressed in a black uniform—an armoured blouse and skirt, with knee-high stockings and high heels—and had long black hair, pale skin, and red eyes. She stopped right on the edge of the sunlight on the office floor and looked at Truman. As the bodyguards stood at the edge of the carpet in front of Truman's desk in single file, she asked, "Are you alright, sir?"

Truman sat back down in his chair, propped his elbows on the table, and interlocked his fingers in front of his face, striking his usual pose. "Never better, Captain Maria. Never better."

Elsewhere...

Damian opened his eyes and stared into the black void. Trapped within its confines, the slightest movement made a noise that echoed at a near-deafening pitch.

"Vell… vell… vell," a voice with a heavy German drawl said behind him. Condescending in tone, sadistic in nature. "Vhut have we here?"

I know that voice. Damian whirled around and looked at the dark figure enveloped in a faint crimson aura standing just a few paces away. "Red," he hissed, hatred and rage boiling up inside him.

FWOOSH!

Floodlights doused the void with blinding white light as a marching band played *Preußens Gloria* behind the figure, whose main features were concealed in shadows cast by the lights. Damian shielded his eyes with his arm, watching as the figure stretched his arms outward and waved them to the music's rhythm.

"*Ja*, it is, mein inferior Dehue friend!"

"I'm not your goddamn friend, and I'm not inferior."

"Nevertheless, it's been far, far too long."

"Not long enough. You're supposed to be dead."

"Dead, but not passed along. It's only a matter of time before I return to ze vorld of ze living. It shall be quite ze party. Quite… ze reunion. You und I, *ja*?" The figure took a step toward him, hands clasped behind his back. "Tell me: vhut should I destroy next? Ze grandest of cities? Ze tiniest of villages in ze countryside? Ze Axis Alliance? Ze Vorld Alliance?"

"It's all the same to you," Damian snarled as he drew his revolver.

Red laughed. "*Ja*! It is! But I vanted your opinion." He said in a sing-song voice, "You never know—I might obliterate someone you care about." He leered, "You... ze great 'Dead Blue.' Vhut a prestigious title you have earned for yourself! Ze Killer of Twenty Million human beings. Impressive, impressive! You have begun a journey full of rampages und violence, und I am pleased for several reasons."

"Because I kill people?"

Red leaned in close. Only then could Damian make out the fearsome, nightmarish expression that looked him dead in the eyes. The wild, crimson hair that struck out over his crazed cardinal-red eyes. The fearsome shadows that emphasized the crescent-shaped, shark-toothed grin that sliced across his face. "Because... you... kill... people. As of late, you have provided me und my men with some *großartig* entertainment."

Damian's gun hand started to tremble.

Red's eyes throbbed with maniacal glee, as if his pupils had their own heartbeats. "Und it's only a matter of time..."

Damian couldn't stop himself from shaking, staring deep into the blood-soaked abyss that Red's eyes reflected from past exploits.

Past exploits that he enjoyed. The souls trapped within the abyss shrieked in agony and terror as they burned in a vast, blazing ocean of blood, its tidal waves hurling them deeper into the storm.

"...Before I wake up... und obliterate *everysing*."

Damian blinked.

Red vanished—

Whispered in his ear behind him, "Exciting, *ja*?!"

Damian lurched out of his sleep, screaming, firing his revolvers with blind terror and rage. The cupboards on the other side of the room splintered; the medical drugs and tools exploded.

Then he stopped. Drenched in sweat, panting heavily, looking around for his enemy. Red had to be somewhere. He had a feeling he'd see those horrible eyes peeking out from the shadows in a corner, or from under the bed. Damian scanned the infirmary.

"Well, I'd say that was a close call," Nurse Kat said coolly as she peeked over her clipboard, which she had raised as a shield. She sat on a chair by the microwave across the room from the door, staring at the cupboards Damian had blasted. "Thirty seconds earlier and you would have had to add me as a statistic to your body count," she added with surprising calmness in her voice.

Damian looked at her, still breathing heavily, his eyes wide. "Hunh…?"

"Have a bad dream?"

"I… uh… yeah, I guess so."

"You 'guess so'?" Nurse Kat looked at her cupboards again. "Bit of an *understatement*, don't you think?"

Damian's revolver disappeared in a wisp of smoke. He looked at the window blinds. Golden sunlight passed through in narrow strips. "What day is it?"

"Still Saturday. The third."

"What time is it?"

Nurse Kat stole a glance at her wrist watch. "About two in the afternoon. You were only out for an hour or so."

"Oh—"

BAM!

Jenny and Aria burst into the room with machine guns. Jenny yelled, "WHAT THE FUCK'S GOING ON?!"

Damian scowled at Aria as she turned her machine gun on him. "Nothing's going on."

"Damian had a nightmare," Nurse Kat said, just before the microwave beeped. She popped open the door and took out a cup of instant noodles with the fork already in it.

"Thanks, nurse," Damian hissed.

"What? A nightmare?" Aria said as she slowly lowered her machine gun.

Jenny looked at the cupboards. "Wait, a nightmare did this?!" She laughed. Aria laughed with her.

Damian scrunched his eyebrows together as the two sisters continued laughing at him. "You know, you bitches have a really shitty response time. Might wanna improve on that."

"At least *we* didn't shoot up a bunch of harmless cupboards because of a nightmare," Aria said with a snicker.

"Toasters, I could see," Jenny giggled, "but *this*…!"

"Okay, I get it!" Damian snapped. "You think it's funny. Laugh it up. Laugh it up! Just remember that it might happen to you someday."

"Doubtful," Aria said.

Damian crawled out of bed, stretched, and headed for the door, pushing between the sisters to get out.

Whap!

Suddenly both sisters grabbed either shoulder and pulled him back, keeping him within arms' length. Jenny leaned forward and said in his ear, "Try not to pull that stunt at the bathhouse again."

Without turning around, Damian said, "What stunt?"

"Oh, you know what we're talking about," Aria said in his other ear.

Damian continued playing the innocent card. "…I don't know what you're talking about."

K-chak!

Damian felt two gun barrels touch the back of his head. "…My memory's returned. I'm cured."

"Thought so," Jenny said. "Remember, Damian, when I said there was nowhere you could run where I can't find you?"

"Yeah…?"

Aria said, "That applies for *both* of us."

Damian blinked, eyebrows raised.

"You don't want us both looking for you, do you?"

"…No?" Damian gulped. "Uh, nurse! Seems you've got two mental patients out of their cells."

"Can't talk now," Nurse Kat said from the corner, scarfing down her noodles. "Eating."

Damian scowled.

"We're not gonna hurt you, Damian," Aria said. "We're gonna let you off with a warning this time."

"You know, for hostages, you're acting *way* out of line," Damian said.

"Remember what else I said, Damian?" Jenny asked. "Back at the house?"

"What?"

"You're *my* bitch, now."

Damian maintained a cocky, unperturbed scowl. "Right. You don't know what you're up against."

"We outnumber you, Damian," Jenny said.

"We *also* know your weakness," Aria added as she slid the barrel of her machine gun down his spine to the spot between his tattooed wings. The movement made Damian shudder.

Jenny smirked, whispered in his ear, "Keep your brother in check for us, okay?"

Damian jolted upright.

"Both of you had better behave for the rest of the trip," Aria said in a menacingly quiet tone. "Got it?"

"G-got it," Damian replied.

"Good boy," Jenny said.

"Will that be all?" Damian asked.

"Yes. You may leave," Jenny said, lowering her machine gun.

"Run along now," Aria sang.

Damian quickly left the room and slammed the infirmary door shut behind him. Then he started down the hall at a brisk pace, eager to get to his room. The hairs on his neck stood up as he walked. *Shit, shit, shit, shit!* "This isn't gonna be as easy as we'd expected, Tyler," he whispered.

"I noticed. We need to be careful around those two."

"Yeah, extra careful. One of them was bad enough. Her younger sister's even worse."

"Can't just leave. Looks like we need to figure out a new plan."

"Can't be too careful these days," Damian said. "There're eyes and ears everywhere you go."

"So now what?"

"The answer's obvious: we prepare for the absolute worst. Actual guns and armour for when my recharge period takes my powers away. At least two escape routes on this ship in case they try something. And then—"

Creak!

Damian turned around. The infirmary door was open just a crack, with two eyes, one over the other, staring right at him.

"Remember to behave," Jenny said.

The sisters shared a collective chuckle, sending another chill down Damian's spine as he retreated to his room, slammed the door shut, and locked it. He put his back against the door and sighed. "Christ. I'm starting to wonder if taking hostages was such a good idea."

"That's what I've been telling you all along, you idiot. Now we're fucked. On this ship, you've got a bunch of murderous psychopaths who are scrutinizing your every move. Outside, the rest of the fucking world is out to kill or capture you. We're fucked either way. What the hell are we gonna do, brother?"

Damian put his ear to the door and listened for a short while. Then he replied in his thoughts, *We're gonna do exactly what we're told to do*... he smirked cunningly *...and behave.*

TO BE CONTINUED IN COBALT ROGUE, VOL. 2

COBALT ROGUE, VOL. 1: THE DEAD BLUE

Author's Notes

Ahoge

Literally translated as 'stupid hair,' it appears as a stray hair sticking up from a (usually) neat set of hair on an anime character. This typically indicates that the character is stupid, with a few exceptions. Whether this means that Damian is stupid or not is something I'll leave for you to decide.

Smith & Wesson Model 500

A revolver that regularly holds and fires five rounds. However, Damian's Model 500 is an exception because it is formed from his own telekinetic energy, therefore allowing him to manipulate its performance and appearance at will. He also prefers the model with the 4" inch barrel. Because this is his favourite sidearm and he uses it several times throughout the story, I often refer to it as his 'trademark weapon/gun/revolver'.

Scionia Army Challenger IV Main Battle Tank

This main battle tank is based off the designs of the British Army Challenger 2 and the Russian Army T-90 Bhishma main battle tank. However, the Scionia Army Challenger IV has the potential to travel at twice the speed of the Challenger 2, and it has eight (in total) HEAT missile launchers fitted into the front and back of the hull. The Challenger IV is also protected by the same three-tiered protection system a T-90 has, with four layers of anti-tank proof aluminum sheets (extending the armoured skirt) fitted over the tracks to protect the road wheels and drive sprockets from enemy fire. Unlike the Challenger 2 (which requires a four-man crew to operate it), or the T-90 (which requires a three-man crew), the Challenger IV only requires a single operator, though it does has enough space to accommodate up to five other passengers. Since Scionia was one of the more advanced countries in the world before the nuclear strike in the Dehue Extermination Project, the Scionia Army Challenger IV main battle tank was acknowledged as the fastest main battle tank in the world since its development in 2018, and was also the first tank to have an EMP (Electro Magnetic Pulse) installed, even though it can emit the pulse by a seven-digit code, with authorization by a higher ranking officer; by law it can only be activated under severely necessary circumstances. The Challenger IV also maintains the unique Scionian tradition of containing a BV (boiling vessel) to brew tea and other hot beverages and prepare boil-in-the-bag meals contained in ration packs.

"Kyoko-Style"

Kyoko-style, basically Chinese-style, but since this is a different world it's got a different name.

Twelve-Shooter Service Revolver

Large service revolver with lightweight armour and a big cylinder designed to hold twelve slugs instead of six. Designed by highly successful firearm developer Shoji Fukushima, of Fukushima Industries. The revolver had been a standard-issue sidearm for medium- to high-ranking Troyan soldiers since 2024, only a year after its first field test.

Terrain Marcher Class 4

Updated model of the Terrain Marcher Class 03, or Dehue Battle Automaton. It's basically a giant robot.

Spiral Suicide

Hallucinatory drug that causes people to commit suicide using unorthodox methods—small doses knock them out.

Works by Alexander Engel-Hodgkinson

Clockworld (One-Shot)
The Tea Party Affair
I Keep My True Love in the Basement (One-Shot)
Reality Glitch ('Jumping for Charlotte' segment)
I Keep My True Love in the Basement/REMIX
Cobalt Christmas
She Watches Me Bury Her

The Final Apocalypse Saga (First two volumes previously published as 'Dark-Boy')
Cobalt Rogue, Vol. 1: The Dead Blue
Cobalt Rogue, Vol. 2: Sky Japan Welcome Party
Cobalt Rogue, Vol. 3: Cemetery Rumble, Part I

www.ingramcontent.com/pod-product-compliance
Lightning Source LLC
Chambersburg PA
CBHW020506020726
47493CB00001B/205

* 9 7 8 0 9 9 5 2 1 7 4 9 2 *